Early Pra

Gordon has artfully nurtured a charming whodunit. Penny...a reluctant detective with a fraught history...proves an engaging and skillful sleuth. Readers should hope that this winning mystery series starring a gardener/detective will be fruitful and multiply.
--*Kirkus Reviews*

In Penny Summers, Gordon creates a smart, endearing sleuth whose personality blossoms forth on every page. As avarice and artifacts collide in the world of Civil War collectors and reenactors, Penny Summers' tenacity and curiosity draw her and the reader into a complex web of deceit where death still lingers long after the guns of the Blue and the Gray fall silent.
  --*Mark de Castrique,* author of the Sam Blackman series

Gordon's riveting tale has it all—a poisonous plant, a reappearing gun, a hidden compartment and, of course, suspicious deaths. We can hope that Penny soon finds herself tangled in another web of deceit, betrayal and murder.
--*Tom Rash,* Asheville Editing

Malice at the Manor

J. Marshall Gordon

Malice at the Manor

Copyright 2018 – John M. Gordon

ISBN # 9781943789801

All rights reserved. No part of this book may be reproduced or transmitted in any form or by any means, electronic or mechanical, including photocopying, recording or by any information storage and retrieval system, without permission in writing from the author or publisher. This book was printed in the United States of America.

Cover design and layout by: WhiteRabbitgraphix.com

This is a work of fiction. Any characters, names and incidents appearing in this work are entirely fictitious. Any resemblance to real persons, living or dead, is purely coincidental.

Taylor and Seale Publishing, LLC.
Daytona Beach, Florida 32118
Phone: 1-386-760-8987
www.taylorandseale.com

To those who carry the scars.

Malice at the Manor

Chapter 1

Strolling through a well-planned garden always brightens my day. And I occasionally pick up an idea or two. As my Grandpa Jack used to say, *Penelope, if you don't learn something every day, you're not paying attention.*

A year ago I'd become a Master Gardener and when I realized that I enjoyed just about every aspect of gardening, I enrolled in the spring semester of Madison Lerrimore's residential design course at Annapolis Community College. A week after the last class, we'd come to North Carolina to visit one of the most interesting landscapes we'd studied.

Madison and I were rambling through hemlocks, sparkling hollies, groves of flowering fruit trees and colorful shrubs at Brantleigh Manor, the finest example of Italian Renaissance garden design in America. Overhead, an iconic Carolina blue sky reigned supreme. Not a cloud in sight.

Our guide was the landscape architect who had laid out

the gardens in 1905. Actually, he wasn't *the* designer, Frederick Law Olmsted, but his twenty-first century doppelganger.

"Here in the Glen—" he harrumphed to ensure our attention "I transitioned to a more naturalistic style—like my first design ..."

I acknowledged his smug smile. Every student of garden design knows the story of Olmsted and Vaux winning the design competition for New York's Central Park in the 1850s.

Between his observations, we followed a winding path through patchworks of flowering trees and shrubs punctuated with sweeps of crayon-bright tulips and sun-dappled daffodils. With photo opportunities beckoning at every bend, I couldn't resist taking shots that I would assemble into a PowerPoint that Madison could use in next spring's intro course. I included Madison in one shot, her short dark hair and lack of make-up contrasting with the luscious pink blooms of the flowering almonds where our Olmsted had once again halted us.

"I designed this entire Glen," he said with a hint of exasperation as he swept his walking stick in a complete circle, "as an arboretum of evergreens ... a *winter* garden if you will. We planted every kind of fir, pine, spruce, and hemlock and several kinds of hollies."

His ruddy cheeks, balding forehead, long gray whiskers, greatcoat and walking stick made him a dead ringer for his portrait in the estate's brochure.

"So much of Brantleigh Manor's landscape has been changed over the years," he continued. "Regrettably, here in the Glen, in *my* opinion, the alterations have *not* been improvements."

As his tone shifted into resentment, my ears perked up.

"After Governor Brantley's death," he said, "wouldn't you know, his widow decided she'd prefer a more colorful plant palette. She had the majority of my evergreens yanked out and replaced with what you see today." He stomped his cane, narrowly missing a buckled shoe. "Without so much as a by your leave!"

It was ingenious, I thought, for Brantleigh to employ docents in the guise of America's first landscape architect. For visitors who might imagine that gardens materialize spontaneously, their presence underscored the reality that all gardens are really collaborations with nature that were birthed in a designer's imagination.

"Really," he said. "How tedious!" His eyebrows furrowed. "By then my Glen was nearly forty years of age ... and growing apace." He huffed impatiently. "She should have asked my opinion."

While my eyes, I'm sure, rolled at his blatant theatricality, it was also true that if Madison weren't wearing her jean jacket embroidered with Grateful Dead bears, I could have easily imagined we were with the genuine Frederick Law Olmsted, more than a hundred years before.

"By then, unfortunately," he said, his face relaxing, "I was in my gra—"

"*Mo-om!* There's a man down there!"

The kid's scream ratcheted up my pulse in an instant. Until that moment, I hadn't noticed either the boy or his mother a hundred feet or so ahead of us. The mom looked up from her phone and glanced at him, thinking perhaps it was a stunt to get her attention.

"Okay, young man," she said, "that's enough."

As they hustled past us she grumbled, "This kid and his

overactive imagination—"

"But *Mo-om* …"

Do not ever discount the testimony of a child, whispered my late lamented Grandpa Jack who occasionally offers observations from beyond the grave.

I dashed to where they had been. Madison and Olmsted hurried to catch up. Nothing appeared amiss.

Tarry! Grandpa Jack whispered. *The boy said the man was* down *there.*

Down there? Where? Then I realized that the mountain laurel on both sides of the path obscured a minuscule creek that crossed under it. I snagged a branch laden with pink posies and pushed it aside. Then another. And a third. OhMyGod—

"The kid was right," I said, my breath catching as my adrenalin bubbled, "it's another Olmsted."

"Penelope," Madison croaked, "you're kidding … right?"

"Unfortunately—" I said, but couldn't say more.

Our docent's double was down there, literally under our noses, in the tiny rivulet.

Déjà vu all over again, whispered Grandpa Jack, who'd always enjoyed quoting Yogi Berra.

Olmsted's eyebrows arched into the shape of violin f-holes as he pulled a phone from his greatcoat and gave up channeling America's first landscape architect.

"Mike. Ned here."

Ned? I'd assumed he was Wayland, Madison's stepfather, who she'd said would be our guide. She hadn't seen him since high school, and a key reason for planning the trip was her eagerness to reconcile with him.

"We've got a problem," Ned said to his phone. "We've

found Wayland. He's either drunk or sick or—"

Dead's what I think, whispered Grandpa Jack.

Madison screamed and quickly looked away.

When we'd met our guide this morning, Madison had hesitated slightly but said nothing. I never guessed that he wasn't her stepfather.

"Just shut up a second," Ned screamed at the phone. "We're in the Glen. And FYI, the kid who found him and his freaked-out mom are on their way back to the Manor."

Ned tapped off his phone and scanned the path. The boy and his mom were long gone. Two elderly women admired an enormous Yoshino cherry in full pink regalia a couple of hundred feet behind us. One carried a cane and the other used a walker. Beyond us, an elderly gray-haired guy dressed in black was either unconcerned or unaware of our predicament. He turned his back and, with a slight limp, continued toward the Waterfall Garden.

"Let's get him up," Ned said.

Madison's hand jumped to her mouth.

I scrabbled down to the little creek and felt the man's wrist for a pulse. I'm no expert but I couldn't detect one. Grandpa Jack, who championed the Great Books program at St. John's College, used to tease me about wasting my time reading mysteries. I'd told him I occasionally come across a tidbit I file away and trust that I'll never need in real life. Which is why I quickly checked Wayland for signs of violence. His clothes appeared free of blood and I could see no holes of the bullet variety or otherwise.

"Ned," I called up, "give me a hand?"

Madison, wide-eyed, stepped back further.

With an arm around his chest, I heaved him like a store-window manikin until Ned, on his knees, could get a grip on his waistcoat. Already stiffening, the poor guy was the literal definition of dead weight. By the time we tugged him up onto the path and turned him over, I was out of breath.

"Holy—" Madison stammered, gasped for air, threw her hand to her face and began to wail.

I knew the horror of finding a family member dead, familiar with the anguish that never completely fades. But, right here and now, what? Call 9-1-1? The F.B.I.? The State Police? Flummoxed, I stared at the dead man. I was like an uncertain zombie. One moment a student of landscape architecture, and the next, an unwilling participant in a grisly scenario. Tomorrow's local headline formed in my mind's eye: EX-NAVY PUBLIC AFFAIRS OFFICER FALTERS IN CRISIS. The day had turned upside down, left me in panic mode, captive in a terrifying new reality.

Madison's stepfather wasn't as tall or as gaunt as Ned, but was outfitted identically. Mud streaked his greatcoat, his waistcoat was unbuttoned, his shoes scuffed. A mountain laurel twig served as a hook for the straw boater he'd lost when he fell. His wig was gone, leaving a crop of thinning buzz-cut hair that made him look like a long-retired Marine. Worst of all was his mouth stretched awkwardly, his face a spasm. I lifted an eyelid. A foggy eye stared skyward.

"He's beyond help," I pronounced.

"My s-step-father," Madison stammered. Her tearful face crumpled into an equally crumpled blue bandana.

My heart went out to my mentor. She and I had become friends almost as soon as her design course began. The weekend before we came to North Carolina she and her partner and their daughter Kalea had helped celebrate my thirty-third birthday at O'Leary's, a few blocks from my Eastport condo.

Ned took charge, gesturing toward a grove of native rhododendrons a couple of yards uphill from the path. "We have to get him out of sight."

Madison's wailing intensified.

"You're not supposed to move a body," I said.

You've read too many murder mysteries, Grandpa Jack whispered.

"He's already been moved," Ned countered.

The dead man's shoes plowed little furrows in the mulch as Ned and I schlepped him toward the rhododendrons. In spite of the pleasant morning, by then I was perspiring profusely, far more than what my Great-Aunt Zelma would call *glistening*. Madison walked alongside us to block the view from the two women who were closing on us, having finished marveling at the big Yoshino cherry. When we laid him down, she stumbled a few yards further up the hillside and upchucked.

Ned clicked his phone. "Michael, update. Wayland's dead."

Grandpa Jack had been right. Again.

When I was growing up in Annapolis, my Grandpa Jack was the dean of St. John's College, and expected me to apply there after high school. Instead I opted for the Naval Academy. In so many ways, especially after mom deserted us, he was like a doting parent and when he died, I was half a world away, a public affairs officer on the USS Enterprise during the Iraq war. In the privacy of my stateroom, I wept, devastated, unable to attend his funeral.

But his death didn't end his caring for me. I still hear his occasional whispers. At first it was unnerving, but these days I'm grateful for his suggestions although sometimes he comes across as a know-it-all.

Chapter 2

"Damned hot in this Olmsted getup," Ned said as he pocketed the phone and shrugged out of his greatcoat. When he peeled off his Olmsted wig, his sandy hair caught the breeze, transforming his head into a circus freak's—the top looking about forty years old, the rest appeared to be in its eighties: mustachioed, bearded, framed by theatrical sideburns.

He glanced at Madison, her tears streaming. "I s'pose you know he was scheduled to've been with y'all today," he said, "but he went for a walk this morning. Didn't come back."

I listened carefully, hoping Ned would explain my confusion over Wayland's absence.

"He said he'd be our guide," Madison said. "But when you met us—" she sniffled "I assumed it was just a last minute scheduling glitch."

"I had a passel of UNC students this morning." Ned finger-combed his tousled hair. "We normally tour only one group a day. But since Wayland hadn't returned, I had to take y'all."

The two women stopped where we'd found Wayland, briefly admired the mountain laurel blossoms that concealed the rivulet, and shuffled on toward the Waterfall Garden.

Two Brantleigh Manor officers, alerted by Ned's call, sprinted toward us. Ned went to the path and motioned them to where we'd brought the dead man. One with an EMT shoulder patch confirmed Wayland was dead. The other got on his radio. Within minutes, Brantleigh's chief of security, a Captain Randall, arrived in a pint-size electric vehicle carrying a sawhorse to straddle the path. A sign on it read:

CLOSED FOR MAINTENANCE.

"I trust you'll bear with us," Randall said with a condescending smile. "Sheriff's deputies and a medical examiner'll be along soon."

It would make my day. Not. Being grilled by boys in blue is my second least favorite thing. Just after finding dead people.

Within minutes, an ambulance, its siren silent and not quite able to keep all four tires on the macadam path, approached. Randall swung the sawhorse aside to let it to pass, then swung it back across the path as the ambulance slowed to a stop.

The M.E. jumped out and identified herself. "Where's my patient?"

"He's already done passed through them pearly gates," said the EMT. Which gave me a chuckle but failed to elicit even a diffident smirk from the M.E.

Moments later, a dark sedan with unblinking emergency lights over the driver's visor was ushered past the sawhorse.

Two plainclothes officers hopped from the unmarked and pumped a haven't-seen-you-in-a-while handshake with Captain Randall.

"I'm Detective Ben Twomey," the taller said to us, extending his hand to Madison and glancing at me. "Deputy Sabillas will take your names and contact information."

"Miss ..." Twomey's probing eyes went back to Madison.

"Madison Lerrimore." She spelled her name and gave him her phone number and home address.

"I believe the deceased was your father-in-law?"

"No sir. My *step*father."

Twomey blinked, recalibrating. "Does that explain why

you're here?"

"Well ... partly."

"Okay, what's going on?"

Madison wiped her eyes with the bandana. "I teach landscape design in Maryland, and Penny—" she nodded toward me "—is one of my students. We're here because Brantleigh is the best example of Italian Renaissance design in the country."

"So," Twomey said, "tell me about finding your stepfather."

Madison turned to me. I raised a finger and took a breath.

"*You* found him?" Twomey asked.

Quick nod. Adrenalin pumped. "What's your last name, Ms. Penny?"

"Summers, sir." Then added my phone and my Aunt Zelma's Flat Rock address where we were staying.

It had actually been my Aunt Zelma who'd helped make the connection between Madison and Wayland. In an email last fall my aunt had mentioned that she had a friend who was seeing a retired history professor from Maryland. Although his last name was different, I knew Madison's stepfather had taught at some Baltimore college. Turned out the retired professor was, in fact, Madison's long-lost stepfather. She was delighted to discover that he lived in North Carolina and worked at Brantleigh Manor. I realized later that must have been the moment she started to think about visiting Brantleigh.

Twomey glanced at Madison then back to me. "Okay ... so tell me."

I explained that a boy had first noticed Mr. Morgan in a tiny creek and that we'd responded and pulled the man out. "He looked like he'd fallen from the path—which I suppose he had."

Twomey groaned. "Don't y'all know any better than to muck up a crime scene?" His displeasure, as a novelist a century ago might have penned, was writ bold across his brows. "Haven't y'all watched any cop shows?"

"With due respect sir," Ned said, almost mockingly, "we had no idea a crime had been committed. We still don't. For all we knew he might have had a seizure or a heart attack. We didn't even know he was dead till we got him out."

"And ... you are?"

"Ned Ferguson, sir."

"So what's with the costume?"

"I'm a docent here, impersonating Frederick Law Olmsted—"

Chief Randall cleared his throat. "Mr. Olmsted designed these gardens when the estate was built."

Twomey made a "whatever" face as Sabillas noted both names.

"Show us exactly where you found Mr. Morgan."

Ned led our little parade back down to the path where I pulled mountain laurel branches aside to give the detectives a clear view of the trickling stream where Wayland had collapsed. Neither seemed interested in going down to it.

"Reckon he might could've already been dead when he fell down there," Sabillas said. "No way falling that little bit would've killed him."

What a brilliant observation, I thought, while Grandpa Jack whispered, *Keep your sarcastic lips buttoned.* We trudged back up to the rhodies but kept our thoughts to ourselves.

"So," Twomey said to Ned, "you were showing these women around the gardens."

"Yessir. But Wayland was *supposed* to've been with them. I only took them because he hadn't shown up."

"Sir," I interrupted, "something that might help determine the time of death."

"What's that?"

"When we pulled him up, rigor mortis had begun. I'd guess he'd been dead maybe five or six hours."

"You're some kind of expert?" Sabillas sneered, then pressed his lips together and dutifully noted my estimate.

No end of things you can learn by reading mysteries, Grandpa Jack whispered with a smirk.

Twomey straightened his shoulders, glanced at Ned, then at Madison, and back to me. "Should I assume that you'd never met Mr. Morgan ... alive?"

I nodded. "Your assumption would be correct."

I read *smartass* in his narrowed eyes. Boys in blue, even of the plainclothes variety, probably didn't enjoy interviewing people like me any more than I enjoyed being interviewed.

Madison, fortunately, picked up the ball. She explained that she'd visited her stepfather late yesterday. "But before then," she said, "we hadn't seen each other for more than twenty years."

Twomey leaned forward. "Explain please."

"We didn't get along when I was in school, and while I was at the university, he and my mom divorced. I'd lost track of him."

"But he wasn't the only reason you're here."

Madison glanced at me, then turned back to the detective. "I've wanted to come for years. When I heard that my stepfather was a docent here, it seemed like a good opportunity to kill two birds with one stone ..." Given

Wayland's demise, I silently questioned her choice of idiom. "... to see the gardens and get back in touch with him."

Twomey thanked her and turned to Ned. "Did *you* see Mr. Morgan today ... uhhh ... before ... that is, alive?"

Ned nodded. "We both got to the docents' lounge about the same time this morning. Around eight. I made my coffee and he had his tea."

I knew Madison had brought a box of gourmet herbal tea-bags for her stepfather that she hoped would help smooth their reconciliation. In fact, she'd gone to see him right after we arrived yesterday. But if the glance she gave me was intended as a message, it didn't register.

"How was he?" Twomey asked.

"Same as always." Ned straightened his shoulders and glanced up to the cloudless sky. "We talked about the reenactment here this weekend. We *were* both going to be in it."

"So ... nothing unusual?"

"Except—"

"Except what?"

"Well, before he finished his tea, he said he needed some air. I figured he had a bit of a hangover."

Madison shot me another undecipherable glance.

"What time was that?"

"I'd guess maybe half past eight ... quarter to nine." Sabillas scribbled the time.

"So," Twomey continued, "you and Mr. Morgan were friends?"

"Of course." Ned shifted his weight. "For about three years. When we met he mentioned that he'd taught history. At the time, Mr. Brantley here was looking to hire another Olmsted docent. Wayland was a quick study—and we're both Civil War reenactors. So, sure, we're friends. *Were*."

"So," Twomey said, "What about enemies? He have any?"

Ned gave it a moment's thought. "Not that I know of," he said to the sky.

Not everyone can tell a lie smoothly. Without quite knowing why, I sensed that Ned had just told one. I tucked his *not that I know of* into my cranial filing cabinet.

"Sir," Madison interrupted, "can I respond to the question?" She glanced at Wayland's body splayed in a bedraggled approximation of a crime-show corpse.

May I, my English-major neurons substituted.

"Which?"

"About whether he had enemies. When I went to his apartment yesterday—" Her voice broke.

"Go on."

"Before I even knocked, I heard an argument inside."

"With? Man or woman?"

"It was a man. I couldn't hear much through the door but—"

"Please tell me what you *could* hear."

"It was about money," Madison said. "And lots of swearing."

Ned continued gazing upward. If Wayland had been his friend, why was he uninterested in what Madison had heard?

Twomey continued his questioning. "Did you," he asked, "know the other man?"

Madison shook her head. "He left pretty quick after I got there."

"Mr. Morgan … uhhh … your stepfather … he didn't introduce you?"

"He just said he was a friend and they'd had a

disagreement. But looking back, I think it was a whole lot worse than just a disagreement."

Madison glanced at me like I might question her assessment. But I was totally clueless.

Twomey watched Sabillas write in his notebook, then handed Madison a card. "You might never see him again," he said. "But if you do, you'll let me know."

"'Course."

"How long are you going to be in the area?"

"We'd planned to see the Battle of Asheville reenactment Saturday. My stepfather was supposed to role-play the defending colonel. But now I ..." Her mouth sagged as she shrugged.

"Sir." Ned interrupted "the reenactment was originally Wayland's idea. He was tight with Mr. Brantley and coordinated everything. It's been advertised for weeks. So, even without him, I'm sure it'll be held."

Sabillas jotted as fast as he could.

"I hope it goes okay," Twomey said.

Ned smiled theatrically. "I'll be one o' them damn Yankees."

Grandpa Jack wondered if it was significant that the two friends would have been on opposing sides.

"After we get the medical examiner's report," Twomey said as the EMTs loaded the dead man into the ambulance, "we might need to talk with y'all again." He turned to Chief Randall. "I believe we're finished here."

Although it felt awkward, Madison and I thanked Ned for our truncated tour. Demonstrating what I thought was a strange lack of compassion, he offered to show us the rest of the Brantleigh gardens as soon as his schedule would permit. Madison was equivocal. We hadn't planned to stay beyond the weekend, and her reluctance to consent to anything at that point was understandable.

When Chief Randall dropped us back at the Manor House entry circle, I wondered if the bronze eagle in the little temple on the hill was staring down. It seemed so long ago that Ned had shepherded us up to where we'd shared the eagle's view of the estate. Rubbing his bronze shoulder for luck had been in vain.

As we returned to the parking area, I debated whether Wayland's death had been natural or premeditated. Then I smiled at the recollection of my mom joking that my nickname should be Curious Georgette because I asked so many questions.

Instead of belaboring this with Madison, as we headed back to Kalorama, I asked if she should notify any of Wayland's biological family.

"I sure don't know anyone and I doubt if my mom would give two figs to know he's dead," she said. "If she ever knew anything about his family, she'd have forgotten years ago."

Chapter 3

After our tragic day at Brantleigh, I piloted our rental Nissan back to my Great-Aunt Zelma's estate in Flat Rock, where we'd arrived yesterday afternoon.

Mid-semester, Madison had asked our class if any of us wanted to visit Brantleigh Manor. Mine was the only hand in the air. When I realized the estate was close to my Great-Aunt Zelma's summer home in Flat Rock, I shot her an email. She'd instantly suggested we stay with her at the Porter family estate, Kalorama. Although a part of me dreaded a return to where my childhood had ended so tragically, the opportunity to visit Brantleigh Manor and see my favorite relative eclipsed my trepidation.

In our separate ways, Madison and I were both shell-shocked. Neither of us said anything for the half hour it took to get back to Aunt Zelma's. I briefly considered telling her I understood the agony of an unexpected death in the family. But then it dawned on me that the impact on me of my little brother's death was worse than a stepfather's, no matter how many good memories she may have shared with hers. In any case, I said nothing. Commiseration, I figured, couldn't really help. It was better to be a supportive friend than to compare degrees of grief.

Madison stared out the window whimpering as we passed through Kalorama's ancient iron gates. "Can *I* do something?" I asked.

"Not a thing," she said.

I felt like I'd been kicked to the sideline, but honestly had no idea how or if I might be any help.

I braked to a stop under Kalorama's porte-cochère. We opened the doors and returned to terra firma. As we stepped between the stone lions that guard the steps to the veranda, the piquant perfume of Koreanspice viburnum did its best to dispel our gloom. At the door, my aunt's standard black poodle André sniffed us and, apparently remembering us from yesterday, allowed us in.

"My goodness," my aunt called, "ya'll have had a long day. Freshen up and tell me about it."

Madison said nothing. I might have nodded, said okay or something, but I doubt it.

"The sun's over the yardarm," Aunt Zee said. "Grab a drink."

I didn't need a second invitation. I poured myself a tumbler of chardonnay and scooped a handful of pita chips. She beckoned to the white wicker chair at her side as Madison perused the higher-octane alternatives.

Great-Aunt Zelma had never married and never moved from Henderson County. She boasts that the Great Smokies of Western North Carolina are in her DNA. She taught history at Hendersonville High until six years ago, allowed to teach beyond the usual retirement age because she'd lived so much of it. She once told me that as a freshly minted teacher in the 1950s she'd spent several evenings with her then elderly neighbor Carl Sandburg discussing their mutual interest in Abraham Lincoln.

"So. How'd it go?" she asked.

I savored a sip of chardonnay trying to find the right words—

"Penelope, what happened?"

I looked beyond her shoulder to the graying Smokies. "Madison," I called, "get yourself a drink and join us." A dark cloud hovering over Mt. Pisgah matched our mood perfectly.

Madison poured a generous dose of tequila and topped it with lime soda, then planted the bottle on the little table between us. She downed half the glass, added more tequila, and began crying.

"Dear God. What on earth?" Aunt Zee stared into the distance. "Something—about Wayland?"

Madison sobbed and nodded.

"He stopped in this morning," Aunt Zelma said.

My mouth dropped open.

"Just his shade, apparition, phantom—whatever."

Kalorama's well water, I decided right then, was contaminated with some mind-altering substance. Or she dipped into her cask of amontillado a little too often.

"During my meditation," she added.

Madison's wide eyes revealed her disbelief.

"Right away I knew something was wrong," Zelma said.

I was as confused as Madison.

"Said he was sorry he hadn't seen me for a while."

"Did he say why," I asked cautiously, "why he ... his reason for stopping in?"

She shook her head. "He was here for only a couple of minutes. As he started to fade I said, 'Don't be a stranger.' He said, 'gotta go', blew me a kiss and disappeared."

Madison slugged down more tequila. "We found him ... dead."

"Oh God," Aunt Zelma said. "He was going to be your docent. What happened?"

"We don't know ..." Madison, face flushed, eyes in pain, slugged another.

"We had a substitute," I said. "Ned somebody. He and I pulled Wayland out of a little creek."

"Ned Ferguson?" my aunt asked. "I know him. A friend

of Wayland's."

"It's been a blur," Madison added. "The police gave us hell for moving him."

Aunt Zee twirled her wineglass and looked up at Madison. "I'm so sorry."

Madison dabbed an eye.

"I haven't seen him since last fall," my aunt said. "Since my friend Lynn was dating him."

Madison was quietly thoughtful for a moment. "D'you think I could meet her? We only talked for a short time yesterday. It'd been so long since we lost touch."

"There're several folks around here who knew him," Aunt Zee said. "I could invite them to dinner."

Madison, tearful, nodded. "That'd be great."

+ + +

Sleep was long in coming. I couldn't get comfortable, wandering in and out of random dissociations and embracing several phantoms on the long road to rest. But I heard nothing from Madison's room.

The night before, after a long chat with Aunt Zee, I'd gone to bed before Madison returned from Wayland's apartment. It must have been close to midnight when I woke to the creaking of her bedroom door. Sometime later, I had my recurrent nightmare: my little brother Josh's splash into the swimming pool and my screaming for help.

But the shrieks had come from Madison's room next door.

Before I could pry myself out of bed to rouse her from the nightmare, they subsided.

I gradually wandered back to the arms of Morpheus wondering what could have haunted her dreams.

Chapter 4

The next morning, at Aunt Zelma's suggestion, I drove Madison to Asheville to visit an earlier Olmsted design, Mr. George Washington Vanderbilt's Biltmore Estate. Yesterday's ominous dark clouds had dissipated, leaving us a bright spring day to enjoy the short drive north on Highway 25, the old Buncombe Turnpike, up to Asheville.

It was interesting to learn that Mr. Olmsted had also designed an evergreen glen for Mr. Vanderbilt. And to find that Biltmore's glen had suffered a similar fate as Brantleigh's, having been altered to become an azalea garden—actually quite beautiful this time of year. But, other than the two glens, there was not much similarity between the two landscapes.

I took several photos of Biltmore's statuary and the pond terrace for the PowerPoint I'd promised Madison. We lunched in a converted stable and did our best to avoid the elephant in the room.

By the time we'd finished wandering in the Walled and Rose Gardens and through the Conservatory, it was late afternoon when we returned to Flat Rock.

In the salon, Aunt Zelma explained what she'd planned. Several neighbors who knew Wayland had agreed to come to dinner and would be happy to share their memories with his stepdaughter.

"The caterer should arrive soon," she said. "Until then, the cocktail hour is extended."

I sat down with a chardonnay and Madison returned to the tequila.

Aunt Zelma sipped amontillado from an antique goblet. She tapped it gently. "I want to tell you about the guests this evening." She raised a finger for each of her four bridge-playing friends: Gwen Vardiman, eighty-ish and plump, with readily shared opinions; Deb Imler, a hub of Flat Rock's rumor network and Aunt Zee's best friend; Winnie Hamrick, also a teller of village tales and, when partnered with Lynn Eavers, a frequent winner at the bridge table.

"Lynn was Wayland's lady friend … until they broke up last fall."

My aunt raised her last finger. "Another neighbor who knew your stepfather is Claude Garner. He's a Civil War enthusiast and reenactor. I taught him in high school, and now he's a teacher himself. Hollywood handsome. And by the way, your Brantleigh docent, Ned Ferguson, sends his regrets."

The Big Ben door chime sounded and Aunt Zelma dashed to the foyer.

"Claude, welcome."

"Wouldn't want to miss a chance to meet your Marylanders," his voice boomed.

"That voice …" Madison whispered, wide-eyed. "It's the guy I heard arguing with Wayland."

Aunt Zelma and the handsome man entered the salon.

"This is my niece, Penny Summers," Aunt Zee said, indicating me, "Claude Garner." Aunt Zelma was correct, movie star handsome. Broad forehead and a dark mustache that curled around his mouth to form a goatee. Like Ned, he looked to be in his forties. We shook hands.

"And this is Madison Lerrimore," Aunt Zelma said, indicating my teacher. "Claude Garner."

"You!" Madison barked.

Garner's mouth opened in surprise, then recovered. "A pleasure to see you again," he said smoothly. "My deepest condolences on your dad's death."

Madison said nothing, but her fevered stare and flared nostrils radiated hostility. Like a desert heat wave had blossomed.

"I had no idea you'd met," Aunt Zelma said, attempting serenity.

"Oh yes," Madison said. "We've met." Then, "Ms. Porter told us she'd invited friends of my stepdad. After what I heard yesterday, I can't imagine you're in that category."

Garner slipped off his elbow-patched houndstooth jacket and hung it on an antique coat tree. "Wayland and I had a business arrangement," he said. "And we didn't see eye to eye on how it was working out." His black golf shirt covered a fitness-center physique. "I'm terribly sorry if we upset you, Ms. Morgan."

"My last name, by the way, isn't Morgan." Madison flipped him an insincere smile. "It's Lerrimore."

"My apologies," Garner said. "Your dad never mentioned he had a daughter."

"*Step*daughter."

When the doorbell chimed again, I went to the door, leaving my aunt to deal with her former student. Madison followed me into the hall. Lynn Eavers introduced herself. Under her blond pageboy, emerald earrings danced above her elegant dark-green sheath. "Pleased to meet you, I'm sure, Ms ...?

"Penny Summers. I'm Zelma's grand-niece." I turned to include my teacher. "This is Madison, Wayland's stepdaughter."

"My condolences, Madison," Lynn said. "But it's a pleasure to meet you."

"Ms. Porter said you and Wayland were friends."

"For a time," she admitted, "more than friends."

"My stepdad and I lost track of each other," Madison said. "I hope you can tell me about him."

Lynn patted Madison's arm in a "you can count on it" way. I led them to the salon, directly to the wine-crowded sideboard, and caught glimpses of caterers bringing covered dishes through the servants' entrance.

A wine and a half later, Lynn was deep in conversation with Garner. My aunt's other bridge partners, Deb Imler, Winnie Hamrick and Gwen Vardiman had arrived. Aunt Zee beckoned us all into the dining room, the term not at all doing it justice. The caterers not only had brought the meal but, as they'd probably done many times before, elegantly transformed the room. A crystal chandelier with what seemed like a million twinkling lights hung over the center of the table where a bouffant bouquet of spring flowers added color to the otherwise silver and white room. A pair of triplet candlesticks stood on either side of the bouquet, all six white candles aflame. The setting was worthy of a magazine cover.

Great-Aunt Zelma sat at the fireplace end of the table, in front of the intricately carved mantel that had been chipped by a bushwhacker's bullet during the Civil War. Possibly the same bushwhacker who murdered my great-great-great Grandfather Percival who'd built the house. An antique oval mirror hung over the mantel flanked by silver sconces with candles alight. Claude Garner sat at the opposite end. Madison and I sat among her friends. When Aunt Zelma offered grace, I surveyed them, trying to remember which name belonged to whom.

After the Amens, "For the benefit of our Yankee visitors," Aunt Zelma announced, "we're having a traditional down-home Southern supper." Madison, who had applied a touch of lipstick for the evening, and I who had not, would be watched carefully for any incriminating Yankee behavior like requesting unsweetened iced tea. There was no chance I'd make that mistake tonight since a large carafe of chardonnay made iced tea irrelevant.

Bow-tied caterers began bringing in platters and bowls with aromas that awakened memories of long-ago summers. I leaned toward Gwen to make room for a caterer to set a dish that looked like rice and beans mingled with bits of bacon.

"That's Hoppin' John," Winnie said from across the table. Resplendent in an antique serving bowl, it could have been pictured in Fine Dining alongside its recipe. "Around here, it's mandatory to serve Hoppin' John on New Year's Day."

"The black-eyed peas are for luck," said Gwen.

"We could use more of that," I muttered under my breath.

Aunt Zelma helped herself to a slice of country ham, slathered it with red-eye gravy, and passed the platter to Madison.

"Miz Porter," Madison said, "Can you give us a clue about these little golf-ball things?"

Gwen Vardiman's corpulence made it unnecessary for her to shift very far to give Madison a nudge. "Laws honey," she said in a smoker's rasp, "I'd thought you'd know a hushpuppy when you met one."

After good-natured chuckling at Madison's expense, I said, "Can I take a couple home? My Doberman barks unmercifully at the delivery man."

"Trust me, they work fine," Lynn said from the other side

of the table, "although I've personally only used them on the two-legged variety."

Laughter that followed set the tone for the evening. "Lynn," Deb said, "has a lot of experience with two-legged dogs." She invited her friend to elaborate on her hushpuppy skirmishes.

More laughter.

It pleased me that Madison seemed to enjoy Lynn's brand of humor.

Lynn, my aunt had told us, was a retired Wilmington police officer, had lived in Flat Rock for the last eight years, and dated Wayland for two of those years until last fall.

"Mr. Garner," Madison finally said, glaring, sarcasm inflecting every word, "please tell us about your friendship with my stepfather and your … misunderstanding."

Garner's mouth distorted into an "it doesn't matter" kind of smile as a forkful of roast chicken went in.

"Since he's gone," Madison said, "I may be the only one who can fix whatever your misunderstanding was. Think about it."

"You might be right about that."

Madison stared meaningfully across the table at me as if I might perform the miracle of uncovering Garner and Wayland's misunderstanding.

Instantly I was ready to bag the reenactment and any help I might offer Madison, and catch the next train out of Dodge. I didn't need Grandpa Jack's advice to stay out of this tangle.

"Ms. Lerrimore," Gwen said, shifting the topic, "this morning's paper said ya'll found Wayland in a creek?" She exuded the unmistakable scent of lavender, no doubt chosen to coordinate with her oversize purple beads.

It seemed thoughtless to put Madison on the spot so I

explained our tour with Ned up to the point where we'd found Wayland. "We had no idea what had happened until we pulled him out."

"We still don't," Madison added.

Grandpa Jack whispered *I'm not the one who reads mystery books, but I smelled trouble as soon as you pulled him out. Something is rotten.* He added, *"and it's not in Denmark.*

"It's a damn shame," Gwen said, as she popped a hushpuppy. "Last time I saw him he looked as healthy as a jackrabbit."

"Lynn," I said, "tell us about Wayland."

"She's never passed up an opportunity to talk about him," Deb said.

"Well ...," Lynn began, patting the corner of her mouth with her napkin, "when I realized he was more infatuated with the Civil War than with me, I tossed him a couple of hushpuppies and told him to come see me after the War."

After a few chuckles around the table, Garner preened his goatee and humphed to affirm that he, too, was a Civil War enthusiast.

"Mr. Garner," Madison intoned in a semblance of geniality, "tell us about the reenactment."

Garner stabbed a bite of ham, and then laid it back on his plate. "Your stepfather and Mr. Brantley actually did the major planning."

"So I heard."

"What you'll see this weekend will be loosely based on the actual Battle of Asheville. It went down only three days before the Appomattox surrender."

"But it was weeks," Aunt Zee said, "before anyone this far south heard about Appomattox."

Garner picked up his bite of ham, had it halfway to his mouth, then set it back on his plate again. "The so-called battle," he said, "was a one-day affair just north of Asheville. A brigade of Ohioans from Tennessee was ordered to attack the city. After your stepdad studied on it, he persuaded Mr. Brantley that a reenactment could be a money-maker, so we cobbled together some reenactors. As you know, he was going to role-play Colonel Clayton, commander of the Asheville militia."

Madison cocked her head. "So who'll play Clayton now?"

"I've asked a historian who likes to get into uniform occasionally. But, except for a handful of militiamen and the colonel himself, no uniforms will be needed. The Silver Grays wore whatever they were wearing when they were called up."

I was curious but Madison spoke first. "Silver Grays?"

"A bunch of old guys who had muskets in their closets. Think aging reservists."

"Who won?"

"Most historians agree the defenders."

"They must have been pretty good to beat the Yankees," she said.

"They probably kept their Enfields oiled and went out for target practice from time to time," Garner said, "but no one really knows. They weren't as good as the Union troops they went to fight, of course, but Colonel Clayton put a couple of cannons on a hillside overlooking the turnpike." Garner finally popped the bite of ham into his mouth and spoke while he chewed. "They lobbed enough cannon balls to convince the Yankees that the Ashevillians weren't going to take any sh—nonsense."

"And the Ohioans?" I asked.

"Apparently about a thousand," Garner said, clearly enjoying the role of historian. After another gulp of wine, his tone became more professorial. "They were led by a Colonel Kirby. Incidentally, I'll play Kirby. Oh, and Ned Ferguson will be one of my corporals. He said he was your Olmsted guide at Brantleigh yesterday."

"Small world," I said.

"When Kirby's troops were spotted," Aunt Zelma said, "Colonel Clayton summoned his militia, alerted the Silver Grays, and rounded up as many civilians as he could."

"Fortunately for Asheville," Garner added, fingering his goatee, "Kirby's intelligence was way off. He thought Clayton had twenty cannons and way more troops than he actually had."

"Maybe Clayton had a double agent," I said, "feeding the Yankees bogus information." I loved conspiracy theories.

"The battle only lasted a few hours," Garner continued, "till the Yankees high-tailed it back to Tennessee. So it probably should be called a skirmish but don't tell the Brantleigh folks. They're hoping to make a bit of ..." He rubbed his thumb and finger together. "Wayland assured them they'd have a horde of paying visitors. Remains to be seen."

"Brantleigh has hosted antique car shows," Aunt Zelma said, "so why not the Civil War?"

After the hoppin' john, hushpuppies, ham, and chicken had made several more circuits around the table, our plates were collected and dessert was brought out: blackberry cobbler with homemade ice cream. When Garner finished, he offered his apologies, saying he had tests to grade, and thanked Aunt Zelma for her hospitality.

"I hope to see you all on Saturday," he said as he left the room. A moment later, the front door closed behind him.

Chapter 5

"Seconds on the cobbler?" Aunt Zelma asked. Gwen, Lynn, and I said yes, and my aunt asked one of the caterers to bring three more dessert servings while she refilled our coffee from an antique silver carafe that Percival and Ellen Porter had brought from Charleston when the house was built. She then signaled for an array of liqueurs and little glasses.

Lynn poured herself a B and B and chugged it. "I'm going to miss that man."

"There's got to be a story there," I said and poured myself a Cointreau.

"We'd actually started talking about getting engaged," Lynn said. "Then it went all to hell in a haversack when he first laid eyes on my daughter. He asked her to have dinner with him, but she said no."

Madison's eyes widened but she said nothing. "It was about the same time," Lynn said, "that he began planning the reenactment. So it was sayonara. Shame he didn't live to take part in the battle he'd—pardon me—fought for."

Deb and Gwen snickered. I would have liked to ask her the age of her daughter but decided not to add to whatever was between Lynn and her memories.

"Pass me the B and B and I'll tell y'all another thing or two." Lynn raised her glass in preparation for a refill. The alcohol seemed to be working its magic. *In vino veritas.*

Aunt Zelma passed me the decanter and I handed it to Lynn. She refilled her glass, downed it and refilled it, setting the decanter within reach.

"I remember—" Gwen Vardiman cleared her throat "—you told us about one of his whimsies you probably won't miss."

Lynn's face colored. "Not important."

Gwen prodded. "Shouldn't we remember him as he actually was, even if there were a few warts?"

After a hesitation, "Okay." Lynn drained the little glass. "The Civil War wasn't his only obsession."

Gwen smirked, the cat who'd plucked a canary feather from her whiskers.

"He asked me to dress like a cheerleader."

"Oh. My. God," said Madison, her face half hiding a recognition of something she hadn't shared with me.

"I never understood that fantasy," Lynn added, then chuckled. "But then, the man preferred herbal tea to coffee, so I knew there was a loose screw," she tapped her forehead, "somewhere up there."

I couldn't believe Wayland's friends were sullying his reputation in front of his stepdaughter.

"I would've never guessed." Aunt Zelma said, and laid her dessert fork alongside her unfinished cobbler.

We were quiet for a moment until Madison raised her glass of Kahlua to Lynn. "Can I ask you something?"

"Just not about cheerleaders," Lynn answered. We chuckled politely.

"Okay. When I saw Wayland Tuesday night, he and Mr. Garner were in a very heated argument. Something about money. Tonight, when Garner told me it was a simple difference of opinion over a business arrangement, I wanted to believe it. But, at the time, it sounded vicious. D'you have *any* idea what it could've been about?"

A frown crossed Lynn's face. "Money? Couldn't tell you," she slurred. "As long as he picked up the check at restaurants. We never discussed money, so I have no idea what was between him and Garner. Only thing I knew of was the reenactment."

Winnie Hamrick jumped in. "About a month ago, I was at the antiques barn on the Greenville Highway. Lots of old military stuff. The owner had an old buckle he'd got from a guy who found it metal detecting."

Aunt Zelma had warned us that Winnie was an inveterate gossip.

"But a week after he bought it, the owner said, another Civil War geek told him it was a fake. Probably cast from the genuine article, the geek said, and artificially aged. Turned out it had come from our very own Claude Garner."

"Well butter my buns and call me a biscuit." Gwen's beads bounced with her guffaws. "I can't believe you've kept that all to your lonesome."

"Wayland has—had," Madison said, "quite a collection of Civil War antiques. Assuming I'll eventually inherit the stuff, so unless they're fakes, I suppose I'll have to find someplace to sell it all. Maybe that antiques barn would take it."

"*Assuming* they're genuine," said Winnie.

Deb turned to Aunt Zelma. "Didn't Wayland meet Garner and Ned at a Civil War Meetup?"

"Right soon after he moved here," my aunt said.

"That's where Ned told him about the Brantleigh job," Lynn said.

"So they were all friends," Winnie said.

"You're thinking if one apple is rotten the whole peck is bad?" Gwen mused aloud.

Chapter 6

When my family used to visit Great-Aunt Zelma in the summertime, I always had the same third-floor bedroom. Without air-conditioning in the house then, I kept the windows open. Ever since, I've always liked to sleep in fresh air. Even though the mansion was now air-conditioned, tonight I had both dormer windows swung wide open. Scattered stars and a few distant lights twinkled through new leaves on the big chestnut oaks. A gentle breeze carried sounds of traffic from the Sandburg Pike, a half mile west.

As soon as I kicked off my shoes, there was a soft knock on the door. "I need to talk," Madison whispered.

I opened the door and she padded in, wrapped in a blue terrycloth robe. What now? I wondered.

"Want a little wine?" I'd stashed a screw-top bottle of chardonnay in my bag.

"Wouldn't mind," she said.

I found two little glasses on the old mantel. "Sorry it's not chilled."

"I never had a fridge in my dorm room." Madison chuckled. "In school my weekend breakfasts were cold pizza and warm beer." She took the wine and set a little book she'd brought with her between us on the fainting couch, an iconic therapist's couch, red velvet upholstery curved up at one end in place of a pillow.

We touched glasses and swigged.

"Can't sleep?" I said, thinking of her first night's terror and hoping we wouldn't have an encore.

"I'm still in shock, meeting that guy, learning his name. Just hearing his voice brought back their argument. Part of me is sure he killed Wayland. But another part thinks the cops will try to blame me since they think he's the reason we came."

"Of course he's *part* of the reason we're here, Madison. But you don't know anything about how he died. Let the Medical Examiner figure it out. Maybe the *how* will suggest the *why*. And then the *who* will become obvious."

Madison took a sip and fondled the little glass. "Garner was yelling and Wayland said something about only selling something for thirty thousand. And before I even knocked, Garner said 'You're lying through your teeth.'"

"I'm listening," I said. But I couldn't think where this might be headed.

"Then Wayland told him the flag was so far gone he had to accept thirty. He said 'I'm sorry we had less to split.'"

"Garner said he'd heard that he'd gotten a million. Then Wayland said well he'd heard wrong. And Garner said, 'You'd better pray that all our rounds are blanks—'"

"He was talking about the reenactment."

Madison pulled her legs up to sit cross-legged. "When I knocked, it all stopped. Wayland opened the door and seemed surprised—like he didn't remember that I'd planned to stop by. He was probably embarrassed to have me interrupt. Anyhow, he didn't introduce me. Mostly I was stunned at how he'd aged, but I did wonder who the guy was. I could see they'd been drinking. They yelled some more and Wayland punched a finger in his chest. 'You'd better hope that I keep what I know about you and your so-called metal-detecting,' he said. They sounded like a pair of gunslingers in an old western."

"Jibes with what Winnie said."

"'Mark my words,' Garner said, 'we aren't finished here. You're in way over your head.' Then he stormed out."

A whiff of breeze came through my windows. Must have swirled through the old boxwoods—it carried a hint of cat pee.

"That does throw a shadow over Wayland's death," I said. But it was probably only the pee-scented puff of air that raised the hair on my neck.

"When Wayland insisted they only had a misunderstanding, I accepted it," Madison said. "But now I have to think there was a lot more to it."

I knew she was still in shock, but there was something in her tone that suggested she'd memorized a script. But who was I to second-guess her sincerity? After Josh drowned, I was incoherent for days.

"We don't know what caused his death. Let's wait to hear what the medical examiner says," I said. "Maybe it was a heart attack."

I could only hope that would be the case. Because if my impression of Ned's deceit was correct and he knew of their argument … perhaps all of the apples *were* bad.

"Now that I know who Garner is, I can call the detective."

"The sooner you call," I prodded, "the sooner he'll be questioned."

She turned to gaze into the night. "Something else."

"What's that?"

She turned back, thoughtful. "You remember Detective Twomey pressed me about my decision to come to Brantleigh?"

"I wouldn't say that he pressed you on it. He just asked you if there was a connection."

"If Garner didn't do it, they might try to link it to me. Or even to you."

This line of reasoning was getting bizarre. "Madison. For heaven's sake, what are you worried about? Detectives look for motive, means, and opportunity. You're clear on all three counts."

She arched her head back, pensive, for a beat. "I guess I panicked when he asked about the connection." She smiled self-consciously and brushed a hair from her forehead. "Nothing. Forget it."

"Not to worry. You explained it clearly."

What was this reversal of roles where I was counseling my teacher? And what, for God's sake, could have led her to imagine detectives might connect *her* with Wayland's death? Or *me*? This wasn't making any sense. Had I been transported to an alternate universe?

"I know. It's probably just silly. But I don't believe he died from a heart attack." Madison hugged herself and briefly closed her eyes. "I feel like I'm just hanging out here, waiting for those detectives to come calling."

I know absolutely nothing about psychology except what little I've read in stories, but Madison's dread sounded like some kind of guilt complex. Which I was sure was completely unfounded. For heaven's sake, she'd wanted to reconnect with him.

"Okay," Madison said, "but I'd bet he was murdered."

Now she was closing in on Grandpa Jack's guess. "But what makes you think—?"

"He told me he had a heart condition but said his cardiologist, just a week ago, told him he was good for another fifty."

"So he was healthy," I said, adding more credence to the supposition of murder.

"Since he'd moved here, he said he'd hiked or biked

almost every weekend ... except when he was channeling Olmsted or working on the reenactment. So he shouldn't have keeled over from a heart attack."

"Madison, you know, stuff happens. A guy I knew had a heart attack on his way out of his doctor's office. The doc had just told him his heart was fine."

Madison just stared.

"So whatever Wayland's doctor told him last week or last month," I said, "wasn't necessarily a preview of coming attractions."

She nodded and changed the subject. "Will you go to the medical examiner's office with me tomorrow?"

"Sure," I said, hoping that would give us answers.

At the end of the semester, Madison had offered to look at a concept plan I'd drafted for a wealthy client. Actually my *first* design client. To my great embarrassment, she'd discovered that I'd miscalculated the number of steps needed from the driveway up to the door of the residence. I hadn't paid enough attention when she'd taught the rise over run calculation for step design. The other error she'd caught was that I'd suggested a trio of shade-loving shrubs when their intended site was in sunshine most of the day. I owed her big-time. Thanks to Madison, my client might never guess I was a total newbie.

Madison set her empty glass aside and picked up the little book, an ancient mini photo album. "Thinking about Wayland ..." She flipped it open, its plastic windows tinted with age. "I don't have many pictures from back then." She stopped and flipped back a page, angling it to me. "Here's me, when I could do cartwheels." A hand-lettered label read: Sammy–7 years.

I stared, thinking I'd seen the photo before. And

confused by the little label. "Is that your sister? Sammy?"

She shook her head slowly. "I used to be Samantha—after one of my grandmothers."

"And your middle name was Madison?"

"Nope. I was Sammy Jean. Got teased about that a lot."

"So you changed your name."

"I'd read a story about a girl named Maddy and convinced my mom." She flipped a couple of pages in the little album and stopped again. "This is the only shot of us together." She was about fifteen, grimacing at the camera, dripping wet, standing beside a much younger Wayland in swim trunks at a pool, a kid on a diving board in the background. She looked like she'd been coerced into standing there, taking time from cavorting in the pool. Then I remembered where I'd seen the cartwheel shot. It wasn't that I'd actually *seen* that photo, just that there was a near twin of it my mom had taken of me and Dad at Aunt Zelma's pool.

I didn't want to guess how many years had passed since that was taken. A reminder that time doesn't stand still. "Must be hard to remember those days," I said.

I refocused on the photo and realized something more. "You know ... we could have been sisters ... you were a blonde."

"Not as light as you, though. I switched to mongrel brown when I started at Towson. Didn't want to look like a good-time girl."

"That where you met Cheyenne?"

She shook her head. "We met in grad school." She turned to the last photo. "Here we are—the Quad at College Park." She held it long enough for me to see that she had changed very little, then snapped the album shut. "You still okay to go with me in the morning?"

"'Course."

"I also want to see his apartment again. Wayland gave me a set of his keys. It's about halfway to Brantleigh."

Might as well. "Okay."

We were quiet for a moment. "Madison," I said without looking at her, "quick question."

"Okay."

"When we were with the detectives …"

"It's mostly a blur."

"Do you remember when Ned said he and Wayland met that morning, Ned with his coffee and Wayland his tea?"

Slowly. "Sure."

"You glanced at me like it was some kind of signal."

"Sorry." She seemed perplexed. "None intended." She unfolded herself and lowered her slippered feet to the floor. "When we lived in Annapolis he used to buy herbal tea at the Peggy Stewart shop. I brought him one I hoped he'd like. He must have taken it out to Brantleigh."

"Did he drink tea to get over a hangover?"

She gave me a look as if I'd lost my brain somewhere between dinner and my bedroom.

"Sorry. Just trying to connect what we know to what we don't know."

She clutched the little album and padded toward the door. "Thanks for the wine." And closed the door behind her.

Her unintended signals and strange logic made me wish I'd majored in psychology.

Later, as I was trying to summon sleep, Grandpa Jack whispered, *By the pricking of my thumbs, Something wicked this way comes.*

Chapter 7

The next morning, Aunt Zelma surprised us with a scrambled egg and smoked ham breakfast.

"Thanks, Aunt Zee." I kissed her cheek. "I expect we'll be back by noon," I said as Madison and I set out for Hendersonville.

Three blocks from the courthouse, we found the Medical Examiner's office. To a yawning receptionist, Madison explained her relationship to Wayland Morgan.

"Let me check." The receptionist sighed and disappeared into an inner office.

Madison drummed her fingers on the tall counter until a man came from the back room with a portfolio.

"Wayland Morgan ..." His finger traced down the paper. "Sudden cardiac death due to arrhythmia."

"That's like a heart attack?" Madison asked.

"Not exactly," the man said. "Arrhythmia just means the heart's regular rhythm becomes erratic. The heart goes into fibrillation. Beats so fast that the blood flow to the brain is interrupted. Leads very quickly to loss of consciousness."

"What could cause it?"

"Often there're no warning symptoms." He cocked his head and scrunched his face. "Do you know if Mr. Morgan had heart problems?"

"Just an occasional irregular heartbeat. PVCs he said his doctor called them. But the doctor said they were harmless and he was good for another fifty years."

"I'm very sorry," the man said. "I'll print a copy of the report for you." He turned to a computer, pressed a few keys, and went to the printer as it stuttered in the corner. When it coughed out the copy, he folded it into an envelope and handed it to Madison. "He can be picked up on Monday. Have the funeral home give us a call."

"Well there you are," I said on our way out. "That should give you some consolation."

Madison rolled her eyes. "Remind me to find an undertaker."

"So you can say goodbye to your murder theory."

"Unless there's some way arrhythmia can be triggered by—I don't know—some kind of poison or something."

"If that were even possible," I said, "the pathologist would have tested for it."

"Hypothetically."

I couldn't understand why my friend wasn't content with the M.E.'s findings.

Grandpa Jack tapped my shoulder. *If you were convinced Garner was responsible for* your *stepfather's death*, he whispered, *you, too, would be looking for a way to connect him to it.*

I decided there had to be more to her reaction than what I was hearing. But dismissed the idea of convening an inquisition when Madison reminded me I'd agreed to go with her to Wayland's apartment. Not that I looked forward to visiting a dead man's home.

I turned west toward Etowah, took a left turn and followed signs through a picturesque valley to the historic Vanderbilt Lodge. We slowed to read a weathered bronze plaque on a granite slab that said it had been built a hundred years earlier as a tuberculosis sanitarium by George W. Vanderbilt. In the 1930s, it had been a psychiatric hospital. If Aunt Zelma were with us, I wondered if she'd pick up on the auras of any resident ghosts. Even imagining that made my skin crawl.

And we were headed to a dead man's apartment.

The circular drive beckoned us to a stone portico over the entrance.

When I turned off the ignition, Madison declared that whether or not Claude Garner had somehow triggered her stepfather's arrhythmia, she needed to call Detective Twomey. A moment later she was saying "… and a good morning to you, sir … Yes … You asked me to call if I learned who my stepfather was arguing with the night before we found him." There was a pause. "Okay … last night Penny's great-aunt—where we're staying—invited people who had known him for dinner. It's Claude Garner." She spelled it. "He teaches at Hendersonville High." She held the phone quietly while the detective noted the information. "Thank you, sir." She tapped it off. "I hope they throw him in jail and toss the key."

Whatever happened to innocence until proven guilty, Grandpa Jack wondered.

"At least he'll have to explain the altercation," I said as we headed to the entrance. At the door Madison punched in the code her stepdad had given her. Inside, she gave the receptionist Wayland's apartment number and said she had the keys.

"You know Mr. Morgan is dead?" the woman said, rather more matter-of-factly than I thought appropriate.

"Matter of fact, I do."

"Two detectives were in here yesterday," the receptionist said. "They searched his apartment, photographed, and dusted for fingerprints. Said they couldn't find anything and didn't seal it off. So as far as we're concerned, you're free to go up."

We ascended in an ancient self-service elevator to the

second floor and followed a long carpeted hall to 243. Madison fiddled with the keys her stepdad had given her until the second latch popped and the door swung open. We went in; both locks snapped behind us.

At one side of the big room, a pair of tall windows overlooked a picturesque stream that plumed downhill around mountainside boulders. Between the windows, a museum-quality cabinet sat with the artifacts Madison had mentioned.

She found a switch that turned on lights over all five shelves. Both Confederate and Union relics were on display: belts, buckles, pistols and holsters, canteens, shell casings, a couple of bugles, and minié balls fired and unfired. Each labeled with its provenance. To my amateur eyes, everything appeared authentic.

On the lowest shelf were surgeon's tools that looked like medieval torture devices. A pair of Mathew Brady photographs showed them in use. Not pleasant.

"If either Wayland or Garner made any of these," I said, "he's done an amazing job of making them look genuine."

"If these are genuine," Madison said, "I wonder how he could afford them."

"Obviously a serious collector," I said.

"He taught a course on the Civil War and Reconstruction but I don't think he collected artifacts."

"He must have caught the bug when he moved here."

"Could be."

"Give me a coupla minutes," I said. "I need to pump the bilge."

"You what?"

"It's Navy slang for using the toilet."

"It's at the end of the hall."

Civil War battlefield maps adorned the walls. In the bathroom, facing the throne, was a sketch map of Wayland's obsession, the Battle of Asheville. An S-shaped line depicted the Union approach on the Buncombe Turnpike and a tight row of little v's represented the defenders' cannons and breastworks.

As I returned to where Madison was rummaging in Wayland's desk, noises at the apartment door brought me to a stop. We looked at each other. A key found its home in the upper lock. Who else had Wayland given keys to?

"What the—?" Madison closed the drawer. "The bedroom," she whispered. "Quick."

We backed into the closet, into Wayland's suits, shirts, jackets, and Olmsted outfits. I leaned against back of the closet and pulled the folding doors closed as far as possible.

A key turned in the second lock and the door groaned open ... and shut. Footfalls moved into the apartment. Through the slightly ajar closet door I caught a slice of the front room. A disembodied hand pulled the center desk drawer out.

When the face leaned to peer into the drawer I recognized the mustache and goatee. "It's Garner," I mouthed. He began sifting papers.

Madison opened the closet wide and rummaged through Wayland's clothes, pulling hangers from one side to the other. Garner stopped in mid-search of the sheaf of papers he'd pulled out.

"Who's there?" Madison called, as if she lived here and guests came and went as they pleased. We pretended to search the closet waiting for Garner's reply.

"Madison?" Garner said. "It's Madison isn't it?"

My synapses went to warp speed. "We're looking for a

suit to bury him in," I said.

Madison's temper returned. She scowled. "You and Wayland had—a disagreement. Did you think you could settle it with his ghost?"

"What I came for," he said with the syrupy ease of a practiced perjurer, "was an officer's uniform for the reenactment."

"I doubt it'd be in a desk drawer," I said.

No response.

"There's a blue uniform at the left end of his closet," Madison said.

"That's it," Garner said, looking relieved. "Wayland said I could borrow it. Thanks."

When he'd left, I said, "The uniform was a handy cover story. He was looking for something else."

"I'm surprised Wayland gave him keys to his place."

"Obviously, in spite of their argument, they must have been buds."

"Whatever he was after," Madison said, "I don't think he found it."

"But you and I might." We headed back to the front room.

"Lead on, Sherlock."

"When we slammed into the closet," I said, "the back wall didn't feel solid."

We shoved his clothes to the ends of the rod. A portion of the wall was a slightly different shade of white. And, sure enough, it was thin plywood.

On the left side three screws held it in place. Madison found three more on the right. We moved all of Wayland's clothes to his bed and, using dinner knives in the screw slots, went to work. It took only a couple of minutes to pull down the plywood. A section of a wall stud had been removed to accommodate what, in an exterior wall, could have been the rough opening for a small window. In the cavity was a slim cardboard box. Inside the box was a frayed American flag stained with age and who knows what. Part of the star field was missing. I'd barely survived higher math at the Naval Academy, but multiplication tables were still accessible so I calculated it had originally had thirty-five stars in a rectangle. Burn holes had damaged several stripes. Embroidered across the middle red stripe: 101st Regt O.V.I.

"Part of his collection," Madison said, "but why not have it on display?"

"Maybe too valuable?"

"If Wayland thought it was too valuable to hang on the wall, let's not leave it here."

Even if we could be arrested for burglary, I said, "Let's get it into a safe deposit box."

"I wonder if it's what Garner was looking for."

"Unlike the uniform," I said, "the flag *could* have been in the desk."

"Okay," she said to the flag, "you're off to safety." She folded it gently to prevent any further damage. Then we slipped it into a dry-cleaner's plastic cover.

That old thing will only be trouble, Grandpa Jack prophesied.

We screwed the fake piece of closet wall back in place and took the flag to the big front room.

On a wall over a pair of armchairs were two photos of Wayland that I hadn't noticed when we arrived. In one he wore a Confederate officer's uniform, ceremonial sword on high, leading a company of reenactors into battle. In the other, he was a sergeant wearing a kepi, aiming a rifle with fixed bayonet at the camera.

Above the desk, projecting from the wall were a pair of deer leg brackets that undoubtedly once cradled that rifle.

"When you were here Tuesday—" I motioned to the deer brackets "—was there a rifle up there?"

Madison closed her eyes, her face up. "You know ... I think so."

"I can't imagine him loaning it," I said, "with the reenactment coming up."

"If it was an original, it's probably worth a ton of money," she said.

"So ... stolen?"

"Garner?"

"But if he took the rifle," I said, "wouldn't he have picked up the uniform at the same time?"

"And why wait till today to search the desk?"

We shook our heads in mutual ignorance and, hoping for hints, began rifling through the drawer that Garner had opened. Madison leafed through bank statements and legal documents. "Check the address of his bank," I suggested. "You can rent a safe deposit box for the old flag."

"Hmmm ... Hendersonville Savings and Trust." She set the statement aside.

I opened one of the smaller drawers: a pair of scissors, box of paperclips, and sticky notes, but nothing of interest. Pulled out another—

"My God," Madison cried. "Surprise! He had a will." She skimmed the paper and tears formed. "I'm his next-of-kin."

I leaned to peer over her shoulder. She wiped an eye with the back of her hand and examined it closely.

I would have expected her to be all smiles. But tears?

Go for it, Grandpa Jack mumbled. *You're the one who detects obscure connections.*

"I assume that means you're his executor. You'll have to find a lawyer."

"Cheyenne's a lawyer."

"But not licensed in North Carolina."

Madison stared blankly for a moment until a mischievous smile brightened her face. "I wonder where he hid his millions."

I nodded at the Civil War collections in the cabinet. "Maybe that antiques barn can change all of that stuff into dollars," I said, "if they're not fake."

"One of Aunt Zee's friends said Garner made bogus buckles. If Wayland needed money to buy real relics, maybe he created fakes too."

We searched every cupboard and closet, large and small, but found nothing that could make bugles, buttons, or buckles or anything else.

"At least your stepdad wasn't counterfeiting," I said.

"Small favors," she said.

We went back to our search of the desk. I opened another drawer. Letters and travel receipts. Madison started through the receipts while I shuffled through the letters. My attention caught on an envelope postmarked Hagerstown, Maryland, but without a return address. Inside, a childishly handwritten missive was squashed into the white space of a magazine ad for expensive bourbon.

After a quick perusal I said, "Take a look," and wondered if it would make more sense read aloud.

"'Dear Wayward,'" Madison began. "Must have been his nickname. 'Thank you for what you done. You know I'll follow you to the edge of the universe to have my way with you.' Then, in parentheses, 'Ha Ha. Can't wait to see you. And meet your adorable daughter. I bet you can guess what will happen then.' And then, squeezed vertically along the torn edge of the page, 'Hardy Ha Ha.' It's signed Angie."

"Not the most educated lady on the planet."

Madison turned the envelope. "Postmarked almost a year ago." She started to flip the letter frisbee-style toward the wastebasket.

"Not yet," I said. I put it back in its envelope with the others and shoved them all back in the drawer.

"Let's get the flag to the bank." Then I glanced around the room. "Did Wayland have a computer?"

"Don't know. I didn't notice one. But it would be unusual if he didn't."

After a last look at the old desk, I said, "Maybe Garner took *it* too."

Chapter 8

En route to the Hendersonville Savings and Trust, Madison and I tried to imagine where the old flag had come from and why it had been hidden.

"He must have spent a wad for it," she said.

"If it's too valuable to display, why have it?"

"Maybe just the thrill of ownership."

"If I were the betting type," I said, looking for a conspiracy, "I'd lay money on there being some sinister reason for keeping it out of sight."

"D'you think it could be what he and Garner were arguing about?"

"Didn't you say that Wayland said something like 'all I got for it was—'? If it had been sold, it wouldn't have been there for us to find."

"What if he *pretended* to sell it?"

It took almost a half hour to get to Hendersonville, find the bank and rent a safe deposit box. We tucked it carefully in the box.

On the way back to Flat Rock, stopped at a red light, Madison's phone trilled. She glanced at it and said, "Don't recognize the number." She put it to her ear and answered. "Hi, it's Madison ... " She listened. "Nice of you to offer, but no thanks. I'm somewhat busy, as you might guess ... Ciao." The light turned green.

"Who?"

"Ned Ferguson, if you can believe it. An invitation to show me the gardens we didn't get to on Wednesday."

"Not both of us?"

"He didn't mention you."

Hmmm, whispered Grandpa Jack.

She turned to me. "Makes no sense."

"Maybe angling for a date?" I said, hoping to inject an ounce of levity.

Madison guffawed and we were quiet for several miles while I tried to conjure why Ned would have made that invitation when he knew that we'd be on our way back to Maryland on Monday.

Madison broke the silence. "Let's stop for lunch before we go back. My treat. There's something I need to tell you."

A blue-and-white checkered sign: ALEXANDER'S ARGONAUT loomed on the left. I glanced in the mirror, snapped the turn signal and braked, waited for a pickup to pass, and turned in.

At a booth, we ordered tumblers of the house Robola while we inspected the menus.

Madison took a gulp. "I ought to fill you in on a couple of things."

"Things I need to know, or just that you want to get off your chest?"

"Both, I think."

"You're sounding mysterious."

Past the usual lunch hour, there were only two couples in the restaurant, laughing at something one of the women said. Not much chance we'd be overheard.

"So my stepdad did some very bad things," Madison said. "With money. He embezzled from companies where he did their bookkeeping." She chugged her Robola.

"You said he taught history."

"He did," she said, staring into her wine, "until the college terminated him for sexual harassment."

What? "Was the accusation true?"

"I never knew." Madison reddened. "And it didn't

matter. He had to leave the college."

There was something she wasn't saying.

The waitress returned and we gave her our orders. Madison asked for a wine refill.

"Wayland learned bookkeeping and my dad hired him for his plumbing company. That's how Wayland and my mom met."

"Okaayyy."

"Let me back up," she said. "When my real dad and mom married, it was one of those 'I can help him quit drinking after we're married' things. It took ten years for her to wake up to the fact that she couldn't."

"Your biological father."

Madison nodded. Maybe there was more to this story than she wanted to tell.

"After the divorce, she married Wayland. Funny thing was that my dad kept Wayland on as a bookkeeper for the business."

"I think I'm following," I said.

"A couple of years later, my dad suspected something wasn't kosher with his taxes. He asked another accountant to look over his books. That guy found mistakes. Then an auditor found more than errors—fraud. A couple of Wayland's other clients hired auditors who found similar patterns. Bingo, a trial, he's convicted, and he's gone. Mom divorced him, and after all his debts and fines were paid, she's had nothing but her social security. That's where I come in."

"Thank God for daughters who care." Somehow I couldn't help thinking that her recitation of Wayland's history sounded rehearsed. If it was, she was a frightfully good storyteller.

"So, it wasn't just that he was hard to get along with that I hadn't seen him for all those years. He was in prison—Roxbury in Hagerstown."

Where the strange letter in Wayland's desk was postmarked. From a girlfriend named Angie. I tried not to let my surprise show.

Our gyro plates arrived piled high with fries and generous dollops of tzatziki.

"So, he got a twenty-year sentence?"

She popped a pair of fries into her mouth. "Almost—eighteen."

"Isn't that a long time for a white-collar crime?"

Madison swallowed. "I hope you can understand how thankful I am that your aunt helped find him. I had no idea where he'd gone after he was released."

Side-stepped the question, Grandpa Jack whispered.

+ + +

I left a few fries on my plate to justify ordering a baclava and espresso. Madison undoubtedly felt superior by having cleaned her plate and ordering a cup of locally-roasted coffee. She paid the bill while I dropped a tip on the table, and we stumbled back to our purple Nissan for the short ride back to Kalorama.

Headed west on the Sandburg Pike, Madison echoed my question: "What drew me to landscape architecture?"

I'd asked because I was a Penny-come-lately to the prospect of becoming a landscape architect. When I started at the Naval Academy, I'd never even heard of the profession. My Navy career had ended four years ago when I returned to Annapolis and began working for my senior prom date's dad in his public relations business. Since then I'd qualified as a Master Gardener and found that, with the exception of mucking in goldfish ponds, I enjoyed all things horticultural. That led me to start my part-time business, Summers Breeze Gardening, and take Madison's design course at Annapolis Community College.

"Interesting question," Madison said. She was in her forties and had been an adjunct instructor in the Horticulture and Landscape Design Department for several years.

I asked her if, like me, she'd first been a gardener.

"I think it started when I was in middle school," she said, "when I began having weird dreams about being lost in a huge garden. Different nights there were different gardens, but the strange thing was, in every one, there was a tower, a like a medieval clock tower that I could see from wherever I was. Different gardens but always the same tower. So in my dreams, with the tower in sight, I knew I wasn't lost. All I had to do was get to the tower and I'd be safe."

Freud, I was willing to bet, would have a field day with those garden dreams. They begged for clarification. Once again I wondered if I should have majored in psychology and studied dream interpretation.

"Eventually," Madison continued, "I began refashioning the gardens in the dreams, changing the flowers, adding trees, moving shrubs, building paths, and like that. The feeling that I was in control in those gardens was, please excuse the word, magical. Then I'd wake up and try to remember how the garden had been laid out. I'd sketch my ideas during study hall and once I constructed a layout of a huge garden on a sheet of foam board with dried flower stems for trees and greenery from the model train store. I bought the tower in the section with model-size towns and bought four cheap watches to be the clocks in the tower. Don't know why that was important, but it seemed important at the time. Then another kid and I built a model garden maze for a science project. That was when I decided I wanted to do this kind of thing for neighbors, figuring out how to make their gardens easier to get lost in. Of course the neighbors *I* knew didn't have space for the gardens I dreamt about. And I think it was my mom who told me professionals called landscape architects got paid for playing with models like that."

"I guess I'd better start dreaming big," I said, "if I'm ever going to use any ideas from Brantleigh."

"Penny," she said, "you've shown a good sense of balance in your concepts. One day you'll have a commission for a landscape design large enough to incorporate something from Olmsted."

When Pigs Fly, I thought, but I could hope.

Chapter 9

A single flower stem of Koreanspice viburnum was the centerpiece on Aunt Zelma's kitchen table but its perfume was no match for an overwhelming Essence d'Oregano. Aunt Zee licked her fingers and looked up from the remnant of a pizza wedge on her plate. "Feta, mushroom, and olive—my once-a-month indulgence."

"Sorry we took so long," Madison said.

"The good news, if you can call it that," I said, "is the medical examiner says Wayland died from cardiac arrest."

"When your time comes," my aunt said, "that's a better way to go than a lot of others I could name."

Zelma's percolator hissed and spit. "Care for some coffee?"

In spite of the heady aroma, neither of us jumped at the invitation.

"With a fresh-from-the-oven raspberry tart?"

We immediately acquiesced.

My aunt chose three mugs from her cupboard. I poured while she opened her oven, pulled out the tart, and cut three squares.

Madison and I summarized our visit to Wayland's apartment, Claude Garner's appearance, and the old flag we'd taken to the bank.

She followed a nibble of tart with a sip of coffee. "Claude and Wayland were friends, so I can't believe he's involved in anything more than preparation for the reenactment."

"I think there was far more between them," Madison said, "than the disagreement Garner claimed. That story isn't over yet."

And I'll wager it won't end with everyone living happily

ever after, Grandpa Jack added.

"Their argument was so heated," I said, "that before she heard the M.E.'s report, Madison was sure Garner had killed him."

"Listen, I've known Claude since he started high school," my aunt said. "Trust me, he's not the type to get involved in anything ... violent."

"Except," I said, "peddling fake Civil War buckles?"

"Oh," she sniffed, "a schoolboy prank."

Madison frowned, tossed me a quick glance, and blew across a bite of tart to cool it.

Aunt Zelma set down her mug. "If there's nothing on your agenda this afternoon, I could take you to Carl Sandburg's farm. It's quite close. You'd love the descendants of his wife's herd of goats."

Madison loves animals as much as I do but I felt drawn to check on preparations at Brantleigh for tomorrow's reenactment.

Madison agreed with me, so Aunt Zee said she'd go to "Carl's place" as she called it to reminisce with Sandburg's spirit, and join us for the reenactment tomorrow.

+ + +

After passing through Brantleigh's twin gatehouses with portals that could have been suitably graced by Swiss guards, Madison and I wound our way to the reenactment area. Pickups and campers and trailers, oh my. Under a warm Carolina sun, blue and tan and gray uniformed men carried bundles of firewood to a gently sloped grassy field where rows of white tents were being erected. An antique American flag ruffled in the breeze where the Yankee reenactors would spend the night. Beyond, a North Carolina battle flag with its broad blue and white stripe and white star in a red field identified the defenders' tent zone.

Confederates unloaded cannons and gun carriages from trailers and maneuvered them to the far side of the field. Two officers huddled over a topographical map. One wore a Confederate tan uniform with gold braid on his cuffs and a wine-colored sash. The other in Union blue looked like Claude Garner.

We passed a row of sutlers' tents where made-in-China Civil War caps and knapsacks were being unpacked and readied for sale by contemporary versions of the traders who followed Civil War encampments selling, at inflated prices even then, food, uniforms, mess kits, and other necessities.

Under a big tent, rows of folding chairs were being arranged for presentations. A schedule nailed to a post told me that between interviews of the two commanders, there would be a fashion parade of women in their Civil War era finery.

Nearby, two women in frilly dresses, their hair adorned with feathers, gave passersby beguiling glances, practicing the artifice of soiled doves. But they looked no more like Civil War camp followers than I would have passed for a wife of Henry the Eighth.

Wood smoke drifted from a few small campfires where women in dresses fashioned from feed sacks prepared vittles for their menfolk.

"This wasn't on my tour."

I recognized the voice but I had to turn to recognize its owner. It's one thing to be told that a man is a Civil War reenactor but it's another to see his familiar form in a blue uniform with chevrons on the shoulders and a kepi cap crushed on his head. "Corporal Wycliffe Lemon, ma'am, at your service," said Ned Ferguson with a practiced nod.

He offered his gentlemanly arms and led us to the Union officer with the claret sash. "Colonel Kirby, may I introduce a couple of Yankees?"

Garner had added the sash to the uniform from Wayland's closet. The gold-fringed epaulettes on his shoulders put me in mind of Admiral Nelson at the Battle of Trafalgar which we'd studied at the Naval Academy. But his cowboy-style hat was circled by yellow cords with tasseled tips, not at all like Admiral Nelson's bicorn. Embroidered eagles adorned his stiff blue collar. Tasseled ends of the red sash hung by his side. His double-breasted frock coat with rows of gold buttons and a sword at his side suggested he was ready for battle. Or, at least, for visitors' cameras.

"Good day, ladies. What a pleasure!"

"Why cuhnel, it's a real pleasure to meet y'all." Madison, mutated into Scarlett O'Hara, curtseyed and baited him with her tongue-in-cheek performance.

Where on earth was Madison going with this?

Garner fingered his goatee. "I assure you, the pleasure's all mine, miss."

She flattered him with a coy smile. "Are your boys going to win this one, or slink away with your tails between your legs like y'all did in 1865?"

"Well, ma'am," he replied in a surly voice, "we've agreed to follow the dictates of history, although, if I were you, I wouldn't say anything about tails between legs near a Union campground." A smile belied his gruff warning.

"But, sir, history suggests your boys were in such haste to get back to Tennessee that they tossed away equipment to lighten their load."

Garner smiled cryptically and turned away.

Nearby, the tan-uniformed Confederate colonel stood

with a group of red-capped artillerymen, instructing them, I supposed, as to where to position their cannons.

"Colonel Clayton, sir," Ned interrupted, "I've rounded up a pair of Yankee spies."

"We're busted," I whispered to Madison.

"... as near the tree-line as possible," Clayton finished with the artillerymen. Then turned to meet the spies.

"This is Lorenzo Peters," Ned said to Madison. "He's filling in for your stepdad as commander of the Home Guard." Lorenzo looked as if he'd walked straight out of a Mathew Brady tintype. A battle-weary gray slouch hat shaded his suntanned, creased, and bristled face. Gold curlicues on his jacket cuffs and three gold stars on each side of his stiff collar indicated his rank.

"Colonel," Ned said, "this here's Wayland's stepdaughter, Madison, and one of her design students from Maryland."

Peters yanked off his slouch hat and offered his hand to Madison. "Miss Morgan, we're all so very sorry about Wayland's death. He was quite the historian and an earnest reenactor." New creases appeared on his forehead. "Have they figured out what happened?"

"The M.E. thinks it was something like a heart attack. And, for the record, my last name's not Morgan. It's Lerrimore."

"I stand corrected and hope y'all will come back tomorrow."

"We'll be here, yes sir. We're anxious to see you fend off Ned ... excuse me, Corporal Lemon here, and the rest of the Union interlopers."

Ned laughed self-consciously.

"Yes, ma'am," Lorenzo Peters said, "you'll see history

repeat itself. Don't be late now." Then he excused himself and ordered his bugler to assemble his troops.

As we walked away, Ned said, "Since he arrived this morning, he's been in a royal funk. This place is so unlike the topography where the battle actually took place. There aren't any overlooks where he could realistically place his cannons. And he's not allowed to dig earthworks."

"At the real battle site, you probably couldn't accommodate visitors," I said.

"More important," Madison added, "Brantleigh wouldn't rake in any admission money."

I was thinking about the battlefield casualties during the war. "Will there be battlefield doctors?"

"Doc Thompson should be here later today," Ned said. "He's got a whole kit of surgeon's knives and saws. And he's always happy to explain the gory details. I for one am happy to be a twenty-first century reenactor rather than a Civil War Billy Yank. You can look for Doc's hospital tent tomorrow."

On second thought, I wasn't sure I'd want to hear any of the gruesome details.

"During the reenactment," Ned said, "in case of heat stroke or whatever, there'll be an honest-to-God modern ambulance standing by."

In her Scarlett O'Hara drawl, Madison sighed. "Thank heaven."

Garner hadn't yet called his troops to muster, so Ned took time to show us where the battle lines would be. He pointed out the Yankees' approach route "yonder," and where the defenders' trenches would be simulated.

"Right about here is where you'll have the best view of the defenders firing at us." He indicated a vantage point just outside the already erected spectator fence.

We thanked him and as he turned to go, Madison apologized for not having time to tour the rest of the Brantleigh gardens with him.

Ned touched his cap. "After the weekend, perhaps."

We started back past Sutler's Row to the mown field that served as the parking area. "Madison," I said, "do you still want to come to the reenactment tomorrow now that Lorenzo will be role-playing Colonel Clayton?"

"Of course," she said, as if there were never any doubt. "We're assuming Garner will be using Wayland's rifle. It'll be a kick to see it in action."

"He doesn't seem to have it with him today."

"Wouldn't need it for the set-up day, though, would he?"

Grandpa Jack wasn't sure.

Chapter 10

Saturday morning, after one of Aunt Zelma's famous blueberry pancake and sausage breakfasts, the three of us headed to the reenactment in Aunt Zelma's Lexus SUV.

We were soon at the end of a slow-moving cavalcade of cars approaching the French Broad River Bridge and the Brantleigh gate. "Looks like Wayland was right," I said. "Brantleigh Manor's going to make money today."

"I wonder," Madison mused, "how many people here had great-grand-dads who were in the war?"

"I've always thought I'd have liked to have been a Silver Gray," Aunt Zee announced. She caressed her white hair and laughed. "Now I'd be eligible."

"You have any of old Percy's guns?" I asked.

Zelma shook her head. "Long gone."

"Were there women among the Silver Grays?" asked Madison.

"There were quite a few women on both sides who disguised themselves and took a man's name to volunteer. So it's entirely possible that there were Asheville women helping to repel those Yankees a hundred and fifty years ago."

Ticket takers outfitted as Civil War veterans in the Brantleigh gatehouses relieved us of a couple of bills, stamped the backs of our hands, and welcomed us to the 150th Anniversary Battle of Asheville. Following signs in Civil War era lettering, we found our way to the site.

There was no doubt this was Dixie—seemed like half the cars and pickups in the field today had the Stars and Bars for a front tag. The Aerie Lodge restaurant was already doing what my aunt referred to as a landslide business, wait-staff hustling among patrons overflowing the patio. It was a crowded but short walk from the parking area to Sutlers Row. Battle flags waved lazily in a light breeze where canteens, tin cups, buckles and buttons, and kid-size rifles were selling at tourist prices.

We agreed that quite a few of today's crowd could tell stories of their Confederate forebears.

"Isn't it strange," Aunt Zelma said, "There's still all this enthusiasm for something that was over and done with a hundred and fifty years ago?"

"Like living history," Madison said, "except it's darned difficult to feel very historic among all these twenty-first-century gawkers."

"Early in the war …" A familiar voice. Wycliffe Lemon aka Ned Ferguson, his musket at 'present arms', was surrounded by listeners. "… the Brantleys owned an armory that manufactured Enfield rifles. But most of the muskets and rifles you'll see today are reproductions. This one—" Ned lifted it higher "—is a copy of an 1842 Springfield, originally made in Massachusetts." We joined his group of fans.

I tried to recall the musket in the photo of Wayland leading troops into battle. But I had never been good at finding elusive differences between two similar pictures. So I couldn't tell if Ned's musket was even the same model as Wayland's, much less if it was the missing one that we assumed Claude Garner would carry today.

He looked up and recognized my aunt. "Ms. Porter," he saluted. "What a fine day for a battle."

Aunt Zelma smiled.

"I'm sorry I couldn't come to your soirée," Ned said.

"There'll be more," my aunt assured him. "And what on

earth are you doing in Yankee blue?"

"I'm one of them dad-burned Yankees today. But rest assured, before the day's out, your Silver Grays will have us'uns headin' back up the Buncombe Pike."

A kepi-capped teen in a Hendersonville Grenadiers tee shirt raised his hand. "What kind of bullets do you use?"

"Good question," Ned said. "Reenactors don't use bullets but we use the same kind of black powder that was used in the war." He reached into his ammunition pouch on his belt and pulled out a small paper tube shaped like a short cigarette. "This is what holds the black powder. See how the end is scrunched?" He showed the end to the group and moved it to his mouth. "When you watch a soldier reload you'll see him take one of these and use his teeth—" Ned pretended to bite off the end "—to rip open the tube." Pretending the tube had been opened, he tipped it over the muzzle of his rifle. "Then he'll pour the black powder down the bore. And here's where it's not real. In the war, he'd have a lead ball to drop into the rifle and use his ramrod to ram it into the powder. In reenactments, no lead balls and no ramrods. You'll just hear a bang and see some smoke. But, just like in the war, we have to reload after every shot."

"Cool," the kid said, and poked his thick glasses back in place.

The bugle call we'd heard yesterday sounded again. "Gotta go," Ned said. "Gettin' ready to march on Asheville. But, if history is our guide, we won't get past the defenders. You Yankees," he said looking at me and Madison, "shouldn't get your hopes up."

Corporal Lemon hurried to join the blue uniforms heading toward the distant hill where they would turn around to begin the assault.

We found the place Ned had suggested we'd have a good view of the action and were soon hemmed in by spectators. On our left, Lorenzo Peters as Colonel Clayton, with the crimson sash, assembled his home guard and Silver Grays. Nineteenth-century civilian clothes portrayed what the Grays had been wearing when the alarm was sounded: blacksmith, shop owner, tradesman. On a hill beyond, the cannons were now aimed toward where the Yankees would approach. Red-capped artillerymen went through their choreographed sequence of cleaning the barrel, ramming bags of gunpowder, loading an iron ball, and setting the primer.

After Colonel Clayton pep-talked his troops, he noticed our gang of Yankee spies and approached with a smile. "Y'all have a great position to see us fight off the Yankees, but you're going to be mighty close to the action. You'll want to cover your ears."

"Ned Ferguson," I said, "told us this would be a good spot."

"That's true," he said, "but you should never trust a Union soldier." He laughed. "But when I see a spectator this close to the action, it puts me in the mind of the story I heard tell of a woman near a Civil War battleground—don't recall which—who was hit in the belly by a stray bullet and later found she was pregnant. Seems the bullet had first torn through a soldier's family jewels."

Madison smiled plausibly, but I knew she wasn't fooled. "Medically impossible," she said. "Must have been a campfire hoax."

"Gotcha," said Lorenzo Peters with a broad smile.

"At reenactments," I heard a man behind me say, "sometimes a soldier'll play gettin' hit, sprawled out there till a battlefield doctor can get to 'em." We turned to face him. His sideburns suggested he was a sometime reenactor. If not, he had seen reenactors pretending to be wounded. His narrowed eyes seemed to hold an animal fury. "Far as I recall," he said, "there was a coupla Yankee casualties in the Asheville battle. Only one o'ourn was wounded."

"Glad that man was only aiming his eyes at us," I said.

"Look yonder!" someone called. We looked toward the distant ridge and drew a collective breath. A tiny battle banner followed by a tight column of blue uniforms was coming into view. Lorenzo Peters called to his bugler. Urgent clarion notes loud enough to be heard in the next county called the Confederate defenders to hustle into position behind a simulated barricade of branches, bring their rifles to bear on the northerners in the distance, and await the order to commence firing.

As the Yankees got closer, Aunt Zelma pointed out the battle flag billowing above the Union flag-bearer. It was like the present-day American flag except the stars were arranged in concentric circles instead of a rectangle. "Looks almost like the one from Wayland's closet," I whispered to Madison. Visitors moved closer to the spectator fence, crowding us in.

"We get many more folks here," Aunt Zee said, "we're going to have to introduce ourselves." Around us, the crowd bustled in anticipation. Smartphone cameras began documenting the action.

Behind us, at the rear of their makeshift barricade, Colonel Clayton with his uniformed Home Guard and oddly dressed Silver Grays waited.

A loud pop and a wisp of smoke from a distant Union rifle. The kaboom of a cannon reverberated. White smoke drifted from the distant battery and a second explosion boomed across the field. The Union brigade kept coming.

Lorenzo Peters gave the order. "Fire at will!"

A series of ear-splitting cracks from the defenders beside us. His admonition had been correct—the sound level where we stood would damage unprotected ears. But we were crowded in. All we could do was cover our ears. The second cannon boomed and billowed white smoke. Smoke tendrils rose from the Confederates' rifles. Riflemen's teeth tore the tops from white tubes and emptied the black powder into gun muzzles. With firing caps in place and guns cocked, the defenders fired again. From where we were, it looked like the oncoming Yankees were coming straight at us. Ned was right. This was indeed a great vantage point. But all it would have taken is a reenactor with real bullets and poor eyesight and ... I couldn't bear to think about it. I'd been fortunate to have been on an aircraft carrier during Iraqi Freedom and not in ground combat.

When the Union column was within a couple of football field lengths, they spread into a wide formation, six abreast, shoulder to shoulder, a second line behind the first. A volley crashed, smoke rose, and the second rank stepped between them. Another volley, like all the popcorn in hell. When the flag-bearer was within a hundred yards, our defenders fired again. And again. The Battle of Asheville raged.

Through the drifting smoke, I noticed Garner, as Colonel Kirby, behind the Yankee flag-bearer, leading his troops toward us. Both his arms were raised, one with his sword extended, the other waved a pistol in our direction. Where was Wayland's rifle?

Madison, fingers in her ears, yelled over the pandemonium, "I can't make out who's who except for the two colonels." At that instant, a clod of dirt jumped from the ground and Madison collapsed. I figured she'd fainted.

I looked down. Blood seeped through her jeans.

Chapter 11

I yelled: "Madison's been hit."
Madison mumbled, obviously in shock.
I yelled again. "A woman's been shot!"
"Get a doctor!" Aunt Zelma screamed.
Spectators peered down, uncomprehending, and backed away. Madison was dazed, moaning and barely breathing.
"Knife!" I yelled. A man tugged a Winchester knife from its belt pouch, opened it, and handed it to me. Thank God it was devilishly sharp. I carefully slit Madison's jeans as far as her knee, pulled it up and away from the damage and pressed my hand over her nasty wound.
"Sir, quick!" Blood seeped between my fingers. "Give me the belt."
The man unhooked his oval CS buckle, yanked the wide leather strap from his pants and handed it down. Aunt Zelma helped me wrap it around Madison's wounded leg below the knee above the wound, snugging it tightly while I kept one hand pressed against the injury.
"Cease firing," Lorenzo Peters yelled. Garner echoed the order to his blue-uniformed troops. One last bang and the reenactment skidded to a stop. Across the meadow, a final cannon thundered. The battle ended.
"Make a hole!" A Brantleigh security officer materialized, pushing the crowd apart to make a lane for an ambulance. "Step aside! Now." Horn in staccato mode, its siren growling, the orange-striped ambulance backed slowly, red and white flashers insistent. As it halted, an EMT yanked the rear doors open and a gurney materialized. Two EMTs in a practiced motion lifted Madison onto it. One opened an equipment case, yanked out a pressure pad and a

tourniquet. He ripped the pad open, carefully lifted my palm, and pressed it in place. The second EMT wrapped the tourniquet below her knee alongside the belt and twisted the rod until the bleeding was nearly stanched. My hands quivered. Madison wasn't the only one in shock.

Techs lifted the gurney, rolled it into the ambulance and locked it down. "Boogie time," one yelled and jumped behind the wheel. The siren yelped. The other tossed me the borrowed belt and jumped in alongside his patient. The rear doors slammed. The siren burped out mini-shrieks as it rolled carefully through the parking area, and gathered speed.

The belt's donor wore a gray Confederate kepi cap over long gray locks. "Thanks," I said, and handed it back. "It may have saved her life." Then he noticed something at my feet.

"Well lookee there." He reached into the trampled grass. "I never seen one o' these. That's been shot, I mean."

"Can I take a look?" He handed the distorted lead ball to me. I turned it in my palm, a bit of blood in a crevice.

"Finders keepers." He grabbed it back.

I hadn't heard that since fourth grade. "Can I borrow it for a bit?" I said. "This minié ball is what hit my friend. It might help us figure out who shot her."

"I don't think so. You'll just keep it." Holding the bullet in one hand, he fed his long belt through the loops of his oversize pants. "I don't trust no Yankee further'n I can throw 'em." Satisfied the belt was in place, he snugged the bronze oval buckle prongs into a pair of holes. He didn't look fit enough to toss a newspaper to a porch.

"What made you think I was a Yankee, sir?"

"If y'all need to ask, y'all ain't as bright as you make out to be."

My aunt stepped closer. "Young man," she bellowed, "you're outnumbered."

Spectators stepped backward, fearing a brawl. The security officer worked his way toward us. Gray Locks glanced at the officer.

"Tell you what," he said. "I'd be willing to loan it to y'all. But I need a promise that I'll get it back."

"You'll take a promise from a Yankee?" I asked. He looked around.

"I'll guarantee it, young man." Aunt Zelma stood an inch or two taller than the man, her arms akimbo. "You can trust a Southern lady."

"Reckon I'm agoin' to have to," said Gray Locks.

I pulled a notebook from my backpack, opened to a blank page, and handed it to him. He touched his shirt pocket looking for a pen but it wasn't there. I handed him a pen.

"Name, rank, and serial number," he said. "That's all you'll get from me."

"You'd better add your address if you want it back," I said.

"Rightee-o." A smile crossed his face and I knew we were on the same side ... more or less. He glanced at the Summers Breeze Gardening card I pulled out. "I don't do any of that computer stuff."

"It's also got my phone and address."

Aunt Zelma took it, added her name and phone number on the back, and handed it to the man who reluctantly exchanged it for the lump of lead and the notebook page.

"I'll be expectin' to be hearin' from y'all right soon."

Chapter 12

At the Henderson County Sheriff's office, Detective Twomey, who remembered me from last week, was on duty. He didn't actually say *You again!* but I could tell that's what went through his mind when I told him I had the bullet that sent my friend to the hospital. He acknowledged that they'd been notified of the accident by Brantleigh Security and a pair of deputies had been dispatched. "Seems like we might should set up a field office out there," he said. "Be on hand for whatever's next." I attempted a polite smile. "I s'pose y'all want to tell me what happened?" I nodded.

I did my best to explain how it unfolded. When I mentioned that our Olmsted docent last week was one of the Union reenactors, he radioed the deputies who were presumably already interviewing witnesses.

I handed over the misshapen minié ball and was assured that it would go directly to the state's forensic lab in Raleigh. I copied our donor's address and explained my promise that the relic would be returned. "My reputation as a Yankee," I said, "is on the line here." Twomey smiled and assured me the lump of lead would eventually be returned to the man.

From there it was only a few minutes to the Belle Mère Hospital. I gave the Emergency Room receptionist Madison's name. "They took her directly into surgery," she said. We were directed to a waiting room.

"I can't stand hospitals," Aunt Zelma said. "Not since Daddy died. I don't even visit sick friends anymore unless they're home."

"Not my favorite place either," I said, "but the fickle finger of fate didn't give us a choice."

I checked my watch. The hospital's cafeteria was open

but neither of us had an appetite.

"That shot makes no sense," Aunt Zelma said.

"But it happened. It can't have been an accident."

"But who would have ..."

"Had to be one of the Union troops," I said.

"In other words ..." Her face was a palace of incredulity. He had been her student, her protégé. "Garner."

"But Garner didn't have a rifle," I said. "He had a sword and pistol."

If it wasn't Garner, Grandpa Jack whispered, *then who borrowed Wayland's rifle?* Aunt Zee's voice tumbled over her brother's. "If he only had a sword and a pistol," she said, tilting her head, genuinely perplexed, "then who shot Madison?"

"If you eliminate the impossible," I said, "according to Sherlock, whatever remains must be the truth." Aunt Zee appeared confused. "Must've been Ned," I said.

Her confusion morphed into disbelief and finally acceptance.

While I pretended to peruse a magazine, my brain replayed everything I thought I knew about everything leading up to the shooting.

Aunt Zee wondered aloud if Wayland's death and Madison's "accident" could be related. But that possibility, too, made no sense.

Grandpa Jack had always said I could add two and two and come up with an orange, but no amount of mental gymnastics revealed any theories that could connect the two events. The maddening thing was, as I realized, the two events *might* be random but if they weren't, there had to be a common denominator.

We scanned *National Geographic* and *People*

magazines, *Psychology Today,* and even an old *Better Homes and Gardens*. Three cups of stale coffee and as many visits to the ladies' later, I inquired at the nurse's station. Madison was still in surgery.

I was attempting to memorize a recipe for barbecued shrimp and grits in *Our State* magazine when a surgeon walked in and introduced himself. Dr. Selkirk wore his surgical mask under his chin; his scrub cap was patterned with flames. "Thanks to your quick action," he said in an unmistakable Carolina accent, "and the on-scene EMTs, your friend's prognosis is excellent. Given the tincture of time, I think she'll make a full recovery."

"What happens now?" I asked.

"I want to monitor her here for at least a week," Selkirk said, "then we'll assess. She'll start physical therapy here and need to continue afterward for several weeks. It'll be a while before she'll be able to put her weight on that leg."

"I didn't say anything earlier," Aunt Zelma whispered. "I didn't want to sound neurotic. But my meditation stones this morning foretold ..."

They *what?*

Selkirk, eyebrow raised, regarded my aunt, but dismissed the transient thought. "Rather complex surgery," he said. "Reminded me of injuries I've read about during the Civil War," he said. "Her tibia was shattered and there was a lot of collateral damage in her musculature. Back then, the battlefield surgeon would have had no choice but to amputate."

I shuddered.

"Fortunately," he added, "it missed her fibula."

All I understood was "musculature." I'd ask my brother Spencer to educate me on leg bones the next time we were together.

"There was," Selkirk added, "something unusual about her wound. Soil particles in the tissue." Bingo, the puff of dirt.

"We found the minié ball," I said. "Must have boomeranged off the ground before it hit her."

"Just think ...," Dr. Selkirk said, smiling sardonically, "I've waited a hundred and fifty years to stitch up a Confederate."

"Sorry to be the bearer of bad news," I said. "She's a Yankee."

"In that case," the surgeon said, his weird smile switching to a genuine one, "it's a good thing the Hippocratic Oath requires us to care for both sides."

He instructed a nurse to allow us to visit Madison as soon as she was taken to a room. But for only a few minutes.

Madison was sedated, her eyes closed. Rhythmic bleeps from wavy-lined monitors punctuated the otherwise tranquil intensive care room. Plastic bags dripped fluids. Her left leg was snared in what resembled a cylindrical basket. Dr. Selkirk explained that it was a fixator to keep her leg immobilized.

I leaned close and whispered, hoping she could hear me. "I'll call Cheyenne."

Madison had first introduced me to her partner and their daughter Kalea when our class met at their house to practice on-site measurements. Then last week, they'd applauded when I blew out thirty-three candles with one long puff.

"Tell ... Melanie." Her eyelids twitched.

Melanie? "Melanie who?"

Aunt Zelma shrugged.

"Thass okay ..." Madison drifted in and out of

consciousness.

Sedatives had done their job. But who on earth was Melanie?

Madison struggled back to the surface. "I don't think ... accident."

"We found the bullet," I said. "The cops may be able to link it to one of the rifles."

Madison's eyed attempted to focus. "I'm ... so sorry our trip ... turned to cra—"

"Nobody's fault," Zelma whispered.

"Wayland ....," she began.

What about Wayland?

"Now I'll never have a chance ... to make up with the old bastard." She closed her eyes and returned to la-la land.

"Did she just call her stepfather a bastard?" Zelma asked.

"She'll be more coherent tomorrow."

"Don't be too sure," my aunt said. "Heavy-duty painkillers can foul up your brain—how do you say—big-time?"

Maybe he was a bastard, Grandpa Jack whispered.

Chapter 13

Back at Kalorama, I sulked while my aunt gradually illuminated her version of a gothic church at midnight. So many candles blossomed from the coffee table in the salon it was difficult to see the bouquet of red tulips she'd brought from the kitchen. Candles flickered everywhere: in wall sconces, on side tables, and in candelabras on the ancient mantel. "That ought to dispel the sinister vibrations," she said. When she'd lit the last candle, she went to the kitchen and returned with the same amontillado and goblets we'd used the first evening, apparently her standard accessories for a heart-to-heart.

I couldn't think beyond the fact that the tulips were the same color as Madison's blood. But I wasn't in the mood to wallow in symbolism, so I summoned a half-hearted smile and sipped the sweet wine.

Aunt Zee sipped as she settled beside me on the plush sofa. "When you and Madison arrived," she said, "the first thing I noticed was her aura. Dusty gray. Since Wayland's death, it's darker. I think she's a messenger."

This was a language I didn't understand. "What ... do you mean ... messenger?"

"I could see she had a load of psychic baggage. What I didn't know, and still don't, is whether she wants to unload it here or take it back with her."

Before this trip, I'd never doubted my aunt's sanity nor even been aware of her professed ability to sense auras and vibrations. Or converse with spirits. My world had always consisted of what I could see and touch. Except, of course, for her brother's, my Grandpa Jack's, intermittent whispers.

"I should have guessed," she said, "when I found my

alexandrite alongside my tourmaline. The accident shouldn't have been a surprise."

"Seems to me," I said, "that if carrying psychological baggage makes us messengers, then we're all messengers."

"Except, you see," Aunt Zee went on to explain, "There's a difference between psychological and *psychic*. A *psychologist* can help you discover your psychological baggage. Whereas psychic baggage is lodged in the etheric body—"

While she motored on about auras and etheric bodies, my thoughts jumped to more practical matters. I realized there was no way I could return to Annapolis on Monday. I needed to stay in North Carolina. I couldn't leave Madison on her own. My new client would have to wait.

"I'm afraid I can't comment on auras or psychic baggage," I said. "But what's happened to Madison has changed everything. If your invitation's still open I'd like to stay until I can see this craziness through."

"You wouldn't be the Penelope I know if you didn't. My invitation's always open."

I excused myself and went to the veranda where there was decent iPhone reception and cancelled our Monday flights back to Maryland.

When I returned inside, Aunt Zelma had refilled our goblets. I wasn't sure if more amontillado would improve my ability to discover whatever was still in the realm of the unknown. But a swallow or two might help. I was willing to go with that possibility.

"So if the reenactment accident *wasn't* accidental," my aunt said, and believe you me, there are no accidents, maybe Wayland's death was not a heart attack or arrhythmia or whatever the medical examiner called it."

"The *shoot*ing was certainly not accidental," I insisted. "But I'm not seeing a connection with Wayland's death—"

"I haven't the faintest either," Aunt Zee interrupted, "but first poor Wayland dies and then what could have been an attempt on his stepdaughter's life—it can't be a coincidence."

Here we go round again, Grandpa Jack whispered.

I was still in shock. My brain cells were slow in connecting. "Be right back," I said. "I need to call Cheyenne." Fortified with another swallow of amontillado, I went back to the veranda and phoned Madison's partner. I tried not to make the *accident* sound as frightening as it actually was, but she immediately jumped into panic mode. I had to tell her that I didn't think it *was* an accident.

"Someone, one of the reenactors," she shrieked, "wanted to hurt her?"

I tried to assure her that no one knew anything for certain at this point and that after the police examined the lead ball they should have some leads. I added that I planned to visit the hospital this evening. But avoided telling her why.

"Tell her Kalea and I will get there as soon as we can. We'll try for Tuesday."

I would need more than amontillado to work up the fortitude to make my second call, to Aidan Reid, to postpone our meeting.

"Cheyenne and Kalea are planning to fly down Tuesday," I told Aunt Zelma.

"I hope you told her they're welcome to stay here."

I picked at a patch of soft wax on a candle. "You're very generous, but I suspect Shy will want to stay near the hospital. Kalea, though, might stay with us. You'll love her."

Aunt Zee seemed to relax. "I know I will."

"Back to Wayland," I said. "I have to agree with you. So if his death was not related to a heart problem—"

"Unless it was somehow triggered by someone who wanted him out of the way."

"Madison said he'd been told by a doctor that his heart was good for another fifty years."

"Ned Ferguson told the detectives at Brantleigh he assumed Wayland had a hangover Wednesday morning when he went for a walk. But walking to clear your head doesn't cause a heart attack."

"It had to be a shock, finding him in the garden," she said.

"Definitely not one of my favorite moments."

"You've always been sensitive."

Where was she headed with this? "What does sensitivity have to do with thinking Wayland might not have had a heart attack?"

Aunt Zelma pushed her goblet in a slow circle. "What I mean is that you seem to be able to sense the unseen. If you think something is not as it appears, you consider the alternatives."

We try, Grandpa Jack whispered.

"So, if it wasn't arrhythmia," I said, "is it possible either Claude Garner or your friend Lynn were angry enough to want him dead?"

Aunt Zelma set her goblet down, and looked me in the eye. "It's a long way from anger to murder. That would take a whole passel of angries."

"Just trying to think of possibilities."

"Lynn had issues with him, sure, but she misses him. That's not to say I've never seen her angry. But she'd never cross the line from protect and defend to transgress and offend."

"Then what about Garner? Wayland undoubtedly knew of his bogus buckles business—"

"I simply can't imagine either of them killing anyone," Aunt Zelma said. "But if you're thinking of painting Wayland with Garner's brush," she said, "you should probably add Ned Ferguson to your palette. Both were chummy with Wayland."

It was time to come clean with my aunt. "I think Ned shot Madison."

Now you've cut your problem down to at least double, Grandpa Jack muttered.

I replied, silently, with a clean variation of my brother's once favorite flip rejoinder: *No kidding, Sherlock.*

I sipped the last of the strong wine.

"Refill?"

I shook my head. A pleasant buzz told me I'd had enough.

Aunt Zelma sipped as she stared into the evening out the window, and finally changed the subject. "How's your friend at the Naval Academy?"

Last year Senior Chief Petty Officer Aaron Hunt and I had sleuthed together in Annapolis to find his girlfriend's killer.

"Aaron? He's at Kings Bay in Georgia now. He's the command master chief of one of the submarine squadrons. We keep in touch, but we're just friends."

She adjusted a red tulip in the bouquet. "Penny ... I'm just saying, King's Bay'd be only a one-day drive from here." I knew she'd get around to hinting about my love life.

"That would be nice," I said. "If there was time. But I need to help Madison get to the bottom of this business and get back to Annapolis."

"What I'm saying is that it can't hurt to check on him while you're so close." A coquettish smirk. "All work and no play, you know."

How to respond without rejecting her sincere concern? "Actually ... he'll be in Annapolis next month and we're planning to have dinner together." I trusted this would quell my aunt's niggling on my love life.

"Still," she urged, "you could—"

"But I need ... I have to get back to Annapolis as soon as possible. It's my first real design commission."

She sat back. "Using what you've learned from Madison?"

I nodded. "And before I see Mr. Reid, I have to fix a couple of problems Madison found with my plan."

My aunt picked at an aging scarlet petal. "Of course I'm not your mother ... or your grandmother ... so please accept what I'm going to say in the spirit it's intended." She tore the old petal and scrunched it between her fingers, looking straight at me.

"You've had a rough go, you know, losing your mother as you did. But I believe your DNA has equipped you for far more than success as a Naval officer. Or for the public relations career you seem embarked on—"

"Don't leave out gardening," I injected, with what I imagined was a self-deprecating smile. The horizon's the limit, I recalled Madison once telling our class, meaning, I supposed, that the view of a garden didn't end at the property line, and design considerations shouldn't either.

"I know it's your obsession—no, I should've said your *passion* now. You wouldn't be here otherwise."

Maybe her stones had helped her see me more clearly

than I knew myself.

"Tell me what's new in Annapolis," she said, decanting another amontillado into her goblet.

"You remember what Grandpa Jack used to say—"

"About biting off more than you can chew?"

I chuckled. "It's my new middle name."

After six years in the Navy, I'd returned to civilian life in my hometown to a public relations job that has kept me and my long-haired Maine Coon housemate comfortably housed and reasonably well fed. A year and a half ago, on a whim, I'd signed up for Master Gardener training and when I realized that I actually enjoyed messing about with plants and planting, I'd proclaimed myself Gardener-in-Chief of Summers Breeze Gardens. In my far from humble opinion, it was a clever play on my last name. I bought a small van and had a friend set up a website offering my services. And because I'd decided to eventually become the *designer*-in-chief, I'd registered for Madison's residential landscape design course that led to this trip.

"I have a lot going on," I said. "But I wanted to see you."

I didn't mention my dread of returning to where my childhood had screeched to a stop.

Twenty-three years ago, on our last family visit, I was asked to keep an eye on my little brother, Josh. I don't remember where my older brother Spencer was, but Josh and I were at the pool and I remember reading *The Secret Garden* when I heard the splash. I panicked and screamed, pinned like an insect, unable to move.

Mom left us later that summer and Dad and Spence and I never returned. Josh's death also left me with the water phobia that nearly got me kicked out of the Naval Academy.

I had, of course, wanted to see my Aunt Zelma but deep

down I also harbored a faint hope that after all these years, seeing my aunt's cursed swimming pool would somehow allow me to step away from the curse of my little brother's death. I certainly didn't expect his young specter to offer absolution. Actually, I couldn't really expect anything. The pool would probably stay damned.

After today, my concerns had to take second place to Madison's.

Since I was now taking my friend under my proverbial wing, I needed to check on her. And solve the Melanie mystery.

Time to get back to Belle Mère Hospital.

Chapter 14

The nurse behind the counter recognized me and waved me toward Madison's room, saying she was resting comfortably.

The only light came from her cardiac and pulse-ox monitors weaving eerie lines across green screens. The basket around her leg was recognizable under the light blanket.

Once acclimated to the gloom, I found a chair and pulled it close enough to take her hand. I gave her what I hoped would be a gentle reassuring squeeze. She didn't wake, but withdrew her hand.

"You're not supposed to be here." Her befuddled voice mumbled strangely in a low register unlike anything I'd ever heard. "Don't start anything." It wasn't Madison's voice. Could the sedatives have changed her that much?

"Madison?" I'd never seen anyone under hypnosis but Madison was obviously in some kind of trance. I tried again. "Madison?" I said softly.

"I'm Angela," the strange voice replied. Ooops.

I quickly decided I'd have to go with the flow. "Angela?"

"I'm the guardian."

"Guarding who?"

"Melanie and Sammy," the voice growled.

Should I get out now? Before I inadvertently created havoc with her psychology.

Grandpa Jack whispered *Go on. Ask her why they need to be guarded.*

I hesitated but then followed his advice. "Why do they need guarding?"

In the time it took before her response, I considered that

maybe I should find out if there was a psychologist on duty who would know how to deal with this sort of thing.

The fuddled voice finally answered: "They're not safe."

"Not safe?" I whispered. "From?"

"The beast with the tail."

I'd had zip training in psychology and began to dread where this might be going.

"Angela—" Madison's own voice, distressed "—don't let him do that again."

Angela: "I'm not as strong as he is."

"Please. I don't want him to do it anymore."

A brighter, younger voice entered the conversation. "Sammy can forget about the beast. It's dead. We can have fun."

"Who are you?" I asked as gently as I could, not wanting to awaken Madison from this trance or dream or whatever it was.

"Silly. I'm Melanie," the new voice answered politely.

It dawned like a solar flare. Not with a bang but with Melanie's meek declaration. She and Angela were my friend's imaginary playmates. Madison's soul was revealing itself in a way it would have never done in daylight.

Who was I kidding? Subconscious probing was as far from my abilities as Baltimore is from Berlin. But I could use my old public affairs officer interviewing skills. "The beast. Did you see it?"

"I hid in the closet," Melanie said.

"Where was Angela?"

Melanie's breaths came in short hiccuppy bursts. "Guarding the door. She screamed. But he came in anyway. It was awful."

I didn't want to imagine the reality of it.

"But we don't need to worry anymore." Melanie again. "The beast is dead." Madison pulled her hand farther away as her breathing softened.

Mine was anything but. Adrenaline surged.

Where had I been? I'd only wanted to find out who Melanie was. Now I'd learned much more than I cared to know. Angela and Melanie had become Madison's imaginary friends when she was sexually abused. Her stepfather?

Not only could I not imagine the reality of what Madison had experienced, my heart pumped with compassion for my friend's horrible childhood. What was I supposed to do with this knowledge? Should I call Cheyenne?

Grandpa Jack said no. Shy would go berserk.

My allegiance to my professor and mentor was shot out of the sky.

No, not true. I still carried the allegiance. It had simply shifted into a new orbit. I looked forward to my third glass of amontillado—at Aunt Zelma's kitchen table, shuffling my thoughts.

The road back to Kalorama was strange. Bleak. Darkness was only part of it. The rest was the unreality in my head. I couldn't imagine the trauma my friend must have endured to produce these apparitions.

Then Felicity Lippert floated back to mind. I hadn't thought about her in a long time. In junior high, behind her back, we called her Lippity Liar. She told us tales we figured she'd fabricated: wild parties, stuff she'd smoked, pills she'd tried, cousins she'd had sex with, and nighttime visits from her Uncle Kiffin. The queen of storytelling, we called her. And we were her handmaidens. Because she knew things we'd never understand, we memorized the intimate details she told us. Yeah sure, Lippy, we said. Where had she learned this stuff? And what on earth kind of a name was Kiffin?

I remember fantasizing about the boys in the stories she'd made up. But we never tried to get inside Lippy's head. As in what her feelings about those escapades were. What kind of a person she was. I wouldn't have even known how to ask the questions. But after meeting Madison's imaginary friends tonight, I had a creepy feeling that Lippy might not have been lying.

Chapter 15

Sunday morning, at Aunt Zee's breakfast table, the headline on the front page of the Hendersonville Gazette was in an extra-bold font: **FREAK ACCIDENT AT BRANTLEIGH MANOR.**

Aunt Zelma read aloud. "Madison Lerrimore, 43, from Annapolis Maryland, was wounded yesterday in what appeared to have been an accidental shooting during the reenactment of the Battle of Asheville at the Brantleigh Manor estate near Etowah. Officials noted that live bullets are never used in reenactments, but the minié ball that had apparently wounded the spectator was recovered and given to police. Ms. Lerrimore was in surgery for several hours yesterday following the accident. Late yesterday, she was reported in guarded condition at the Belle Mère Hospital. Ms. Lerrimore, a landscape architect, teaches garden design at Annapolis Community College—"

"Accidental shooting?" I mused aloud. "Not a chance."

"Then let's call it an attempted murder."

"But why? That's what I'd like to know."

"You *and* the sheriff," Aunt Zelma said, and went on: "Investigators are looking for a connection between Ms. Lerrimore's shooting and the death of her stepfather, Wayland Morgan, the Brantleigh tour guide who was found dead on the estate last Wednesday."

"Count on it," I said to the paper.

Aunt Zelma opened to an inside page and snapped it into submission. "It goes on to say that the sheriff's office hasn't made a connection between Mr. Morgan's death and Madison's shooting but they're following every lead. And then it says, and I quote, 'After the accident brought the reenactment to a halt, the reenactors' muskets and cartridge cases were examined. Nationwide, reenactments never use live ammunition. No evidence was found that a lead bullet had been fired yesterday by any of the reenactors. A deputy sheriff, however, told this reporter that the State Bureau of Investigation forensics laboratory is examining what appears to have been a minié ball recovered from where Ms. Lerrimore was wounded. It is hoped that an examination may link it to the weapon that fired it.'"

I knew whose weapon had launched that blob of lead. But I sure as hell didn't know how to prove it.

"The Henderson County sheriff," Aunt Zee continued, "has given the go-ahead for today's reenactment as scheduled."

"That gives me an idea," I said. I slugged the rest of my coffee, pecked my aunt on the cheek, and headed for Brantleigh Manor. I showed the ticket taker my faded hand stamp from yesterday, and went to the reenactment site.

Wisps of wood smoke rose from cook-fires among the tents where diehard reenactors had spent the night. Several, already in uniform, wandered into the battle zone, sipping coffee from tin cups. Only a few other visitors had arrived this early. On the hillside, red-capped artillerymen were gathered at the cannons. I found Lorenzo Peters morphing into Colonel Clayton for the day's reenactment.

"Miss … ah … Penny Summers, isn't it?"

I smiled. "Good memory, sir."

"You can knock off the sir." His earnest reenactor expression relaxed. "It's Lorenzo."

"Lorenzo, then. The Gazette said all yesterday's reenactors' muskets were checked and no evidence of a lead ball was found."

"The cartridge cases too." Lorenzo adjusted the tassels of his dark red sash.

"What's your guess?" I asked. "Accident or intentional?"

"Hard to know. But in all the reenactments I've ever been at, we've never had an actual ball fired. It would have been difficult for someone to pour black powder in the bore and drop a ball on it without someone noticing," he said. "But not impossible."

"But wouldn't the ball need to be rammed?"

"No ramrods are ever used in reenactments," Lorenzo said as he snugged the sash into place. "And since it wasn't rammed, that would pretty much guarantee a loss of accuracy. In any case, there's no way to know if the shot was aimed intentionally."

"The ball wouldn't have been in the rifle, it seems to me, if it weren't intended to be fired," I said. "What would be the point? It had to have been shot on purpose."

"You might could be right, Miz Penny." His puckered brow undoubtedly reflected his disbelief that any responsible reenactor would have deliberately jeopardized another.

"But, in the midst of firing and reloading, no reenactor would have been watching any of the others. Right?"

"You're correct there, too, miss," Lorenzo said.

"The surgeon at Belle Mère said he found soil particles in Madison's wound."

"That signifies the ball ricocheted off the ground before it hit her," he said, looking thoughtful. "And that suggests that the weapon was either aimed too low or the shooter didn't compensate for the downward arc of the bullet."

"Or the inaccuracy from not ramming," I said.

"Exactly." Lorenzo appeared dejected.

"Seems like it might not have been an accident," I said.

Lorenzo wiped his brow even though the sun was far from its zenith. At midday in June, even North Carolinians begin to wonder if global warming might not be fiction.

"Well," he said, "it might have been the first shot from a preloaded musket."

"But not firing for however long after the shooting began—wouldn't that have been noticed by the men nearby?"

"Again, not necessarily," Lorenzo said, "because, as you said, they were totally occupied in firing, loading gunpowder, firing, and reloading."

"Which wouldn't help at all in figuring out which gun it came from."

"I read in the Gazette," Lorenzo said, "that the ball was being examined in the state forensics lab. If they find rifling marks, they might could be matched to the rifle that fired it. But some reenactors' weapons are smoothbore replicas of muskets made without rifling. If it was fired from one of those, there'd be no signature on the ball. Then too, a musket is generally less accurate than a rifled gun."

"Lorenzo, I'm thinking that the distance between whoever shot it and Madison, rifled barrel or not, an unrammed bullet, and the soiled lead ball all point to the shooting being intentional. I think it was its inaccuracy that saved her."

"One thing is certain, Miz Penny. The ball that hit Miss Lerrimore came from Claude Garner's brigade. All of my Silver Grays were facing the other direction."

Grandpa Jack didn't miss a beat. *Don't forget that you were standing precisely where Ned Ferguson suggested.*

How could I learn if what Ned used was a smoothbore? As a stand-in for a detective, this was getting way above my nonexistent pay grade. "Lorenzo ... is there some way you could take a look at Ned's musket today to see if it's a smoothbore? He told us where we should be for the best view of the action. So, if the shot was deliberate, my money would be on him. And there's something else that leads me to suspect him. His friend Wayland Morgan's musket was missing from his apartment yesterday."

"I was at the gun show with Wayland when he bought that musket. It's a copy of an 1842 Springfield, a smoothbore."

Probably the one Ned brandished in his lecture yesterday, Grandpa Jack whispered.

"I'll file that tidbit away. Thanks."

"But if you need to know what Mr. Ferguson is using today, the only person who might could check it for you would be Claude Garner. Ferguson's one of his Yanks."

"Garner and Ned travel in the same circles. He'd know I was on to something."

We exchanged a fragment of a military salute.

"My lips are sealed," Lorenzo whispered.

You are *on to something,* Grandpa Jack muttered.

Chapter 16

When I returned to Kalorama, I found a note from Aunt Zelma on the foyer console. She'd gone to Hendersonville for groceries. In her absence, I passed up the amontillado for a glass of Biltmore chardonnay, and made the call I'd dreaded.

My Pinocchio nose began stretching as soon as Aidan Reid's answering machine picked up. I explained that my workshop in North Carolina was extended for another week and promised my client that I'd be in touch to reschedule our meeting just as soon as I returned to Maryland. I clicked off and hoped that when he heard it, he'd decide to stick with me for the time it would take me to modify the concept plan to repair the problems Madison had found and avoid displaying my inexperience.

I had definitely bitten off more than I could chew. There was the not so minor matter of proving that Ned fired the bullet that bounced into Madison's leg and, at the same time, helping to find her stepfather's murderer *and* preparing for Cheyenne and Kalea's arrival. I'd last seen Madison's partner and their daughter at my birthday dinner the week before coming to Flat Rock. I didn't know Cheyenne well, but Kalea and I had hit it off right away.

I wasn't sure if Madison's pajamas would fit over the fixator on her leg but I figured I could do my friend a small kindness by taking her a pair with her robe. André, the big poodle, followed me to her room. It was similar to mine only in that we both had four-poster beds and elegant antique marble-top dressers with tilting mirrors. In the dresser's top drawer, her underwear lay neatly folded. Her terrycloth robe and pajamas were in the second. I rolled them together for their trip to the hospital and paused when I noticed that her laptop sat between a pair of cranberry-glass hurricane lamps on the marble top.

Moments later, Curious Georgette was feeling only slightly guilty sitting in an antique rocker with Madison's MacBook.

Password? Landscape? No. Her partner's name? No. Then I had it. *Kalea,* their eleven-year-old (going on eighteen) daughter. I opened Safari. Four sites were bookmarked: ACC, Annapolis Community College, and NYT for her online news. Third was The Peggy Stewart, the tea and coffee shop named for the ship set on fire in Annapolis harbor, Annapolis's "Boston Tea Party," where Madison had bought the tea for her stepfather. The fourth was a plant database, a natural for a landscape architect. Thinking I might learn a thing or two, I opened the site to the page she'd visited. It described the details of a plant I'd admired at the National Botanic Garden: Carolina Jessamine aka Jasmine. Scrolling down, I checked its details: hardiness zones (7-9), soil preference (rich), flowers (cascades of tiny yellow blossoms), bloom time (early spring), and a note that the vigorous vining plant was South Carolina's state flower. Now I could honestly say that I'd studied it. However briefly.

I scrolled a little further and found a bold warning: "All parts of this plant are poisonous. Children who mistake this plant for honeysuckle have been poisoned." And on and on. "... gelsemine ... strychnine-related alkaloids ..." I looked out her window to the not-so-distant mountains and let this sink in. Then back to the laptop screen. Jessamine, I found, was often planted in southern gardens to cover unsightly fences, tumble over stone walls, and soften hillside terraces.

If Madison had begun a design project in North Carolina, she hadn't mentioned it. Curious Georgette closed the MacBook.

André chose that moment to drop his muzzle on my knee. I flashed on Cookie, my flop-eared Dobergirl, whose intuitive gaze always confirms her perceptive understanding. I doubted that André's telepathic abilities were close to Cookie's, but fuzzeling dogs' ears can lead to insights, which I badly needed, or reminiscences. Mine unfailingly either begin or end with Mom whom I hadn't seen since I was ten.

Dad, who had somehow managed to raise me and my older brother Spencer, and was able to pull a few favors from friends in the state government to grease my appointment to the Naval Academy, had since retired to a gated community. Since I left the Navy after only six years, he'd been on my case. If I'd stayed in uniform, he'd argued, I'd soon be the public affairs officer for the Commander-in-Chief of the Atlantic Fleet and retire after a tour as the PAO for the Chief of Naval Operations. Then I could make the world a better place any way I'd want, with a comfortable retirement. He'd taught at the Naval Academy for twenty-five years so I suppose he had good reason to think that life was all about winding down comfortably. Not me, foolish brat that I was. Maybe he'd come around when I had a flourishing landscape architecture practice. Unfortunately, that wouldn't be anytime soon.

I remembered Mom with little Josh on her lap telling us made-up-on-the-spot fairy tales that always involved children walking through magical doors into wonderful fantasy worlds. After she deserted us, on some level I understood that she had gone through a similar portal to some wonderful place that could only exist in the mind of a story-teller.

With Madison's pajamas and robe under my arm, André followed me down the wide staircase. As I hit the last step—my brain went into free-fall, assembling herbal tea, Carolina Jessamine, and sexual abuse.

I sat quickly, unable to move, and barely registered André bumping into my back. The tea Madison had brought from Annapolis infused with gelsemine had poisoned her stepfather.

We'd come to North Carolina so she could kill Wayland.

I didn't need Grandpa Jack to alert me that I was in a huge can of worms!

Should I go directly to the police? Or encourage Madison to turn herself in before an investigation discovered the terrible truth? I was lost in a strange landscape with neither a map nor a docent. Madison was my mentor, my friend, and dear Kalea's mom. And now I realized she was a deeply wounded soul.

Ultimately I decided there was no way I could betray her. I would never want Kalea to endure the heartbreak I'd gone through when my mom left us. It would have to be Madison's choice of how to proceed. She would have to make the fateful decision for herself.

Her pajamas and robe in hand, and a confrontation in mind, I headed to Hendersonville.

But far more than a confrontation with Madison was on my mind. How was I supposed to deal with the realization that my friend had, in effect, murdered her stepfather? If I didn't report what I knew, wouldn't I be some kind of an accessory after the fact? Like driving a getaway car? My conscience scrambled to make sense of what was right but I had no ledges to hang on, no pillars of justice to lean against.

At the Naval Academy, our ethics classes dealt with questions like under what circumstances might one disobey an order from a superior officer, not whether one should report a friend who'd murdered her stepfather.

+++

At the first Hendersonville stoplight, my phone did the mazurka. Cheyenne's number on its screen.

"Penny," she said, "how's Madison?"

"You got my message."

"Called the hospital last night but they said she was asleep."

"I'm on my way to see her right now."

"I tried to talk with her this morning," Cheyenne said. "She seemed pretty tired."

My brain was fully occupied. Only a few neurons available to converse with Shy. Could she hear the tension in my voice? "Probably still sedated," I said.

"Kalea and I'll be on the Delta flight Tuesday. It gets to Asheville about two in the afternoon. Can you pick us up? No, never mind … I'll rent a car."

"I'll meet you there. By the way, my aunt would like you to stay with us. It's a pre-Civil War era mansion. Plenty of room. Eight bedrooms. Only three in use. Actually only two while Madison's in the hospital."

"You're twisting my arm." She sounded genuinely appreciative. "Sounds wonderful, but we'd prefer a hotel close to the hospital."

"I figured you might."

Cheyenne let a long moment pass. "You sound upset. What's going on? Something you're not telling me?"

She sounded panicky. I'd tried not to let my understanding of Madison's real purpose in coming to North

Carolina show in my voice. "Do you know of any other reason Madison might have had, aside from visiting Brantleigh, to come to North Carolina?"

"Only that she wanted to reconcile with her stepdad."

"Nothing else?"

"Tell me what you're thinking."

"Not thinking anything. Just wondering." My virtual fingers were crossed.

"There's something wrong, Penny. I can feel it." I must not have succeeded in hiding my epiphany. "Something about the shooting?"

"The shooting? No." My overactive imagination was at warp speed. I couldn't tell her what I was trying not to think. "I'll meet you and Kalea at the airport. And get you to Hendersonville. Madison will be happy that you're coming."

We hung up. Maybe Madison had never told Shy about her stepfather's abuse. Even married lovers could have secrets.

Entering Belle Mère's parking garage, Grandpa Jack nudged me. *It's possible those two aren't as close as you thought.*

What's that supposed to mean, I wondered.

What else might they not be telling each other?

"The only disconnect I know of," I whispered to myself, "is Cheyenne's lack of interest in Madison's profession."

Chapter 17

I exited the elevator on the Surgical Recovery floor and passed the nurses' station. "She already has a visitor," said a nurse who recognized me. "Not that she's awake yet."

I'd taken a single step toward Madison's room when alarms sounded. Two panicked nurses raced ahead of me.

I don't know who was more surprised. Ned, who was straightening Madison's pillow, the nurses, or me. Madison was still in la-la land.

"What are you doing?" the senior nurse screamed at Ned.

"When the alarm went off I tried to wake her."

"That's our job."

Ned glared. "Y'all weren't here!"

The alarms stopped. The senior nurse turned to her colleague. "Sandy, go call security."

"Hey, hang on a minute," Ned complained as Sandy hurried off.

"No, *you* hang on," the nurse demanded. "You just stay where you are."

"Penelope—" his anger barely under control "—can you tell this nurse who I am? I brought her flowers and some of her stepdad's stuff."

"I see the flowers. Nice, Ned. What other stuff?"

The nurse's narrowed eyes could have blinded him with daggers.

Madison's eyelids fluttered. She frowned but didn't wake.

"Wayland's mug," Ned said, "and his new box of tea. From our break room." He nodded to where he'd set the coffee mug with an X-rated image of Little Red Riding Hood. Beside it, the box of teabags bore an image of the

Peggy Stewart in flames.

"Very thoughtful." I knew he could hear the sarcasm.

Brisk footfalls in the hall announced the arrival of a pair of security officers, male and female, hospital patches on their shoulders and silver shields on their pockets.

"What's happening?" the male with a pencil mustache asked.

"We're not sure," the senior nurse replied. "This gentleman was in the room when the patient's pulse-oximeter suddenly dropped. He said he tried to wake her but I think he'd had a pillow over her face."

"No way!" Ned glowered, feigning innocence.

Not the brightest crayon, Grandpa Jack whispered.

As they escorted him from the room, the female officer whose name tag read OTIS asked me to visit the ground floor security office. "I'll be only a minute," I said.

Madison's eyes were closed, her monitors checked by the nurses, her breathing regular. Satisfied their patient was on course and on glide path, as medics on my aircraft carrier might have said, they went with the security detail, leaving the door ajar.

I was bumfuzzled. A zen bumper-sticker I'd seen yesterday came to mind: "Don't believe everything you think." I didn't know if Ned had attempted to suffocate Madison or if Madison herself had somehow triggered the alarm. Finally decided that if I were to wager on the truth, my money would be on Ned attempting to kill her—again.

I leaned over my friend. "Madison … you missed the excitement." She moved a hand and attempted to open an eye.

"It's Penny." The eye opened. "Blink if you can hear me. Okay?" She closed her eye and opened it again slowly.

"Cheyenne and Kalea will be here in a couple of days." That got her attention. She forced both eyes open and tried a smile. But didn't say anything.

"I brought your pajamas and robe. They're on your I-V pole."

Her dry lips attempted to say thanks.

"Ned Ferguson brought flowers and a couple of your stepdad's things from Brantleigh."

"Tell him thanks," she murmured as her eyelids rolled back down.

The confrontation about Carolina Jessamine and herbal tea would have to wait. "Hasta mañana," I said, and left the room as quietly as possible, waved toward the nurse's station which earned me a polite smile, and punched the elevator's down button.

I found the door marked SECURITY and knocked. It was opened by a rotund woman in a dark gray uniform. "The door on the right, Ms. Summers." Behind the other door, I could hear Pencil-Mustache with an obviously rattled Ned Ferguson.

"You have no right to hold me," he yelled.

"Not holding you, sir," the officer said, "detaining you. If you have nothing to hide, you won't mind answering a few questions. We have to learn why the patient's pulse-ox crashed while you were in her room."

I entered the indicated door as Officer Otis asked for my full name and relationship to the patient. Easy ones.

"Seeing as you're a friend," she said, "may I ask a couple of questions?"

"No problem," I said, trying to suppress my disdain of police asking questions.

Never volunteer more than you've been asked, Grandpa

Jack reminded me.

"What can you tell me about Mr. Ferguson's relationship with Ms. Lerrimore? Or is it the other way around?"

This was not an easy one. I took a deep breath, hoping for inspiration.

Just the facts, Grandpa Jack reminded me.

"Mr. Ferguson was our landscape docent at Brantleigh last Wednesday."

"Had he and Ms. Lerrimore met before then?"

"I'm pretty sure they hadn't."

"Okay, go on."

"Ferguson was also one of the Civil War reenactors yesterday when Ms. Lerrimore was wounded."

"You were there?"

"Yes."

While Officer Otis wrote on her notepad, I hoped she'd ask if I thought he could have fired the accidental bullet. What I might say, though, would be only hearsay, of no real value. Just the same, I would have liked a chance to share it.

Muffled footsteps. Outside our door, the door to the other room opened. Ned's profanity became louder. His protestations continued as he was escorted out of the hospital.

"In your opinion, Ms. Summers, and I know it's only an opinion, do you think Mr. Ferguson's visit to Ms. Lerrimore was anything other than that of a friend visiting a friend?"

"First of all, I don't think they should be considered friends," I said. "But to answer your question, I think …" I faltered.

Officer Otis blinked and kept her expectant smile.

She asked you point-blank, Grandpa Jack said.

I shifted in the chair and took a breath.

"Okay. Friday, the reenactment setup day, he showed us where to be close to the action. Right beside the spectator fence. That put us almost in the line of fire from the Yankees. And he role-played one of the Yankee attackers coming toward us."

When she said nothing, I went on. "I can't help but suspect that he fired the shot. He knew exactly where she'd be standing. When it didn't kill her, I think this was a stupid second attempt to smother her."

Her eyebrows soared. "Have you spoken with Brantleigh security or the police?"

I nodded. "The state's forensic lab in Raleigh is looking at the bullet we found and, as I understand it, will try to connect it to the reenactor who fired it."

"Thanks."

As I was leaving, I overheard Officer Otis talking to the officer who had interviewed Ned. "We need to get with whoever's on top of the reenactment accident. This thing may be related."

That would be the sheriff, Grandpa Jack whispered, echoing Pencil-Mustache.

Chapter 18

I hadn't planned to tell Madison I'd invaded her computer. And I wasn't looking forward to confronting her with what I'd learned. But I had no stomach for my other option. I'd tell her what I knew and let her decide when and where to turn herself in.

Using the stairs gave me two minutes of aerobic exercise on the way back up to her room. I knocked.

"Come on in," her groggy voice burbled.

"Madison, we need to talk." She opened her eyes. "Are you awake enough for a chat?"

"I think so." A fleeting smile.

"Good. Because I have a confession to make."

She smiled. "I'm no priest so don't expect absolution."

I chuckled. Good humor meant she was processing what she'd heard.

"I peeked in your MacBook."

"What were you looking for?"

"I wasn't Googling. I'm naturally curious—okay, maybe a bit nosy. Anyway, I looked at your recently visited sites." She didn't seem annoyed but apparently was unable to imagine what her online activity might suggest.

"Anything interesting?"

"Matter of fact, there was. Carolina Jessamine."

Her face changed slightly. "I remember."

"And I found the order of herbal tea you bought for Wayland."

Wrinkles between her eyes. Realization dawning?

"Ned Ferguson brought that tea from the docents' lounge. You remember the nurses rushing in and yelling at him?"

"Sort of."

"What I'd like to know ... is ... is the connection between the Peggy Stewart tea, Carolina Jessamine, and us coming to Brantleigh."

"What do you mean?" I watched the actress prepare her next line. "Besides getting reacquainted with my stepdad and visiting Brantleigh, there's nothing else."

Gently, I said, "I think there is."

"Sorry to disappoint." Her voice was weak, but close to confrontational.

"Here's why. I sat with you late last night. Your sedation put you in some kind of quasi-hypnotic state."

"Really?" Her frown deepened—she'd worked out where I was headed.

I stepped through the ring of fire. "Yeah," I said gently, "I met Melanie and Angela."

Madison's face reddened. Her nostrils flared as she looked away. Without her consent and without her even realizing it, I'd invaded her sanctum sanctorum.

I spoke even more softly. "I haven't told a soul and I won't, but please tell me what's going on."

Madison deflated into a crying child. I had again stepped into totally unknown territory. My pulse pounded.

She snatched a wad of tissues from a bedside table and snorted into them. Finally, her tears subsided enough to talk. "You promise you won't tell? Anyone? Police? Not Kalea and not Cheyenne?"

"Promise."

She sank back into her pillows. Her tear-stained eyes found mine, her face contorted.

"Tell me," I said.

She fought the return of tears. "Those garden design

dreams ... where Melanie and Angela and I explored the gardens together but they always helped me get back to the clock tower. Where I was safe."

Grandpa Jack assembled the facts: Madison's interest in landscape architecture originated as a way of coping with childhood abuse. Her interest in beautifying the natural world emerged as she repeatedly escaped to her dream gardens.

"Oh ... Penny. I've tried to let the past be past." She inhaled and released it. "But when Kalea showed signs of puberty, it all came back." She whimpered. "Wayland touching me. And ... at that age I wasn't interested in boys—*or* girls. I was a child."

I was barely breathing, our conversation halted as I searched for words that could never express the depth of my empathy. I settled on "How horrible."

"When your aunt confirmed that Wayland was here ... I ... I'd hated him for so long."

I stayed quiet.

"I could finally even the score. Prison had been too good for him. Just thinking about Kalea ... He needed to disappear—permanently." She hiccupped. "Deserved to die. Even if I'd have to do it."

It stung to realize that I had a friend who hated another person enough to devise a murder.

"I could do what I'd dreamt of doing for a long, *long* time. The plan just fell into place." She stared at the ceiling. "Oh God ... " She began crying softly again.

"When we found him," I whispered, "your shock seemed real."

Between tears, Madison smiled Mona Lisa style. "Trust

me. It was a shock."

"So the reason Wayland was in prison had nothing to do with embezzling money."

Madison stared, took in a long breath and exhaled slowly.

"Good guess," she said, apparently sensing freedom in shedding the fabrication. "I knew I couldn't continue letting him … I knew it was wrong. A couple of times I tried to tell my mom but she told me to stop lying, like I was trying to get him in trouble because I was jealous or something. I finally told Jennifer—my best friend—and she insisted we tell our school nurse. The nurse called the police and Child Protective Services. Long story short, he was arrested that same day. I missed a half day of school but no one besides Jennifer knew what had happened. That was the end of the seven worst years of my life."

"You testified in court?"

"Not *in* the courtroom. They had a separate room where they had a CPS woman interview me. I couldn't see him, but she told me he could see me. I didn't care. I told her exactly what he'd done. I was glad to have him in prison. Anywhere he couldn't get near me."

I took a breath and held her hand. "So, you did it with poisoned tea bags."

She began with whimpers, then began to cry real tears, and reached for another tissue. She pulled her knees up as far as the fixator would allow, and leaned her head into them, shuddering with each new wave of sorrow. Eventually she raised her head.

"Have you told the police?" She sniffled. "Could I be charged with murder?"

There was the real question. Who would tell the cops?

Could I? Would I?

"No one knows except you and me," I said.

She put her head in her hands. "I put dried Jessamine in only one of the bags." she sobbed.

Really? "Just one?" Was that like one member of a firing squad firing a blank so that no one could know if he'd fired a fatal round. Only when Wayland had succumbed would she know the fatal round had been fired.

She nodded. "I figured we'd all be back in Maryland by the time he used the doctored one."

"Which is why finding him was truly a surprise."

"I only had to add a little to my act." She closed her eyes and let out a long breath, apparently grateful to shed the pretense of being a dutiful step-daughter.

While I tried to get my head around the fact that Madison was a murderess, I changed the subject. "You've never said anything to Cheyenne about Wayland's abuse?"

She shook her head. "I've been so ashamed and humiliated. No, I never told her about it. I was afraid of what she'd think of me."

"But you're legally married. She loves you."

She angled her head slightly, pondering. "I'd never trust the not testifying against your spouse thing. So, I didn't tell her about my plan with the teabag either."

Here I was again. Ready to counsel my teacher. As if I understood the workings of the universe. Which I most certainly never have. But the truth would eventually emerge. Wouldn't it?

I attempted a suggestion: "If I were you, I'd get this off my chest before the police come calling."

Madison gaped but said nothing. Was she considering the idea?

"That first night," she said, "I'd hoped we could bury the hatchet." She inhaled deeply and spewed it back out. "But I flashed back … to when I was twelve …." Her eyes squeezed shut. Tears dribbled. "I had to follow through. It had to be done. I handed him the box of tea bags. And told him we'd meet him at the gryphons in the morning."

I could see Madison was exhausted. I gave her a hug and reassured her that I'd not told anyone. She collapsed into her pillows while I picked up the Peggy Stewart box and the X-rated mug and headed back to the car. Drew in several restorative deep breaths. Made sure the gearshift was in neutral, turned the ignition and attempted to engage my wobbly brain. The strange thing was that Madison was still my friend, teacher, and colleague.

According to an ancient playwright, friends demonstrate their love in times of trouble.

Chapter 19

What I'd learned plunked me astride a dragon on the devil's carousel. Jimi Hendrix's "Star-Spangled Banner" squealed off key while lurid images of grotesque creatures followed me until I finally stepped off the merry-go-round with the sobering realization that I had to let the medical examiner know about Wayland's poisoning. It was a terrible decision but, to keep faith with myself, I had no other choice.

Being Sunday, there was no answer. I left a voicemail. When the M.E. called back I would spill the proverbial beans, and law enforcement's finger would point to my friend. I had no idea how I would deal with the cloud of guilt I knew would descend.

Then Grandpa Jack reminded me that it was my own streak of curiosity that had landed me in this ethical basket of snakes.

Thanks a lot!

Should I call Cheyenne about Ned's second attempt to kill her partner? While neither seemed to have been planned carefully enough to guarantee success, I was glad that both were now in the hands of professional investigators. So, for now, I could see no reason to heap any added worry on Shy.

When I turned onto the Sandburg Pike, my phone mazurka'd. It was a Henderson County detective, Coleen Jackson.

"We're talkin' with a Mr. Ned Ferguson," she said in her delightful Appalachian accent, "about an incident at Belle Mère. We have a statement from an Officer Otis at the hospital explaining what happened. Mr. Ferguson disputes their conclusions and suggested you'd vouch for him."

"I've met Mr. Ferguson," I said, "but don't really know him. What kind of vouching does he have in mind?"

"He says the hospital security made a huge mistake."

Go with the flow, Grandpa Jack counseled.

"As I told Officer Otis, I think Mr. Ferguson attempted to smother Ms. Lerrimore."

Chapter 20

Monday morning when I came down for breakfast, Aunt Zelma was slumped over the table. The box of tea bags from Annapolis and a half-empty mug were on the table. Her breaths were shallow, her eyelids drooped, and her skin cool. Her pulse was weak. She mumbled something I couldn't understand, but, in fact, I did understand.

She was a listless marionette as I dragged her to her SUV under the porte-cochère.

Wishing for a siren, I tore down the driveway. I ran a couple of red lights but Flat Rock's finest weren't around to take the bait. Rushing your aunt to a hospital doesn't leave many neurons available for introspection. But "How could I have been so stupid, thoughtless, irresponsible ...," echoed. My last thought as I screamed into the hospital entrance was that if Aunt Zelma died, not only would my stupidity lead to a charge of negligent homicide, but I'd never be able to forgive myself.

I jerked to a stop, raced in and yelled, "My aunt's been poisoned. Probably gelsemine." Two attendants looked at me as if I'd spoken Klingon. When I yelled again, they followed me, gurney in tow. The doc on duty was a tall woman with dark hair in a bun and horn-rimmed glasses only a few years out of style. She understood the poisoning part so I knew she'd get Aunt Zelma's stomach pumped. And said she'd look up the gelsemine part. I said it's from Carolina Jessamine, to which she nodded knowingly as they disappeared into a treatment room. "Please, God," I said to the door, "let her be okay."

Outside, waiting for my adrenalin level to sink back into the safe zone, I phoned the M.E. again in case yesterday's message hadn't been heard. A Dr. Buchanan answered. After a beat, he said, "It seems we haven't yet heard from a funeral home."

"Uh ... There'll be a delay with that. His stepdaughter was wounded at Brantleigh Manor on Saturday. She's in your ICU."

"Read about that. The paper said it was an accident."

"We're not certain." Why was I sounding like a detective not revealing everything she knew?

"Luckily for her—" Buchanan chuckled "we don't charge extra for customers left in the chiller."

Without mentioning Madison's name, I explained why I thought he should test Wayland for gelsemine poisoning. He acknowledged that their basic tox screen would not have found gelsemine.

"If I tell his stepdaughter your fees kick in after thirty days," I said, "would that give you time to make that test?" Buchanan agreed that the additional test was warranted. We rang off and I went back to the waiting room.

The dark-haired doctor entered the room. "Ms. ...?"

"Summers."

"Ms. Summers, your aunt is out of danger but we'll need to keep her for several hours at least."

Thank God!

"She's on oxygen and taking stimulants including, you may be interested to know, another plant product—digitalis."

In Master Gardener training I'd learned that all parts of the Foxglove plant are poisonous. But, paradoxically, it can be used as a stimulant. Strange how things come together.

"Can I see her?"

"She has difficulty speaking but she hears just fine." The doc led me to her curtained bed.

"How're you feeling?"

"Nether bevverr."

"Do you remember making tea this morning?" She nodded. "It was an herbal blend that Madison brought from Maryland." Another nod of recognition. Instead of explaining how the tea-bag had been contaminated, I settled for solace. I leaned close. "Your doc promised that you'll be fine. But she wants you to stay awhile. Rest. I'll be back for you as soon you're cleared to leave. She'll call me."

The doc's jacket had a cat pin on one lapel and a dog on the other. Good with the pediatric crowd, I guessed and, no doubt, the geriatric. I gave her my phone number and promised to return as soon as she called.

+ + +

Back at Kalorama, I found the tea bag Aunt Zelma had used, still soggy in her little teapot. Sniffed it. Smelled like damp hay. An ordinary tea bag. I wondered if the Peggy Stewart tea shop would bag any herb mixture you brought to them and run it through their tea-bagging machine. With that in mind, I counted the bags. Ten. Of course. There'd been a dozen. Minus Wayland's and the one Zelma used, there were still ten in the box. The tags were all alike. The strings all looked the same. The bags all looked alike. The staples were all ... were *not* alike. There was an extra bend in the staple wire on my aunt's soggy bag. It had been opened and re-closed. Since Madison claimed she'd only tampered with one tea bag, I double-checked the rest of them. Only Aunt Zelma's had a re-bent staple.

I picked up the saturated tea bag and held it, transfixed.

"You little imposter," I told it.

My dancing phone broke my concentration. I clicked the green spot. "Penny for your thoughts."

"Medical examiner's office. Dr. Buchanan."

"Oh hi."

"Ms. Summers, I have to thank you for your call this morning." The resonant voice had confidence woven through it. "After we spoke, I did a complete tox scan on Mr. Morgan and found something that might interest you."

Now I knew Wayland hadn't been poisoned with gelsemine, but confirmation would be nice. "What was that?"

"It wasn't gelsemine."

Okay. Madison was already off the hook.

"It was Conium maculatum."

Unless it was a plant I might specify for a client's garden, the last thing I needed was another Latin name.

"Poison Hemlock," he said. "The poison is coniine." He pronounced it coney-een.

"Like what Socrates drank?"

"The same. Works like curare."

"Cure what?"

"Coo-rah-ray," he said slowly. "South American tribes use it on their blow-pipe darts. Or at least have in the past. Native Americans used it on arrowheads."

His information seemed too good to be true. "You're absolutely sure it was … coney-een?"

"No question."

Could Madison have mistaken Conium maculatum for Carolina Jessamine? I went back to her MacBook and looked up Poison Hemlock. There were no similarities between it and Carolina Jessamine. There'd been no confusion. Thank

God, Madison wasn't guilty of anything except *intending* to kill her stepfather.

Back to square one, Grandpa Jack whispered.

So, Madison was not a murderess. But was I off the hook? What about my conscience? Could I live with the knowledge that my mentor and friend had premeditated a murder? The concept was so outside my moral code I had no way to make sense of it.

My aunt had been right. Madison had toted a dark aura to North Carolina. And it had put my aunt in the emergency room. If I had been aware of the aura, and what it foreshadowed, would I have come with her?

Most of my outrage, though, was not aimed at her but at myself for becoming an accessory to a crime. Like Lady Macbeth, there was blood on my hands too.

+ + +

Low-hanging pewter gray clouds spread a pall over the afternoon. Rain after midnight my car radio warned. It took several minutes to find a space on the tightly packed Belle Mère visitors' parking deck.

I thought about asking Madison if she wanted the good news or the bad news first. But I decided, for once, I'd ditch the flippancy.

"Okay," I said, "you remember yesterday when Ned brought Wayland's mug and the box of tea bags from Peggy Stewart's?"

She nodded.

"This morning I had to rush Aunt Zelma to the emergency room. She'd made tea with one of those bags."

"Oh. God."

"But she's okay. She was pumped in the ER."

"Oh Penny … She could have died." Madison wasn't

acting. She was stunned.

"The hospital identified gelsemine."

She put her face in her hands. "Like I told you, I only added it to one bag."

"On the tea bag she used the staple was bent a little differently. You'd opened the bag, added the leaves and re-closed it."

"I am so very sorry, Penny." Madison whimpered, then abruptly recovered. "So Wayland did die of a heart atta—"

I interrupted. "Let me back up." Madison's eyes widened in expectation. "Yesterday I called the medical examiner and suggested he should check Wayland for gelsemine poisoning. Your name was not mentioned."

"You *what?* Oh sweet Jesus!"

"Madison, listen. When he called back he said he'd done a complete tox screen. Wayland was killed with Poison Hemlock."

"Poison Hemlock? You're … I mean the medical examiner … is sure it was Poison Hemlock? Conium something?"

"He's certain."

Madison stared and released a long thoughtful breath. Her expression was a mix of despair, solace, and what else I couldn't imagine.

In that instant, it dawned on me that my friend had been cheated out of a normal childhood. She'd been betrayed. By her stepfather's sins of commission and her mother's sins of omission. She'd devised her plan to poison Wayland very recently but the seeds of that idea were embedded in her long-ago trauma. And the PTSD she has lived with every day since.

Actually, her strategy to avenge her stepfather's betrayal

wasn't much different from my reaction to my mom's desertion all those years ago. Not that I could have murdered my mom, but for months I tried to conjure an appropriate punishment—*if* she ever returned. I was totally furious that she would skip away into some fantasy world because Josh had drowned.

But whose fault was that?

Madison and I both had Lady Macbeth stains on our souls. Stains we could never scrub clean.

Chapter 21

Tuesday morning Aunt Zelma and I sat across from each other at the small kitchen table. We'd just finished our orange juice. "Coffee?" Aunt Zelma asked.

"No tea?"

Aunt Zelma, back to her perky self, regarded me with a *need you ask* expression.

"Sorry. My snarky streak."

"Coffee?" she asked again.

"Sure. Black."

"This is from Costa Rica." She poured the beans and started her grinder.

While she poured the grindings and boiling water into her coffee press, I spilled the beans. Told her about snooping in Madison's laptop.

"She'd bought tea at Peggy Stewart's and researched Carolina Jessamine."

"Carolina Jessamine? When Jack and I were kids Mother warned us to not mistake it for honeysuckle. She said we could die from gel-something in it."

"That's why I knew I had to get you to the emergency room." My aunt deserved the truth.

"You *what?*"

"The tea bag you used yesterday had Jessamine leaves in it."

"How would you know that?"

"Madison added them hoping to kill Wayland."

"You think she wanted to kill …? Why on earth … when they'd just reconnected?"

"No idea," I lied. "I'm not sure it matters now."

"Of course it matters. That woman's aura is far from

serene." I needed no additional evidence that my aunt could see beyond the visible. "Why on earth would she—"

"Long story."

She decanted the fragrant elixir into a pair of commemorative mugs.

"Wayland was murdered," I said. "But not with Jessamine. Poison Hemlock. Like Socrates."

My aunt frowned, confused.

"Which means," I said, "that Madison is *not* responsible for his death. You used the only poisoned tea bag. Someone else murdered Wayland."

I inhaled a slug of coffee while Aunt Zee globbed strawberry preserves on a toasted bagel. I sensed her brain trying to discover a reason for Madison to try to kill her stepfather. Or, perhaps, brooding on her close call with gelsemine poisoning.

Turned out it was the latter. "If you hadn't figured out what Madison had done, you wouldn't have … you saved my life."

Fortunately, she didn't ask to hear the "long story" of Madison's intention. I also didn't want to think about my negligence in leaving the box of tea—probably on the kitchen table—where my aunt could find it.

"Then who poisoned Wayland with whatever it was?" she asked.

"Would your friend Lynn know someone with a grudge? A very *big* grudge?"

"You'd have to ask her. I'm sure she'd be glad to gossip. But what could she know now that she didn't last week?"

"Maybe she's had time to think it through. Remember something."

My aunt glanced down her list of favorites, found her

number, and I added it to my contacts.

"What scares me though," I said, "is that Ned was in Madison's room yesterday when one of her monitor alarms went off. I think he tried to smother her. And we've agreed he fired the bullet that sent her to the hospital."

Aunt Zee wrapped her hands around the warm mug and peered into it, probably trying to fuse the Ned Ferguson she knew with the one who could have twice attempted to kill Madison.

I added a spoonful of the preserves to my English muffin and took a bite.

My aunt finally put her mug down and picked up the front page of the morning Gazette. "Listen to this. 'The sheriff is requesting anyone who was at the reenactment last Saturday to report anything that could lead to the identification of a reenactor who fired a lead ball toward spectators.'"

A sip of Costa Rican coffee helped me reply. "How many calls do you imagine that'll get them?"

"It would only take *one*," she suggested. "But they could get dozens."

Yours'll be one of them, said Grandpa Jack.

"I'm off to the airport," I said. "Cheyenne and Kalea are due in at two."

"They're welcome to stay here, you know."

"I told Shy, but she wants to stay near the hospital. I'll lobby Kalea to stay with us." I didn't mention that I'd secretly adopted Kalea as a surrogate niece.

On the way through Hendersonville I stopped at the high school. An office assistant told me Mr. Garner was in class. I left a note asking him to call.

When I got on the interstate, I phoned Lynn and laid out

my dilemma. She was happy to give me the lowdown on Wayland's personality foibles, but nothing about enemies or grudges. She suggested that I talk with Garner and Ned Ferguson. Not much help.

Then I called the sheriff's hotline, identified myself, and explained my suspicion of Ned. They probably chalked me up as another publicity nut. But it was done.

At the airport, I parked and got to the arrival area just as Delta's two o'clock passengers were heading toward the luggage carousel. Kalea spotted me. "Aunt Penny!"

"Hey Kiddo!"

Her raven hair echoed her sparkling dark eyes. Center-parted, it hung below her shoulders. Tan cowboy boots strutted beneath a high-low floral skirt. I promised to teach her how as a midshipman I'd learned to shine shoes until you could see your reflection.

Cheyenne pulled up beside us and I swung arms around both of them. "Welcome to Beer City USA."

Shy looked to Kalea. "Honey, we're in the wrong town." Kalea rolled her eyes.

"Wait till you see the bumper stickers," I said.

Cheyenne's burgundy wrap dress complemented her dark auburn hair and, as usual, matched her lipstick. I conveyed Aunt Zelma's invitation again, but she had booked a room at the Blue Ridge Inn, walking distance to the hospital.

Under a Carolina blue sky furrowed with rows of cirrus horsetails, Cheyenne and Kalea followed me in their rental to the Belle Mère.

"Well, it looks like they let just any old body into this hospital," Madison said, grinning, when we walked in.

"You'd better be glad," Cheyenne retorted, "they didn't

turn you away when they heard your Yankee accent."

Madison slipped a second pillow behind herself to sit straighter. "Oooch."

"Mom," Kalea said shyly. "How are you?"

"Fine as frog's whiskers, as they say around here. Actually the leg still hurts, but my magic pills keep that under control."

"Promise me you won't get addicted," Kalea added. "They're dangerous."

Madison squinted and twisted her face to look deranged. "I may have to hold up a bank to support my habit," she said. "But I'll let you drive the getaway car."

"Only if it has jet-assist and retractable wings," Kalea joked.

"We've missed you," Shy said, smiling through happy tears.

Kalea examined the fixator. "You might have a problem going through airport security," she said.

Shy planted a burgundy kiss on her partner's lips.

Madison managed a weak smile and looked from her partner to their daughter. "Melanie."

Kalea looked up, confused. "She doesn't know me?"

Shy, to no one in particular, "Who's Melanie?"

I feigned bewilderment.

Cheyenne patted Kalea's shoulder. "She'll be back to her old self soon."

I wished I could be as confident.

Kalea grabbed my wrist. "D'you think your aunt would let me stay with you?"

"She's hoping you will." Kalea broke into a happy smile and hugged me.

We promised to be back soon and left the surgical

recovery floor and headed to where Shy's rental and my little Purple Porcupine were parked side by side. We transferred Kalea's bags to my back seat and headed to Flat Rock while Cheyenne drove the three blocks to the Blue Ridge Inn.

"Something's wrong," Kalea said. "Maddy-Mom didn't recognize me."

"I'm sure it's only because of the painkillers and sedation," I said. And hoped that was all it was.

"She'll get her memory back as soon as they let her out of there," Kalea said with cheerful assurance.

"I'm sure."

After a pause, "So what happened to her stepfather?"

"Did Shy tell you we found him at Brantleigh?"

"Sure. But how did it happen?"

"I don't know. But I have suspicions."

"Shy-Mom said you thought he'd been murdered."

Grandpa Jack nudged me. *You owe her a straight answer.*

"Okay. The medical examiner first thought it was a heart problem but then discovered he'd been poisoned. I don't think he knows how and nobody knows why."

Kalea pooched out her lips then opened them. "I could probably help."

Didn't expect that, did you? whispered Grandpa Jack.

"Really?" Kalea never ceased to amaze. "How?"

She unclipped her seat belt and reached into the back seat. She returned with a book.

"I've been studying for the Junior Police Academy."

I glanced at the book. *"Forensics for Dummies."*

"I'm going to be a Crime Scene Investigator."

Isn't every kid? whispered Grandpa Jack.

I stopped for the light at the intersection with Brownell

Highway. I hated to waste an opportunity to find something that might help me learn how or who had poisoned him. "Punkin, you want to see Mr. Morgan's apartment?"

She made a face. "I suppose."

"Madison lent me the keys. There's a lot of Civil War stuff."

Her face reflected a lack of enthusiasm for Civil War memorabilia that matched my own.

"But," she said, brightening, "I could start my investigation."

Under the long portico, several residents sat in white rocking chairs, reading, e-mailing or texting.

"Cool" was Kalea's appraisal of the old elevator as she piloted it to the second floor. After a couple of back and forths on the handle that jerked us up and down and back up, we stopped only a short step above the floor. She pulled the accordion door open, hopped down and followed me to Wayland's apartment at the end of the hall.

The door opened to a scene very different from what I remembered. Books askew. Pillows sliced open. Desk drawers tossed, their contents scattered.

Chapter 22

We stepped gingerly into Wayland's apartment. Kalea's eyes widened.

"Who made this mess?" she said, picking up a handful of couch stuffing.

I could almost hear her forensic gears beginning to grind. "Hang on," I said. "I need to call the sheriff." I pulled her back into the hall.

I yanked out my phone and started to punch 9-1-1. Kalea pulled my fingers off the phone.

"What?"

"I *am* going to be a Crime Scene Investigator." She was serious.

"You've been watching too many detective shows."

Her plaintive "Ple-e-ease," as she sparkled with anticipation caught me up short.

Why not? I was certain it had been Garner. Madison and I had been here last week. Any detective would have to ask *me* if anything was missing. We went back in. Kalea beamed when I closed the door behind us.

"Those ripped cushions look like what Cookie did the day you left." She and Cheyenne had volunteered to dog-sit my Dobergirl while I was in North Carolina.

"She chewed cushions?"

"A couple."

Ahhh … the joys of canine motherhood. "I'll get them fixed when I get back."

"She missed you big time," Kalea added, as if that excused Cookie's destruction. She pushed aside a stray lock of hair. "The first thing a C.S.I. needs to do is become the perpetrator. Put yourself into his brain … or hers."

Perhaps she hadn't seen too many detective shows. "You know, real-life detective work isn't as fast and slick as the shows depict it."

Kalea gave me a look that could only be translated "Duhhh." I steeled myself for a Grandpa Jack lecture on underestimating the younger generation.

"So you'll major in criminology when you get to college?"

Kalea crouched and began to collect strewn papers. "Aunt Penny, does the Navy really have an NCIS?"

"They're mostly civilians. So you don't need to join the Navy. I've also heard they sometimes take interns."

"Cool." Kalea righted another upside-down drawer.

I studied the room. Pictures torn from the wall, chairs upended, and desk drawers upside down. The desk might have once been a schoolteacher's. Pencils, papers and a couple of computer discs were splayed nearby. Wayland, it appeared, *had* a computer.

On the wall over the desk, deer leg bracket cradled the rifle—*Wait*! Madison and I had noticed Friday that there wasn't a rifle on the wall. Now, it was back!

Another nudge from Grandpa Jack. *If Ned was the reenactment shooter, then he "borrowed" the smooth-bore Springfield and trashed the place when he brought it back.*

Regardless, the locks would need to be changed.

Kalea picked up the wide center drawer. She tilted it this way and that. "There's something strange about this one." She turned it over and sighted across the bottom.

"What?"

She knocked on its bottom. "This wood is different."

"Newer?"

Kalea turned the drawer right side up, angled it, and drew a conclusion neither I nor the searcher had guessed. "It has a false bottom." She shook it like a Christmas present. A barely audible muffled thump.

"Now," she said, "how do you get into it?"

"Your first test as a C.S.I."

Kalea said nothing, and, one at a time, studied all four sides. Then the bottom, and finally the inside again. "The bottom was added after it was made," she said, "so there's gotta be …"

"Would Miss Sherlock like a magnifying glass?" I asked.

She glared like I'd used a dirty word and reexamined the inside of the drawer. Several knots in the newer wood. She pressed one near the left front corner. The drawer bottom popped up. "Check this out." The source of the muffled thump lay there like a medieval treasure exposed to light after centuries of darkness. Enclosed in dense foam, the compact laptop sported a sticker: I ♥ CIVIL WAR HISTORY.

Eager eleven-year-old hands extracted it from its soft bed. Nested beside it was its charger and what looked like a safe deposit box key. Kalea handed me the key, snapped the laptop open, and fired it up.

The desktop image was the same photo that lay on the floor in its broken frame: Confederate Major Wayland Morgan, sword raised, leading a company of reenactors toward the camera.

Kalea's fingers wandered around the trackpad. A box appeared in the center of the screen. She shook her head. "Needs a password."

I remembered an old haversack hanging in Wayland's entry hall, went for it, and handed it to her. "Drop the laptop in here. You can work on it at Aunt Zelma's." She dutifully readied it for us to take to Kalorama.

On the floor near where an upper drawer had landed, I scooped up a splayed stack of bank statements and letters.

The top one caught Kalea's eye as it had mine. "Some kid wrote that one," she said, and snatched it.

I looked over her shoulder. "Not very legible handwriting." I said. "Angie's probably one of Wayland's old girlfriends."

Kalea stumbled as she read. "'Thank you for what you … uhhh … what you done. You know I'll follow you to the edge of the … universe to have my way with you.' That Angie is some kind of weird."

I put it back with the others and slipped them into my backpack. It would take time to comb through them all.

A 24/7 locksmith promised to arrive within the hour to change the locks. On our way out, I alerted the building manager and cajoled him into asking the locksmith to leave the new keys and the invoice with him.

On our way to Flat Rock I phoned Cheyenne at the hospital. "How's the patient?" I asked.

"She's in and out. Did she meet someone named Melanie down here?"

"Don't think so." Cheyenne couldn't see my Pinocchio nose. "She's mentioned the name but I've no idea who she's talking about."

"Maybe a playmate when she was a kid?" she said.

"Is she awake enough to talk?"

Muffled voices as Shy spoke off-phone, then returned. "Not quite. Anything you want me to tell her?"

"Tell her Kalea and I stopped at Wayland's apartment. It'd been trashed."

"You called the police?"

"I know who did it, so no. We don't need the cops on this one."

"But you ... let Kalea enter a crime scene?" A peeved parent. "That is *not* okay."

"All's well that ends well."

"You'd better hope so. Penny, if you were anyone else, I'd have you bring her back here immediately. She's only eleven, for crying out loud."

"By the way, I think your young C.S.I. found what Garner'd been looking for. Wayland's laptop. And tell Madison her stepfather's old musket was returned."

"Hunhh?"

"She'll understand."

+ + +

"You must be Kalea." Aunt Zelma greeted us at her door. "Welcome to our little mountain nest." Unmistakable happy dimples on her face were proof of her delight in welcoming a youngster to Kalorama. I remembered those dimples from when I was the youngster.

"It's very nice to meet you, Ms. Porter."

"Make it simple. Okay? Just Aunt Zelma." Kalea nodded. "You have a pretty name."

"It means beloved flower in Hawaiian."

"It matches you perfectly."

Kalea blushed. "Aunt Penny said I should ask you to tell me about her great-great-great grandfather."

"And so I shall. But first, tell me about yourself." Aunt Zee led us to the kitchen where she'd made tuna sandwiches.

Between bites, Kalea explained how she planned to become a C.S.I., how she'd found Wayland's laptop and that she would dope out its password so she and I could conduct forensic research. Lingo from TV shows.

"I'm happy you're here," Aunt Zee said. "And I'm hoping I'll have a chance to meet Cheyenne soon."

"She's at the Blue Ridge Inn," I said.

"She wants to be near Maddy-Mom." Kalea sipped her milk.

Aunt Zelma smiled warmly. "I understand."

Kalea gulped the last of her milk. "If you'll excuse me," she said, taking the haversack, "I'll get to work." From the salon, we heard the laptop snap open.

"What a polite young lady," Aunt Zelma said. "You'd think she was a Southern child."

"She's always had two adults for family." In the background, the lolloping of youthful fingers on laptop keys. "Of course she plays with kids in the neighborhood, but she's the leader of the pack."

"Seems like she's eleven going on nineteen."

I wished I could claim kinship with this wunderkind but my gene pool was dormant.

"Got it!" Kalea screamed.

Aunt Zelma and I joined her on the couch. "Tell us," I said. "What's the word?"

"It's a password. Letters and numbers."

"We can keep a secret," Aunt Zelma said.

She shut it down and reopened it to demonstrate. "Okay, it's capital C and W, for Civil War, and 1861 slash 1865. Appropriate for a Civil War geek, don't you think?" She looked up with a triumphant grin. When she'd finished, a score of folder icons appeared, nearly obliterating Major Wayland Morgan, sword drawn, marching into battle.

Kalea and I could now march into Wayland's laptop and begin our digital forensic research. What a whiz!

Chapter 23

Kalea and I lugged her suitcase and overnight bag up to Madison's room. Aunt Zelma stayed in the salon with her latest from the Flat Rock Library.

We took Wayland's laptop next door to my room and sat side by side on the fainting couch. The music of crickets and katydids flowed through the windows at our backs. The laptop lay across Kalea's knees.

"Let's look at his emails," I said.

"No problem." She clicked the envelope icon. "He had two accounts. AOL and Gmail."

"Go for the AOL," I said.

She clicked again and waited. Finally, "Nothing in or out since last Tuesday." She clicked twice more. "Okay, here's the last one. From somebody with initials C.G. He wrote 'I'll expect some answers tonight.' What d'you think that's about?"

"C.G. is Claude Garner. He's the guy Madison heard arguing with her stepfather the night before we found him."

Kalea's eyes brightened with the confidence of a detective who's nailed her case. "Then this Garner probably killed him."

"That's what your mom thought."

"But not you?"

"He may have had some part in it but I don't think he actually did it."

"At least he's on our list of suspects."

"Agreed. Now let's look at the entire inbox for the last year."

We read them together, from the earliest to last Tuesday's. Except for reenactment planning, the correspondence mostly concerned Wayland's purchase of a tattered Civil War battle flag and its subsequent sale which Garner accused him of selling for much more than Wayland reported.

Interesting but it didn't explain the old flag Madison and I had found.

Reading on, we followed the seeds of disagreement between the two men as it germinated and flowered into threats.

The emails revealed the story. Garner had heard of an old Yankee battle flag from a reenactor buddy near Hot Springs. The story unfolded that a hundred and sixty years before, Colonel Kirby's regiment carried the banner from Tennessee to what became known as the Battle of Asheville. When the Ohioans were repulsed and retreated, the battle-scarred flag had been tossed into the woods near the Woodfin farm north of Asheville, where it was found the following day by a young Wylie Hepworth.

The banner was crumpled in a musette bag for the next eighty-some years until Wylie's son Thomas cleaned out his attic. Thomas had framed it, hung it on his living room wall and watched it fade until he willed it to his daughter, Anna, a college professor in Boone. Anna knew the old flag had some value, but since she'd never married, she had no one to pass it down to. After her eightieth birthday she'd tried, unsuccessfully, to find someone to buy the damn thing. Eventually the word got to Garner. His first thought was to drive up to Boone, offer the old lady a couple of thousand and sell it to a Yankee collector for twice that. Easy money. His second idea was to put Ned Ferguson on it assuming Ned, with his docent experience at Brantleigh, could sweet-talk some collector out of several more thousand. They'd share the profit, of course.

Within a week they'd met Wayland at a Civil War Meetup. When Ned discovered that Wayland had taught history, he told him about the docent opportunity at Brantleigh and mentioned the dilemma about the flag. Wayland, apparently sensing an opportunity, assured them that, as a Yankee and onetime history professor, he could both walk the walk and talk the talk — not only acquire the flag for a bargain, but find a wealthy collector or a museum with a large endowment to purchase it at an inflated price. Garner and Ned greedily agreed to let their new friend look for a well-healed purchaser and split the profit three ways.

In an email last October, Wayland had described Boone's treacherous wintry streets when he knocked on Anna Hepworth's door near the Appalachian State campus where she had taught. "Weatherbeaten and shrewd" was how he'd described the lady to Garner, cc'd to Ned, at the end of the day.

"She wanted $30,000 and I offered her $20,000. I told her it would be a nice sum to leave to her favorite charity," he'd written. By then, the onetime low paid history professor had undoubtedly realized there was more than a few thousand to be made.

"I ain't a goner just yet, Mr. Morgan," she'd replied. "Got some livin' to be done still. And your dollars'll help me do it."

Wayland then explained that he'd sweetened the kitty, so to speak, to $25,000. He'd told her that was as high as he was allowed to go. Miss Hepworth finally agreed to the compromise. Given the size of this outlay, Wayland wrote that he'd have to lay it on thick to some collector to make enough for "all three of us" to get a decent share of the profit.

A few weeks later, presumably as a result of rumors in the small world of Civil War collectors, Garner emailed that he'd heard the Hepworth woman had accepted $10,000, not the $25,000 Wayland reported. Wayland replied that Garner had been misinformed. Garner, obviously concerned, replied that he would borrow the flag and have it assessed while Wayland trolled for the promised wealthy buyer.

"I wonder how much the flag was really worth," Kalea said. "And how much do you think mom's stepfather really paid that woman for it?"

"Unless we find more records, we may never know."

Kalea yawned. It had been a very long day for my C.S.I. partner. "Bedtime," I said, "for C.S.I. interns." Kalea nodded and went across the hallway to brush her teeth. I settled her in Madison's four-poster and returned to my room, ready to burn more of Wayland's laptop battery and Great-Aunt Zelma's midnight oil.

Alone, I perused Wayland's Gmail archives to learn the other half of the story in his correspondence with prospective purchasers. In these, his knowledge of the Civil War shone brightly. He had reeled in a Civil War nut, the CEO of the Knowles Apothecary, one Grover Knowles who had acknowledged that he'd amassed millions brewing Carolina Blues tonic. The bottom line was that Grover had topped an offer of $950,000 from a major museum.

None of the emails to or from Grover Knowles mentioned the final price which had apparently been decided in a telephone conversation, but an email exchange confirmed the date Wayland would deliver the flag, a Sunday in mid-February, only a week after Garner had returned it along with a duplicate created by someone he referred to as Our Betsy Ross.

I guessed that the flag Madison and I had found in the closet wall was the original which had been copied to create the counterfeit he'd sold to the unsuspecting Grover Knowles, not the 1865 original he'd wangled from the elderly Anna Hepworth.

Among Wayland's checkbook stubs, I found a payment to an "A.H." for $25,000 in October the year before. Then last February a deposit was recorded: $55,000 from Knowles Apothecary. The first week of March, he'd written two checks for $10,000 each to Claude Garner and Ned Ferguson. I opened the calculator app on my iPhone and made some deductions from my guesstimate of $975,000 that Wayland may have received from Mr. Knowles. If Wayland's check stubs told the truth, he'd apparently skimmed upwards of $940,000.

As could be expected, the emails gave no indication of where it had been stashed. Reason enough, I was certain, for the verbal saber-rattling Madison had witnessed.

Wayland had scammed the scammers.

Chapter 24

"Knock knock." Kalea's voice as her knuckles rapped on my door the next morning.

"Abandon hope, all ye who dare to enter." The quote wasn't quite right, but the best my sleepy brain could retrieve. I'd fallen asleep in my clothes sometime after two.

"Wow, you look like you've had a whole hour of sleep," my C.S.I. teammate said, sweeping into the room like a dorm room inspector. For a moment I tried to recall the dream she woke me from but it had evaporated. Kalea was fresh-faced, in clean jeans and a black tee-shirt emblazoned with an NCIS's Abby quote: I love it when you talk geek.

"Got five full hours," I said with a yawn. I could have welcomed five more, but bright May sunshine flooded through the dormer windows.

By the time I'd drifted off, I realized I needed more help with the tangle of clues than a bright eleven-year-old could provide.

A year ago, when he was stationed at the Naval Academy, then Senior Chief Petty Officer Aaron Hunt had helped me track down his girlfriend's killer. We'd stayed in touch by lobbing the occasional e-missive through cyberspace. Which is how I'd learned of his advancement to master chief, the topmost rung of the enlisted ranks. His last email, about a month before Madison and I came south, said he'd saved some leave and wondered if I would be in Annapolis in June. Said he needed to visit the Academy and hoped we could get together for dinner. Straightaway, part of me was ready to leap at the chance to see him again. A larger part was afraid to admit it. So I'd said maybe. Now, my so-called sensible self could justify an invitation to assist in this convoluted investigation on two counts. In the first place, we needed someone to pose as a good ole boy to pry information from Ned and Garner. In the second place ... I missed him. If he could get leave to help out, we could reconnect on neutral territory.

Your heart just missed a couple of beats, Grandpa Jack added.

I forced myself up and yawned twice on my way to the bathroom. I would send Aaron an email today.

"So ... you stayed up," Kalea chided, following me. "Don't deny it. What do you have to say for yourself, young lady?" Echoing one or both of her moms.

I debated how much to tell of what I'd learned from Wayland's Gmail account. Through my toothpaste, I mumbled "I was busy with Mr. Morgan's email." I finished with the toothbrush and rinsed. "Interesting stuff."

"I'll bet." Snarky. "Are you gonna tell me or will I have to bribe you?"

"I'll let you bribe me. But later. I'm in the shower for a couple of minutes."

Five minutes later, Kalea was perusing Wayland's emails while I pulled on clean socks and tucked in my new Michael Jordan Tar Heels tee-shirt. A moment later, Kalea closed the laptop and sat beside me, studying my face in the antique dresser mirror while I brushed my hair into a ponytail.

"Maddy never uses makeup," she said, "but Shy always does."

"Cheyenne's in a profession where it's expected."

"Have you ever used makeup?" she asked.

"Not since I sneaked lipstick to middle school." I snapped on a scrunchie. "My dad didn't approve. And now it's too much trouble."

I admired our faces, side by side in the antique pockmarked mirror. We were a darned good-looking team.

+ + +

"There you are," Aunt Zelma said as we joined her in the kitchen. "Top of the morning." Although her old teapot was on the table, it was the savory aroma of coffee, bacon, toast, and jam that we'd followed down the stairway. "You two find anything interesting in Wayland's computer?"

"We learned a lot," Miss C.S.I. replied, "most interesting." Winked for my benefit.

Aunt Zelma poured milk for Kalea while I loaded two plates with toast and bacon and poured myself a much-needed jolt of caffeine. Between us we brought Aunt Zelma up to speed on the revelations from Wayland's emails: The connivance of Claude Garner in the apparent swindling of an elderly Boone woman for an extremely valuable Civil War battle flag, its subsequent sale, and Garner's suspicion that Wayland reported less profit than he'd actually reaped. "Which explains their argument," I said.

"I still think Mr. Garner killed him," Kalea said.

"Don't think so," I said. "Look. If Garner hoped to get money from Wayland, it wouldn't help at all for him to be dead."

Kalea seemed to consider this as she folded a rasher of bacon into a slice of whole wheat toast and took a chomp.

My aunt tapped her teapot. "You should try this," she said. "It's from a half-Cherokee woman down near the South Carolina border. She grows her own herbs and uses a recipe handed down from her Cherokee grandmother."

Could Cherokee herbal tea account for my aunt's abilities to visit other dimensions?

At least it's better than the tea she drank yesterday, Grandpa Jack whispered. *And thanks for locking the barn after the horse was stolen.*

He was angry because I'd only belatedly hidden the teabags in my room. I was still beating myself up for that.

"I'm sure the tea's wonderful but right now I need all the caffeine I can get. Late night at the office." I gave her a genuine smile as I poured what was left in the coffee press into a travel mug. Kalea accepted another travel mug with hastily prepared instant hot chocolate.

On the road to the hospital, my phone began dispensing Chopin's mazurka. It was Garner—responding to the note I'd hoped he wouldn't ignore. I gave Kalea the hush sign.

"Thanks for the call back," I said. "As I'm sure you know, I'm trying to help Madison figure out how her stepfather died."

"Gathered that."

If you want a direct answer, Grandpa Jack always said, ask a direct question.

"Do you know anyone who might have been angry enough to murder—" I held the phone away from my ear as his expletives exploded through telephonic cyberspace. Glad I hadn't put him on speakerphone.

He'd been interviewed by county detectives. When I asked what he'd told them, his retort again stung my eardrum.

"Okay," I said, "What about your friend Ned? When the detectives asked him if he knew if Wayland had enemies, I had the distinct impression he lied through his teeth."

After another non-answer, I closed the phone. "Mr. Garner says he was at school early all last week grading exams."

"And you believe him?" Kalea asked.

"He said the police interviewed him. And two other teachers at the school vouched for him. So that theory is busted. We'll have to accept that it wasn't Mr. Garner who poisoned Wayland."

"Then who?" Kalea asked.

"Then who, indeed? Not a doggone clue."

At the hospital, we found Shy sitting on the edge of Madison's bed.

Kalea hopped on the other side. "You're so much better."

"I feel better," Madison said.

"Yesterday you thought I was Melanie."

Cheyenne put a hand over Madison's. "You said it had been so long since you'd seen her."

Madison closed her eyes. Her shoulders twitched slightly.

"Did you have a playmate named Melanie?"

Her eyes still shut, Madison shook her head.

"A niece?" Shy asked.

Her partner continued slowly shaking her head.

Shy and I exchanged a glance but neither of us pursued it.

"Anyway, I have to get back to Annapolis," Cheyenne said. "I've booked a Saturday flight."

Madison turned to Kalea, "Will *you* stay? At least till they let me out of this funhouse?"

"I want to help Aunt Penny break this case."

I gave my young assistant a wink.

"I kinda figured you might," Cheyenne said.

"Until the Police Academy," Kalea added.

"Deal," said her mom.

I asked Madison if she knew Kalea and I visited

Wayland's apartment yesterday.

"Totally tossed," Kalea said.

"That's all Shy told me," Madison said.

"But," Cheyenne said, "Our friend here allowed Kalea to invade a crime scene."

"Sweetheart, I think we should trust Penny …"

Shy looked away and said nothing.

"Did she mention," I said, "that Wayland's musket was back over his desk?"

Madison's eyebrows lifted. "Really?"

"Whoever tore the place apart must have put it back. I figure it must have been Garner looking for the original flag."

"Whoever it was, Aunt Penny had the locks changed," Kalea added. "He won't be back."

"Your brilliant C.S.I. found Wayland's laptop. And a safe deposit box key."

"Okaayy." Madison wore a tell me expression.

"Under a false drawer bottom," Kalea said. Her impish face glowed.

"She not only found it," I said, "but puzzled out his password."

Both women beamed at their young sleuth.

"We went through his emails," I said, "and found that Wayland, Garner, and Ned pulled a scam that involved buying and reselling an antique Civil War flag. Probably like the one we found. Wayland was the buyer and seller. A lot of money changed hands. He was supposed to split the profit with the other two, but apparently kept the lion's share."

"So, my dearly departed stepfather was a crook." She took a breath. "Why am I not surprised?"

"Since there's not much in his checking account," I said,

"I think we should see if there's money in a safe deposit box. The key Kalea found may be to the unshared loot."

"Go for it," Madison said.

Cheyenne, unsmiling, had a faraway look.

Could she be wondering, Grandpa Jack whispered, *how much money is in that box?*

"Subject change," I said. "I'd like to take Kalea and Cheyenne out to Brantleigh tomorrow." It was a long shot, but I had a faint hope that I might get a ray of insight into Wayland's demise by visiting the gardens again. "You don't mind?"

"Go ahead. Just leave me here with Nurse Ratched," Madison joked. "I won't complain. But don't bother Shy with any design theory. Bores her stiff. Takes a royal mandate to prod her into visiting a garden."

Cheyenne's face made it clear that she wasn't at all interested in visiting Brantleigh. Kalea, on the other hand, seemed eager to visit the scene of the murder. "I might pick up some clues."

A knock on the door and Madison's lunch was brought in. The tray was placed and the rolling table positioned. "Sorry. No cocktails today," the server said, smiling. "Barrel-aged Cranberry-Apple is our libation-du-jour."

Madison laughed. "No tip today."

"So, Maddy," Shy said, when the server left, "New subject. I want to take Penny and her Aunt Zelma to lunch."

"What's the occasion?"

"To show our appreciation," she said, "for caring for you, my dear."

"I can survive on spam and Jell-O," she said, and pouted theatrically. "Enjoy yourselves."

On our way down the elevator, I phoned my aunt.

Once back in sunlight, I said, "My aunt says it's sweet of you and if you're serious, recommends Season's. Just a few miles from her place."

Cheyenne and Kalea followed me to Aunt Zelma's.

"I'm afraid you may have Madison longer than you bargained for," Cheyenne said after my introductions.

"No worries," Aunt Zee said. "She's a sweetheart. We'll get her back to you good as new."

I hoped she'd be nearly as good as new in a month or two, but between now and then there'd be weeks of physical therapy and she might wind up with one leg shorter than the other.

"She will be good as new," Kalea promised.

Our table at Season's overlooked the restaurant's front garden. Tulips and pansies of every hue posed for camera-toting couples on their way in. After our waitress handed us menus and hurried off with our drink orders, Cheyenne said Madison had told her about Wayland's will.

Aunt Zelma brightened. "A couple of years ago, Wayland asked if I knew a good lawyer. Turned out he'd never had a will. But he never told me that he'd had one drawn up."

Cheyenne opened her napkin and arranged her silverware. "It leaves everything to Madison Morgan."

Kalea pushed aside a lock of raven hair that had wandered onto her face. "I didn't know her last name was Morgan."

"It was Wayland's last name," Cheyenne explained, "so when her mom was married to him, he must have adopted her. When she started college, her mom divorced Wayland so she changed it back to her biological father's name."

Kalea frowned briefly, then wrinkled her nose. "He must

not have known that."

"It was a long time ago."

"When Wayland asked if I knew a lawyer," my aunt said, "he only said he'd decided to make a will. Since he never mentioned a family, I assumed he was a bachelor."

"Unfortunately," Cheyenne said, smoothing the napkin in her lap, "my Maryland Bar membership doesn't permit me to work in North Carolina. I've contacted a local lawyer here who'll handle the name discrepancy and probate the will."

The waitress returned with a Pepsi, two chardonnays, and an old-fashioned for Aunt Zelma. I nodded at the nearest plate on the table to my right. "I'll have what he's having."

The waitress glanced at the table. "The hickory-smoked pork. My favorite." She nodded, took the others' orders, and left.

"Could you get a power of attorney from Madison," I asked Cheyenne, "that would let us have a look in Wayland's safe deposit box?"

As soon as our waitress returned with our spinach, strawberry, and pecan salads, Kalea plucked a strawberry from the pinnacle of her salad and as deftly as a magician weaves a playing card into thin air it arrived in her mouth.

Although Cheyenne glanced out the window at the vibrant sweeps of tulips, I wondered if dollar signs, not spring color, glimmered in her mind's eye. Wayland's ill-gotten flag money would eventually be Madison's ...

Grandpa Jack cleared his throat. *Could Cheyenne and Ned be shooting at the same duck?*

Cheyenne drizzled balsamic vinegar over the spinach then held her salad fork suspended. "If I remember my banking law," she said, "the bank would probably let

Madison open the box, but only with a bank officer as witness, to see if his will or a life insurance policy is there. Since she already has his will, there's no point in taking chances on a bank officer getting a peek at any valuables."

Keep your thoughts to yourself, Grandpa Jack whispered to me softly.

Back at Aunt Zee's I asked Kalea to fetch my iPad. "It's on my dresser." The prospect of having Aaron to assist in untangling the questions surrounding Wayland's death released a few of my normally imprisoned butterflies. Maybe I wouldn't have to wait until Annapolis to share a candlelight dinner with him.

She scampered up two flights as only an eleven-year-old can. When she returned, I fired it up and, while she watched over my shoulder, tapped out:

Aaron — Hi from Flat Rock NC. Our visit here hasn't gone exactly according to plan. Remember that my design course professor, Madison, planned this trip after learning her stepfather lived near Hendersonville and had a docent job at Brantleigh Manor? (Note that I use the past tense.) During our tour with another guide, we found him—dead. But that's just the beginning. At a Civil War reenactment (where no real bullets are ever supposed to be used), Madison was shot and seriously wounded. She survived the surgery but will be in the hospital for at least another week. The local gendarmes haven't arrested anyone but I'm pretty sure I know whodunnit.

I've poked in her stepdad's computer and read quite a few of his emails. He and two others (one of them I'm sure was Madison's shooter) were involved in a scam that I think led to his death—and, I suspect, her "accident."

I'm not happy to admit it but I could use the help of a fresh face of the male persuasion. One who could work undercover as a Civil War geek. I'm thinking that with your South Carolina accent you'd be ideally suited for the part. Could you spare a few days? If it doesn't gross you out, you could stay for free in the apartment of the late Wayland Morgan who now languishes in the medical examiner's cold storage.

Say yes and I'll treat you to dinner at Twelve Bones Barbecue up in Asheville, the favorite of a recent president.

Cheers! Penny

"If he says yes," Kalea said, her pout this time unmistakable, "You'll be spending more time with him than with me."

"Don't get your knickers in a twist," I said. "You're my C.S.I. assistant. Aaron will be our undercover aide." I hit send and closed the iPad.

Chapter 25

When my alarm went off the next morning, Kalea was already up, anxious to see where Wayland had been found. After Cheyenne reluctantly agreed to come with us, I decided to treat them to the noon mansion tour. Meanwhile, Curious Georgette could sniff for any evidence that could help solve the mystery. Thanks to reading a mystery or two, I'd learned about the Locard theory that a criminal always leaves some trace evidence at the scene of the crime as well as unwittingly carries something from it. There was no reason I couldn't be the one to find what had been left.

I scrambled for the bathroom. After a quick shower, Kalea and I followed the scent of fresh baking down the stairs.

"What's *that?*" Kalea's nose wrinkled at a serving dish of creamy, lumpy goo set beside a basket of fluffy orange-colored biscuits.

"One of our famous Southern breakfasts, my dear," Aunt Zelma assured her.

"So what *is* it?" Kalea demanded.

"Sweet potato biscuits with sausage gravy," Aunt Zelma said. "A Kalorama specialty."

I remembered my first visit here and being equally squeamish when I met this breakfast for the first time. "Just split open a biscuit," I said, "pile on the gravy ... and enjoy."

+ + +

"I'll take it." Cheyenne's first view of Brantleigh Manor.

"Mom, even you can't afford that."

"Gotcha!"

"Gotcha your own self!" Kalea laughed.

Shy uncapped her camera and took a couple of shots of Kalea and me beside the big gryphons at the entrance. Then, using my camera, snapped one of Kalea and me destined for my condo.

I bought tickets for the noon Manor House tour. A week ago, we'd breezed through the house too quickly to learn much.

"We have a couple of hours to look around the gardens," I said with a glance at my watch. "Need to be back here by quarter to twelve."

"You promised," Cheyenne reminded me, "not to bore me with any designer talk."

"Cross my heart." At least Kalea and I'd get a quick look at where we'd found Wayland.

I took them first to the little temple at the end of the long lawn where Madison and I had rubbed the eagle's shoulder for luck. Probably as useless today as it had been the first time. Kalea touched the eagle tentatively but Shy refused, as she said, "to have any part in a pagan ritual."

Back in front of the mansion, I turned for a quick look at the landscaped lawn but kept my designer's mouth shut about the importance of a focal point in a vista. Instead, we went around the mansion, through the Parterre Garden and up the Double Italian Garden Stairs to the Pond Garden. Cheyenne snapped a photo of Kalea posing beside a dolphin fountain. As we wandered on, she took several more of Kalea with sculptures she said she'd get enlarged for her office.

We dawdled over the array of colors in the Rose Garden and in the Quincunx, I snapped a shot of Kalea pretending to hide behind a tree trunk. In the Glen, past the flowering cherry, Kalea asked where we'd found Wayland. I lifted the mountain laurel branch that had concealed him.

With a downward glance, "Ooooh," Kalea squealed.

Shy looked over her daughter's shoulder. "It's only a dead animal."

It wasn't a ghost and it wasn't an animal. It was Wayland's Olmsted wig with only a few straggly gray hairs around its edges. Kalea lay on the path, reached down to retrieve it, pulled it up, and stuffed it in her backpack.

"He either lost his balance or was pushed," she said. "Whichever, the poison must have acted very fast." For a nanosecond I pursued the possibility that the wig should be handed over as evidence. Then I thought if the detectives hadn't found it, they didn't need it now. Whatever had killed Wayland wouldn't be on the wig. Assuming we could figure out how he had died and who'd dunnit, it could become part of Kalea's presentation at the Junior Police Academy.

After she zipped up her backpack, we continued on the uphill path along the waterfalls to a wooden bridge across the upper falls. Again I held my tongue about focal points.

While Shy and Kalea admired the view, Grandpa Jack tapped my shoulder. Knowing I'd been pondering how to pry information from Ned Ferguson, he suggested I might talk Ned into taking *me* instead of Madison to visit the gardens we hadn't seen last week. *Brilliant*, I replied silently.

As Cheyenne snapped a photo of Kalea and the cascade, I glanced at my watch. "Scheisse," I said, to protect Kalea's tender ears. "We're gonna be late."

We rushed off the bridge which set it swaying, hurried back down the Waterfall Garden path, through the Glen and the terrace gardens, and finally, out of breath, trotted down the Italian Stairs, through the Parterre Garden and dashed back around to the front of the Manor. We hurried past a group of elderly visitors and up the steps between the gryphons, breathing hard, fearing we had missed our tour.

A gray-haired docent welcomed us and glanced at our tickets. "That tour hasn't started yet," she said. "Catch your breath." Which is what we were trying to do. She raised a finger to keep us a moment while she welcomed an elderly trio, then turned back. "Y'all put me in mind of a couple last week who ran up here so out of breath they could hardly explain that they'd seen Governor Brantley's ghost."

"Cool," said Kalea. Cheyenne was quiet, not caring if anyone had seen a ghost or not.

"What gave them the ghost idea?" I asked.

"It was the wife," the docent said. "She said she'd seen him talking with what she assumed was the Angel of Death, dressed in black. She'd turned to tell her husband and when she turned back, both the ghost and the dark angel had vanished.

"The husband piped up. 'Well, that's what ghosts do, dear, appear and disappear when you're not expecting them.' His wife just glared." The docent chuckled. "It was like we were in an Alfred Hitchcock movie."

The docent turned to usher in other guests, then turned back to us. "The woman said something like, 'I saw him, Edgar, don't say I didn't.' When I asked her why she thought she'd seen the governor's ghost, she said he looked like he'd walked right out of the guidebook. 'It had to be him and the Angel of Death,' she said. 'Who else?'"

"So, what'd you do?" Kalea asked.

"Didn't want a heart attack on my hands, thank you very much. So, I told them to have a seat and, like you, to get their breath back. After a minute or two, the woman said, 'Oh why didn't I get his picture? Then you'd know I'm not making this up. And, Edgar, if you'd turned around faster, you could have told this woman I didn't imagine it.' I didn't fancy calling her a liar so I said we've had reports of ghost sightings from time to time."

"You get many?" I asked.

"Once in a long while, but mostly inside the house," the docent said.

Kalea beamed in anticipation.

"Only later, I realized it was a strange coincidence," the docent continued. "It was the day one of our Olmsted docents died."

Kalea and I exchanged skeptical looks. "Did the lady say if the Death Angel had an umbrella?" Kalea asked. "Might have been like a KGB assassination."

"She didn't mention one," the docent said, motioning us toward our tour group.

The day Wayland died? It didn't take a reminder from Grandpa Jack for me to realize that Wayland, as Olmsted, would have been dressed as if he were a gentleman visitor from a hundred years ago. From a distance, easily mistaken for a phantom. My C.S.I. aide and I would discuss the docent's story later in private.

I wondered if Agatha Christie could have used this dubious sighting to kick-start a story.

Indubitably, whispered Grandpa Jack, whose literary preferences as a tutor emeritus of St. John's College, were usually limited to his beloved Great Books.

Thinking of Agatha, I recalled her theory that every murderer is somebody's old friend. If the ghost *was* Wayland in his Olmsted get-up, I thought, then the man in black might have been ... *I knew not.*

"Vivid imaginations, these mountain people," Cheyenne

interrupted. But my train of thought had left the station. I knew none of Wayland's friends, old or new, with the exception of Ned and Garner.

"I've never heard so much blarney," Shy huffed on our way to the Great Hall.

In any event, the docent's anecdote had stirred the plot of *our* mystery. But why, I wondered, hadn't Cheyenne picked up on the docent's tale as an avenue to tracking down Wayland's murderer? Some lawyers, I supposed, wear blinders to stay focused on their case. Or perhaps it was simply a lack of interest in Wayland's death.

Our mansion tour was, as I'd remembered, a room after room blur of Gilded Age elegance. But it was almost impossible to concentrate on the docent's spiel while I pondered who might have been the man in black. Unless the "misunderstanding" between Wayland and Garner was key to a much darker altercation, Wayland's death seemed to have been senseless. But could Ned have had a role in this? Possibly, I concluded, but only if the attempts on Madison's life were somehow connected with Wayland's death. It couldn't have been a coincidence that he'd been at the reenactment as well as in Madison's hospital room when the alarm sounded. But unless Ned lied about his Olmsted gig that morning, he could hardly have been Wayland's assassin.

While Kalea scouted for resident wraiths, Cheyenne marveled at the antiques and artwork. My ears perked up briefly when the docent explained how politicians here, in 1920, had plotted to defeat the state's ratification of the women's suffrage amendment to the Constitution. It was the year Great-Aunt Zelma was born. I couldn't picture the troglodyte misogynists who had kept this state from ratifying the amendment until fifty years later.

"What a spooky mansion," Kalea declared, as we walked back into sunlight and returned to the car. "If I were the governor's ghost, I'd much rather be in the garden than cooped up in that place."

Driving back to Kalorama, I considered replaying my ponderings for Cheyenne, but ultimately decided that she had no interest in Wayland's demise or who might have caused it. *With the possible exception of the money her partner might inherit,* Grandpa Jack added.

Cheyenne interrupted that train of thought. "I still think Madison might have met someone named Melanie here."

"Not that I know of." My nose again stretched. Curious Georgette had done a lot of wondering lately. Now it was whether by questioning Madison's faithfulness, Shy could be revealing some guilt of her own.

There I was again, sinking into the quicksand of trying to deal with my friends' psychology.

"Mom," Kalea said, "since when have you become a worrywart?"

"Could Melanie be an imaginary friend?" I suggested.

"What?"

"Imaginary, like not an actual person."

"She does have a good imagination," Cheyenne said. "Did she ever tell you about her Green Room club in high school?"

I shook my head as I made the left turn toward downtown Hendersonville.

"According to her scrapbook, she was a pretty good actress."

Remembering her performance in the Glen when we found Wayland, "A Renaissance woman," I said.

"She and a friend wrote a one-act play they called

Conjunctions," said Cheyenne. "About secrets not staying secret."

"Maybe Melanie was the co-author?" At least I was trying to stay on script.

"Can't remember but I don't think it was a Melanie."

"Perhaps a classmate?"

"Possibly. She'd originally planned to major in theater. If she hadn't caught the landscape architecture bug, she said she'd have wanted to be a stage designer."

"Seems like a comparable talent to designing landscapes," I said.

Cheyenne nodded, her attention elsewhere.

"Could there be some other side of Madison," I said, double-checking that Cheyenne hadn't known of the abuse, "that knows Melanie?"

She frowned, considering the possibility. "I've never thought she was role-playing."

The proof of her acting ability, whispered Grandpa Jack.

Like the Mona Lisa smile Madison wore when I complimented her on her reaction in the Glen when we found Wayland.

Quod erat demonstrandum, said Grandpa Jack.

+ + +

When we dropped Cheyenne back at the Inn, she headed off to the local lawyer with Wayland's will.

On our way to Belle Mère, Kalea and I talked about tracking down the Angel of Death. Kalea suggested that maybe the Brantleigh ticket office would remember him.

Out of the mouths of babes ….

At the hospital, Kalea ran up the five flights to the Surgical Recovery floor. I, on the other hand, at the ripe old age of thirty-three, was thankful for the elevator. Why hadn't

I run my usual six miles last weekend, I asked myself. Grandpa Jack whispered that he *had* reminded me Saturday morning.

"Dr. Selkirk says my recovery's on track," Madison said, "which means I should be out of here sometime in the next decade." It was nice to see her humor had returned.

I told her Cheyenne was on her way to the lawyer who would handle Wayland's will.

Kalea explained our Brantleigh visit. "We have an idea about your stepfather's murderer."

"Really?"

Kalea told her about the governor's ghost and the Angel of Death dressed in black. "Aunt Penny thinks the ghost was actually your stepfather and the Angel of Death was whoever poisoned him.

"So," Madison smiled sardonically, "put an ad in the paper for an Angel of Death."

"I don't think Ned was the man in black," I said, "but I do think he wants to hurt you for some reason. I think he fired the shot that brought you here. And why he was here last Sunday."

"Assuming you're right, what could be his purpose? What on earth could he want that I'm keeping him from?" Madison's eyes bored into mine as she cracked a smile. "And don't start with me about ending a sentence with a preposition. That's the kind of silliness up with which I cannot put."

"I have no idea why Ned seems to have you in his crosshairs," I said. "Which is why I've decided to beard the lion in his den, or in this case, his garden. I'll ask him to take me on the rest of the tour in your place. It'll give me a chance to grill him."

"Yes, we know …" She mimicked me, "Where were you on the morning of—?"

I had to laugh. "Trust me. If there's a connection I'll find it."

"Be careful."

"I'll make sure she's safe," Kalea said.

I glanced at my assistant. "Sorry, Punkin. You won't be on that mission."

"Until you earn your credentials and are issued a badge and gun," Madison said, "you won't be playing with the big boys."

Chapter 26

Before leaving Hendersonville, I drove to the bank where we had stowed the old flag. "I'll just be a minute," I said.

A manager examined the key Kalea found. "I don't think it's a safe deposit box key," he said. "Looks like it might be to a home safe."

I thanked him and tucked it back into my backpack's smallest pocket. I had to agree that it wasn't like the flag's safe deposit box key.

"Bad news and good news," I told Kalea back in the car.

"What's the bad news?"

"The key you found isn't for a safe deposit box."

"That's bad news?"

I headed us toward Flat Rock. "The good news is that the key might fit a home safe. The money might be in his apartment."

She strained against the seat belt. "Let's go find it."

"Curb your enthusiasm. Wherever it is, it's not going anywhere."

Kalea pretended to pout. Or maybe it was real. "If it's there," she said, "we'll find it."

I explained that Ned was our guide the day we found Mr. Morgan. "He seemed like a nice guy, but, between you, me and—"

"—the lamppost," she interrupted.

"You should avoid clichés like the plague," I said, pretending impatience with my smart sidekick.

"Okay ..." she said, "but nice guys aren't always nice. Could he have used some kind of poison that didn't work immediately?"

"Possibly." What *had* Ned been doing that morning? He'd said he was with a group from UNC, but there was no way to confirm it. I punched his number on my phone and when he didn't answer I left a message. In Madison's place, I said, I'd be happy to go back to Brantleigh and take photos for her of what we'd missed. He wouldn't need to know that I had already covered some of those parts with Cheyenne and Kalea.

"What we need to do this afternoon," I said, "is follow up on your suggestion to I.D. the man in black."

We drove to Brantleigh and parked at the ticket shop just inside the gatehouses. After a family of four headed to the Manor House with brochures in hand, we stepped up to the counter. The agent was a middle-aged prep-school type wearing a V-neck sweater and bow-tie.

"My uncle told me he'd be in town," I began, making it up as I went along. "Wednesday a week ago. He visits Brantleigh whenever he's here. And I'm worried. When he visits he imagines he's a Brantley heir who'll eventually inherit the whole estate." I tapped the side of my head. "You know, a trifle weird? But I never heard from him, so I'm hoping you could help me figure out if he came and didn't call me, or maybe changed his mind and never came." Kalea rolled her eyes. But I had to admit that, even to me, my story sounded lame.

After a passing frown and a glance into his memory, he said, "Miss, was that the day our Mr. Morgan was found?"

Mr. Memory. Wonderful. "Now that you mention it, I believe it was the same day." My prevarications are all in the name of research, I would explain later to Kalea.

"I was here that morning," the man said.

"Great. Maybe you remember a gentleman—he wears

black a lot—who would have come in early. He comes early to avoid the tourists, he says, as if he weren't one. Since he always uses his credit card—"

"Unfortunately," the agent said with a wry smile, "it doesn't matter if he used a credit card or not, we wouldn't have a record. We don't keep track of names, just the ticket purchased. In his case, if he came alone, we'd only have a record of an adult entry on that day. Sorry."

I fished in my well of make-believe. "He's a big guy, usually wears a black sweater and ball cap." My wooden nose stretched farther. "Probably the Steelers."

"Anything else to jog my memory?"

I dug deeper. "He's retired … wears a mustache." No reaction. "A small mustache."

The man tickled his chin with a knuckle. "Does your uncle have sideburns?"

Another shot in the dark: "He did the last time he was here."

"Well, then, I do remember." Lucky guess. "He was alone. A bit unusual for a family-oriented place like this. His sideburns were really bushy—reminded me of one of my Mensa buddies. Don't think he had a mustache though. But as I recall he got a senior discount. That'd make him at least fifty-five."

"Thanks," I said. "That's him. He must have shaved off his mustache and didn't bother to call me. I'll give him a proper tongue-lashing."

I thanked the man and complimented his memory.

"Enjoy your day," he said, and glanced over the counter at Kalea. "You've got a right cute kid."

Back in the sunshine, Kalea exploded. "I put a curse on anyone who calls me cute." She rolled her arms around each other like a taffy-pulling machine, tapped each elbow with the opposite fist, and pointed both index fingers back toward the ticket office.

"But you are, you know."

"You're demented."

"No names," I mused aloud, "so there's a dead end—if you'll pardon the expression."

"That is so incredibly funny," Kalea said, "I forgot to laugh."

How long had it been since I'd heard that?

Chapter 27

"You are truly spoiling us rotten," I told Aunt Zelma Friday morning. She beamed as we feasted on her sausage patties and strawberry-smothered waffles.

Mornings were always special during my childhood visits to Flat Rock. Breakfasts on the veranda were invariably more than special—they were memorable. Now, twenty-three years later, I was drinking Costa Rican coffee from the mug I'd sent her from the Gulf. It read USS ENTERPRISE CV-65 on one side. On the back, IRAQI FREEDOM 2007. Although I keep mine on a bookshelf, it's a reminder of a time I mostly want to forget.

Kalea and I filled Aunt Zelma in on our visit to Brantleigh and the docent's tale. Kalea elaborated on our speculation that the ghosts were Wayland and his killer.

"If Wayland's murderer was there," Aunt Zelma said, "they might have a record."

"We checked," Kalea said. "The ticket-man didn't have a name but he remembered an old guy with bushy sideburns. We think he might be the man in black that the docent told us about."

Between bites of strawberry-smothered waffles, we watched the sky over Mount Pisgah turn fretful. Kalea and Aunt Zec counted three dragons among the increasingly raggedy clouds while I checked the weather-guessers on my smartphone: fifty percent odds on rain all day. When I checked my email, an inner whoop.

"You're going to have a chance to meet Aaron," I said, and explained to my aunt that I'd asked him to help with our research. "Says he'll start at 1700." I translated the military time to five P.M. "Says he'll lay over about half way so he'll get here about noon tomorrow."

"He's welcome to stay here," my aunt said with a meaningful smile. "Bedrooms are going begging."

"That would be great, thanks, except I don't need any of your nosey friends knowing he's here."

"You want to keep him to yourself," Kalea said, smirking.

"He'll stay in Wayland's apartment," I said, and explained that he'll be snooping into the Civil War flag scam."

"Like undercover?" Kalea asked.

"Exactly."

Aunt Zelma frowned.

"I promise you'll meet him before he goes back."

"It'll be nice for you two to get together again," she said. "How long has it been?"

"He went to King's Bay last July. It'll be fun to see him but I only asked if he could help us dig into the flag scam."

Aunt Zelma said unh-hunh like it was a double-entendre while Kalea muttered "Yeah-sure."

"He'll just help with that side of the investigation," I insisted. "It won't be a tryst."

"Is that some kind of a pretzel?" asked Kalea.

"Sometimes," said Aunt Zelma, with her own version of a Mona Lisa smile.

I choked out my last slurp of coffee.

+ + +

The rain had begun. Kalea and I were on our way to Wayland's apartment, while thoughts of a safe full of money danced in our heads. At a Hendersonville stoplight, there were only five cars ahead of us and four waiting to head south. No comparison with rush-hours in Annapolis.

"Do you really think there'll be a wad of money?" Kalea asked.

I increased the speed of the wipers, now thrashing at the deluge. "We'll see, won't we?"

Kalea stared ahead, temporarily mollified.

"Wait … let me take a look …" I twitched two fingers over my head like Martian antennae. "I see a bundle of—"

"Maybe you've inherited the second sight," Kalea scoffed.

I don't believe it's possible to see anything beyond what's visible. But since I sometimes receive suggestions from Grandpa Jack, they might be considered glimpses beyond the perceptible.

"Do you think it's possible," I said as I nosed the Nissan into a parking spot, "there could be a gene for the second sight?"

"There're more things in heaven and earth than are dreamt of in your philosophy." Kalea's smile was solidly in the smug zone.

Fifth-graders in Annapolis were studying Hamlet?

I picked up the new keys and the locksmith's bill on the way to the elevator.

Wayland's apartment still looked like a tornado had blown through. Desk drawers askew on the floor, couch cushions oozing stuffing, pictures and frames trashed. The false bottom was back in its place, but the drawer was still on the floor, empty. Kalea knelt beside it and began assembling newspaper clippings, paperclips, pens, and pencils into what she determined was satisfactory order.

"I don't think straightening the room is going to help us find any money."

She aligned a few empty CD jewel cases, placed them in

the back of the drawer, and stood. For a moment we looked at each other, uncertain where to begin.

"Okay," she said, "If you lived here, where would you hide your diamonds?"

"Good question … if I had jewelry to squirrel away, where …?" That's when I thought of the old flag. "The closet."

I opened the doors and shoved clothes to one end. Garner had found the hideaway. The faux wall had been taken down.

"Cool," Kalea said as she helped me slide the panel out of the closet. The space behind it was empty.

I shoved an Olmsted outfit back to the middle of the rod.

"What's back there?" Kalea said, pointing to a plumbing access panel at the end of the closet.

"Plumbing connections."

"For what?" She looked at me like I was dumber than a pair of doorknobs.

Grandpa Jack squeezed my shoulder. *The hall's on the other side.*

I tried to avoid admitting my stupidity. "Uhh … just for grins, let's take a look."

"We need a Phillips screwdriver," Kalea said. "Did Mr. Morgan have a tool box?"

"Right," I said, trying to keep up with my clever assistant.

Wayland's toolbox was almost in my face—beside a spare Olmsted wig. Kalea found the screwdriver he had probably used to install the dummy panel. As she removed the second screw and pulled the door away, Grandpa Jack whispered *Voilà!* A digital keypad stared mutely, ready for a password.

"Maybe he has another one in another closet that opens

with a key," I said, putting the key back in a pocket.

"I'll try his laptop password."

"C W," she said. "1861—slash." She glanced up. "There's no slash."

I looked over her shoulder. Red numbers in the window read 291861. At least its batteries were alive. "Try the pound button to enter."

"Okay." Tap. "Nothing."

We could be here all week trying various six-digit combinations. If the key was backup for when battery died, where was the keyhole?

"Aunt Penny, what d'you think this is for?" She touched a shiny circle embedded in the gray door.

"Certainly not a keyhole. What do *you* think it's for?"

"Could be a cover for a keyhole."

My stupidity had returned.

Kalea had already taken a flat screwdriver from the toolbox and was prying off the metal circle. The keyhole, as she had surmised, was revealed. The key fit. The safe's door sprang open.

"You do have the second sight, Aunt Penny," Kalea blurted.

We counted nine hundred-thousand-dollar bundles. Underneath were a few more bills and a copy of a receipt: Received of Grover Knowles, $900,750 cash. Wayland had been an inveterate record-keeper, even if it confirmed that he'd been a con artist.

"What'll we do with it?" Kalea asked.

Much as I distrusted Cheyenne's apparent interest in Madison's inheritance, she'd learn about this money eventually. And her advice would be free. "Time to call a lawyer." I pulled out my phone and speed-dialed Shy.

"Leave it in the box for now," she counseled. "Until the estate is closed out, no one needs to know."

"If Garner or Ferguson ever learns how much Wayland stiffed them," I said, "couldn't they file suit against his estate?"

"Only if there was a written agreement," she said. "But since we haven't found it, I doubt there is one. Verbal agreements, they taught us in law school, aren't worth the paper they're written on." We both laughed.

"Maybe I'll be a lawyer first and then a forensics investigator." Kalea said, cocking her head with an "it could happen" look.

"You'd be a double-threat," I said, closing and locking the safe.

+ + +

The next morning, Kalea and I headed to the Asheville airport in time to see Cheyenne off. We'd see Madison on our way back. As we merged onto the interstate, my phone mazurka'd. Ned.

"About Brantleigh," he said, "I don't have any gigs on Monday. Could that work for you? I mean, if you're still up for seeing the rest of the garden. Wouldn't want you to go back without seein' the whole nine yards ... Sorry, no pun intended."

"Monday's good," I said. "What time?"

"Morning, say nine? We could meet at the gryphons. But don't look for Olmsted—" he chuckled "—he won't be there."

My agenda was ready.

You'd better understand that Ned has one too, whispered Grandpa Jack.

I turned in toward the short-term parking. "I'm really

happy my moms let me stay. Summer is sooo damn boring in Annapolis—"

"Please don't use a word with me that you wouldn't use at home."

"What word?"

"You know damn well what word I mean."

Kalea laughed. "This summer'll be specially boring 'cause the Blue Angels won't be at the Naval Academy graduation. Their gas money ran out."

Cheyenne's flight was ready to board. "Promise to help Aunt Penny and not be a pest?"

Kalea flipped her an exaggerated two-fingered salute. "And I promise to be back in time for the Police Academy."

Cheyenne returned the salute. "You'd *better* be back by then." She hugged her daughter and turned to me. "At the first sign of insubordination, put your assistant on a flight home."

Kalea grinned as I said yes ma'am.

"Stay in touch," Shy said as we hugged. "And thanks for all you're doing for Maddy."

+ + +

Dr. Selkirk was in Madison's room. His scrub cap du jour featured intergalactic spaceships. His badge reel read ROCKET DOC.

"How's Mom?" Kalea asked.

The surgeon beamed. "I'm almost ready to kick her out. Well, roll her out."

"Said if I'm good he'd release me Tuesday." Madison twisted her wheelchair to us and Dr. Selkirk's smile confirmed the plan.

"I'll see her again on Monday and prepare the discharge," Selkirk said. "Give us a buzz Tuesday morning to confirm, but she should be able to get out of here before lunch."

After he left, Madison wore a smile but blurted an *oooch* as she repositioned her legs.

"I can't believe what you found in the wall safe," she said.

"Shy-Mom said we shouldn't think about it until your stepdad's will is closed, whatever that means," Kalea said.

I put my finger to my lips. "Mum's the word." We said good-bye and Kalea gave her mom a snuggly kiss.

On the way to Kalorama, I fired up my phone, handed it to Kalea and asked her to check for email.

"There's a new one from an A. H.," she said. "That's Aaron?"

"Tap it and read, please."

"'On the road again. Will arrive mid-day Sunday,'" she read. "He wants you to call in the morning with a rendezvous address and he'll give you his etta."

"His what?"

"Etta. He spelled it with capital letters: ETA."

"Punkin, that's military talk for estimated time of arrival. Anything else?"

"Just mush. 'It will be great to see you again,' he says. Exclamation point. Then, 'Fair winds. Aaron.'"

She looked up from the phone to me. "You're blushing."

Chapter 28

I found a parking spot near the entrance of the Vanderbilt Lodge Sunday afternoon where Kalea and I would await Aaron's arrival. The gently aged architectural matriarch seemed subdued. With the exception of one resident who exited the Lodge, nodded, and headed to her car as we approached, the mountainside was quiet. In spite of wonderful weekend weather, there were no readers, knitters, or dreamers in the rocking chairs. We had our choice.

Our two cans of Pepsi sweated tiny puddles on the ledge over which I stayed alert for Aaron's approach. While I opened a newspaper, Kalea dug her forensics book from her backpack, propped it on her knees, and began the chapter on profiling.

The Hendersonville Gazette's lead editorial dealt with the state legislature's attacks on voting rights and teachers' salaries. At the bottom of the page over a short single-column article, a headline announced: BATTLE OF ASHEVILLE ACCIDENT PROBED. Edward "Ned" Ferguson, one of the Yankee reenactors and a docent at Brantleigh Manor where the event was staged, was interviewed again by Henderson County detectives on Friday about the gunshot that wounded a spectator last Saturday.

No wonder Ned hadn't returned my call until yesterday. If he showed up tomorrow, I would have my *own* interview with the creep.

While we waited, I searched online for Civil War in Western North Carolina. I found references to the Battle of Asheville as well as the Brantley armory that manufactured Enfield rifles in the first years of the war. And was surprised to find that the Civil War enthusiasts Meetup group Deb

Imler had mentioned had a meeting scheduled the next day. I copied out the details of the meeting and also found some convenient history about a Kershaw's Brigade that Aaron could adopt for his bonafides. He'd be able to hit the ground running.

Just after two, as his email predicted, his dark blue Mercedes, top down, entered the circular drive. I made like a 1940s landing signal officer, stretching both arms straight out signaling "on glide path." When I slashed my throat signaling "Cut Engine," he came to a stop directly in front of us wearing, not a white silk scarf, but an embroidered Navy golf shirt and a broad smile. Watching old "Victory at Sea" episodes at the Naval Academy hadn't been for naught.

As he opened his door, I leaned in to give him a quick hug and said simply, "I'm really glad you're here."

"And who's this?" he said.

"My C.S.I. partner, discoverer of hidden laptops, decipherer of pass-codes, and F.B.I. profiler-in-training. Kalea."

"I'm pleased to meet such a talented deputy to the best sleuth in the hemisphere." Kalea beamed.

"Kalea, my friend Aaron Hunt."

"Nice to meetcha," she said.

He stepped out and stretched. I leaned up to give him another hug, inhaling his tropical aftershave. What I'd waited for. What I hadn't imagined was that he'd return it and land a cheek peck.

"Okay, enough mush," Kalea said.

We broke our clinch. While he went to the trunk for a bag, I tipped his seat forward to reach a bag on the back seat. "Let's get your stuff up to the room."

Kalea grabbed a stack of shirts on hangers that he'd kept

pressed under the back-seat bag. Aaron led the way with his bag and an overnight kit. "Your email sounded like you're in a regular pickle," he said. "Sorry I couldn't bring a white horse to carry y'all to safety."

"You're here. That's enough."

"Mr. Hunt," Kalea asked, "Do you believe in white horses and fairy tales?"

"I didn't used to, but I'm coming around."

"That's good," she said, "because some strange things are happening around here."

"We'll get to that," I said. Kalea piloted the clankety elevator to the second floor.

"Sorry we haven't found a crime scene cleanup company," I said, fitting the new keys. The room still looked like a giant storm had passed through.

"It's so home-like," Aaron said.

"We thought you'd appreciate the lived-in look," I said.

"Whoa." He'd noticed the cabinet of Civil War antiques. I flipped on the display lights. "Is that stuff for real?"

"Looks real to me," Kalea said.

"Many moons ago," I said, "Madison's stepdad taught history. When he moved here he got obsessed with the Civil War." I picked up the photo of Wayland in his Confederate uniform, frame askew and glass broken. "Became a reenactor. He was to have been the commander of the home guard in the reenactment last weekend."

"Where Maddy-Mom got shot," Kalea added.

We stepped over the desk drawers and ripped-open pillows that we'd not cleaned up when we'd been intent on finding the home safe. The bedroom, too, still held evidence of the rampage: dresser drawers dumped, the framed print of Van Gogh's Starry Night on the floor.

Kalea hung Aaron's shirts on the closet rod while he plopped his bag on the bed.

"Kalea, let's make this place habitable while Aaron gets settled."

I re-hung the print and, together, we replaced dresser drawers.

In the front room, Wayland's rifle still hung on the wall over his desk. We slid desk drawers into their slots and picked up the broken glass from the Major Morgan photo.

When Aaron appeared, he said, "How 'bout a SITREP?"

"Military talk for situation report," I said to Kalea.

"You sailors have tons of those ananyms."

"Acronyms." Then to Aaron: "Lunch first. Then we'll get you up to speed."

The old elevator clanked its way down to the lobby. There were only a few patrons lingering in the sumptuous Mountainview Grille. Grand in a Vanderbilt kind of way. Gold-framed portraits of Edith and George hung on either side of a wide marble fireplace, the mantel decked with fresh flowers, chandeliers crafted from tangled antlers hung from the ceiling, and a small bouquet graced every table. We unfolded cloth napkins that matched the burgundy-colored curtains. Glancing at the leather-bound menu, I discovered immediately that the prices reflected the Michelin star imprinted on the cover. "Nothing but the best," I said, my finger tapping the prices, "for guests of the Vanderbilts."

Aaron ordered a barbecued ribs platter, baked beans, German potato salad, and a draft Gaelic Ale. Since Kalea and I had eaten only a couple of hours earlier, we ordered salads.

When the waitress left, Kalea held up her fork and tapped the table like King Arthur awaiting his roast. "Mr. Hunt, are you going to figure out who murdered Maddy-Mom's stepdad?"

"I feel like I've—like I've walked into the middle of a movie and only have a hint of what it's about." He turned to Kalea. "How about you first tell me about your mom."

Kalea put her fork down. "'kay ... Her name's Madison. Her leg was hurt pretty bad when she got shot last weekend. She'll be a while recovering from her surgery."

"That's what Penny's email said."

The waitress brought my wine and Aaron's beer.

"May I start at the beginning?" I said, "Before the accident?"

"Sure—'cept it wasn't an accident." Kalea flipped her ponytail in mock annoyance.

While Aaron dug into his barbecue, I started with our Brantleigh tour, finding Wayland, and explained what we knew about the battle flag scam.

Aaron set down his ale. "So, you'd like yours truly to scope out what those dudes are up to."

I nodded. "There's something hinky going on that I'm quite sure a man could work out. Your Carolina accent fits perfectly with the Civil War enthusiast guise I've dreamed up for you."

Aaron nodded with an "okay, go on" look.

"You'll be Clement Pritchard, a wealthy developer from Florence, South Carolina." Kalea's eyes widened as she realized how many tricks a sleuth needed up her sleeve. "A Myrtle Beach real estate developer." I dove into my backpack and pulled out a Stars and Bars bow tie. "Your great-granddad was in the Seventh South Carolina Infantry and was discharged after being wounded at Chancellorsville. In 1863. Remember, the 'Seventh' was part of Kershaw's Brigade. Kershaw. Okay?"

"I've got to memorize all that? You sure you can't do this? Seems you've become quite the historian."

"Child's play, my dear, compared to what you've learned about submarine electronics."

Aaron smiled his acceptance and tapped the side of his head. "Fire away, then."

"You're a very wealthy amateur Civil War buff hoping to buy the original flag from Fort Sumter for your private collection." I pulled out a packet of freshly printed business cards. "And here're some cards."

"Clement Pritchard," he read. "Commercial real estate. Investment, development, and management. Not sure about the Dixie flag in the background though."

"Matches the tie," I said. "So … after you hand these out, you'll need to be ready for calls from our 828 area code."

"Pritchard here …" His South Carolina accent had eroded only slightly during his nearly twenty years in the Navy.

"Perfect."

+ + +

At the hospital, Kalea led us to Madison's room.

"Mom. You have visitors."

Madison closed her book and dropped it on the bed table. "I remember the movie," she said, "but the book's better." I glimpsed the author's name, Pat Conroy. She angled her head at Aaron. "Hi."

"Aaron," he said, and held out his hand.

They shook. "Nice to meet you."

I'd explained to Madison on our flight to Asheville about meeting Aaron last year after finding his girlfriend in a goldfish pond. "I hadn't known you were a Sherlock," Madison had said. "Just an unwitting Nancy Drew," I'd told her, with a smile intended to be self-deprecating.

"I understand you've been giving Penny ideas about becoming a twenty-first century Olmsted," Aaron said.

"I cannot tell a lie," she said, facing me and letting her eyelids dip for an instant before extending her hand to our new colleague.

"Did Penny explain that I've been invited to co-star in her new reality show?" Aaron's eyes met mine. "We're calling it Capture the Flag."

"We've got the flag," Madison said, "but ... we need help connecting it with my stepdad's death."

"And maybe your so-called accident," Aaron added.

Madison frowned. "We don't think it was an accident."

Aaron studied Madison's squiggly heart-beat line on the monitor for a moment and then turned back to her. "If this Ned character purposely loaded a bullet at the reenactment to shoot you, d'you have any idea why? Could there be any connection to your stepdad's flag business?"

"All we know," I said, "is that Ned and Claude Garner set up a scam and Wayland scammed the scammers."

Aaron turned to Kalea. "Do *you* have a theory?"

"Well ... I'd say someone didn't want Mom to have the money—"

"What money?"

"I've ... forgotten," Kalea muttered weakly.

"Tell you later," I said.

"No one's supposed to know," Kalea whispered.

"It's okay for Mr. Hunt to know," I said. "Just not now."

Madison pushed herself higher in the bed with a muffled *oooch*. "My stepdad had some money which, if I survive my war wound, I'll eventually inherit."

"Based on what Penny explained at lunch," Aaron said,

"I can see some connections."

"I'll fill you in later," I promised again.

Madison turned to me. "If you're still planning to go back to Brantleigh with Ned tomorrow—" she glanced meaningfully at Aaron "—I'd take backup."

Chapter 29

We left the Mercedes at the hospital. I didn't want to take a chance his car could be connected with either me or Aunt Zelma.

The afternoon sun was parading through fast-moving raggedy clouds over Mt. Pisgah when we turned in between Kalorama's big iron gates. Kalea preceded us to the steps. "I'd like you to meet Penny's friend, Aaron," she said to my aunt. Aaron extended his hand.

"My Great-Aunt Zelma Porter," I said.

"My pleasure, Miz Porter."

"Honey, if I were fifty years younger ..." She winked over his shoulder at me. Had she started on her amontillado early?

"Aunt Penny, you're blushing."

I frowned at my surrogate niece. "Your mom said I could send you home for insubordination."

Mock salute. "Yes sir, ma'am. It won't happen again sir, ma'am." Aaron and Aunt Zelma snickered.

"You folks ready for supper?" Aunt Zelma asked.

When I canvassed my charges, Aaron, who's hungry most of the time, was noncommittal. Kalea lifted her chin and one shoulder in a "whatever" posture. My aunt led us to the kitchen saying she'd slap some sandwiches together.

Aaron admired Zelma's collectible hogs and piglets grinning at us from nearly every shelf. "Don't ask," I said. "It'll take her mind off the story of the first owner's murder she's waiting to tell you."

"Can I take a rain check on that?"

+ + +

With shades of sunset glowering behind Mt. Pisgah, I

wished Aunt Zelma luck in her checkers match with Kalea, and started back to the hospital with Aaron to get his car.

"I'm glad you asked me to join you," he said as we headed down the lane.

"We needed a third person for our sleuth brigade." With a self-conscious smile: "For some reason your name topped our list of candidates."

"Aw shucks, ma'am. Much obliged."

As I turned onto the Sandburg Pike, he added, "Been thinking about you."

I felt like saying "me too," while my tongue-tied self concentrated on staying in my lane.

"I'm looking forward to coming to Annapolis. I've missed you."

My pulse ratcheted. Ever since getting dumped by my fiancé, I'd kept my heart under wraps. A squeaky "me too" was all I could summon.

"It's the truth."

"You're a silver-tongued rascal."

He laughed. "I'll take your word for it."

Traffic from Flat Rock into Hendersonville was almost nonexistent, but it took a conscious effort to brake for the occasional stoplight. I was too aware of Aaron beside me.

From the hospital, in our own cars, we caravanned to the Vanderbilt Lodge. I suggested a nightcap at the Pub to introduce him to his undercover persona. Like the Grille on the opposite side of the lobby, it was luxurious. A chandelier of interlocking antlers hung over our café-table.

"Let's talk business for a minute," I said.

After the waitress took our order, Aaron said, "If you insist."

"I've found a Civil War Meetup group for you to work

up your bona fides."

"And that's because …"

"They have a dinner meeting tomorrow. You may meet some of the actors in *our* mystery, but at least you can get a sense of the Civil War fervor around here."

"Will I have to remember the Seventh something and Kershaw's Brigade?"

"That could help," I said, "depending on who you meet."

He sighed "—The things we do for—"

"Hey, hey, don't get melodramatic. You volunteered."

After a beat, he said, "Roger that."

"It'll be at the Stone House restaurant. I've never been there but your GPS shouldn't have a problem."

Generous pours of dark rum and chilled chardonnay arrived. We sipped tentatively and shared silly smiles.

A world of difference from my junior prom date at the Little Campus restaurant in Annapolis, when my first glass of wine was still several months in the future. But the giddy feeling was the same. Aaron and I were friends … well … maybe getting to be better friends.

The waitress set down a saucer of cheese bites with a dollop of what looked like Aunt Zelma's fig jam. Sampling both, I said, "We need a reason for Clement Pritchard to be here."

Aaron sipped rum and put down the tumbler. "There was a billboard on the interstate about a gun show. Maybe he's searching for an original from the 'recent unpleasantness.'"

"Good. Ties in with your Fort Sumter flag quest."

I described Wayland's friends who might be at the Meetup: Claude Garner whose broad forehead and goatee should be easy to recognize, Ned Ferguson with a narrow face and sandy hair and eyebrows shaped like violin f-holes, and Lorenzo Peters, whose weather-beaten whiskered face resembled a vintage Mathew Brady portrait.

"Okay." He laughed. "That's easy enough. Mathew Brady, Ned Peters, Wayland Ferguson—wait, he's the dead one."

"I can see your mind is like a steel trap—rusted shut." I baited him with what I hoped was an endearing smile. "You've been underwater too long."

"Run those names by me once more?"

"I'll send you the cheat notes in the morning."

We'd returned to the easy-banter communications style we'd had in Annapolis. But neither of us mentioned our sleuthing the year before.

"Aaron, is Naptown still on your summer schedule?"

His face reddened. "I have to admit, that was a ploy to see you." He hesitated. "I don't really have a meeting at the Naval Academy." I reached across the table for his hand. He took mine and squeezed. "North Carolina, though, is a nice alternative."

I tightened my grip.

By the time we parted, the rain had started. On my way back to Kalorama, between wiper slaps Grandpa Jack inquired if my priorities were upside down by letting tomorrow's date with Ned take precedence over staying at the Lodge with Aaron.

Probably, I admitted.

Chapter 30

Monday's Gazette lay in its rain-spattered plastic pouch at the gate. Near the bottom of the first page was a photo of Ned and an article: REENACTOR QUESTIONED IN ACCIDENT PROBE. It restated what we'd known about the shooting and added that Mr. Edward "Ned" Ferguson, a Brantleigh Manor docent and reenactor who role-played a Union attacker, was arrested on charges of malicious wounding and the felony use of a firearm. Bail was set at $100,000.

"I wonder if Mr. Brantley posted his bail," I said across the breakfast table.

"Shouldn't they charge him with attempted murder?" said Kalea.

"And this is the guy you're meeting today?" Aunt Zelma's meaning was clear: I can't believe you're going anywhere with him.

"If he shows up, he's the one I need to pry information from. Don't worry."

"It's hard for me to believe this is the same Ned Ferguson I've known."

Kalea was disappointed that she couldn't come with me. "I'd be your backup."

"Don't worry," I said, "I'll tell you the good stuff when I get back."

The day was overcast with a light drizzle left over from yesterday's rain. My umbrella was in the car.

Ned waited at the gryphons as arranged but it was as clear as the frown on his face that he carried a monster chip on his shoulder. "I saw the paper this morning," I said, in an attempt at pleasantry. "Wasn't sure you'd be here."

"Mr. Brantley posted my bail," Ned barked.

Why not bark about his innocence and wrongful arrest?

You're not the only one with an agenda, Grandpa Jack reminded me.

"Lead on, McGruff."

No response from Ned so I doubted he appreciated the misquote. (English majors rule!)

"We'll start from where we found Wayland."

On full alert, I followed him around to the Parterre Garden at the back of the Manor.

The drizzle became a steady rain. Umbrellas on high, we ascended the double stairway, wound through terraces and on to the Glen. Taking purposeful strides, Ned was a man on a mission.

He wore cargo pants, a Tarheels hoodie, and a dapper pub cap over his sandy locks. Was his umbrella poisoned tipped? I glanced around thinking the presence of other visitors would deter him from following any physical agenda, but we were alone. If a weapon were needed, I had only my umbrella.

"They honor Olmsted's memory here, but have they kept his designs?" Ned was already on a rant. "Certainly not in the Glen."

We passed the creek where we'd found Wayland and continued toward the Waterfall Garden where Brantleigh Creek tumbled around and over rocky outcrops. I oohed and aahed like it was my first sight of the falls. From beneath my rain-pelted umbrella I grabbed a couple of shots and hoped Ned would understand that I really intended to create a PowerPoint. Which was true for heaven's sake.

On our trek up the path alongside the falls, Ned explained Olmsted's engineering to keep the waterfalls looking perfect, even when there was too much rain. "Above the waterfall, as you'll see, there's a pond. There's a dam at this end of it where the falls start. What you can't see is a spillway under it for when it rains too hard for too long."

"Like today?" I lifted my umbrella slightly and looked where Ned pointed. I saw only the wooden bridge that Cheyenne, Kalea, and I had visited last week. I asked him to hold my umbrella above my camera while I took an upward-angle wide shot with the bridge at the top.

There was no one ahead of us as we hiked up. No one following us, either. We were alone. The rain had undoubtedly kept fair-weather visitors either at home or in a pub like the one at Vanderbilt Lodge where I imagined Aaron was nursing a rum as he crammed for the Meetup tonight. Meantime I'm thinking I may have been too self-confident in not suggesting he shadow me here.

After the final rain-slicked stone step, the bridge shuddered slightly as we both stepped onto it. The railings didn't appear very sturdy, but that was probably just my overactive early warning system.

I'd learned hypervigilance on the Big E's deck during flight operations. "If you're going to be a hotshot Navy photographer," our senior chief had warned, "keep your head on a swivel up there." His advice paid off because I was never sucked into a jet intake or chopped into propeller hamburger while I snagged, in my humble opinion, some great photos. Which was more dangerous, I wondered, an aircraft carrier deck during flight operations, or confronting an angry conspirator with something to hide?

Madison's advice echoed: *If I were you I'd take backup.*

Too late for second-guesses, Grandpa Jack said.

"From here," Ned said, "you can see the dam." The stream poured smoothly down to its obliteration among boulders fifty feet below. I snapped a wide shot of the dam and another down the waterfalls.

Time for answers. "Mr. Ferguson—"

"Ned is fine."

"Ned, then, thanks for taking time to show me the rest of the gardens."

"My pleasure."

"Can I ask you something?"

He said nothing. Just nodded. Perhaps a smirk.

"You know I'm helping Madison try to figure out how her stepfather died."

"All I know is what I read in the paper. Heart problem."

"I read that too. But I don't believe it and neither does Madison. By the way, the M.E. has revised his conclusion. It wasn't arrhythmia."

Ned seemed genuinely surprised. "What was it?"

"We're not permitted to say," I fabricated, "because it's now a criminal investigation. Suspected murder."

That spooked him, but he tried not to let it show. "They have any suspects?"

"Why do you think Mr. Garner had an argument with Mr. Morgan the night before he died?"

Ned swallowed hard. He knew. But said nothing.

"Ned, when you talked with the cops, can I assume they wanted to hear about the reenactment accident as well as the hospital episode?"

His eyes widened and his eyebrows did their furtive curvy thing but relayed no humor. Surprised at this new confrontation, he snapped. "Why do you care what the police asked?"

"I care because I'm upset and angry that Madison was badly wounded. And because you seem to be in their sights."

You're pushing him, Grandpa Jack warned.

"I think you should stick to learning what you can from Mr. Olmsted," he said, "and not poke your nose into what doesn't concern you."

"Ned," I said, my anger building, "no one tells me what to be concerned about. You ought to be able to answer a straightforward question without getting your panties in a wrinkle."

Ned smirked. "I can't think of any reason they wanted to talk with me," he said, attempting to sound reasonable, "except that I was in the area when the accident happened."

"Ned," I said forcefully, to remind him that *I* was asking the questions, although I also realized I was both figuratively and literally on shaky ground. "I haven't forgotten that you recommended where we should be for a good view. I think you wanted us in that precise position."

"No reason at all beside what I suggested. It was the best vantage point for the action." Ned scanned the area. Confirming we were alone? My alert warning system flashed.

"Ned, I don't believe you killed Wayland but I think there's a link between Wayland's death and the reenactment … uh … accident and you seem to be that link. At least you know what that link is. What is it?"

Had I pushed too far?

For a fraction of a second, he processed the question. Then his face shifted almost imperceptibly. "Good heavens, you have an imagination," he said, like he was quoting from some Southern gothic story.

I moved to the other side of the bridge and turned to see Ned leaping at me.

I only had a moment to slash my still open umbrella at

him twice before he wrested it away and slammed me against the railing. It grunched and cracked.

I screamed. No response and no one in sight.

Ned pinned my arms behind me. Then briefly he released his right hand to punch my face.

Warm blood crept from my nose. I twisted my head away and used my free left hand to grab his flailing right hand, which I succeeded in doing—but for only a moment. He grabbed my left arm and pinned it again. This was awkward as neither of us had a hand free to do battle. He faced me and would have been quite vulnerable in the crotch department, but he had me immobilized against the cracked railing. Both umbrellas now discarded. Both of us getting soaked.

I kicked his ankle, hoping to knock a foot out from under him, but my effort only triggered a taunt: "Wow. You're one tough little lady." With a sarcastic laugh, he stepped back just enough to raise a knee and slam it against me with the obvious intent of breaking the cracked railing at my back. The railing groaned again, but he hadn't hit me hard enough to break it. I jerked sideways and because the bridge was slippery we pivoted so that he was now backed against the damaged railing, off-balance. He briefly let me go to regain his footing which gave me the only chance I needed to use my knee where it would hurt the most. He screeched and bent forward, truly in pain now, in enough agony that he lost the plot, giving me the fraction of a second needed to back off slightly and slam him. The impact, plus his weight, splintered the railing.

It opened like a double door into the void. "Whaaa thufff …" he bellowed as he staggered backward into space. I caught a millisecond's glance at his bulging eyes as he began a slow-motion tumble. After the *kalump*, I screwed up my nerve and peered down. He lay crumpled on a stream-splashed boulder, the water tinted pink on its way to the next fall.

I was drenched. But it was the shock of only narrowly surviving the encounter, not the rain, that left me shaking uncontrollably.

Chapter 31

My pulse raced and adrenalin urged me to finish what I'd started. Except I pretty much knew it was already finished. I kicked his umbrella over the edge and picked up mine.

My face felt like it had been hit by a locomotive. I pressed a bandana to my nose and stepped carefully down nearly-vertical wet steps to the base of the waterfall where Ned had fallen. My arm, back, and chest muscles complained with every step. I descended cautiously, unwilling to compound my injuries, through a grove of bamboo, to the cascade-washed boulders where Ned lay. I stepped out onto a stone in the stream to see him clearly. He was definitely not revivable. I bent down, rinsed my bandana and wiped my nose again. Only a small spot of red.

Madison, I realized, would be furious. Not to mention Kalea and Aunt Zelma. And, of course, Aaron.

The rain had abated and a stray shaft of sun poked a ragged hole in clouds. I had to get to the mansion and report the accident.

Just three steps up, I caught the glint of something shiny lying in the bamboo grove. A curious magpie, I pried through the stalks to reach whatever it was.

It looked something akin to a garden hose nozzle. But no hose connection. Had no idea what it might be. Dropped it into my backpack to wonder about later.

My muscles burned, but I finally retraced my steps to the Glen and followed the path to where we'd found Wayland. Still no other visitors in sight. The drippy overcast had convinced today's visitors to tour the mansion, rather than the sodden gardens.

I fought the jitters and took another swipe with my damp

bandana that told me my nosebleed had mostly stopped.

I walked as quickly down the stairway as I dared to the parterre where a security officer stepped into his electric vehicle. "Sir," I called, gasping, "Hang on. An accident."

"Where?" He stepped back out.

"There's a dead man on the rocks under the waterfalls bridge. It's Ned Ferguson."

The officer turned to his lapel microphone and relayed the emergency. "Wait right here, Miss …"

"Summers."

Within minutes, Captain Randall arrived in his own two-seater. His face could only be described as a scowl. "I believe we've met," he began and stared briefly at my bruised nose.

"Yes sir, we have."

"Aren't you Ms. Lerrimore's friend from Maryland?"

"Yessir."

"Hop in, please. Officer Sheppard, follow us." Using a switchback side trail off-limits to the public, we were up at the bridge in record time. My escort looked over the broken railing. Officer Sheppard opened his notebook, prepped for note-taking.

"Okay, Miss Summers," Randall said, "tell us what you know."

I briefly considered saying that I'd just started up the Stream Valley when I heard a scream so I came up and found the bridge railing broken. I went down to see if the guy was okay which of course he wasn't so I went back to the Manor and told this officer. And, just as quickly, realized that would set off warning bells on his internal lie detector. Still in shock, I decided the truth would probably be the best bet.

"I had questions about the reenactment that I hoped Mr. Ferguson could answer," I began.

After explaining our rendezvous and Ned's attempt on my life, I couldn't backtrack and suggest that Ned, guilty of the reenactment wounding, decided to end his life.

Sheppard ran his pen up and down the side of his nose and added to his notes. Randall pondered the wet bridge planks. "Corporal Sheppard, get this path blocked, and call for an ambulance … ten-forty, no siren. We'll meet it at the greenhouse."

The corporal made the 9-1-1 call, noted my phone number, gave me his card, and gave me a lift back to the parking area. "You should get your nose checked out. If I'd be you, I'd hustle to Belle Mère's emergency room."

I sat in my car, wet, exhausted, sore, my pulse and breathing accelerated. Calling Aaron, my fingers jittered on the phone. "I've finished with Ned," I managed to say. "If you're not too busy memorizing names and faces, you up for lunch?"

"Penny?" He must have sensed my tremblings. "Penny, what's happened?"

"I … I'll—"

"*Sweetheart.* Are you okay?"

"Uhhh …"

"Can I come get you?"

"I'm okay," I finally managed. "I'll meet you at the Grille in about fifteen."

Chapter 32

The waitress, in a 1920's frock and frilly apron, set down our drinks. "Your sandwiches'll be right out." My respiration now nearly normal, I picked up my chard and clinked with Aaron's dark rum.

Ned's bulging eyes stared from my wine. I took a long slug to erase the image. Aaron spooned an ice cube into his rum, lifted his glass, and instead of sipping, stopped and stared. "Now tell me." He leaned over to touch my nose gently. "Why is your cute nose turning purple?"

"Ned of the S-curved eyebrows won't be at the Meetup tonight."

"Why's that?"

"He's dead."

After another gulp I explained the altercation and my much-too-late wish that I should have asked him to shadow me.

Our waitress returned with the first lump crab sandwich I'd had since coming to North Carolina. On a focaccia roll with tomato remoulade. My appetite, however, wasn't up to what the menu had predicted.

Aaron picked up his bacon-cheeseburger but before his first chomp said, "I'd've tossed that creep over the railing myself."

If I were an actress a hundred years ago, I might have sent the back of my hand to my forehead and whispered "My hero!" But that's exactly what went through my mind, hormones surging. Instead, I said, "You know I'm no shrinking violet."

"I hope you know that I wouldn't be attracted to one. Pardon me if I'm being too forward, but you're wonderful just the way you are." The jelly returned.

Aaron nibbled a dill pickle slice and sensuously swirled a French fry in a glob of ketchup. "I still wish you'd asked me to shadow you. I feel like I missed my first test. We both should have listened to Madison."

"I probably wouldn't have accepted the offer."

"Did Ned say anything that would link him to Wayland's death?"

"He flipped when I suggested he knew of a connection between Wayland and the reenactment shooting."

"Flipped?"

"Said I had a wild imagination. But his body language made it clear he knew."

"One small step for the detectives …"

"New subject. You ready to become Clement Pritchard?" I asked. Aaron would take the next step at the Meetup tonight.

"Whose ancestor fought in Krenshaw's brigade."

"*Ker*shaw's."

"Back to the crib notes, then. And I'll practice my accent. All in the interest of justice."

"Don't forget your calling cards."

"How could I?"

"And your new bowtie."

"I'll keep the image of the wonderful woman who created my new persona in mind all evening."

After a moment basking in the glow of those words, I downed the last of my wine and realized that I'd eaten only half my sandwich. "I'm off to the hospital—need to talk to Madison." I plunked a pair of twenties on the table, hoping they would cover our lunch bill. "My treat," I said, leaned across for a kiss, and stood. "Break a leg at the Meetup."

"Easy for you to say. Don't go busting any more bridges."

I'd survived and didn't need any coddling that might restart the PTSD reflex. As I contorted myself back into the Nissan, aches were reawakened that had faded while I was with Aaron.

+ + +

On Belle Mère's Surgical Recovery unit, I fell in behind Madison's wheelchair headed toward her room, her fixator leg stretched ahead of her as if pointing the way. I followed her in and sat beside the dormant pulse-ox monitor.

"How'd it go?" Madison said, tugging the wheelchair rings to jerk the chair this way and that to face me.

May as well tell her flat out, Grandpa Jack suggested. It wasn't the time to be flip.

"Remember the rickety bridge over the top waterfall? I said. "Ned broke the railing and fell to his death."

Madison scowled in incomprehension. "All by himself?" Madison said doubtfully.

"He had a little help from a friend."

Madison's livid glare softened. "Just happy you weren't hurt."

My stanched nosebleed was no longer obvious and clothing hid most of my increasingly colorful bruises. "I didn't say I wasn't hurt. But don't blame yourself. You warned me."

"So, Mrs. Lincoln," she said, "other than that, how did you like the show?"

Searching for a witty rejoinder that wouldn't come, I remembered the gadget I'd found in the bamboo. I pulled it out of the backpack and held it for inspection.

"Found this near where Ned landed. You ever see

anything like it?"

Madison leaned to examine it closely.

A nurse chose that moment to bring Madison's mid-afternoon meds.

"'Fraid not," Madison said.

The nurse zoomed in on it. "I haven't seen one of those for years."

Seemed I'd come to the right place. "What is it?"

"Jet injector. Gives supposedly painless injections, like for children and at boot camps where they'd inoculate a whole platoon without using needles."

She gave Madison the little cup with her pills and watched as she slurped them with apple juice.

"So they were used for shots," I said. "But not now?"

"There were concerns that some types of hepatitis could be transferred from one patient to another. So they haven't been used since my mom's nursing days."

"How does it inject whatever it … injects … without a needle?"

"It uses an almost microscopically tiny stream under very high pressure."

"It was near a waterfall at Brantleigh. Any ideas? 'Course I've no idea how long it'd been there."

"Pretty sure it's stainless, so it wouldn't rust. I can ask our lab to have a look."

My aches settled in to stay when I got back behind the wheel. But when I turned the ignition, I felt a ripple of panic. A Ned lookalike bent on revenge would jump at me. Though the weather was comfortable, I shivered.

At Kalorama, every muscle I used to unwind from the Nissan screamed for a long hot shower. Kalea watched as I ascended to the veranda like an old lady with arthritis. "Holy crispus," she said. "You pick a fight with Mr. Ferguson? Your Aunt Zelma's going to throw a hissy fit. Not to mention Aaron when he sees you."

"Don't worry about Aaron. We had lunch together."

"What on earth happened to you, young lady?" Aunt Zelma had come into the foyer. "I've been so worried."

"I had a minor misadventure." I'm not sure which detective novelist I sounded like but, to be truthful, I felt pains in more muscles than I knew I had. But, for the sake of melodrama, to paraphrase the poet, I'd emerged from the struggle, bloody but unbowed.

I explained how it had happened.

"During my meditation," Aunt Zelma said. "I realized you were sorry you hadn't asked Aaron to go along."

Chapter 33

"My great-great grandfather, Thomas Pritchard, served in the Seventh South Carolina Infantry, part of Kershaw's Brigade. Wounded at Chancellorsville." Aaron rehearsed his fictional heritage aloud as he clipped the new Stars and Bars bow tie over a crisply-ironed white shirt. He would never have worn this tie anywhere near a Navy base, north or south. But tonight he was Clement Pritchard from Florence, South Carolina, an ultra-wealthy Myrtle Beach developer with a full measure of Southern hypocrisy. The Meetup would be his entrée to a community of Civil War devotees. "I am now Clement … Clement," he said aloud. And to himself, there'd better not be a singalong about the land of cotton.

The Stone House restaurant stood alone at a rural intersection with farmland in every direction. It had been hand-built of river rocks many decades ago as a two-pump gas station. Where cars once refueled, the restaurateur had enclosed a dining room.

"Come in, come in." A paunchy gray-haired man wearing a string tie welcomed Aaron at the door. "I'm Trevor." His smile allayed any concern Aaron might have felt as a bogus Civil War enthusiast. "Don't believe we've met. But I'm bein' forgetful now an' again." Inside, in the front corners of the room, were the two stone columns that had once supported the gas station canopy.

"You're right, Trevor. I don't think we've met … unless you were at the gun show yesterday. I'm Clement Pritchard." He stretched out a hand. "From Florence."

"This here's Glenn Lunsford." Glenn was in his forties, aviator glasses, long sandy hair, beard and mustache. Had to be a reenactor.

"How're y'all?" Glenn said. The dining room was the smallest Aaron had ever seen. Four tables, and only one of them could seat more than two.

"Can't complain, thanks," Aaron said. "Except for all the damn Yankees retiring around here. Changing our landscape slow but sure. They're plumb taking over my condos down to Myrtle Beach."

"Ain't that the truth." Glenn nodded toward the bar.

"What'll it be, gentlemen?" A barmaid smiled as she polished a tumbler.

"Make it a pair of Wild Turkeys, straight up." Glenn glanced at Aaron. "Make 'em doubles?"

"Sure." Aaron nodded. Bourbon would be the price of admission to this old boy group.

Whiskies in hand, Glenn introduced Aaron to a friend. "Like you to meet Colonel Garner. He swings both ways," Glenn belly-laughed. "That jess means he reenacts Union and Confederate both. Any rank." And laughed again. To Garner he said, "This here's Clement Pritchard, from Florence?" Then to Aaron, "Claude teaches history down to Hendersonville, does the reenacting circuit most every year, and still finds time to metal detect in battlefields."

"Not *in* battlefields, Glenn," Claude protested. "Near battlefields. Don't ever want to get on the wrong side of the park police."

So this was the Claude Garner part of the flag scam. The Claude Garner who, undoubtedly, created his "detected" buckles and buttons. Handsome Claude Garner with the large forehead and dark goatee.

Aaron and Glenn sat side by side at the hand-hewn table, two chairs on each side and one at each end. Aaron took a chair facing the bar. Garner sat opposite, facing the restaurant's door. "I like that tie, there, Pritchard," Garner said. Aaron nodded and sipped gently, unused to bourbon straight up. The restaurant door swung open and Garner glanced toward it. "Here's another colonel," he said, brightening, as a craggy-faced man walked around the table and sat beside him. "Where you all been hiding sir?" Garner said. "Haven't seen you since the battle." For Aaron's benefit, Garner added, "Lorenzo Peters and I commanded the reenactment troops at Brantleigh Manor a week ago."

Aaron feigned scratching behind his ear. "Didn't I hear that someone got hurt there?"

"Damn shame," Peters said. "Kind of tars and feathers us all. Whoever nicked that woman was in Claude's unit, but we've never found out how it happened or who fired it. The police are still working on it."

"They've arrested one of my Union reenactors," Garner said, "but he's out on bail."

Aaron stretched his hand across the table. "It's a real pleasure to meet y'all."

A tall wan-faced man sat at one end of the table, and used his boarding-house reach to shake Aaron's hand. "George Ashford."

Aaron reached for Ashford's. "Clement Pritchard." Hoping his drawl sounded natural. With his vocal chords lubricated with Wild Turkey, and surrounded by good old boys, the drawl should come back real good, he thought. Aaron winked at Garner over another sip of whiskey. "Real good," he said as he put it down carefully. He'd need food soon, though, to give the whiskey something to work with.

From the other end, a black-haired middle-aged man leaned in to shake Aaron's other hand. "Hack Bivins."

"Hack ... a pleasure."

"Been to Afghanistan?" Bivins asked. "You look military to me."

"Navy Seal a while back. Can't talk about that."

"Heard you're from Florence. What's happening with our Southern brethren?"

"At the moment," Aaron said, "we're raising money to keep the Fort Sumter flag in Charleston. We need to out-bid a museum in Richmond."

"That would be something that Mr. Garner might help with," Peters said. He turned and raised his eyebrows at Claude. Aaron presumed it was a signal that both men knew of the battle flag business.

Garner's response was immediate. "So you've got a Fort Sumter flag."

"You misunderstood. I don't *have* the flag. But I know who has it and they want to sell."

"You pullin' my leg, man?" Glenn Lunsford said. "You actually see a Fort Sumter flag, hit's got to be a fake. Major Anderson hauled it down and Major *General* Anderson raised it back up after the war. But it weren't the original."

"Sure looked like it to me," Aaron said.

"You ever come across any Gillmore medals?" Garner asked.

"Doubt if I'd know one if it bit me," Aaron said, smiling.

"You ought to. Bein' from around Fort Sumter and all. A Union General by the name of Gillmore gave 'em to soldiers who served under him trying to capture the fort. They weren't ever official Army issue."

"Funny, never heard of 'em."

"Only a few hundred made so they're not ever many for sale. Descendants tend to keep them in the family."

"Makes sense to me."

"I found one I've put on eBay for $750.00. I've had a couple of offers, but I'm not taking anything less."

What a crock, Aaron thought to himself. Garner's partnered with a crooked craftsman and created an imitation. "Where'd you find it?"

"A pawn shop in Knoxville. It's really fine. French-finished. Original brass. Only one small ding." Garner opened his wallet and displayed a photo. "It's actually worth thousands but I'm not asking anywhere near that much."

"I'll ask around," Aaron said, "when I get down to Charleston."

"You might get lucky with a northerner," Garner said. "Since it was a Yankee medal."

"What'll it be worth to me?" Aaron asked.

"Half be okay?"

Aaron mmm'd. "Can I raise the asking price to an even grand?" Handed Garner one of his new cards.

"Sure," Garner said. "Let me know." And gave Aaron a card.

"I've just joined a gang of thieves," Aaron said aloud to himself on his way back to the Lodge.

Chapter 34

The next day I awoke in a sweat. Ned's terrified eyes sliding down to his death wouldn't fade. I sat on the edge of the bed while my pulse rate subsided. My sleep shirt was so damp, instead of tucking it under the pillow, I would hang it up to dry.

Kalea knocked once, walked in and stopped just inside the door, staring. "You see a ghost?"

"In a way," I said. That was a delicate way to say it. "Give me a couple of minutes, Punkin. I'll meet you downstairs."

In the kitchen, I reminded my aunt that Kalea and I were leaving to have breakfast with Aaron.

"Hang on a second," she said, and handed me the morning Gazette. I might have expected it but it was a surprise nevertheless:

ANOTHER BRANTLEIGH MANOR DOCENT DIES
A second Brantleigh Manor landscape docent was found dead Monday in the estate's gardens. The name of the victim is being withheld pending notification of next of kin. Ms. Penelope Summers, a visitor from Maryland ...

You're the common denominator, Grandpa Jack whispered sardonically.

I didn't appreciate his absurd accusatory tone. He hadn't teased me that way since I was three when he said he'd heard from Santa that I would only get a lump of coal on Christmas. But maybe Madison was onto something when she suggested that either of us might be considered a suspect in Wayland's death. And that was *before* I contributed to

Ned's demise!

+ + +

Kalea and I met Aaron in the lobby of the Vanderbilt Lodge. After hugs for both of us, we walked into the Grille.

Kalea took one look at the two stuffed bears guarding the Vanderbilt portraits at the fireplace. "Gross!" she yelped.

A different waitress this morning, wearing the same Carolina blue frock and apron, gave us morning menus. Within minutes, our OJs and coffees arrived.

"Seems like it was only last week we were comparing Pinocchio noses in Annapolis," I said. Aaron reached for my hand. I put my other hand over his as our eyes met.

"Where has the year gone?" he said with a rueful smile.

"You two are awfully cute, you know," said Kalea, and pulled out her phone to document the event.

"Takes one to know one," Aaron said.

Kalea blushed. And said she would put her taffy-pulling curse on him.

"How're you doing?" he asked me. "Looks like our damsel is no longer in distress."

Three breakfast plates were arrayed on our waitress's arm. "One over-easy and bacon." Mine. "Pancakes and sausage." That went to Kalea. "And, for the man of the hour," she said, "Belgian waffles with two poached." With the plates on the table, she refilled our coffees. "Room for cream?"

"The Navy way … black," Kalea told her. "And can I have a hot chocolate?"

"Sure, honey. Be right back."

To Kalea, Aaron said, "You don't miss much."

"She's a C.S.I. in-training."

Kalea gave him a half-smile.

The Pink Panther theme began on Kalea's phone. "Morning Mom … Yep … Everything's cool …"

Our waitress delivered Kalea's hot chocolate.

"We're picking her up today … Uh-hunhh … Love you too."

Aaron's Belgian waffle, smothered under blueberry syrup, was already mostly missing in action. "You should've been a fly on the wall at the Meetup last night."

"Tell me."

Half a poached egg went down the hatch. "I got compliments on my tie."

"Of course," I said. Kalea rolled her eyes.

"Two of your friends were there," Aaron said. "Claude Garner and Lorenzo Peters. Interesting guys."

"You talked with them?"

"It's a small group in a very small place. Of course."

"I'm sure you wowed 'em."

"Garner scoffed at my Fort Sumter flag idea."

"Surprise, surprise. He has his own flag game."

"He apparently has a new one. Gillmore medals."

"Gillmore medals? Never heard of 'em."

"Yes, ma'am. A Union general by that name made them for his troops that tried to take Fort Sumter."

"So what's the game?"

"Undoubtedly the usual. Make 'em to sell on eBay. Apparently they're as rare as dinosaurs' teeth, worth thousands if you can ever find one but he's asking $750 and asked me to hawk it for him."

"If it hasn't sold on eBay," I said, "he must have earned a big-time reputation for fakes."

My phone chose that moment to sound off.

"A penny for your thoughts."

Laughter at the other end. "Detective Twomey, ma'am."

For Aaron and Kalea I whispered, "The detective we met at Brantleigh."

"Yes ..." His voice seemed casual but you can't be sure with a cop. At least I couldn't be sure, particularly since I'd assisted with Ned's fatal fall.

"Since Mr. Ferguson's ... mmm ... incident at Belle Mère hospital last week and his death yesterday ... we obtained a warrant to search his condo."

Here it comes.

"Now please keep what I'm telling you under your hat until tomorrow's Gazette."

"Cross my heart et cetera."

"I knew you'd want to know about the reenactment incident."

Maybe this call was not about Ned's death. "That's right ... sir."

"We found a mold for lead bullets like the one that wounded Ms. Lerrimore."

Why was I not surprised?

"And one of Saturday's reenactment visitors brought in a smartphone video from the event. At one point, there's a Yankee who appears to aim his musket toward the spectator area. The smoke makes it difficult to make a positive ID but we think it's Mr. Ferguson."

I remembered onlookers using their phone cameras.

"Strange thing. When we examined Mr. Ferguson's rifle we hoped we might be able to connect it with the bullet you found. But the barrel on Ferguson's was rifled and the S.B.I. is now positive that the ball that hit Ms. Lerrimore was shot from a smooth-bore musket."

I tried to remember what Lorenzo Peters had explained

to me about rifling in Civil War weapons. And then remembered the disappearance and reappearance of Wayland's rifle.

"Detective," I said, "there's something I should have asked you."

"About what?"

"The reenactment incident."

"I'm listening."

"When Mr. Morgan's apartment was searched after his death, was there a Civil War rifle on the wall over his desk?"

"Give me a second. I'll check our inventory. Although if there had been a weapon, I'm sure I'd have remembered it." I caught Aaron's eye but couldn't communicate my curiosity over Wayland's rifle.

Twomey came back on the line. "Sorry to keep you waiting. There was no weapon of any kind on our inventory. Why'd you ask?"

"Before the reenactment, Wayland's rifle was cradled in a pair of deer leg brackets above his desk. The day after, Madison and I noticed the brackets were empty. But last week, the gun was back on display. I'd assumed Wayland's friend Claude Garner might have borrowed it with the uniform he was lent. But if the ball couldn't have come from Ned's rifle, I'd guess Ned borrowed Wayland's, used it at the reenactment and returned it later."

"Interesting possibility. Could you let Ms. Lerrimore know that we'll pick it up and check your theory?"

I knew I would risk another scolding from Grandpa Jack for reading more great mysteries than Great Books, but added, "While you have it, you could check for fingerprints."

Silence at Twomey's end clearly implied *smartass*.

Chapter 35

Looking forward to springing Madison from her hospital sojourn and getting her back to Aunt Zelma's, I took Aaron and Kalea, and a bundle of her clothes up to her floor.

"We're here to pick up Madison Lerrimore," I said to a nurse at the desk. She reached for a clipboard and ran her finger down the page. Kalea went directly to Madison's room.

"Dr. Stanton has signed off. So, Ms. Lerrimore's, if you'll pardon the expression, ready to roll. Oh, by the way, she's going to need a walker. I'll have one here when she checks out."

When Aaron and I arrived at her room, Madison was on the phone to her partner and Kalea had already begun loading her mom's stuff into her backpack.

"Gotta go," Madison told Shy, as a wheelchair appeared, maneuvered by a pony-tailed attendant. In comparison with his collections of tattoos on both arms, my tramp stamp from Barcelona was a wimp. Mine had served admirably, though, as a symbol of independence after my faithless fiancé broke our engagement. I'd almost tossed his ring in the harbor until I realized it could help keep the male officers on the carrier from hitting on me. I still wore it.

I handed Madison a skirt and a new tee-shirt that, inside a silhouette of the state, read: Y'ALL COME BACK NOW.

"If you give me a little privacy," Madison said, "I'll get changed."

After a minute, she'd not only changed, but sported an orange fright-wig she must have bribed a nurse to get.

"You're the best-looking clown in North Carolina," Aaron said, as she lowered herself into the wheelchair.

"Can I borow it for Halloween?" said Kalea.

The attendant folded down the foot-rests and helped with her basket-enclosed leg. At the nurses' station, paperwork was signed and dated. Noticing the clown wig, the nurse laughed, and handed her an envelope. "Dr. Stanton wants to see you back here Tuesday a week. There's also a note from him for Ms. Summers. By the way, you'll be hearing from our physical therapy team. And let us know right away if you have any problems."

As Madison tucked the envelope in her backpack, Aaron picked up the folded walker, and we headed to the elevator.

Kalea stood beside the wheelchair. "I can walk with you at Aunt Zelma's."

"I'll be expecting you to," Madison said, "but don't expect me to go hopscotchin' for a day or two."

"We'll just walk around the veranda," Kalea said, "until you can go up and down stairs."

"I'm not a cripple," Madison insisted. "It just takes me three times as long to get anywhere as your average bear."

An elevator stopped for us but only had room for two: Kalea and Aaron got on with the folded walker. I stayed with Madison and touched the down button again. Madison spoke softly, "I've had a lot of time to think."

"About?"

"About moving here. Maybe find a teaching job at Cullowhee or UNC."

As Aunt Zelma would say, that surprised the starch out of me. "*Why,* for heaven's sake?"

"For starters, Dr. Stanton. He performed a minor miracle on my leg and I'd like to have him see me through. Secondly, I'm impressed with the range of plants that thrive in this zone. One of our landscape architecture professors, originally from Chapel Hill, often trumpeted the opportunities for LA's in the Carolinas."

"That'll sure be a surprise to Cheyenne."

And Kalea, whispered Grandpa Jack.

"I'll have to break it gently," she said.

"I'd been looking forward to taking your advanced course next spring."

"Don't worry. Yet. Only thinking about it."

The empty elevator returned. The valet rolled Madison in and we floated down to the lobby.

Through wide doors into warm sunshine, we caught up with Kalea and Aaron at the curb. "Madison," I said, "let me take a shot of you for Cheyenne."

"Okay. Say 'Free at Last.'"

I snapped it and read aloud as I added text: The clown is free at last! Hope you'll come down for a reunion.

"Hang in there," I said. "I'll get the Purple Penguin."

I headed into the parking area and mulled over Madison's announcement. I'd feel abandoned if she moved to North Carolina. I'd come to depend on her for my garden design education. Plus, I valued her friendship. Wondering if she would really move from Annapolis left precious little of my brain available to recall where I'd parked.

When I finally found the purple beast and brought it to the entrance, Aaron helped Madison in, and settled her walker in the trunk. Kalea jumped in the back with Aaron. As I slipped it in gear, the attendant saluted. "Y'all take care now." He smiled at Madison's tee. "And don't you come back no more," he sung. "You hear?"

The empty wheelchair performed a wheelie as he hurried it back inside.

Chapter 36

"I need a detox clinic to recover from the hospital food," Madison announced as I pulled in to Sho-Nuff Barbecue.

Aaron retrieved her walker from the trunk and Madison navigated it to the PLACE ORDER HERE counter and ordered a pulled pork sandwich with extra sauce. "Slaw on the side and … a Highland IPA."

I tallied votes from Aaron and Kalea. "Make it three," I said, "two more IPAs and a—"

Kalea scanned the menu board. "Ginger beer."

The order taker handed me a wood paddle sporting a hand-painted 27. "Help yourself to the drinks," she said. "In a few minutes we'll bring you the best barbecue you've ever tasted."

We descended on a table where Madison performed a desultory half-circle pirouette while Aaron deftly replaced the walker with a chair. "Thanks," she said and sat sideways favoring her fixator leg.

Several diners' heads turned when they noticed her bright clown wig, but they didn't stare. In this part of North Carolina, weird was considered normal.

I brought Kalea's ginger beer and our brews from the cooler.

After a sip of IPA, I asked to see Dr. Stanton's note.

Madison unzipped a backpack pocket and retrieved it. I read aloud: "Ms. Summers. Our lab found an alkaloid residue in the inoculator you brought in. Because it could be a poison, we forwarded it to the State Bureau of Investigation lab in Raleigh. They can determine if it's atropine, strychnine, or morphine, or perhaps something as innocuous as caffeine." Kalea was confused. She hadn't heard of the jet inoculator. "They have your contact information and will be in touch. Sincerely, Ed Stanton, MD"

"What's that all about?" Aaron asked.

"Some kind of medical thing I found near where Ned fell. A nurse said their lab might find residue that could help figure out when it was used."

"Poison," Kalea mused excitedly, "but not on the tip of an umbrella."

"You'll know more," said Madison, "when the S.B.I. weenies get back to you."

"Their forensic pathology lab," Kalea clarified.

"Too bad labs don't get results as quickly as the C.S.I. shows suggest."

Grandpa Jack punched my shoulder. *Could the injector have delivered the coniine that killed Wayland?*

Sho-Nuff's barbecue *was* to die for. We licked our fingers and lingered over our brews while Kalea roamed the restaurant snapping pictures to send Cheyenne. Restored, Aaron and Madison reversed their entry maneuver and we returned to the car.

I parked the passenger side beside Kalorama's front steps. Madison said she'd had some step therapy at the hospital but this would be her first real-world test. Kalea took the walker up to the porch while Aaron and I, our arms under her shoulders, helped her negotiate the four broad steps. Only a single "Ooooch."

"Bless your heart, Madison," Aunt Zelma said. "I'm glad to have you back."

Kalea and Madison paraded her new walker on the veranda. In the salon, Aaron and I snuggled close as we pondered his next move as Clement Pritchard.

Later, Aunt Zelma and I fixed salads of spring greens and salmon splashed with raspberry vinaigrette.

My cell phone's mazurka began. "Penny for your ... Ohhh, Cheyenne, hi. Just a sec." I handed it to Madison.

"Yes, it's true," Madison said. "And no, my fright wig isn't covering a shaved head."

Chapter 37

I talked Kalea and Madison into allowing me to leave with Aaron. That would give Madison time to break the news to Kalea about the possibility of transplanting herself to North Carolina. My assistant agreed only after a promise that I would pick her up in the morning for a strategy breakfast at the Lodge.

Aunt Zelma winked at Aaron. "Don't keep her out past her bedtime," she whispered. I feigned embarrassment and grabbed Aaron's hand as we left.

On the road west, a quick flash over the ridge and a growl of thunder warned of the weather-guessers prediction. Approaching cars' wipers whipped. Another half mile and we were in it. Headlights glistened off the wet road. I switched on my wipers and tried to ignore the mesmerizing flop-whop-flop-whop.

Aaron said that when it rained this hard, his father used to say the rain-man done run out of cats and dogs and gone alookin' for tigers and wolves.

Then he began to tickle my neck. I fought the wheel to stay in my lane. His tickle became a caress. I reached across and squeezed his knee.

Could I imagine being with this man? We hadn't seen each other for nearly a year. Had he thought about me as often as I had about him? It was possible. I would have liked to think it was probable but, even so, would it lead anywhere? I had to admit that I hoped it would.

Grandpa Jack whispered, *Nothing ventured, nothing gained.* I whispered back that this was my life. I would not be persuaded by a Ben Franklin maxim.

The turnoff to the Lodge was less than ten minutes

ahead. "I'll give you an hour to stop that," I said. The neck caresses had moved to my shoulders.

"I'll have to stop when you drop me off. Unless … of course, you decide to come in."

I felt myself warming to the suggestion. Que sera, sera.

"Invite me up and I'll consider my options."

"You can change course whenever. You're in charge."

I found a parking spot, pulled the key from the ignition, and pulled his face to mine. Then, sans umbrellas, we splashed our way to the door.

+ + +

Wednesday morning, I kissed Aaron's nose and saw his morning eyes for the first time. Right then I knew it wouldn't be the last.

"That clock right?" I asked.

"If you trust a dead man's."

"Kalea's gonna be one unhappy bunny."

Aaron laughed, lightening my counterfeit concern.

I showered as quickly as I'd learned at the Naval Academy, popped an ibuprofen, put on yesterday's jeans and covered my beginning-to-fade bruises with my ASHEVILLE—CESSPOOL OF SIN tee.

"Take your time," I said, as I dashed out. "I'll get Kalea and meet you back here in the Grille."

"Roger that," he said and gave me a sweet slow kiss on his way to the already warm shower.

By the time I got to Kalorama and parked, the ibuprofen had kicked in, and my bruises were relatively serene. Funny how I hadn't noticed them last evening. André barked up a storm. Too early for guests, the big poodle probably thought. Or perhaps it was a welcoming bark. Whichever, if I'd had a hushpuppy in my pocket, he would have had a treat.

Kalea came to the door, squinting suspiciously. "You said you don't use makeup. So how come you have blush on this morning?"

Aunt Zelma came into the foyer, smiled and winked.

"You about ready to roll?" I called to Kalea as I started up to my room. I changed into a Hendersonville Apple Festival tee and stepped into clean jeans.

+++

As I accelerated through Kalorama's gate onto Beulah Road, Kalea broke the silence. "New email on Wayland's laptop."

"Really? Who from?"

"The man he sold the flag to. Grover Knowles."

"What'd he say?"

"He basically said he'd had the flag appraised and learned it was a fake. He wants his money back."

"Did you tell your Mom?" She nodded. "What'd *she* say?"

"She doesn't think he could get any money back, especially with Wayland gone, but couldn't he come after it?"

"If Wayland delivered the flag to him," I said, "he'd have no idea where to find him, even if he were still alive."

Stay tuned, whispered Grandpa Jack.

+++

Aaron looked up from a menu. "My two favorite detectives," he said, rising. "Miss Penny and Miss Kalea. G'morning."

Kalea stared, presumably checking his face for a blush. "And a good morning to you, Mr. Hunt." With a straight face.

"Touché," Aaron said.

We started with OJ's, two black coffees, and a hot chocolate for Kalea.

After the waitress took our orders, Aaron said Garner had called while I was picking up Kalea. "Get this: He says he has a project he needs help with. He wants Clement Pritchard to find some money he says Wayland owed him."

"Shall we let him in on the secret?" I asked Kalea.

"If he learns the secret handshake," she said.

"I feel like a ventriloquist's puppet," Aaron mumbled, "who hasn't learned his lines."

We laughed. I explained how Kalea found the laptop, our perusal of Wayland's emails, and the money in the wall safe.

"You're the fifth person … no, sixth," Kalea said. "Penny, me, Aunt Zelma, and both my moms. Now you have to swear to—"

The waitress materialized with our platters and topped our coffees. When she left, Aaron continued. "Garner wants to meet Clement Pritchard, to explain the deal. Something about the flag Wayland sold."

"Don't forget your good ole boy accent," I said, attempting to mimic it.

Aaron looked up from his French toast. "Ah don't reckon I kin forget it."

"You'll be like a real double agent," Kalea said. "Cool."

"Speaking of that old flag," I said, "Kalea found an email from the buyer on Wayland's laptop."

"It sounds like I'll need an intelligence briefing before I sally forth," Aaron said. "Who's the email from?"

"Grover Knowles," Kalea said, and explained the message to Aaron, who held his fork motionless absorbing the fresh information.

"It's like I've been written into an Elmore Leonard

story," he said, as he put the fork down. "Two guys are both after a safe deposit box full of money and I'm the stooge who knows where it is."

"It's ironic," I said, "that the missing money isn't what led to Wayland's murder."

"And you know that because …?"

"Both of his partners have, or in Ned's case *had*, solid alibis."

"This Knowles guy obviously doesn't know Wayland's dead," Aaron said, "and he certainly has no way to know that his email was intercepted, so no worries—"

My phone chose that moment to begin its mazurka. I recognized the number and put my coffee down. "Penny Summers … Yes I did … Yessir …" I mouthed *police* to Aaron and Kalea. "Well, Detective, that's interesting. Here's why. The Brantleigh docent who was found dead two weeks ago? The Medical Examiner decided he'd been poisoned with Conium maculatum."

I closed the phone. "News update. That jet injector I found was what was used to kill Wayland." Kalea and I locked glances.

"I knew it," Kalea said. "Like a poison-tipped umbrella stab. He never saw it coming."

"The man in black," we said, nearly in unison.

"The Angel of Death," Kalea said, for Aaron's benefit.

"And who's that?" Aaron asked.

Kalea told him the story from the Brantleigh docent.

"According to Detective Sabillas," I added, "the S.B.I's fingerprint specialists are already on it."

"Things are getting curioser and curioser," Kalea quoted.

Chapter 38

It was late afternoon when Kalea and I returned to Kalorama. Soon, she and Madison were perambulating the veranda. Great-Aunt Zelma and I discussed the Grover Knowles dilemma when my phone sounded off again. Now what? I was weary of the mazurka.

The unknown caller enunciated clearly: "This is Fabian Mills from the State Bureau of Investigation in Raleigh."

"Yes?"

"We received an injection apparatus from the Hendersonville Belle Mère hospital that apparently you brought in."

"That's right."

"I hope you don't mind me contacting you directly rather than through Detective Sabillas."

"Not at all."

Here's what we're up against, Ms. Summers. There are at least two sets of partial prints on this thing. And since we believe the injector was used to poison Wayland Morgan, we'd like very much—to put it mildly—to ID the prints."

"Of course."

"Would you do something for us?" Without waiting for a response, he continued. "We'd like you to visit the Hendersonville Police and have your fingerprints recorded."

"Mine are probably on file somewhere since I was in the Navy. But I'd be happy to."

"Thanks. It'll save us time. The Belle Mère lab people used surgical gloves, so we're assuming some of the partials are yours. If we can eliminate them, we might be able to discover who killed Mr. Morgan."

Five minutes later, Kalea and I were on our way. North

to Hendersonville, a left on King, another left on Fifth and we were there. Kalea couldn't wait to learn about fingerprinting. She'd be the most experienced member of the Junior Police Academy. We found the desk officer had been alerted. After I explained that my niece planned to become a CSI, he took us to the booking room in the back which, at this time of the afternoon, was empty of arrested folks. Unlike the ink-pad and card system I had encountered in preparation for admission to the Naval Academy, they had what looked like a huge copying machine with a green glass surface. The fingerprint specialist slipped on latex gloves and typed in my information.

"Just put your right hand on the platen," she said, adjusted its position, and tapped a button. Instantly, a digital version of my hand print was scanned and recorded.

"Really cool," said Miss CSI and FBI profiler-to-be.

Each finger was scanned, much like my inky fingers were printed more than a dozen years ago at the Annapolis Police Station. When we'd finished, the tech said they would be at Mr. Mills' lab in Raleigh within minutes.

+++

We were back at Kalorama in time for sandwiches and sweet tea with Aunt Zelma and Madison. A fresh bouquet of late tulips was centered on the kitchen table's dark green tablecloth.

"Guess what," Kalea began. "We'll know soon who the Angel of Death is."

Madison's head tilted as she raised her eyebrows.

"If the S.B.I. can identify some fingerprints, they'll know who killed your stepdad." Kalea chewed on her sandwich for a moment and turned to me. "Maybe it was the woman named Angel."

Kalea, clearly, had the proverbial memory of an elephant. Madison looked confused.

"Remember the childish letter we found in Wayland's desk?" I said. "You were going to toss it."

"Ohhh …" She nodded. "*That* one."

"It was signed 'Angie' not 'Angel,' but you remember the letter? On a magazine page?"

"Okaayyy," Madison said.

"There was something weird about it," Kalea said. "She wrote that she couldn't wait to see him again. And Wayland would know what would happen then. It sounded to me like she was threatening him. Not hoping to make love again." She said *make love* like the words were a dead rat she held by the tail.

Madison and I looked at each other. I began to think Kalea could be right. The saved letter was still in my backpack.

My phone again. While I listened to the caller I was thinking that I absolutely needed to find a new ringtone. I said yes ma'am a couple of times and rang off. Kalea had been searching my face for clues to the substance of the call.

"On the road again."

"With your assistant?" Kalea asked.

"You can start the siren." She excused herself and practically bounced to the door.

To Aunt Zelma and Madison I explained. "Wayland's murder investigation has been turned over to the S.B.I. in Asheville. A Special Agent Lisa Brown wants to see me." I chugged the last of my tea, picked up my backpack and followed Kalea.

Without a siren, it took forty-five minutes. A small sign identified the building as the S.B.I.'s Asheville Regional

Office. Gray evening clouds gathered against a rosy horizon as I pulled into a visitors' spot near the door. A man in civvies exited the building, said "Hey" in our direction and headed to an unmarked car.

"An undercover agent," Kalea whispered.

The lobby was decorated in generic government tan, relieved only by framed scenic views of waterfalls and mountains wreathed in the ubiquitous haze of the Smokies.

"Looks like a sorta normal place," Kalea said.

"What'd you expect? A Gotham City skyscraper?"

She gave me her look but said nothing.

"Special Agent Lisa Brown asked me to come in," I said to the agent in a glass cave. She made a call and handed us visitors' IDs.

"I need to check your backpack."

"Sure." I unzipped it and passed it to her.

She poked around and patted the pockets. "Thanks." And handed it back.

A moment later, a Latina in an ochre trench-coat style jacket and dark pants entered.

"Penelope Summers?"

"That's me."

"Thanks for stopping in," Lisa said.

"This is my niece, Kalea. She's here to take notes since she wants to follow in your career."

"An F.B.I. profiler or C.S.I.," Kalea clarified as we followed Agent Brown to her office.

"Think about starting with the S.B.I.," she told Kalea. "You'll have a better chance at the F.B.I."

Kalea beamed. We took two of the visitors' chairs.

"When our meeting here is finished—" the agent swiveled her chair toward Kalea "—I'll give you a short quiz."

Kalea saw by my grin that her leg had been pulled.

The agent's small office was tan like the lobby with three tall gray filing cabinets valiantly attempting to break the monotony of the windowless room. On her desk was a picture of her two curly headed children with their uniformed police officer dad, all smiles.

She opened a red multi-pocketed project folder and a pad of forms. "As I said, the Henderson County Sheriff has asked us to take over the Wayland Morgan case," she said. "And handed it off to me, being closer to the scene of the crime." She held up a file folder and smiled. "Lucky me."

Kalea was devouring each word.

"What I've heard, Ms. Summers, is that you found Mr. Morgan."

"True."

"And you've been some help to the detectives."

"I guess you could say that."

"The reason I asked you to visit is because I want to share some information."

Like I could help her find the guy?

"As you know, the power injector you found was sent to our Raleigh lab to determine the type of alkaloid residue in it."

For Kalea, following this conversation was like watching a tennis match, her attention on Lisa, then to me, and back to Lisa.

"Once the lab recognized the alkaloid, our fingerprint people started working it." Lisa glanced at her notes.

I said they'd already taken my prints.

"Right. Here's what they have. Eliminating yours, they found several partials but couldn't get any hits. But AFIS did find several individuals who might have left the partials."

"Is there any way to track those people," I said, "to see if any of them knew Mr. Morgan?"

"We only know one person," Kalea said. "Actually we don't know him—"

"Punkin," I said, "we know several people—" Lisa Brown held up a finger, ready to referee the debate.

"I meant the Angel of Death," Kalea clarified.

"And who would that be?" Lisa asked, interested.

"At Brantleigh Manor—"

"It's what you'd call hearsay," I said, glancing at Kalea to signify that I would explain it. I told her what the Brantleigh docent related. "My niece jumped to the conclusion that the man in black had somehow assassinated Mr. Morgan."

"We had hoped we might identify whoever had used that injector, Kalea," Lisa said, "but the partial fingerprints didn't have enough minutiae, as the experts call them, to identify an individual."

"Those partial prints," Kalea insisted, "could have been the man in black."

"Possibly," Lisa said.

"Back to my question," I said, "about cross-checking the people your system identified. Assuming the killer and Wayland weren't strangers, I know a few things about Wayland that might help."

"For instance?"

"Okay. He used to live in Annapolis, taught college in Baltimore, had an accounting business, was in prison—"

"Stop right there. Where and when?" Kalea looked at me, wonderment in her eyes at my knowledge of her mom's stepdad.

"Roxbury ... in Hagerstown ... Maryland."

"Isn't that where his girlfriend's letter was postmarked?" Kalea asked.

"Good memory, Kiddo."

"If he met Angie when he got out," Kalea said, "she'd know exactly when that was."

I explained to Lisa that we learned about her from a letter in Wayland's desk.

"That's the one," Kalea said, "that I thought was so weird."

"She thought it could have been a threat," I said.

"Could you bring it in?" Lisa asked. "I'd appreciate a look."

"I have it," I said, as I unzipped the backpack pocket with the sheaf of Wayland's documents. I riffled them to the letter and passed it across.

"Just drop it, please." She opened a lower drawer, pulled on a pair of latex gloves, found an evidence envelope and slipped it in. "Coated paper," she said.

"So," said Kalea, "there could be fingerprints on it."

"Young lady," Agent Brown said, smiling, "you'll be at the head of your CSI class."

When the envelope was sealed and labeled, Lisa Brown examined the letter through the plastic. "I'm—" She stopped and looked more closely. "'Ha Ha,'" she read. "'Can't wait to see you. And meet your adorable daughter. Hardy Ha Ha. Angie.' I can see how this could be interpreted as threatening. And maybe a warning for his daughter, too."

"*Step*daughter. Her name's Madison."

Kalea tensed. "Maddy-Mom might be ...?"

If Agent Brown sensed a risk for Madison, then until the guy was caught—

"I'm thinking out loud here," Lisa said, glancing at a document from her red folder. "One of the names AFIS gave us was an Angelo somebody."

Angelo—Angie?

She went to a filing cabinet, pulled the bottom drawer, yanked out an oversize envelope, and slipped the Angie letter inside. "We'll courier this to Raleigh and let them try to lift prints." With another smile for Kalea, she added, "As you suggested, with this kind of paper it's sometimes possible. Then I'll get on to Roxbury."

Back on the highway, I pondered if there was anything I could do to help the S.B.I. find Angelo somebody before he materialized to threaten Madison.

How can you help, Grandpa Jack whispered, *without understanding the threat?*

"If we knew where he was coming from," I told Kalea, "we could head him off at the pass."

"Translate please."

I hadn't realized that she might have never seen a cowboy movie. "It's from old movies set in the West where the sheriff's deputies would figure out where the bad guys would have to ride their horses through a narrow pass between mountains. So, in our situation, I'm thinking if we could get inside Angelo's head, we could discern his motive and discover if he was a threat to Madison."

All we had was that after doing prison time, he'd used a power injector to kill Wayland Morgan with an herbal poison called coniine. And he might be targeting Madison. But learning his motive, the why of it, would be exceedingly difficult. Again, if I'd majored in psychology, I'd be better equipped.

Chapter 39

Fanny Mulligan's pub in downtown Hendersonville was nearly deserted Wednesday afternoon as Clement Pritchard waited for Claude Garner's teaching day to end. At the bar, Aaron sipped a double shot of sweet tea bourbon on the rocks, his father's favorite when they lived in Walterboro. His dad always had a tot at the end of his shift at the Naval Shipyard.

Kalea was right. He'd become a double agent in the den of thieves. He wasn't sure he was enjoying it. On the other hand, he'd signed on to this mission knowing he would be in the unfamiliar world of Civil War aficionados. Undercover. And he'd agreed with Penny that the flag scam was undoubtedly the key to the verbal altercation Madison had witnessed and probably linked to Wayland's death. So suck it up, he said to himself, and play the role.

A jingle at the pub's door ended his musing.

Garner's houndstooth jacket with the requisite elbow patches complemented his auburn hair, goatee, and a Civil War soldier's dog-tag in the vee of his open-collared shirt.

"What's your pleasure, Colonel?" Aaron asked when Garner approached.

"Wild Turkey, thanks," and to the bartender, "straight up."

"Make it a double, please," Aaron added.

"With lemon sir," Garner added.

When it was poured and garnished, Aaron laid a twenty on the bar, picked up his bourbon, and led Garner to a table. After a perfunctory handshake, "Tell me what's up."

"Long story," Garner began, giving the lemon twist a twirl and taking a sip. "I doubt if the Florence paper carried it, but a couple of weeks ago, one of Brantleigh Manor's docents was found dead. Doesn't seem the police have it figured yet. Anyway, the dead man was Wayland Morgan and he was a friend of mine."

"There was an article about that, come to think of it. About the same time as the reenactment accident."

"That was the weekend after Morgan died."

"What did this Gorman do?"

"It's Morgan—"

"Sorry. I have a touch of dyslexia," Aaron pretended.

"—Morgan took designers around the gardens. Out near Etowah, about a half hour west. That's where they found him."

"Designers? As in garden designers?"

"A lot of landscape architects, as I understand, think they're pretty important. Especially if you want to study the last design of a guy by the name of Olmsted. But all that's beside the point. Wayland Morgan—" Garner's voice became confidentially low "—had a business arrangement with me that involved a lot of money."

Aaron leaned closer, pretended difficulty in following the thought, wondering why Garner chose to confide in him and how deep Garner would dig himself in.

"He sold a Civil War artifact worth close to a million dollars—and the deal was that he'd split it with me." No mention of the originally planned three-way split.

"And he didn't?"

Garner nodded. Aaron sipped his bourbon, a façade of sociability. "Whatever was it that was worth that much?"

"An antique Civil War battle flag. You don't see them very often. Rare as hen's teeth."

"Like your Gillmore medal?"

Garner smiled. Maybe a yes.

"So Gorman—sorry, Morgan—sold it but didn't split the profit."

"Right. He went and got himself killed. Now there's a good chance his stepdaughter will inherit that money if we don't get it first."

"What makes you think I could find it? Why not your own self?"

"Simple. The principals know me. Matter of fact, the stepdaughter used to think I killed him. Might could be she still does. You've got no history here and you seem like you'd look the other way if there's a buck to be made."

"Seems like it would be harder to find it with him dead. You know, not much blood in a dead turnip."

Garner summoned a half-hearted chuckle. "You got that right. I did threaten him, though, if he didn't fork over. Actually the day before his death. But I sure didn't kill him." Garner picked up his glass and put away a sizable chug.

"So, how much d'you think I could find?"

"Might be somewhere close to two million."

Aaron frowned. "For an old flag?" Ooops. He'd forgotten he was supposed to be trying to buy an original. "We hadn't figured to need anywhere near that much for the Sumter flag."

"Actually, Wayland had two," Garner said. "The original and a replica. I think he sold em both. The replica was aged pretty convincingly to make it look old, so, for two different wealthy collectors ... Would've been easy money."

Aaron lifted his sweet tea bourbon, stopped part way to his lips, wondering how to proceed. "What'd be my cut, assuming I could run it to ground?"

"Let me think on that," Garner said, and paused. "Might

could be near a half million." Another pause. "Depending of course on how quick you'd latch on to it."

Aaron conjured a conspiratorial smile. Surprised that he'd been taken into the con man's confidence, like an F.B.I. informant in the mafia. "Any idea how I'd start?" Aaron tried to imagine himself a made man.

They focused on their drinks for almost a minute. "I'd be you," Garner finally said, "I'd try to get to the stepdaughter. Her name's Madison Lerrimore. She'll inherit unless you can divert it."

Aaron leaned closer.

"She's some kind of a professor in Maryland. Came with one of her students to the Brantleigh gardens. I've met her twice now. First time was at Morgan's apartment when I uhhh ... encouraged him to ante up. Big surprise there because I hadn't known he had a daughter ... sorry, stepdaughter. Her student's name is Penny. Met them a second time at an old mansion in Flat Rock. Kalorama. The owner there is the student's great-aunt. And I can tell you, Penny's one snoopy bitch. Don't get tangled up with her."

"Penny ... hmmm." Aaron tapped the side of his head, repeating the women's names and the name of the mansion. "Now where is this place?"

"It's about a mile in on Beulah Road, off the Sandburg Pike south of Flat Rock. You know that area?"

"I'll find it," Aaron said. "I could be a Bible salesman." He laughed.

"Something that might help," Garner added, "Miss Madison was at the Belle Mère hospital for a couple of weeks. Just got out Tuesday. She's the one who got hurt at that reenactment."

Once more, Aaron pretended to ponder, moving his glass

in a wet circle, the sweet bourbon diluted by melting ice. Was Garner's deck missing a card?

"I can't imagine the hospital would give me her contact info. Confidentiality and all that."

"Probably not," Garner said, "but you might find a chatty nurse, you being a pretty good sweet-talker."

I haven't chased a nurse, Aaron reflected, since Honolulu on my first WestPac cruise. "Is it just my overactive imagination, Colonel, or could your friend's death and the reenactment accident be related somehow?"

"I wouldn't know anything about that, Mr. Pritchard."

Master Chief Petty Officer Aaron Hunt had counseled enough sailors in his career to put Garner's face and words together to know that was a carelessly rendered bald-faced lie.

Chapter 40

Kalea and I sat in the Purple Panther outside the Hendersonville Police Department. My digital fingerprints were en route to Raleigh.

"You want to go back to Maryland with me next week?" I said.

Lisa and the State Bureau of Investigation would be able to track down Angie or Angelo or whomever, and I'd be able to get back to Annapolis and the Reid design. Madison could stay at Aunt Zelma's until she was ready to get back. Unless she decided to stay in North Carolina. I'd at least been able to help in the search for her stepfather's murderer.

"What about Maddy-Mom?"

"The sooner she gets back to Annapolis, the safer she'll be from that Angelo guy."

Kalea seemed thoughtful but said nothing.

"Shy can take her home in a few days," I said. "She'll need physical therapy but she can get that in Maryland."

"And Aaron?"

"He'll probably go back to his Navy job next week, too." Thinking of Aaron, I tapped my phone and punched his number. "Are you still in H-ville?" I nodded his reply to Kalea. "I'm ready to follow through on my Twelve Bones promise." I gave him the address and less than ten minutes later we parked beside his Mercedes. Within a few more, we were seated inside.

Without opening her menu, Kalea said, "We have good news."

"We hope," I added.

Aaron put down his menu and cupped a hand behind his ear.

"The S.B.I. has narrowed their fingerprint match list down to a dozen," I said.

"That's *good* news?"

"They're trying to match one of them with prints from the prison where Wayland served time."

"Either an Angie or Angelo," Kalea said.

After the waitress took our orders, Aaron raised his water glass. "Congratulations. Mission accomplished."

"Not quite," I said, "but I think the S.B.I. can take it from here. What's our double-agent learned?"

"Didn't get anything from Garner we don't already know. But it was kind of a kick joining his nefarious gang. He thinks I can hijack the money he assumes Wayland squirreled away before Madison finds it or inherits it."

"But if he has no idea where it is, what makes him think you could find it?"

"He suggested I could find a way to meet Madison. So I have to keep him on a string. And convince him somehow that I can meet her and maybe dream up a phony investment plan to beguile her. But I'll have to keep meeting with him to scope out the whole story."

"You could say you happened to run into her student at Twelve Bones."

"And that would actually be true," Kalea suggested.

Aaron sighed. "He warned me about her, a nosy bitch named Penny."

"Yup," said Kalea. "She's a piece of work, all right." We all laughed.

"By the way," Aaron said, "your detective friend Sabillas came by this morning. Said you'd given him the idea that Wayland's gun was borrowed for the reenactment. Needs to check something about the rifling."

"Sorry. Should have warned you."

The waitress arrived. "These are barbecued in our special sauce," she said as she delivered our platters, "but you can smother them in any of these." She set down a trio of sauces: Carolina, Texas, Tennessee, and Kansas City style. "Can I get you anything more?"

Aaron assured her we were fine, which I thought was easy for him to say. He hadn't been called a bitch. As soon as Aaron's fingers were covered in sauce, he adopted his Pritchard voice to rehearse his call to Garner. "You won't believe who I ran into at Twelve Bones."

+ + +

That evening, after delivering Kalea back to Kalorama, I found Aaron, still in his Pritchard attire, at a bistro table in the Lodge Pub. I perched on the opposite stool and caught the eye of a dark-haired man with acne scars sitting alone. He glared like we'd met before, but I had no idea who he might be. After a quick kiss with Aaron, I glanced back to him. Now he was staring at Aaron.

"You know the guy over there with the pock-marked face?" I tipped my head toward the man. Aaron looked in his direction. The stranger was about my height, sported a bulbous nose, and wore a corduroy golf cap over his dark curls, the brim snapped to the front of the cap. I imagined a silver-topped cane slicing the air as he paraded on a city sidewalk.

"Could be a retired Navy type I met somewhere. But no, I don't recognize him."

"Just wondering."

We finished our nightcaps and went up to the apartment. It was hard to forget it had been Wayland's when Madison and I first visited. Aaron was busy kissing my neck when a battery of insistent knocks reverberated the door.

"Who is it?" Aaron called as we disentangled.

"Guess." Gruff.

If the old door had been fitted with a peephole, Aaron might not have opened it. It was the ogler from the Pub. Peeved.

"Wayland Morgan," he said, jabbing a finger at Aaron. Not a question.

"I'm not," Aaron said.

"You didn't answer my email, so I've had to come all this way to get my money back for that worthless flag."

"I have no idea what you're talking about." He turned to me. "You know anything about a flag?" Then back to the man. "Sorry. You've got the wrong room." Aaron started to close the door. The man jammed a foot and an elbow into the apartment.

"Right room," the man insisted. "We need to talk."

"I don't think so," Aaron said, and shoved the door against his bulk. The intruder didn't back away.

"Take my word for it, Mr. Morgan."

Aaron acquiesced. "Then come on in, sir. But the name's not Morgan." He offered his hand. "Clement Pritchard. This is my friend, Corinne. Yours?"

"Grover Knowles. Don't pretend you don't know me."

Aaron motioned him to the couch. The ripped cushions looked like they'd been liberated from a dumpster.

We sat on matching armchairs, cushions upside-down. "Sorry to disappoint. I am not Wayland Morgan," Aaron insisted.

"And that's a fact," I said. "Wayland died two weeks ago."

Grover raised his gravelly voice. "I don't believe either

one of you," he yelled. "Write me a check."

Aaron raised his eyebrows and held out his hands in a "what can I do?" attitude. "Why do you think Morgan owes you money?"

Grover Knowles stared as if I belonged in a home for lunatics. "I didn't know the flag was a fake," he said.

"What flag? What fake?" Aaron asked.

Knowles' anger boiled. He stood and yelled, "What flag? You idiot! That damned old battle flag."

I glanced at Aaron. Neither of us wanted the man to have a heart attack. "Oh really?" I said. "Might have heard him mention a battle flag."

"I should have had it appraised before I forked over any money," Grover continued, paying me no attention and apparently convinced Aaron was still stalling. "You knew it was a re-pro-duction!"

I took the picture of Confederate Major Wayland Morgan from the wall. "Is this the man who sold you the flag, Mr. Knowles?"

He looked carefully at the photo then across to Aaron, suddenly deflated. "Are you sure he's dead?"

"You're welcome to ask him," I said. "He's in cold storage, compliments of the Henderson County Medical Examiner."

Grover glared at Aaron. "Then who the hell are you?"

"How did you know Morgan lived here?" Aaron countered.

"Triangulated on his cell phone. No problem. So tell me how I can get my million back and I'll tell my lawyer to let it go."

"I have no idea where Wayland may have put whatever money you're talking about," Aaron said. Which was technically true.

"I'll sue his estate. It was a deal."

"In writing?" I asked.

"In the South, a man's word is as good as a contract," Grover said.

We hadn't found an agreement among his papers so I parroted Cheyenne. "A verbal contract is only worth the paper it's written on. That's what they teach in law school."

"My lawyer will see about that," he announced and rose to his feet, almost as grumpy as when he arrived. Then he noticed, apparently for the first time, the cabinet of Civil War relics. "Those Wayland's?"

Neither of us replied but I couldn't help thinking Knowles must be from the shallow end of the gene pool.

"Reason I'm asking, you sell that stuff, you probably could write me a decent check. Maybe not the whole thing, but—"

"That's all part of his estate," I said. "It'll be a while till it's probated. But I doubt that you're mentioned in his will." Grover's face reddened as he headed to the door. Realized he'd drawn the short straw.

"Hang on a second," Aaron said. "Wayland's stepdaughter may want to liquidate this collection. Would you tell us the name of your appraiser?"

I gave Aaron my "not a bad idea" look.

Grover pulled a wallet from his jacket, extracted a card, turned it over and wrote out contact information for Civil War Appraisals, Ltd., in Columbia, South Carolina. "Talk to Hubert," he said. "He's got the most experience. Been on Antiques Roadshow. He's good on uniforms, flags, bugles, anything."

"Thank you, Mr. Knowles," Aaron said. "I'll let

Morgan's stepdaughter know of your interest in recovering whatever you paid for the flag."

Grover's muffled footsteps faded on his way to the elevator.

"Brilliant," I said. "He didn't get our names."

"But he knows where we live."

"We?"

Chapter 41

The views from the mountain-flanked road from the Vanderbilt Lodge back to Flat Rock Thursday morning were as good as it gets. An occasional farmstead punctuated the soft green Appalachian ridges that folded into increasingly grayer ones as far as you could see. History lay gently on these mountains. Hills that had witnessed Yankee forays and Confederate counter attacks. Where so many men had died not all that many years ago.

Chopin's mazurka interrupted my musings. "Penny for—"

"How 'bout a dollar?" It was Kalea.

"Fifty cents?"

The haggler offered a quarter then gave up. "Shy-mom called last night to say she would get here sooner than she'd thought. She's coming in today on the same flight we were on. Gets to Asheville at two. That's the good news."

"And?"

"Belle Mère's physical therapist called this morning. She's decided Maddy-Mom needs physical therapy."

"No surprise there. When?"

"She thinks a couple of times a week for at least a month. Maybe more."

"Where?"

"She said they'll send therapists out here," Kalea said. "She wants her to start tomorrow."

Twenty minutes later, both Kalea and Aunt Zee met me beside the lions at Kalorama's front steps. Madison was hobbling around the house with her walker, Kalea said, prepping for her first session with the therapist.

"How's Aaron?" Aunt Zelma asked, with a meaningful

smile.

I tried for a Mona Lisa look and hoped the quiver in my chest wasn't noticeable. "News flash. Grover Knowles showed up at the Lodge last night."

"How on earth did he know where to come?" Kalea asked.

"Said he triangulated on Wayland's phone calls."

"Fill us in," Aunt Zelma said. "What happened?"

"He was in a royal snit. Assumed Aaron was Wayland. After all, we were in his apartment. Knowles was livid about the fake flag and insisted his money be returned on the spot. After I convinced him that Wayland was dead and we had no idea where any of his money might be, he suggested that Wayland's Civil War relics could be sold to reimburse him."

"I'd think that would be fair," Aunt Zelma said. "Do you think she'd agree to make restitution that way?"

"I'll bet she has her own ideas for whatever she inherits," I said. "But Aaron got the name of the appraiser who told him the flag was bogus. Madison's going to need an honest appraisal when she's ready to sell the collection."

Kalea turned to be sure that Madison was out of earshot. "Did you know," she asked me, "that Maddy-Mom's fallen in love with North Carolina? And she might decide to move here?"

I didn't want to admit that Madison had mentioned it to me the day we picked her up from Belle Mère. "Why would she want to do that?"

"Said she'd like to be close to the mountains. She thinks the air is cleaner here."

"How would that be for you?" I said.

"Like having divorced parents, I guess. I'd have to decide who I wanted to live with." She frowned and let out an exaggerated huff. "Wouldn't be fair."

For Kalea's sake, I hoped it wouldn't happen. And, I admitted selfishly, for mine too.

"Are you guys going to stand out there all day?" Madison called through the open front door.

When we'd finished lunch, I asked Madison if she wanted to go with us to the Asheville airport to meet Cheyenne.

"Tell her I'll see her when she gets here," Madison said.

Something's out of whack between those two, whispered Grandpa Jack.

I raised my palms. "Whatever." Marriage counseling was waayyy beyond me.

"Shy'll be disappointed," Kalea said, running around to the passenger door. "You know how she can be."

"Au contraire," Madison said. "I told her I want to get this therapy going and be able to get back to Annapolis sooner."

"If you go back, Mom."

"*If* I go back," Madison echoed sotto voce.

"Hang on," I said. "Got something for you." I fumbled in my backpack, found the contact information for Civil War Appraisals, and explained where it had come from. "Grover said to ask for a Hubert Washington."

"If Shy-Mom acts weird when she gets off the plane, s'probably because she's had a gin or two," Kalea said when we hit the interstate. "She doesn't like flying any more than Maddy."

I turned the radio off. "I'd've never known."

"Like when they went to Hawaii for their honeymoon. You know, before my adoption was final."

"Where they chose your name."

"Uh-hunhh. And where Maddy-Mom got sick."

"You think they had too many Mai Tais?"

"I don't know but she had a couple of Bloody Marys in Baltimore before we got on the plane to come here, so I'd bet she had a few on those flights across the Pacific."

My phone danced. "I have some news," Agent Lisa Brown said.

I mouthed "Agent Brown" to Kalea and switched to speakerphone. "We hoped we'd hear from you."

"The good news is that we found your Angie. Not a girlfriend. He was an inmate at Roxbury."

"Really?"

"Angelo Scappare. Partial prints on the jet injector and your letter matched what Roxbury sent us. He was the only person with a name like that they'd had while Mr. Morgan was there."

Wayland's murder is solved! Grandpa Jack shrieked.

Not so fast, I said. Although a guy was identified, I didn't think it was time yet for celebration.

"The not-so-good news," Agent Brown continued, "is that Mr. Scappare is on parole in Tennessee and his parole officer hasn't seen him for a couple of weeks."

Ooops, said a subdued Grandpa Jack.

Mark Twain once said it ain't so much what we don't know that gets us into trouble; it's what we *do* know but ain't so. Madison and I were perfect examples, certain that either Ned or Garner had killed Wayland because he'd cheated them. And gotten caught up in the old flag scam before we'd even known there was a man in black out there somewhere.

And now you're chasing another sure bet, Grandpa Jack observed smugly.

"Don't worry," Agent Brown said, bringing me back to

reality. "We'll nail him."

"What about motive?"

"They don't have details, but apparently Mr. Morgan and Scappare shared pictures of their families. Seems that after Mr. Morgan was released, he got cozy with Scappare's family out in western Maryland. Wound up getting his niece pregnant. So we're assuming Morgan's death was Scappare's revenge."

I couldn't comment, especially with Kalea at my side. I wouldn't even mention that his post-release behavior echoed the reason for his incarceration.

He should've been on the sex offender list, whispered Grandpa Jack.

And what difference would that have made?

"There's a warrant out for his arrest," Lisa said. "Violating parole. He's on our 'Be On the Lookout For' list."

"So now we just wait for him to be picked up? Or to simply reappear?"

"Based on the letter you gave us as well as the fact that at Roxbury he was in cognitive behavior therapy for a couple of personality disorders, we ought to prepare for his reappearance."

We?

But she was providing me with more data points. Maybe I could, at last, begin to poke in the man's psyche. "They mention what the personality disorders were?"

"Hang on." A moment later, "Narcissistic and antisocial. Oh ... and they said before prison, he'd been a nursing assistant at Saint Nicodemus Hospital in Franklin. Near Nashville.

Now it isn't just any man's brain you need to crawl into, Grandpa Jack whispered. *You need to find your way into a psycho.*

"I wonder if the hospital would still have inventory records from whenever he was there. They might find they were missing a jet injector."

"You want to apply for a job? We're advertising for an office assistant."

I laughed.

"And, by the by," Lisa Brown said, "I hear through the grapevine that you may meet my colleague next week."

"Not sure what you mean."

"Jocelyn Brantley's an S.B.I. agent here. Her grandfather is throwing a party next weekend for an old friend who's going to open a Civil War museum."

"If you mean Tobin Brantley, I'm amazed at the coincidence. The reason Madison and I came here was to visit Brantleigh's gardens."

"Stay tuned. I'm sure you'll get an invitation."

I wasn't at all sure I ever wanted to see Brantleigh Manor again.

+ + +

A darkening sky and stiff breeze was our welcome to the Asheville airport. In spite of the threatening weather, Cheyenne's flight was on time. Kalea and I waited near the gate. At the same time we spotted her, she saw us. She hugged her daughter. "Where's Maddy?"

"She's practicing her walking," Kalea said. "Starting physical therapy."

Cheyenne nodded without smiling. "'kay. I'll get my luggage and the rental."

"My aunt insists you stay with us this time," I said.

Cheyenne tilted her head. "Very nice of her, but I'll have to stay this first night at the Blue Ridge Inn. Too late to cancel."

"We'll wait at the rental exit," I said. "Look for my Purple Polecat." Cheyenne's expression softened as she turned toward the luggage carousels.

Kalea and I waited in the car. "Had your fill of North Carolina yet?" I asked.

"Not if Maddy-Mom's going to stay."

"We don't know if that's what she'll decide, so you may as well get ready to fly back with them. You anxious to get to the police academy?"

"That's not till August."

"Nice to look forward to something fun."

Not the first time I'd seen her sulk. "I hoped we could go camping or something."

"I wasn't ever a girl sprout," I said. "Never hiked or camped. But I'll tell you what. How about a zip-line this weekend?"

"Awesome." A huge smile illuminated her face. She'd seen the billboards too.

A flash in the mirror from Cheyenne's headlights, a gash of lightning in the gloom, and a nearly instantaneous crash of thunder. The rain began in earnest as we wound our way out of the airport, back to the interstate and headed south to Hendersonville. By the time we got to the Inn, my wipers were at warp speed whopping salvos of sloppy raindrops. With blotchy glimpses through the wipers, I navigated to the curb just beyond the Inn's entrance. Cheyenne stopped behind me and a doorman with a huge umbrella met her. She retreated under the portico while he returned for her bags.

At my prompt, Kalea rolled down her window and yelled. Shy looked in our direction and Kalea called, "We'll meet you for brunch tomorrow." The message was loud enough for the doorman to turn to us with a smile, perhaps wondering briefly if he, too, was invited. Cheyenne waved back, gave Kalea a thumbs up, handed a valet her car keys, and followed her luggage inside.

"Something's bothering Shy-Mom." Kalea was wrapping and unwrapping her messenger bag shoulder strap around a pinkie. "It's like she's not a mom anymore."

Instantly my protective instincts took center stage. I could attest that losing a mom, figuratively or literally, was a serious calamity at her age. "She's got a lot going on." Then quickly added: "I'm sure," hoping it was true. "She has whatever cases she's working on, on top of Madison's injury."

"She has an intern at work now. She came over one afternoon before we first came down. Looks like she just graduated from high school. They had drinks and then went out somewhere that evening. Seemed like they were best friends."

"They probably had a lot of lawyer stuff to discuss."

"I'll bet they got together while I was here with you and Maddy-Mom."

Don't discount the opinion of a child, Grandpa Jack reminded me.

Chapter 42

Aaron had practiced his opening: "Man, you are not gonna believe who I met at Twelve Bones yesterday."

At the other end of the line, Claude Garner waited for Clement Pritchard to get to the point.

"Being away from home makes a man pay attention. Know what I'm saying?"

"I hear you."

"There was this delicious babe at the next table." Aaron was doing his best to be the good old boy. "Million-dollar smile—"

"Got to get back to the classroom, Clement. Get to the point."

"I turned on my charm …"

Such as it is, Garner was probably thinking.

"I tell you I could have dropped my shorts. Turned out to be that Penny woman you warned me to steer clear of."

Garner said nothing.

"We got to talking. Since she's from up north … anyhoo, said she had no interest in a Gillmore medal or any other kind of Civil War paraphernalia. Really into gardens. But she mentioned her friend, Madison."

"She's the one I told you would inherit Wayland's money."

"Right."

"I've seen his collection," Garner said. "Worth some green."

"I told her I could appraise it."

"Good job."

"Penny says this Madison isn't able to get around very well, so she's going to show me the stuff. Out west of

Hendersonville somewhere. I said I'd look it over but explained that I'd need to meet her friend who's inheriting it. Point being, when I meet the Madison woman, I may be able to find out if she's found whatever money Raymond ... *Way*land didn't split with you. And offer her an investment opportunity she can't refuse."

"If you find out she does want to sell the collection, low ball your appraisal. I might be interested in that, too."

"No problem, Colonel." *Den of thieves, indeed.*

+++

My third attempt to reach my brother Spencer was the charm. "Where've you been hiding?" he asked.

"In plain sight," I said. Spencer was a respected doctor, a pediatric neurosurgeon at Johns Hopkins in Baltimore. I'd caught him en route from the hospital to his gated subdivision in his horsey northern suburb. So I went straight to the purpose of my call. "Hope you're up for Twenty Questions." When he said nothing, I went on: "Drop the zero, actually there're only two."

"What mischief have you gotten yourself into this week?" Typical Spencer. But I'd learned long ago to disregard his barbed insinuations.

Knowing a bit of Dutch courage would help me survive whatever jabs my brother might lob, I'd poured myself a tumbler of chardonnay. Took a sip. "This time I ask the questions and you get to answer," I said. "Ready?"

"Are you going to give me a category?"

"Psychology."

"Good," he said. "So long as it's not anatomy or physiology. It's been a long day."

"Wouldn't want to make it too easy." When he didn't offer a retort, I said, "What's a man like who's been diagnosed with antisocial personality disorder?"

"That's too easy. What's the second?"

"Same man. Narcissistic personality disorder."

"I hope you're not thinking of dating this guy."

"But he seems so sweet."

Spencer burst into laughter. "If you'll stop shoveling hogwash, I'll do my best."

"Okay. This is the guy who probably killed my design professor's stepfather. Had a prison term, present whereabouts unknown."

"Sis, I have warned you about meddling with society's underbelly."

"Spence, drop the cute clichés. I'm a big girl. And I promise not to walk down any dark alleys."

His tone changed. "Antisocial personality disorder simply means that your guy has no empathy for others and has no problem breaking the law to get what he wants. He can seem charming and has a big ego."

"Reminds me of a guy I dated in high school. I think he's still behind bars."

"You ready for the narcissistic?"

"Shoot."

"Overlaps a bit with the antisocial characteristics. Thinks he's God's gift to the world, full of fantasies of power and success but of course doesn't think of them as fantasies. Needs admiration but can be rude to the same people he wants to be flattered by."

"All in all, then, a great guy," I teased.

"You know what he was in prison for?"

"Something at a hospital where he was a nursing assistant."

"Must not have poisoned patients or he'd still be behind

bars—or dead."

"Funny you'd mention poison," I said. "He apparently used a plant poison in an old pressure injector."

"Clever bastard."

"So now I'll be on alert for a clever bastard who fishes for compliments."

"When you find him never let him go."

"Or all through my life I may dream alone?"

"You're impossible."

"Love you too, Spencer. Now don't worry about your little sister. And tell Janisse I said hi."

Chapter 43

"Civil War Appraisers." Hubert Washington's smooth Southern accent washed over Madison. "How may I help you?"

"Mr. Washington. You were recommended by a friend."

"We always appreciate referrals."

"My stepfather died recently and I've come to North Carolina to liquidate his estate. He had a lot of Civil War stuff. Bugles, belts, buckles, buttons, cartridge cases, a surgeon's kit, officer hats and shoulder-boards, and several regular soldier caps, the kind that look smashed. All in a display cabinet."

"I get the picture."

"And I don't have any use for any of it. There's also an old flag. Looks like an original. It's beat up enough. It's in a safe deposit box but I can show it to you whenever you could look at the other things."

Washington let out a long exhalation. "I saw one of those recently," he said. "Turned out it was an expensive fake."

"Really?" she said convincingly.

"Where are you located?"

Madison told him.

"I don't travel for appraisals, unless the item is very heavy or difficult to transport—like a cannon. You'd need to bring the items to us."

"But ..."

"What?"

"Do you remember seeing an article about a woman who was wounded at a reenactment near Hendersonville a couple of weeks ago?"

"I did see that."

"I was the one. I'm out of the hospital but in physical therapy. Can't get around much."

Hubert said nothing for a couple of seconds. "Let me check my calendar." He was quiet again. "I might could come up Saturday a week. Could that work for you?"

"Should be fine. Let me give you the number of my friend, Penelope. She doesn't need a wheelchair or a walker and I can't go anywhere yet without one or the other." A slight stretch of the truth. "Penny can give you directions or meet you and take you to the apartment. Matter of fact, I'll let her know you'll be in touch." Madison repeated the number from memory.

"Strange area code."

"We're from Maryland."

+ + +

Aaron's phone began to hum the Navy Hymn. The screen displayed Claude Garner's number. "Pritchard here."

"Any luck?" Claude Garner asked.

"I'm set up to see Wayland's collection tomorrow. Penny says I could meet Madison over the weekend."

"Where're y'all going to meet?"

"Penny gave me directions to Wayland's apartment. As soon as I work up some numbers, she'll introduce me to Madison."

"Good, good."

"But here's another thing. Could you front me a piece of the reward you mentioned? Maybe five hundred? I'm hanging out here longer than I expected. Five would get me at least through the weekend."

Garner laughed.

"What's so funny?" Aaron asked.

"Nothing." On the one hand, Garner probably thought,

Pritchard's information could have come from someone else. On the other hand, if Pritchard was on track to get his hands on Wayland's two million? Or even one?

"If it'll keep you on the trail. Wouldn't want my bloodhound to lose the scent."

"I've got the scent, all right," Aaron said. "I just need to eat occasionally and pay for a few more days at my motel. Whenever you can ante up, I could meet you at the Blue Ridge bar again. Seems to be the center of the universe around here when the sun goes down."

"Would cash be okay?"

"No problem. When?"

"Say nine?"

+ + +

In the Blue Ridge Inn, Aaron checked his watch for the third time since the goggle-eyed tail-wagging cat at his end of the bar showed nine o'clock. Then glanced up from his sweet-tea bourbon to see Garner scanning the crowd from just inside the door. Aaron stood and raised his arm. Then sat back to watch Garner jostle his way to the bar.

"You feel the hormones bouncing around in here?" Garner asked. The majority of the crowd was from the nearby community college. On a platform in one corner, bluegrass musicians tuned their guitars, banjos, and fiddles. Behind them, a woman with a big blond braid over her shoulder tested the strings on her bass fiddle. When the tuning faded, one of the fiddlers, wearing a woolen cap, dipped into a clog-dance melody that sparked the others into action.

"A cross-section of Hendersonville society," Aaron said. "Can I get you a beer? Or," thinking quickly, "Wild Turkey?"

"WT neat would be fine. With lemon."

A waitress acknowledged Aaron's signal. He ordered.

Garner pulled a letter from a hip pocket of his jeans. "Something's coming up I think you might be interested in."

"Interested? How?"

"If you can stick around till next weekend, you could meet a really big player in the Civil War antiques world."

"I was hoping to find your money and get back to Florence."

"I've made a big sale. An original 1865 battle flag."

"Like the one Gorm ... *Way*land sold?" Aaron said.

Aaron feigned astonishment, guessing that Garner imagined Pritchard's brain to be permanently bourbon-fogged. "You're one lucky bastard. Where'd you find this one, and who'd you sell it to?"

"Since the Battle of Asheville in 1865, it'd been in one family," Garner said. "The Yankee flag-bearer must have dropped it after the battle in a rush to get back to Tennessee. So this farmer, on his way into town the day after the battle, found it tossed in the woods. His family'd kept it ever since."

"Worth a bit, I bet."

"The old lady I bought it from had no idea. Probably close to a million, but I gave her ten grand."

"So who's the new owner? You get some real money?"

"A wealthy collector, name of Boscovus Dillingham." Garner wore the grin of a kid who'd done a wheelie the entire length of his block. "It'll hang in his new museum."

"You think I could meet him?" Aaron asked with feigned enthusiasm. "If he's got a ton of money, I have some high-dollar items I'd be willing to part with."

Garner looked dubious. "You could at least make his acquaintance."

"I'm in then. I'll call my executive assistant and tell her

I'll be staying until ... When did you say it was?"

"Saturday a week." Garner handed Aaron an envelope. "Directions to the reception. And the little something we spoke about."

"That'll give me a little more time to find your missing money."

"Here's the thing. I'll get paid for the flag at the reception. You might've heard of Brantleigh Manor."

"Isn't that where the stepdaughter and her student went?"

"Penelope must have told you a lot."

"Chalk it up to my Southern charms." Aaron allowed himself a wolfish grin.

"So ... Mr. Brantley's holding a grand reception, at least that's what his invitation calls it, to honor Mr. Dillingham and his new museum. The invitation says there'll be a surprise announcement. Well, sir, only I know what that will be. And now you too. It'll be his new flag ... no, not new ... his hundred and fifty-year-old battle flag. From the Ohio regiment that marched on Asheville in 1865. He'll unveil it at the reception."

"I'd be honored, Colonel," Aaron said quietly, his words oozing South Carolina honey.

"You'll also probably have a chance to meet Penny's Aunt Zelma Porter. She's the reigning queen of Carolina history around here. In fact it was in her high school class that got me interested enough to study on it. Zelma'll undoubtedly bring your Penelope, and possibly Miss Madison."

"I'll have that lady in my pocket before then," Aaron said. "I gar-un-tee she won't pass up my offer to double her money. Investing in my Myrtle Beach development'll be a no-brainer."

Behind the wheel of his Mercedes, ideas flared like rockets into the night sky. If the amperage of his synapses had been connected to the county grid, the road back to the Vanderbilt Lodge would have been brightly lit.

Chapter 44

Friday morning, Madison, at Zelma's stove, whisked what would soon be an omelet. Nearby, Aunt Zelma arranged meditation stones. Kalea and I were set to leave for breakfast with Cheyenne at the Blue Ridge Inn.

"Warn her I'll be working out with the physical therapist when you all get back," said Madison.

"Maybe we shouldn't," Kalea joked. "She might get jealous."

Madison folded the omelet and lifted it onto a plate. "Ha!"

+ + +

On the outskirts of Hendersonville, Aaron called. "Speakerphone," Kalea whispered.

"Penny for your thoughts."

"A bottle of champagne," Aaron said, "if you'll help me concoct a story. I told Garner I'd have news for him tomorrow, but I need some help inventing it."

I laughed. "I thought making stuff up was second nature now."

"Another thing. Garner told me last night about a reception at Brantleigh and I want to tell you about an idea I had."

Probably what Lisa Brown had mentioned. "I can be out there sixish."

"Don't you mean *we'll* be there at six?" my C.S.I. assistant whispered.

I braked for the left turn toward downtown Hendersonville. "This conference will be only for the top brass." I showed her my fist, Naval Academy ring up.

Cheyenne was in the lobby with both bags, ready to

decamp.

"You sleep okay?"

Her smile was lopsided. "I guess."

"It'll be quieter at Aunt Zelma's."

"Penny's aunt has your bedroom picked out," Kalea said.

"We're running on empty," I said. "How's the food?"

"Last night's menu wasn't bad. But their breakfast buffet … well …"

"Better than nothing?" said Kalea.

Single file, we loaded our plates with miniature pastries and tiny sausages. We claimed a table and went back for coffee and juice.

"I was in the Pub last night." Cheyenne was unwrapping a miniature apple Danish. "Saw a guy who looked for all the world like your friend Aaron." Took a bite. "Tried to get his attention. But he didn't recognize me."

I kept my thoughts to myself.

"He wasn't wearing jeans and a golf shirt, so it probably wasn't him. But I could've sworn …"

I opened my mouth to explain—

"There was another guy at the table," she went on. "I couldn't make out what they were saying but it sounded like he was telling the Aaron lookalike about some event."

"Did he have a Stars and Bars tie?"

"Matter of fact … How'd you know?"

"Because I bought him that tie for his Clement Pritchard identity."

Cheyenne, quizzical, munched and swallowed a bite of her ersatz Danish.

I explained Aaron's undercover mission for Claude Garner. "So if you ever see him in that getup, pay him no attention."

"We'll all need to join actor's equity," Cheyenne quipped.

"You need some background." I summarized what we knew of the flag scam and the "missing" money and why I'd asked Aaron to help.

"Speaking of the money," Shy said, "I'll talk to Madison about investing it. It'd be nice to have it earning instead of just lying there."

As a lawyer, Grandpa Jack whispered, *she should know the bank would report a transaction that large to the IRS.* Which got me to wondering if a lawyer who would certainly know the rules might harbor an ulterior motive.

Kalea brought Cheyenne up to date on everything that had happened while she was in Maryland. About Aaron's arrival and the Meetup. She didn't mention that I'd stayed with him—not that it was anybody's business.

"A second member of the scam gang is dead," Kalea added.

"Unfortunately," I said, "I saw him die."

"*What?*"

I had to explain the altercation on the bridge one more time.

"And now the man who bought the fake flag wants his money back," Kalea said. "And we met an S.B.I. agent—"

"Because the S.B.I. has taken over Wayland's murder investigation," I said, "since they discovered he was killed with poison hemlock."

Cheyenne met my gaze. "The M.E. identified the poison?"

"At first, we thought it might have been something different but it was ultimately identified as what killed Socrates. Poison hemlock."

Ooops, said Grandpa Jack.

"What do you mean? Who's the *we* that thought he'd been killed with a different poison? If *we* means you and Madison, how would she have had any idea?"

I had to backtrack. Neither Cheyenne nor Kalea knew Wayland's demise was the real reason Madison wanted to come to North Carolina.

"We ... uh, found an injector near where we found him," I said, distorting the chronology. "The cops sent it to the S.B.I. lab in Raleigh where they found coniine residue. Better known as poison hemlock. Since the Medical Examiner told Madison that Wayland died from a heart condition, she suggested he should check again. So after a full tox screen he concluded that Wayland had actually died from the poison hemlock. The S.B.I. then came to the obvious conclusion: the injector had been used to kill him."

I hoped I had given her only a few slightly misleading details to prevent any further awkward inquiry. Kalea glanced at me but didn't comment.

"This injector was like a hypodermic?"

I did my best to describe the gadget.

"I guess that makes sense," said Cheyenne, frowning slightly.

She had apparently followed my spurious reasoning. If so, her ability to follow a statement in court was not her strong suit. I just hoped I'd never need to cough up the whole truth. I also prayed she wouldn't press Madison on the subject.

We bussed our plates and flatware into a pair of plastic tubs and paid.

"No comparison to Aunt Zelma's breakfasts," Kalea proclaimed. "I'd give this place just one star."

Kalea and Cheyenne put Shy's bags in her rental. Then they tailed my Purple Platypus to Aunt Zelma's.

As I turned onto Beulah Road, the darkening sky became drizzly. What was it with the quickly changing weather around here?

In the foyer, out of the gentle rain, sounds of shuffling came from the Music Room. Madison appeared, then came to a stop, her therapist steadying her with a rainbow-striped gait belt.

"Three times around," she announced, slightly out of breath. "Tell them how well I'm doing," she said. "No, don't bother … maybe tomorrow."

Cheyenne moved toward her partner but Madison shook her head. "Later."

Shy seemed surprised at the rejection and Kalea gave me a look that reminded me of her suggestion that Cheyenne might be losing interest. I briefly wondered if her interest in Madison's inheritance was only in my imagination.

"Cheyenne," Aunt Zelma called, descending the stairs. "It's a pleasure to see you again. Leave your bags right there. We'll get you settled after lunch."

"For what Madison's been through," the therapist said, "she's doing great."

"I'll be working with Greg twice a week," Madison said. "We're trying to rebuild my atrophied muscles." She grimaced. "No—really. Anyway, I should be good as new." With a sardonic smile she added, "Someday."

Greg shadowed her back to her walker, each step triggering a wince.

"We're finished for today," he said. "I'll see you next week."

"I'll be here." She laughed. "Barring the rapture."

Kalea and I helped Aunt Zee make salami and pimento cheese sandwiches and a fresh tomato salad dressed with balsamic vinegar and basil. We took everything to the veranda and the five of us settled around a small coffee table. The lingering perfume of Koreanspice viburnum and goblets of chilled chardonnay transformed the al fresco meal into the realm of superb.

Around the fountain, two gardeners weeded the bed where poppies and coneflowers were emerging to take the stage from bleeding hearts and bellflowers. The Allegretto movement of Beethoven's Seventh wafted gently from their nearby boombox.

"With that for a prelude," Aunt Zelma predicted, "this summer's flower display should be spectacular."

After a sip of wine, I brought Aunt Zelma up to date on Aaron's sleuthing.

"Can he stay another week?" Aunt Zelma asked.

"He wants to finish his project for Garner in the next day or two. So I doubt it. Why?"

"I had a message this morning."

"During your meditation?"

Aunt Zelma laughed. "Right after. A phone call. An old friend—he's actually only a few years older than me—Tobin Brantley—the owner of Brantleigh Manor."

"We didn't see him when we toured the mansion. Our docent said he and his wife lived almost like hermits in one wing."

"Well, Tobin and Mera are coming out of their hermitage a week from tomorrow. They're hosting a reception for an old friend. *Older* friend. Senator Boscovus Dillingham is donating his collection of Civil War paraphernalia to a new museum." She faced me. "Tobin knew of your visit and that you were my grandniece, so he insisted you come along. I asked if another friend might join us, although I didn't know if Aaron would still be impersonating a Civil War collector. Tobin said of course. Bring him along."

"Will anyone else we know be there?" I asked.

"Tobin mentioned that Claude Garner would be there."

"Maybe the guy I saw with Aaron last night," Shy said.

"Probably," I said. "I'll get the details tonight." That prompted curious glances from both my aunt and Kalea.

"Do you think my moms and I could go?"

"Of course," Aunt Zee said. "Crashing a party is one of life's blessings."

Both moms looked uncertain.

"Between Tobin and Dillingham, they know just about anyone who is anyone around here." She laughed. "I don't think we're on the same team politically. But they invite me to anything related to history."

Kalea coughed to get both of her moms' attention. "Aunt Penny and I are going on a zip-line tomorrow."

"Sounds scary to me, young lady," Cheyenne said.

Life is scary, mused Grandpa Jack.

Chapter 45

When the grandfather clock on the stairway chimed four, I rushed upstairs and changed out of my jeans and tee into a date-worthy boat-neck blouse and pants.

"What's your hurry?" Aunt Zelma asked when I returned.

"A strategy conference," Kalea said scornfully, "with our double-agent. C.S.I. assistants are not invited."

If Kalea enjoyed the attention of an adult of the male persuasion, I couldn't fault her for choosing Aaron. Not exactly eye-candy, but a near miss. And a good soul.

I hugged them both. And headed toward Hendersonville to catch the road to the Lodge. Mesmerized by the peaceful countryside, I switched off the radio to allow my thoughts to roam.

After happily contemplating my contributions to Aaron's "Clement Pritchard" deception, my brain switched to the critical dilemma: If I were Claude Garner, what would I want to hear from my con-artist sleuth who was on the point of finding Wayland's slice of my pie? After several minutes' with no help from Grandpa Jack, I realized this was not a problem that lent itself to a unilateral solution. Aaron and I would puzzle it out together. It was also nice to know that Aaron and I had a bottle of champagne and all night to grapple with the puzzle.

A bit before five, I parked at the Lodge. A quick look into the Grille told me Aaron was still in his room. The old elevator made its grudging way to the second floor and I traipsed to Apartment 243 where the door was closed. Since Grover Knowles' appearance, Aaron had kept it locked.

"Knock, knock," I said to it.

"You're early," said a surprised Aaron dressed as Pritchard.

"Is that a problem?"

"Quite the contrary," Aaron said with his wonderful smile.

I replayed the hug I'd given him the day he arrived. And embellished it with a kiss. He responded as I'd hoped he would. A tighter hug. And a second kiss. "As promised, champagne."

"My hero," I said, with only a hint of irony, when he handed me one of Wayland's Dollar Store tumblers, half full of bubbly. He poured another for himself.

"I can stay silver-tongued a little longer with this instead of rum."

Our thirsts slaked, we descended to the ground floor and approached the Grille. "Just two?" the hostess asked. We nodded and asked for a booth. Since the Friday evening crowd had not yet materialized, our waitress arrived quickly.

"I'm Tiffany," she said, "and I'll be your connection to the kitchen this evening." Her introduction and cute smile guaranteed a generous tip if Aaron picked up the tab. "Can I get you something from the bar?"

"A bottle of your best California chardonnay, please," I intoned in my best prom-date voice.

A few minutes later, the wine was decanted into elegant stemware of a type that had never seen the inside of Wayland's cupboard. Tiffany slipped the bottle in a chiller bucket and handed us menus. We ordered salads and put the menus aside.

"Cheers." Aaron said, and we clinked.

"Cheyenne told us she saw a man who resembled you chatting with another guy at the Blue Ridge pub last night."

Aaron's eyes twinkled. "Might have been my twin brother."

"You're a natural. Hollywood watch out."

"I'd be typecast as a wealthy Southern fraud!"

"She finally decided it wasn't you. So I filled her in about your undercover assignment."

Aaron laughed. "I fed Garner the line about how you'd let me inventory Wayland's collection and meet Madison. And asked him for an advance on my cut. He fronted me five hundred and invited me to a reception at Brantleigh Manor a week from tomorrow."

"Aunt Zelma was invited to that too," I said. "Mr. Brantley told her to bring me too. And my Maryland friends."

"I'm willing," Aaron said. "Got a couple of ideas about making it a special reception."

Tiffany brought our salads and a basket of warm cornbread and satisfied herself that our wine didn't yet need refilling.

"You ready to order?"

We gave her our orders, unrolled red cloth napkins, and began stabbing the salads.

"Aunt Zelma tells me," I said in my best imitation Junior League socialite accent, "the event will be a highlight of the Henderson County social season."

"Garner assured me that the highlight will be the unveiling of a Civil War flag that'll be an exhibit at the new museum. Seems he's conned Dillingham into buying the flag."

"Déjà vu all over again," I said, echoing Grandpa Jack. "Pretty ballsy of him to try the same scam again."

"Claude's his name, conning's his game."

"Maybe I should offer to sell him a bridge over the French Broad? No ... he already has one."

"Something fishy this way swims." Aaron said, trying to sound Shakespearean. "The flag's undoubtedly a copy of the one Wayland sold to Grover."

My brain began to grind. "What if ..."

"What if what?"

"I'm thinking ... I'm thinking."

Aaron stared, awaiting my oracle, while Tiffany reappeared with our dinners.

"You remember I told you Madison and I found an old flag in the back of Wayland's closet—"

A movement near the entrance caught my eye. A familiar face. Partly in shadow. I looked back to Aaron and dredged my memory circuits. A bit like trying to remember a tune while listening to another. The face was buried in there somewhere.

Aaron noticed my brain grinding. "What?"

Then I remembered. "Don't turn around. Garner's on surveillance ... just inside the door."

Garner pretended not to have noticed us but I was certain he had. Which is why he was here.

"He's obviously checking out my story about meeting you to see the antiques. Glad I stayed in costume."

"It's positively you, dahling." I held my wine glass, extending a pinkie.

"So where's your cigarette holder, my dear?"

"Problem. He might have seen you arrive alone."

"I told him you'd given me directions," Aaron said. "We came separately."

"I suppose."

"The bottom line is that he doesn't completely trust me."

"Tomorrow you can call him with the report he wants."

"I'm waiting breathlessly to hear what that'll be."

Tiffany reappeared, lifted the wine bottle from the bucket, topped off our glasses, and disappeared.

"If I understand the ruse," I said, "this evening you're supposed to be listing Wayland's items. Wouldn't an appraiser need to check references before tallying his valuations?"

"Makes sense to me."

"So to stretch the process, you could tell him that you'd inventoried everything today. Then it could take a couple of days of research before you could come up with valuations. But suppose your reference books are in Florence. You'd have to go home for them."

"The deal is that as soon as I finish the appraisal, you'll introduce me to Madison. And that's when I sweet-talk her into investing in my development company."

"Perfect."

"So, to expedite my introduction to Madison, I'll make a WAG."

"Wild ass guess."

"Good enough for Garner."

"Then your appraisal will be a piece of cake. "

"At the risk of changing the subject … I also told him you were cute as apple pie and I planned to seduce you."

"Don't BS me, Mr. Master Chief."

"No lie. Can I lure you to my lair?"

"*Again?*"

Our dinners demolished, we returned to the lobby. Garner had moved to the rack of tourist brochures near the entrance. We boarded the old elevator and ascended, ostensibly to assess Wayland's antiques.

We started with a twenty-five and added the apartment number to become the bottom line of the appraisal: $25,243.00. Who knew? The collection might be worth at least twice that figure. Or not. We agreed that Aaron should promise Garner that if I received the appraisal tomorrow, I would introduce him to Madison on Sunday. "That should curb his fervor for a couple of days."

Then Aaron explained his suggestions for the Brantley's reception. I digested his scenario and suggested a modification.

"Brilliant," said Aaron, after which the second part of the evening began with kisses too numerous to count.

Chapter 46

Saturday morning was exceptionally special because Aaron and I awoke in the same bed at the same time and tangled ourselves into an encore of the night before.

After returning to planet Earth, I buzzed our imaginary valet to bring OJ and coffee.

"Didn't we give Roger the weekend off?" said Aaron.

"We also gave Stanley and Jeff the weekend off," I said. "No Gulfstream. Guess we'll have to stay in Carolina."

"Nothing could be finer …" Aaron attempted to sing, off-key.

I croaked the second line without any key at all.

Midmorning, Aaron phoned Garner. "Need to thank you for the pocket money, Colonel. It covered dinners for me and Penny at the Lodge last night." Aaron winked at me over our orange juice on Wayland's breakfast table and flipped to speakerphone.

"One of your moves?" Garner asked sardonically.

"As it turned out she's as lonely as I am. Had no idea my charms could work that quickly."

For a fraction of a second I pasted on my best minx face.

"Both your cars were still in the lot at midnight," Garner said.

"You're keeping score?"

"In a way," Garner admitted.

"Then score one for the home team."

"Way to go, soldier. What about Wayland's collection?"

"I haven't found anything counterfeit. It must have taken him quite a while to pull this collection together."

"Every bit of spare change he had, he dropped it on artifacts. Started when he got the Brantleigh gig."

"I've listed everything in the cabinet and told Penny I'd work up the valuation and get it to her later today. Some of his stuff I've got a pretty good idea. For the rest I'll pull some figures out of the air. Not to worry. She said she'd set up a meeting with her friend Madison as soon as she had the numbers."

"Stay in touch. I'll double your reward if you can find my missing money this week."

"Don't think there'll be a problem. Should have it by the Brantleigh shindig," Aaron promised. "I'll see you there."

When they'd rung off, "Before our friend smells a conspiracy we'd better split up," Aaron said. I pouted as suggestively as possible, but agreed. After a quick kiss at the Lodge door, I left Aaron to buy stationery. He'd make two copies of his bogus appraisal, one for Madison and another for Garner.

As I jumped in and started the Nissan, my twisted neural connections coughed up Sir Walter Scott's axiom about weaving tangled webs "... when first we practice to deceive." I hoped we'd planned well enough to continue the deception until the reception.

On the Sandburg Pike, Cheyenne called to report that Madison had talked with the appraiser I told her about. "He's agreed to take a look."

"Great. When?"

"She gave him your number. She assumes you can arrange a visit to the apartment. Mr. Washington suggested next weekend."

"*Perfect*. I'll see you in a few."

"Roger dodger."

Cheyenne's always been a little priggish toward me. It might be that she thought Madison might leave her for me.

But both of them knew I didn't swing that way. Or it could have been that she resented my easygoing way with Kalea. Whatever bee buzzed in her bonnet, I never took exception to her brusque manner.

When I called Aaron with the news, he said he'd coordinate Mr. Washington's visit with the reception this weekend.

It was nearly noon when I arrived back at Kalorama and parked under the porte-cochère. Kalea hopped down the steps. "Maddy-Mom's sleeping in this morning," she said soberly. "Shy-Mom's eating breakfast."

Her matter-of-fact tone of voice signaled that her happy camper personality had taken a holiday. I hoped zip-lining would bring it back. If she still harbored the idea that Cheyenne was losing interest in motherhood, she was suppressing it well.

I said Cheyenne had thanked me for tipping off Madison about Hubert Washington's appraisal firm.

"She didn't say anything to me."

"I'm sure she's totally focused on Maddy's recovery," I said. "They haven't seen each other for almost a week. So be glad they care about each other."

"Maybe." My heart did a half gainer.

"Now, can you do something for me before we head out to the zip-line?"

She perked up with a nod.

"Can you find Grover Knowles online? Knowles Apothecary or something. I need his phone number. You can use my iPad. In my room on the dresser I think."

"Am I allowed to ask why?"

"I want to invite him to the reception next weekend."

"You what?"

"I'll explain later. Aaron and I have a plan."

Yes, ma'am."

Claude Garner wasn't the only one who could talk with a smirk. Kalea saluted and started up the old stairway two steps at a time. Smart-aleck.

It was time to call the gendarmes. Detective Sabillas's number was buried in my phone somewhere. Found it.

"Detective Sabillas? This is Penny Summers."

"Glad you called. A report came in yesterday and I meant to call you."

"About Mr. Morgan's Springfield?"

"Anybody tell you you're psychic?" Sabillas asked.

I laughed. "Don't you start. I'm beginning to think that the water around here makes you all see ghosts. Or at least makes you receptive to visiting other dimensions. Anyway, what news?"

"The forensics folks at Raleigh can only say that Mr. Morgan's musket may have fired the bullet that struck Ms. Lerrimore. Morgan's musket is a smooth-bore model and since there was no rifling on the ball, there's no way to tell with any degree of confidence."

"That's what I thought you'd find."

"What is certain is that the bullet was not fired from a rifled musket."

I was about to ask if they'd been able to lift any fingerprints when Kalea thumped down the staircase and handed me a slip of paper with "GK" and a number. Sabillas, I figured, could deal with the fingerprint question. "Narrows it down. But not by much," I said. We rang off. He didn't need me to tell him whose fingerprints he should expect to find.

"Thanks Kiddo." She saluted and led me to a short sofa

in the salon. Surrounded by the kind of classic elegance that is only found in the homes of the upper five percent, I placed a call to a member of the one percent.

"Speakerphone," Kalea whispered. Grover's secretary answered.

"May I speak with Mr. Knowles?"

"May I tell him who's calling?"

"Of course. We met Mr. Knowles last Wednesday when he was looking to meet Wayland Morgan. My name's Corinne Pemberton." Kalea's face said Hunhh?

"He's on another call. Can you hold a sec?"

Before I could answer, Grover's voice blustered onto the line. "Corinne. Yes. How nice of you to call." *How nice?* He was making nice to cover his embarrassment at the mention of Wayland's name.

"Mr. Knowles, I have a favor to ask. We'd like you to visit us again—"

"Unless you've been able to correct the misunderstanding we spoke of, I wouldn't see any point in making the trip."

I wanted to begin by saying "Here's the thing …" But I didn't. I left the speakerphone on because Kalea needed to hear what I had to say, and explained to Grover about the reception at Brantleigh Manor. "My friend Clement Pritchard, who you met at Wayland's apartment, also has an interest in Civil War flags. He'll call you and explain the scenario."

He couldn't understand why I wanted him to bring his worthless flag, but agreed.

When we disconnected, I ran the whole thing past Kalea.

"That'll be mega-cool," she predicted. Her good humor was returning.

André, the big lovable poodle, awoke and jumped down from the opposite couch when he heard Aunt Zelma's Lexus come to a stop outside. I ran out to move my little car so we could more easily bring groceries into the house. André and Kalea lent their support, psychically in his case and physically in hers.

Over ham sandwiches and pickles, Kalea and I explained next Saturday's plan to Aunt Zee. "Apparently Tobin's granddaughter, Jocelyn, will be there," I said. "She's with the S.B.I. in Asheville."

"Should be an interesting party," my aunt said.

Kalea, anxious to get to the promised zip-line, quickly finished eating. "Ready to zip?"

On the way, I cautioned her to not discuss our reception plan to anyone at all. She saluted.

I then called Aaron to let him know Grover Knowles had reluctantly agreed to come to the reception with his flag after a preliminary look at the Civil War artifacts for Madison. "I said you'd confirm the details with him."

"The appraisal is ready," Aaron said. "I've gun-decked enough numbers to make it look genuine."

"Your Navy years haven't been wasted," I replied. I explained to Kalea that he meant the appraisal "guesstimates" had been made up.

Aaron laughed. "If Garner has started shadowing me, I'll need to be seen arriving at Kalorama with the numbers for Madison."

"It'll be a treat for us to meet Mr. Pritchard again," I said. "Shall we—" I winked at Kalea "meet at Kalorama, say nine?"

"Roger that."

+++

At Zippity-Doo-Dah, there were three others in our two o'clock group, a mom and dad with a boy not quite Kalea's age. We hiked to the platform, our orange helmets and body harnesses snugged, as our guide explained the procedure: Attach the harness, clip on the zip, ready your camera, step up on the stump, and jump into space for the ride of your life. Ahead of us the boy was hesitant so his dad (braver than me) agreed to be point man. Halfway down the slope he screamed, "Yeee-ha!" Then the kid. Finally, his mom.

Kalea and I watched them roll down the long sagging cable and, in the distance, land bird-like in a big tree. "Piece of cake," my fearless niece said. Yeah, I thought, like jumping off a high platform into the Naval Academy swimming pool. Which had not been a piece of cake, not even in hindsight.

Kalea did the drill, turned slightly so I could snap a photo, yelled "Geronimo!" and jumped into the void. It was now or never. I clipped on, readied my camera, stepped on the stump, and screeched a tentative "Yeee-ha!"

Rolling above treetops ... glimpses of distant mountains. Skimming above earthly distractions, it was akin to the euphoria I sometimes have on an airplane. En route to the second platform the euphoria changed to melancholy. I remembered my thoughtlessness that had almost killed Zelma. Like Josh's death, another guilt I'd carry with me forever.

Then other guilts sprang up, starting with Ned's demise. And poor Aaron. Former upright citizen, sworn to protect and defend the Constitution against all enemies, foreign and domestic, bear true faith and allegiance, etc., etc. Now plunged into a forged identity, deep in subterfuge, preparing to con a con man. Because he was willing to help me.

But the journey has had a few pleasures, Grandpa Jack added with a wink.

While Kalea helped me onto the last platform, I looked forward to gliding to a different kind of landing at Brantleigh on Saturday.

Chapter 47

That evening, candle flames danced around the dining room but the mood was uncharacteristically depressed. Kalea had entertained everyone with an animated account of our zip-lining expedition. But the apparent strain between Madison and Cheyenne was affecting us all. Even Aunt Zelma seemed gloomy. Conversation was at a standstill.

The mood couldn't have descended any further so I risked nothing by asking Shy if she'd broached the subject of investing the money we'd found.

Madison glared. "And I said absolutely not."

I then brought up the Brantleigh reception next weekend.

"Sounds like it'd be something Madison might like, but I'll skip it," Cheyenne said. "Been there."

"You'd miss meeting some very interesting people," Aunt Zelma said.

"Aaron and I have planned a surprise," I said. "Should be fun."

Say no more, whispered Grandpa Jack.

"I'll think about it." End of discussion.

"Aaron will be here in the morning," I said. "Part of his double-agent assignment."

+ + +

After we loaded and started the dishwasher, I was online, internet shopping for the transit level and compass I'd need to make the revisions to my concept plan for my client, Aidan Reid. Madison and Shy were on the veranda. Muffled fragments of exasperated conversation filtered to the salon where Kalea pretended to be absorbed in her forensics book as she listened for snippets of her moms' conversation.

In the Music Room, Aunt Zelma had her basket of

meditation stones on her lap. I watched her choose one, close it in her fist, close her eyes, then trade it for another. Back to my iPad, I punched in my credit card numbers and completed the order for my new tools.

Aunt Zelma began to sniffle. It was the first time since Josh drowned that I'd seen her in tears. They slipped down her cheeks to a bandana she pulled from her sleeve. I sat and put my arm around her, but that only resulted in a full-fledged eruption. Kalea came to sit on her other side, leaning against her, wiser than her years, acknowledging Aunt Zee's sadness by simply sharing it.

"What's happened?" I whispered. This was the opposite of my aunt's usual cheerful exuberance that she'd had at dinner.

"Nothing." But the tears continued.

"You can't expect me to believe that."

"Really. Nothing," she managed to say between snuffles. "I have ... no idea ..."

"Upsetting news?" I asked.

She chunked the obsidian she'd been holding into the basket. "No." And snuffled again.

I took her hand and held it. Like Kalea, accepting her grief. She picked up the bandana to pat her eyes and cheeks and said nothing for almost a minute.

"One winter when I was young," she sniffed, "I think I was reading Doctor Doolittle, but that's not the point. I started to cry and had no idea why. I wasn't sad or anything. Mother tried to comfort me but I couldn't stop crying. After a while I stopped but I knew in my bones that something bad was happening. I could feel it somehow, but couldn't see it. I couldn't go back to reading so I just stared out the window at the snow on a pine tree and tried to concentrate on the feeling."

"Like now?" Kalea asked.

"I suppose so," she said.

"A police car drove up. That made it worse. I was so frightened I couldn't talk. A couple of cops came to the door kicking snow off their shoes. When they knocked, Mother answered the door. 'You Missus Porter?' one asked. My mother nodded. 'Your son Jack has been taken to Belle Mère,' he said. Well, I can tell you mother went frantic. '*What happened?*' she yelled over and over so loud and so fast they couldn't answer. She could hardly catch her breath. They calmed her down enough to tell her that my brother who'd been sledding with buddies, had apparently slammed into a fence post. Turned out he'd ruptured his spleen. He was only at Belle Mère for a couple of days, but he never went sledding again."

I squeezed her hand.

"It takes something like that," Aunt Zelma said, "to remind us that we're really very fragile beings."

Kalea and I hugged her. "That was your Grandpa Jack," she reminded me, but she hadn't needed to. He'd told me about his boyhood accident on one of our Annapolis walks.

"I haven't had a crying spell like that since the night before little Josh drowned," Aunt Zelma said.

I said nothing. I didn't want to sound either skeptical of her visions or scornful of her prescience. I shuddered at the recollection. Kalea snuggled closer. Movement out the front window caught my attention as Madison leaned closer to Shy on the big wicker sofa and began explaining something. Might have been her idea of moving to North Carolina.

"But you need to remember," Aunt Zelma said, "those tears came to me in our house because something bad happened to a family member."

"I'm your only family here and I promise to be careful," I said.

"Me, too," said Kalea.

"It might not be anything," my aunt said and tucked an arm around Kalea.

I could have offered a platitude: I wouldn't worry. But I didn't. That might have risked the wrath of the goddess. I decided I should worry, but not let it ruin the day. But, probably like Kalea, I pondered the future of Madison and Cheyenne.

"So, if we get through the evening," I said, "we should be home free?"

"Should be." Aunt Zelma said. I may have been the only one who caught the lack of conviction in her voice.

"We'll be the carefullest," Kalea said.

Chapter 48

Sunday morning, Aunt Zelma's big grandfather clock finished its Big Ben prelude and began chiming nine when the front door chime gonged its version in a discordant counterpoint. Kalea ran to open the door.

"Reporting as ordered," Aaron said. His stars and bars bow tie was clipped neatly between the collar tips of his white shirt.

"Whatever," said Kalea.

"So, how's the adorable detective duo?" Aaron asked.

My apprentice scowled and began churning her arms. Aaron was confused.

"She puts a curse on anybody who calls her adorable or cute."

With an ingratiating smile, "But you are, you know."

She gave him an exaggerated glare.

"Come on in," I said. "Aunt Zelma's at church, Cheyenne hasn't finished breakfast, and Madison isn't down yet."

The kitchen smelled of freshly-baked cinnamon pecan rolls and freshly-brewed coffee. Shy's tee was a raucous red that could summon a bull to its coup de grace. She munched her cinnamon roll without smiling. Bits of pecan tumbled to her plate.

"How's the patient?" Aaron asked her.

"Haven't seen her yet this morning," said Shy. "She should be down soon."

"Care for coffee?" I asked.

"Navy way please." And, sotto voce, he whispered that all the players for our Brantleigh reception scenario were confirmed.

I chose another mug from Aunt Zelma's collection. Filled it and topped off mine. "I just hope Madison—"

"What?" Cheyenne glanced up from the remnants of her pecan roll.

I reminded her of the appraisal "Pritchard" had of Wayland's Civil War antiques to keep Garner hooked until the Brantleigh reception.

Aaron swigged his coffee, and slapped his appraisal on the table.

Cheyenne picked up the sheaf, scanned each page and flipped to the last. "Are these numbers anywhere in the ballpark?"

"Garner assumes I know Civil War antiques," Aaron said, "but I really don't know squat. I pulled these out of my left ear ... just for show."

Cheyenne looked up. We don't have any room for all that stuff at home," she continued. "Not that I can imagine Madison even wanting it. She'd rather have the money for whatever it's worth."

Swallowing the last of his coffee, Aaron said, "Can we get this show on the road? Just to go through the motions, it would be good if I could talk briefly with Madison before I call Garner."

"Kalea," Cheyenne said, "would you go see if she's ready to join us?"

Kalea darted through the foyer and dashed upstairs. A moment later she screamed.

"Call an ambulance!" Kalea yelled as she ran back down to us. "She won't wake up."

We raced up to her room. She was asleep, her head hanging over the bedside. Vomit pooled below. Aaron jumped on the bed, turned her and started mouth-to-mouth resuscitation. Not a job for the weak. After three ventilations, he realized she was breathing, shallowly.

Kalea clung to Cheyenne, wailing. "Please! Call. An. Ambulance!

I pushed my fingers against Madison's wrist. "There's a pulse ... but very weak."

Cheyenne remained motionless.

I yanked out my phone and called 9-1-1." I gave the dispatcher our address, described Madison's condition and explained that she'd vomited. "Yes ..., she's breathing, but barely. And yes, a weak pulse." I listened for another long moment. "No sign of physical injury ... and yes, she's lying flat." Another couple of seconds and I closed the phone. "An ambulance and a deputy are on their way."

Cheyenne rushed downstairs to await them.

If I'd had supernatural power I would have slammed the ambulance driver's accelerator pedal to the metal. Instead, I went back to her bedside and focused all the psychic energy I could summon. *You can do it,* I told her. Her face was pale and swollen. Survive! I leaned in to hear a nearly inaudible asthmatic wheeze.

I felt a nudge at my elbow. *The ghost of the Unknown Bushwhacker waited a long time to wreak his revenge,* Grandpa Jack whispered.

Madison would undoubtedly recognize the irony of the idea, but she wouldn't hear it from me. I whispered back, *Give me a break.*

It seemed like hours but must have been only minutes.

Sirens screamed on the distant Sandburg Pike. The wail changed as they downshifted onto Beulah Road.

And wound down into silence when they turned into the estate.

Chapter 49

Tires scrunched on gravel, doors slammed. Cheyenne called, "Third floor," and followed what seemed like a herd of uniforms pounding up the stairs.

The first EMT looked carefully at Madison, checked her breathing and pulse and dug into his big orange jump bag. "Looks like an allergic reaction." He pulled out a syringe and a small bottle, drew a dose, and jabbed it in her thigh.

"Her name is?" the other EMT asked.

"Madison Lerrimore," Cheyenne said.

"Next of kin?"

"I'm her partner," Shy said. "Cheyenne DeBruhl."

"And," Kalea said, "I'm their daughter. Kalea." He added Kalea's name to his notes.

"Mom seemed fine yesterday," Kalea said, then, in a whisper, "She was doing great with physical therapy."

Deputy Sheriff Cooper introduced himself. "What was that about physical therapy?"

"She was recovering from surgery," Cheyenne said.

He pulled a notebook from a top pocket and began taking notes.

"She was the woman who was wounded at the reenactment." My two cents' worth.

"Read about that," Cooper said. "Damn shame."

"That fixator," Kalea said, "keeps her tibia lined up until it heals." Then sobbed against Cheyenne.

I leaned into Aaron's arm. Out the window, motion. A white van encircled by a bold orange stripe scrunched to a stop behind the sheriff's cruiser. Paramedics in blue shirts spilled out, clambered across the veranda, and rushed up.

While they spoke with the EMTs, one pulled on sterile

gloves and inserted a catheter in Madison's wrist to start an IV, and the other unfolded a stair chair. "We'll have her on the way to the ER in a minute," the first said, "but we need to get some Zantac and Benadryl started."

Officer Cooper gestured to an open candy box. Only a few chocolates lay uneaten. "She allergic to chocolate?"

"I bought those for her," Cheyenne said. "She's a chocoholic." Brief smile.

He looked closely at the candy, then glanced to the dresser and Madison's laptop, across the windowsills and the mantel.

"Were any of you nearby?" he asked. Cheyenne, Kalea and I nodded.

"I'm in the next bedroom," I said, pointing to the wall behind Madison's bed.

"Kalea and I," Cheyenne said, "are around the corner."

"Did any of you hear anything during the night?" We shook our heads. "Or this morning?"

"Nothing," I said.

Cooper keyed his shoulder radio. "Dispatch, Cooper, over ... I have a suspicious anaphylaxis, adult female."

The paramedics rolled Madison's chair to the stairway and began her journey to Belle Mère.

What could he mean—suspicious?

Certainly not intentional, Grandpa Jack mused.

But if not chocolate, I pondered, something in last night's dinner?

"Request forensics," Cooper continued. "Roger that. 127 Beulah Road, off the Sandburg Pike, about twelve miles south of H-ville."

We followed Madison down the stairs and into the ambulance. Aunt Zelma's Lexus swerved onto the grass to let it pass. She didn't need psychic powers. "What's happened?"

The EMTs headed to their fire truck. One handed Cheyenne a card. "I really think she'll be okay," he said. "We've seen cases like this. Two days at Belle Mère. At the most."

"Madison had an allergic attack," I told Aunt Zelma. "A deputy sheriff's upstairs who thinks it's suspicious. Forensic investigator's been called."

My great-aunt dropped into an overstuffed chair and let out a long breath. "Oh for pity's sake," she said. For a moment she gazed through an old window at a distorted view of Mt. Pisgah, then back. "Oh God … my crying last night."

When I was a public affairs officer and editor of our shipboard news, it was my job to keep up with everything on board the aircraft carrier. Since then I haven't considered myself a news hound or ambulance chaser. But today …

"I'm following the ambulance," I said.

Kalea jumped up and started for the door. As much as I would have preferred that Aaron come with us, he said he had to call Garner, so he'd stay at Kalorama. I had no idea what he might say to him, but didn't argue. It was safer that no one, especially Garner, guess that Clement Pritchard and I were in cahoots.

Cheyenne asked Kalea to phone her with any news. I couldn't believe that Shy wasn't going. There was definitely something amiss in that marriage.

On the way, I checked with Kalea. "Why do you think Shy-Mom didn't come with us?"

She clicked her phone on and off a couple of times and watched houses at the edge of Hendersonville sweep past.

"Any ideas?"

"I think she doesn't love us as much as she used to."

That might explain a few things, Grandpa Jack whispered.

I kept my NASCAR driver tendencies mostly under control and we still made it to Belle Mère in twelve and a half minutes and lucked into a parking spot close to the ER entrance.

Chapter 50

It's in my nature to imagine the glass half full rather than half empty, but in the few seconds while the emergency room receptionist focused on her computer screen, I tried not to imagine Kalea's reaction if Madison didn't survive. Dear God, no.

The receptionist gave us an institutional smile. "She's with one of our best, Dr. Smythe."

With a glance at my C.S.I. assistant, I did my best to keep my anxiety hidden. Kalea would be worried enough for both of us.

"We don't allow visitors in there while she's in treatment," said the receptionist. "But you're welcome to wait right over there. I'll let you know when she's been taken to recovery."

Kalea and I retreated to a waiting area where patients with less than life-threatening conditions and their caregivers waited their turn. Kalea faced a mute screen on which Andy Griffith was explaining something to Opie. I poured myself a cup of worse than day-old Navy coffee.

Wayland's death and the earlier attempts on Madison's life seemed like a prologue to today. But even if her condition was extremely serious, I wasn't ready to think it had been an attempt on her life.

But ... whispered Grandpa Jack, *couldn't this be connected in some way to Wayland's murder?*

If so, I thought, it would take someone more psychically astute to make the connection.

Aunt Zelma had a word for this feeling of confusion and helplessness. I was bumfuzzled.

"I'm scared," Kalea said.

"I know, Kiddo. Me too." It was spooky to be back at the hospital where Madison's leg had been put back together, where she had begun healing. Where, in the middle of the night, I learned why she had planned this trip. Where she had warned me against meeting Ned at Brantleigh on a gloomy wet day. The same emergency room where I'd rushed my comatose Aunt Zelma—

Something like a gentle breeze brushed my shoulder. On the TV, Barney burst into the station. For an instant, I thought Grandpa Jack had shuffled back into his mortal coil.

"Ms. Summers?"

"Yes?"

Dr. Marian Smythe introduced herself and led us to Madison's bed.

Kalea cringed at the sight of her mom with tubes in her nose. "What's all that?"

"Oxygen," the doctor said. "It's helping your mom breathe."

Madison looked far more peaceful than she had this morning. Some of her natural color had returned to her face.

"We're probably going to need to keep her for a few days."

"Please explain," I said, "what's going on."

"Ms. Lerrimore has had a severe allergic reaction. Although she hasn't regained consciousness, with the tincture of time, I feel sure she will."

Kalea frowned. "What's that mean?"

"What it means is that her brain hasn't awakened yet. We don't know when this allergic reaction happened. But we can guess it may have been last evening or during the night. Has either of you any idea if she ingested anything unusual yesterday?"

"Not that I know of," I said. Kalea shook her head.

The doctor flipped a page in Madison's chart. "The med techs noticed a box of candy by her bed."

"Mom loves chocolate. She can't be allergic to it."

"Let's go sit," Dr. Smythe said.

The idea of leaving Madison lying there unconscious as if she were dying made me nauseous. Kalea, though, seemed to be on some kind of autopilot.

Dr. Smythe's empathy seemed genuine. Medical schools, I thought, must finally be coaching interpersonal skills. We followed her to a consultation room and sat at a tiny coffee table.

"Can we get back to the question," I said. "What happened?"

"Anaphylaxis is what happened."

Kalea frowned. "What's ... a-fan-a-lax?"

"Anaphylaxis is ... a type of allergic reaction," Smythe began. "It closes your throat and stops your breathing."

"How do you know that ... afan ... is what happened?"

"Several things. Hives, constriction of her trachea and bronchial tubes, and her tongue was swollen," Dr. Smythe said.

"How did it happen?"

"It's triggered by something the person is allergic to. Even if they don't know they have the allergy. Do you know if she had any food allergies? Fruits, vegetables, spices, milk, or eggs?"

"I have a friend in Maryland who's allergic to peanuts," Kalea said. "We can't even bring a peanut butter sandwich to school."

"People can be allergic to bee stings," Dr. Smythe said.

"Can't be that," Kalea said. Last summer she was stung

by yellow-jackets that came out of the ground. They hurt for a while, but—"

"So what could have triggered this?" I asked.

"We don't know," she said. "In a situation like this, we call it idiopathic anaphylaxis."

"Let me get this straight," I said. "You're calling it idiopathic simply because you can't identify the trigger."

"That's the size of it."

Recent events came to mind. "Any chance it could have been a poisoning?"

"There aren't any poisons we know of that could trigger an anaphylactic reaction."

"So what could have … no, *might* have caused it?" I asked.

"Nuts and some seafoods, typically shellfish, can trigger anaphylactic shock," she said. "But, other than the chocolate, we don't think Ms. Lerrimore had eaten anything since dinner."

"So what's her prognosis?"

"She'll recover, but it may be several hours." She chuckled. "You two staying here won't speed her recovery."

Dr. Smythe took both our phone numbers and promised to let us know when Madison was awake.

In spite of the EMT's assurance, I was worried for my friend and mentor. She had endured enough and I didn't believe there was anything like karmic punishment for trying to kill her stepdad.

Chapter 51

Back at Kalorama, we joined Aunt Zee and Shy in the salon. Kalea explained that Madison had "a-fan-a—"

"Anaphylaxis?" Aunt Zee said.

"That's it. Mom wasn't conscious yet but the doctor said she'd probably be able to come home in a couple of days."

Cheyenne listened halfheartedly as I expanded on what we'd learned about anaphylactic shock or more precisely what we hadn't learned. "The doc called it idiopathic," I said. "Means they don't have a clue."

Cheyenne turned her attention back to her laptop.

To an investment website, I noticed.

Aunt Zee pulled her basket of stones toward her, selected a rough-hewn dark blue crystal, and held it up to sunlight streaming through a window.

Aaron was in the kitchen adding a splash of water to his tumbler of rum. His phone lay on the kitchen table.

Kalea gestured to the door. We walked across the veranda and down between the lions. Fading blooms on the Koreanspice shrubs signaled the preparation for next spring's display. In the perennial bed around the fountain, late tulips, poppies, and purple coneflowers nodded in the sun. My mind was on Madison and I had no doubt that Kalea's was too. We headed across the lawn toward the formal rose garden until Kalea stopped so suddenly that I nearly tripped. We stood beside the stone marker of the unknown bushwhacker. "Something's definitely wrong between my moms."

I'd sensed a shift but been afraid to acknowledge it. "Has Madison said any more about staying in North Carolina?"

Kalea was thoughtful. "I s'pose that could be their

problem."

"They're both under a lot of stress—"

"Especially Shy-Mom. She acts different."

I embraced Kalea in a hug unlike I'd ever given anyone before. She was so vulnerable, so young, but so mature for her age. She was almost exactly the same age I'd been when my mom deserted our family. It was the worst time in my life and I'd never completely gotten over it.

But it's hard to remember feelings from back then—except the awful emptiness when she left.

I released my young friend. "Let's get Madison well again," I said. "Maybe everything will straighten itself out." I leaned into another hug and kissed Kalea's cheek. It was painful to see her usual optimism in a nosedive. Hoping to sound an upbeat note, I added, "We have the Brantleigh reception to look forward to." Kalea attempted a brave grin.

Back inside, Aaron was doing his best to maintain a pleasant tone of voice on his phone and nearing the bottom of his drink. "I'm being recalled," he mouthed as I reached for the Glen Fiddich.

Kalea, on the sofa, was back with her forensics book.

My aunt, with her basket of stones, was arranging a miniature Stonehenge meditation circle. She placed the craggy blue crystal in the center and considered the effect.

"Mind if I join you?"

She turned her head. "Sure, but don't expect an explanation."

I sat apart so as not to disrupt—what was it—her psychic energy field? "Someday," she said, "you'll mature into your psychic self and won't need me."

I took a tentative sip of Scotch.

Aunt Zee smiled enigmatically. "By the way … your

Saturn return—"

"My *what?*"

"Saturn return." She looked up from her arrangement of stones. "Saturn makes a revolution around the sun—"

"Have you become an astrologer too?"

She laughed. "Isn't everyone?"

My turn to laugh.

"Has anyone ever told you you're a typical Taurus?"

I took another sip. "Not anything I've ever wondered about."

"I could fill you in." She glanced at her Stonehenge circle and back to me.

"Back to our ringed planet." I inhaled the single malt's smoky fragrance and reluctantly tuned in to my astrology lesson.

"It takes Saturn about twenty-nine and a half years to make a full cycle around the sun. Or … from wherever it was the moment you were born … till it returns to the same place."

To say I wasn't interested in Saturn, its cycles, or its rings would have been an understatement. But I said nothing. Through an open window, I began hearing crickets or perhaps it was the first chirrups of late summer locusts.

"Your Saturn returns, more or less every thirty years, are pivot points in your life."

My recent return to civilian life at the age of twenty-nine could qualify as my first.

"So it's usual," she continued, "to consider Saturn's first return—as your transition to adulthood."

"Are you suggesting that I'm a freshly hatched adult?" Without intending to trivialize my aunt's ideas, I had to smile. Crystal-crunchers can harbor curious beliefs.

"What I am suggesting," she said, is that your early thirties is a time for assessing where you've been and where you're going. And I've been under the impression that you and your Navy friend were on a connection course."

Did I need this well-intentioned prodding? Deserve it? That was a subject I had no interest in pursuing. Especially today. *So change the subject,* Grandpa Jack suggested.

"Are you hungry?" My stomach had been sending signals. "But I doubt if you feel any more like putting a meal together than I do."

My aunt exhaled forcefully, annoyed at my shift. "We could send out for pizza."

An hour later, Aunt Zelma, Shy, Kalea, Aaron, and I sat looking at each other over a pair of pizzas, one vegetarian and the other loaded. I poured tumblers of chardonnay for Shy and myself and, ignoring Grandpa Jack's whisper about contributing to the delinquency of a minor, a finger for Kalea. After a sip, my young assistant surprised us with a smile of approval.

Aaron had another dark rum grog and Aunt Zelma poured herself an amontillado.

"I might have known," Aunt Zelma said.

"About what?" said Cheyenne.

"Madison's gray aura."

"Gray aura?" said Shy. "What d'you mean?"

"Aunt Zelma has what's called the second sight," I said. "She sees things that none of us can see, and sometimes even before they happen. So you can interpret that any way you like."

Aaron helped himself to a wedge of the loaded pizza but said nothing, communicating his total disbelief in the existence of auras or the second sight.

"If I'd had any sense," Aunt Zelma said, "I would have connected my tears with Madison. I'm so sorry. I thought when we'd all gone to bed the danger was over."

Chapter 52

"I need to call Garner," Aaron said as he tucked the last morsel of pizza into his mouth.

If Garner had been monitoring Clement Pritchard, I wondered if he'd seen the sheriff's cruisers or the EMS van this morning. Not that they could be seen by driving past Kalorama's big iron gate. The emergency vehicles had been out of sight beyond the bend of the boxwood-lined drive. But if he'd only seen Aaron arrive, by now he should assume that "Pritchard" and Madison and I were in a huddle over his appraisal and the "Myrtle Beach investment opportunity."

André, Aunt Zee's big poodle, followed Aaron and me down the steps from the veranda, and, after a short visit to the shrub border, accompanied us on a hand-holding tour of the grounds. Like planchettes wandering the surface of a ouija board, we found ourselves approaching the cursed swimming pool.

"What'll you tell him?"

"What else? That Madison's back in the hospital," Aaron said. "D'you think she'll be okay?"

"She's a tough cookie."

"This whole charade," Aaron said, "depends on her approval."

"She'll be on board," I said, with my fingers crossed. "I'll explain it to her. She'll be cool."

"Then what?"

"You need to keep the pretense going with Garner."

A pair of sun-warmed Wedgewood blue Adirondack chairs at the edge of the pool beckoned. I twisted mine away from the water so I wouldn't hear the dim echo of Josh's splash. André lay between us on the flagstone deck, head on paws, a portrait of canine contentment.

Aaron stared into the water. I reached to squeeze his hand. "You've got to keep him on the hook."

"Right. But how?"

"You could tell him I took your appraisal and the inheritance investment idea to Cheyenne," I said. "And she said she'd discuss it with Madison as soon as she's back from the hospital."

A pair of dragonflies helicoptered briefly over the swimming pool then darted off in search of unchlorinated water.

"Might work," Aaron said. "As long as I can get my theoretical hooks on Wayland's theoretical flag fortune by the weekend."

"You could embellish your tale by saying that Cheyenne agrees that they'll search for any of the flag money that Wayland kept. But she's sure that Madison will agree with the plan so she's written an earnest money check."

André raised his head to check out another dragonfly on reconnaissance. Chomped the air and returned to the land of contentment.

Aaron gave my hand a quick squeeze and fist-pumped the morning air. "You're a genius," he said. "But if Shy meets him at the reception, she might have to confirm the story."

"If she decides to attend."

Aaron smiled, nodding thoughtfully. "What about Madison?"

"Fingers crossed. But our scenario will work even if neither Madison nor Shy are there."

André rose, did his imitation of a runner's stretch, and stood expectantly as if to say "It's time for a reward for guarding you." With no hush puppies in my pockets, all I could do was fuzzle his ears.

Aaron gazed at a pattern of tiny wind ripples on the pool surface, tapped his phone on, speed-dialed and, for my benefit, switched to speakerphone.

"Claude?"

"How's it hangin' man?"

"Our golden goose almost bought the farm last night."

"What farm?"

"It's an expression for kicking the bucket," Aaron said. "No actual farm."

Panicked: "You mean the stepdaughter's dead?"

"She nearly died. She's back at the hospital."

"God ... Now I might never get my share."

What exactly would be a fair share of a criminal scam? Grandpa Jack pondered.

"Not to worry, Colonel." Aaron shoveled our rehearsed hash. "All in good time ..." After the assurance of Cheyenne's earnest money, Garner seemed reluctantly pacified.

"Do what you need to do," he said. "I'm counting on you. Big bonus if you have it by Saturday."

"For God's sake, man, what do you think's jazzing my jets?"

He clicked off the phone and gave me an affectionate grin. In the gloaming, a gentle breeze wafted the last remnants of Koreanspice perfume across our path as we dawdled back to the mansion.

+ + +

Mid-morning Tuesday, Aaron and I were sipping coffee in Aunt Zelma's kitchen. In the center of the table, flowers that Kalea and I had gathered yesterday tumbled from an antique cut-glass vase. "Cheyenne's at the local lawyer," I said, "discussing Wayland's will."

Aunt Zee had taken Kalea to play with the youngest descendants of Mrs. Sandburg's dairy goats.

Aaron and I were both looking forward to watching our reception scenario unfold. "Everything set for Saturday?" I asked. "Did Mr. Washington agree to meet us at the Lodge?"

"He's actually anxious now to have a look at Wayland's goodies cabinet before the reception."

"And …?"

"He'll only have time to make a preliminary appraisal so you can warn Madison not to expect a full valuation."

"What about—"

"Everything's cool. Jocelyn and Knowles are as good as waiting in the wings. How about Kalea?"

"She's good with it. And how's Clement Pritchard?"

"Pacing the Green Room. But—F.Y.I., the reception will have to be his last appearance. I have a verbal leave extension, but I need to get back to King's Bay on Sunday. The Deputy Commander wants me on deck bright-eyed and bushy-tailed Monday morning."

I cringed. "I'll miss you. I've been hoping we'd have more time."

"Not half as much as I'll miss you."

That, of course, led to a kiss and my suggestion to accompany him back to Vanderbilt Lodge.

The front door opened. Kalea and Aunt Zee walked in. For some reason, neither of us had heard footsteps on the veranda. "You two should do kissy-kissy," Kalea said, "when you're by yourselves."

It wouldn't have helped if I'd pointed out to her that until she barged in, we had been very much alone.

+ + +

I was worried that I hadn't heard from the hospital so, from Aaron's car, I phoned. The operator patched me through to Madison's room.

"Dr. Smythe is ready to kick me out," she said, "so if your aunt's willing to have a troublemaker back at Kalorama …"

Chapter 53

It's Saturday and Hubert Washington is examining a tarnished oval Civil War buckle from the top shelf of Wayland's display cabinet. "CS" is centered in the oval. He examines it briefly and turns it over. "These days I have to look carefully for counterfeits," he explains.

We've confirmed that he understands his role in our scenario. And, satisfied that he knows the road from the Lodge to Brantleigh Manor, we agree to rendezvous there, and leave Hubert examining a pair of squashed kepi caps.

My pulse increases as Aaron accelerates back toward Flat Rock to pick up the Kalorama contingent. If the afternoon unfolds as planned, it will not only spotlight Boscovus Dillingham's announcement of his Civil War museum but also launch Claude Garner toward his rendezvous with destiny.

Aaron and I walk our way through it. Step by step. Everything except my anxiety level is in readiness.

We park under Aunt Zelma's port-cochère only a half hour behind schedule. Our cohorts are on the veranda, finishing lunch. Madison seems fully recovered from her bout with anaphylaxis and Cheyenne has apparently decided to join the party. She wears a bright crimson dress that closely matches her lipstick. Madison, having graduated from the walker to crutches, wears a flowing skirt that mostly conceals the metal basket around her leg. My aunt has found a black velvet dress for Kalea that had been mine twenty-some years ago. To avoid her taffy-machine curse, I promise not to tease her about being the Lady in Black. Aunt Zelma's tangerine chiffon gown seems perfect for her position as the reigning queen of Western North Carolina history. She smiles at my choice of a white outfit topped with a red-white-and-blue infinity scarf as if this were the Fourth of July.

Aunt Zelma's not the NASCAR ace Aaron would have been, but the odds for our safe arrival in her SUV are significantly improved with her in the pilot's seat. Kalea in the co-pilot's seat explains the essentials of DNA profiling to Aunt Zee. Without the breeze I enjoyed in Aaron's convertible, I'm acutely aware that Western North Carolina is much warmer this week than when Madison and I arrived. In the middle row, Madison chats confidentially to Cheyenne. From the back seat, all I can make out is "... the flag Penny and I found in his closet ...."

With a scowl I can feel punch right through me, Cheyenne says, "What *about* a flag in Wayland's closet?"

Madison gives her the short version. "Penny and I think it was copied to make what Wayland sold to Grover Knowles."

I could add that it's worth a barrel of money. But I don't. One of Grandpa Jack's adages was that some things are better left unsaid.

Crossing the old Brantleigh Bridge across the French Broad, we see that the estate has been embellished for the event. The left gatehouse is topped with the North Carolina flag and the other, where I might have expected to see the infamous Stars and Bars, flies the original flag of the Confederacy, three broad stripes: red-white-red and, on the blue field, a circle of stars.

In front of the mansion, Aaron stops to straighten his bow tie and comments on the elaborately-carved fountain in the entry circle.

"There's a reproduction of it in a famous garden in

Georgetown," I tell him. Madison rewards me with a wink for remembering that field trip.

Under Brantleigh's red, white, and blue bunting-draped portico, Tobin and Mera welcome us. "So wonderful of you to come," they tell Aunt Zelma.

My aunt embraces Mera and endures a cheek-kiss from Tobin. "I'd like you to meet Penny, my grandniece from Maryland," she says. "And Penny's friends Madison and Cheyenne ... and their daughter Kalea." Kalea executes a mini-curtsy.

I tell them how much Madison and I enjoyed visiting their gardens.

"Madison," Tobin says, "we're terribly sorry about your accident at the reenactment."

She braces herself on one crutch, "I am too." Nods imperceptibly and smiles stoically.

I refrain from picking an argument over his use of the term "accident." After all, we're his guests.

"So glad you all could be here," Mera says. Then, glancing at Aaron, "And ...?"

"My second cousin ... at least twice removed," Aunt Zee improvises, "Clement Pritchard, from Florence. He's quite the Civil War enthusiast."

Mera extends her hand.

"The pleasure is all mine," Aaron gushes.

The Brantleys direct us through to the Great Hall.

The elegance of the huge room once again overwhelms.

Aaron is wide-eyed, in awe of the elegant floor-to-ceiling Palladian windows flanking the French doors to the parterre, and the two huge fireplaces that anchor each end of the big room. Above the south mantel is a magisterial portrait of Tobin's grandfather, the stern Cameron Brantley at his governor's desk, a North Carolina flag behind his shoulder.

Displays of red, white, and blue flowers in crystal vases on both mantels. On a grand piano, photos of Tobin as a child and of Tobin and Mera with dignitaries and political luminaries. Antique tapestries and gold-framed oil portraits adorn the walls. A Chopin nocturne turned low plays from hidden speakers.

Aunt Zelma points out an old-world-style fresco on the vaulted ceiling. "The marriage of Bacchus and Ariadne," she says. It's easy to imagine we've been transported to an Italian Renaissance villa.

Trompe l'oeil fresco cherubs on the ceiling appear to hold aloft the two most elaborate chandeliers I've ever seen. Around the room, rococo chairs, couches and love seats also give the impression of having come from an Italian castle. In each grouping, a glass-topped coffee table displays Civil War artifacts.

At the north fireplace, a flurry of chairs face tan curtains on a massive easel that hide Claude Garner's "surprise." We mosey to the opposite end where Henderson County's old money crowd is gathered at a broad bar. We ask for wine and a Sprite for Kalea. I'm handed a bulbous wineglass with a generous pour of oaky French Chardonnay.

Aaron excuses himself and slides into the library. He's back in two minutes and orders a sweet tea bourbon on the rocks.

"Mr. Washington?" I ask, between sips.

Aaron nods.

"Knowles?"

"Yep."

"The S.B.I.?"

"The tall woman—" he nods toward a statuesque pony-tailed blonde "—Jocelyn."

"The flag?"

"Ready." Kalea's Cheshire cat grin assures me she's primed.

All I need to know.

"The Gazette sent a photographer," Aaron adds, sipping his bourbon.

The photographer Madison and I had posed for at the bronze eagle is at the other end of the bar. I glance toward him. He nods briefly and returns to snapping Henderson County's upper crust.

Aunt Zelma's bridge partners Lynn and Gwen are already here. Madison introduces them to Cheyenne and explains Lynn's former connection to her stepfather. Lynn's wearing the same green sheath she wore to Zelma's catered Southern dinner. Emerald ear pendants swing under her blond page-boy just as delightfully today as then. Gwen, apparently a frequent guest here, brags that she and the Brantleys are donors to nearly every philanthropic cause in the county.

Cheyenne appears piqued by having to make nice with Aunt Zelma's friends, or maybe she's simply uninterested in the ornamentation in this museum-like house—acting like a sulky child who's been told to give up a play date to gain the munificence of a wealthy aunt. Madison and I wander to admire an antique bird's eye view of the entire Brantleigh estate—no doubt a gift from Frederick Law Olmsted to Governor Brantley when the landscape was new.

Movement at the arched opening. Claude Garner and Lorenzo Peters come through together. Peters, his craggy features easily recognized, goes directly to the bar. Garner, in khaki slacks and his houndstooth jacket, spots Aaron and makes a beeline for us. Aunt Zelma greets him, a history teacher to a former student. "If I were you," she says, "as soon as the Senator's museum opens, I'd plan to take my class."

"I'm sure it'll be great," says Garner, with a self-effacing smile.

Aaron offers a collegial handshake. "Good to see you again, Colonel."

"Mr. Pritchard—" Garner glancing at me "—it appears you've made some progress."

"Sir," Aaron says in his Pritchard voice, "I'd like you to meet Penelope Summers, who was kind enough to show me Wayland's artifacts and convey my appraisal to—"

I offer my hand. "We met at my great-aunt's house."

"A pleasure to see you again," he says. "I was sorry to hear about Mr. Ferguson's death."

"Sad," I say, attempting to match Madison's acting ability. "He was a superb Olmsted interpreter."

Garner's smile morphs to mischievous. He glances at Aaron. "Let me grab a bourbon, then you and I can settle our business."

The three of us amble back to the bar. I stay close since Garner thinks Aaron's seduced me—or was it vice versa?

"I assume that's the new flag you mentioned," Aaron says, motioning to the easel.

"It's not *new*." Garner whispers angrily as he accepts his bourbon from the bartender. "It's an original."

"Sorry," Aaron whispers insincerely. He asks for a refill while I sip my wine tentatively, knowing I'll need all my senses to perform in our scenario.

"So," Aaron whispers, "how much did you get for it?"

"Dillingham wanted to spend a day with it before

finalizing the purchase. He's going to write me the check this afternoon."

"How much?" Aaron asks again.

Garner pretends to not be sure. Finally, under his breath, "Just south of a million."

"Blazes," says Aaron, "I'd no idea a battle flag would go for that much."

"Originals do, and they're damn difficult to find."

Aaron appears to be deep in thought, his eyes on Bacchus and Ariadne. "That's about the same as you said your friend sold the other flag for."

"You're right. About the same." Smirking, Garner adds, "But this time the money's not going through a crooked *middle*man."

"Speaking of middlemen, here's what got our ball rolling." Aaron hands Garner the bogus appraisal. It's immediately tucked in a jacket pocket.

"Penelope and I've met with both of the ladies—" Aaron angles his head toward Madison and Cheyenne who look up from their chat with Lynn and Gwen, having been prompted to reflect enthusiasm for Pritchard's investment scheme "—and we've searched for money Wayland may have squirreled away." Aaron's sorrowful expression reminds me of a kid with a bad report card. "But so far—no joy. What can I say?"

Garner stammers, "But you ... said ... by today—"

"I'd hoped to have it for you today but Madison's only been out of the hospital a couple of days." Aaron reaches into his jacket and hands Garner a bulging Vanderbilt Lodge envelope. "Earnest money ... just till they can find it or the estate is settled. So," he says, with an artificial smile, "never fear. You'll get—"

"What Wayland stole," Garner huffs.

Drinks in hand, I let Aaron and Garner wander to a settee under a wall tapestry depicting the Garden of Eden. Decorously arranged foliage obscures Adam and Eve's X-rated zones. Aaron chatters quietly, reaffirming the story we concocted.

Looking forward to showing my appreciation to Aaron tonight, I rejoin Team Kalorama, plucking cubes of cheeses, grapes, and strawberries from the hors d'oeuvres. At the bar, conversations and convivial laughter continue, punctuated by smiles.

Chapter 54

Movement at the arch catches my attention. A man, alone, comes into the Great Hall. He's elderly, has a slight limp and wears jeans, the default uniform for men of almost all income brackets in this part of the world. Mostly, the blue variety. His are black. Vietnam vet?

As he comes closer, I see he's a reenactor: unkempt hair, mutton-chop sideburns. Eyebrows up, something's surprised him. Then I realize it's not surprise, he's aloof. He's among strangers.

Kalea guides us to chairs under a tapestry depicting Plato in his Groves of Academe. I'm focused on the man. I don't hear Shy and Madison presumably discussing their return to Maryland. The man scans the crowd. Looking for a friend?

Bingo! Black jeans and mutton chops—It's the *man in black* with Mensa sideburns. A slight limp! The man who was watching the day we found Wayland. The man who explained about reenactors role-playing wounded soldiers. Angelo!

I look around hoping no one noticed my quick intake of breath. This was not the image of the sociopath I'd conjured. Although he'd been clever at hiding from his parole officer and the S.B.I., I realize that I might have expected him to show up today hoping for an opportunity to wreak his revenge on Madison. He's at the bar, wallet in hand, unaware the drinks are free.

"Kalea," I whisper, "you up for a Junior Police Academy test?"

Angelo Scappare accepts a tumbler of something, turns from the bar and glances our way.

"What's up?" says Kalea, her face brimming with

anticipation.

Angelo zeroes in on Madison. A blink of recognition? Then turns to me. And back to Madison.

"There's an S.B.I. agent here."

Her eyes get large. "What's *he* here for?"

"*She's* Mr. Brantley's granddaughter. Jocelyn. She works in the same office with Agent Brown."

I shift my eyes to signal Kalea to look toward Angelo. She glances ... turns back ... and whispers, "The man in *bla*—?" Her eyes enlarge again.

"Jocelyn's the tall blonde." I motion toward her chatting with her grandfather. "Wander over to her, quietly get her attention and let her know that Agent Brown connected this Angelo guy to Wayland's death and he's *here* stalking his second target."

Kalea nods and wanders toward Tobin Brantley and Jocelyn as if to listen in on their conversation. I return to the others and debate whether to tell Madison her stepfather's murderer is in the room. Quickly realize that might lead to a confrontation we wouldn't be able to control. So, no. Except to Aaron. And trust the S.B.I. cavalry will soon be galloping toward our pass.

I sidle up to Aaron and ask to have a few words alone. Hoping Garner thinks we're discussing Wayland's artifacts, I take thirty seconds to bring him up to speed.

"You're sure?"

"Kalea's telling Jocelyn."

Angelo's antennae continue twitching in my direction. I look back at Aaron, doing my best to appear nonchalant.

While Jocelyn casually glances around the room, Kalea returns. Without a visible reaction, Jocelyn recognizes the missing parolee, excuses herself from her grand-dad and heads to the library. She holds the door for an elderly cigar-smoking gent with amber-tinted aviator glasses maneuvering his wheelchair into the room. The guest of honor. Boscovus Dillingham rolls his wheelchair toward the covered easel.

Angelo briefly tracks the wheelchair then returns to his vigil. Madison chats with Cheyenne and Aunt Zelma, unaware of danger.

Kalea, reporting to me, her back to Angelo, gives me a surreptitious thumbs-up. "She's calling the S.B.I. duty officer," she whispers. "Says no worries, they'll be on their way."

The S.B.I. office is up the highway in Asheville, Grandpa Jack whispers. *Not exactly around the proverbial corner.*

My pulse accelerates. How many options are there for a mentally unbalanced attacker at close range?

Jocelyn comes back and follows the wheelchair to where Tobin Brantley waits like a bridegroom. She whispers to Senator Dillingham who pulls an envelope from a jacket pocket and unfolds a sheet of paper for her inspection.

Jocelyn hands the document back and gives a furtive smile in Aaron's direction.

Garner is happiness personified. The moment he's waited for. He smiles at Aaron, acknowledging their comradeship. Aaron fingers his Pritchard bowtie.

Tobin Brantley, standing beside his friend's wheelchair, claps for attention. The hubbub recedes. His stentorian welcome draws our attention.

We find five chairs at the end of a row and I take the one on the end, ready to play my part. Madison is beside me, where I can guard her.

I'm wary, as Angelo, carrying his unsipped drink and feigning interest in the activity at the easel, moves closer.

"Back in the 1940s," Aunt Zelma whispers to us, "Boscovus Dillingham was a very young senator. Exceedingly wealthy. Now owns the finest collection of Civil War artifacts outside of the Smithsonian." I stumble through the mental math and realize he's in his late nineties.

The photographer from the Gazette materializes.

"Ladies and gents," Tobin begins, "friends of the South and friends of Senator Boscovus Dillingham. Welcome."

Garner and Aaron smile broadly.

For entirely *different reasons*, whispers Grandpa Jack.

I nurse my panic by pretending to follow Mr. Brantley's introduction and note that Aaron is able to mask his with a purposeful grin.

Angelo, his back against a Palladian window, follows Mr. Brantley's words but keeps an eye on us. As long as he keeps his distance, I won't need any of the moves that sent Ned to his death. My pulse ratchets higher, hoping for Agent Brown's speedy arrival.

"Thank you for taking time from this lovely weekend," Tobin Brantley says, "to honor your friend and mine, Senator Boscovus Dillingham." Brantley glances at the long-retired senator and claps. Dillingham nods as we all applaud. Angelo hesitantly joins in.

When the applause slackens, Brantley continues. "On the hundred and fiftieth anniversary of the War of Northern Aggression … we're celebrating an incredibly generous gift from Senator Dillingham to the citizens of Henderson County ... and the nation. His entire collection of Civil War accoutrements—"

"Tobin," Boscovus interrupts, "could you refrain from using language us ole southern boys weren't never learned?" Laughter.

For the zillionth time I glance at the archway hoping to see Agent Brown with whatever troops she'll bring to subdue Angelo. I wipe perspiration from the back of my neck.

Tobin resumes. "In other words, the senator's incredibly large collection of genuine Civil War stuff." Tobin glances at his friend again, they both laugh, and more laughter ripples the room.

"This man is a living legend," Tobin says. "We're glad to be your friends. Take it away, Boscovus."

The photographer moves close and frames a shot of the Senator in his wheelchair beside the curtained easel in readiness for the promised highlight of the afternoon.

Angelo slides imperceptibly slowly along the wall, closer to the action. And to us. No Agent Brown.

"Long ago, I promised not to fail all y'alls' parents, and I don't intend to start now." Laughter erupts again. "So if you have no objection, folks," Dillingham says, "I'll stay in this contraption rather than try to stand and, more than likely, fail at that." Laughs and more applause. "I would have won again in '56, don't you know, and kept on working for you … might still be in Washington … if Mr. Stevenson hadn't been so popular hereabouts." Another round of applause.

Dillingham raises his palm. "But let me tell y'all what's happening right now in Henderson County. First, we're going to convert the old courthouse into the Museum of the Civil War. And it'll be no never mind to me if y'all want to call it the Dillingham—"

We stand and applaud even more loudly. The Gazette photographer snaps several of Boscovus pausing and us applauding.

"Y'all know I've collected a few things here and there that were everyday items among the brave men who fought in the War of Northern Aggression." Murmurs of approval. "And a few things them Yankees had, as well. Most of those—" he sneaks a glance at Tobin "—ac*coote*rmonts will be at the museum ... and ... anything more I can add before I join the six-feet-under gang."

Laughter and applause.

Tobin takes the microphone. "There won't be enough space for everything to be on display at the same time." Tobin gestures that his friend's collection is too wide and too tall. Followed by laughs. Tobin hands the microphone back to Dillingham.

"The centerpiece of my museum," Dillingham says, "will be what I'm about to reveal." He rises hesitantly from the wheelchair, fondles tasseled cords at the easel, prepares to open the curtains. "Drum roll please." A crisply uniformed snare drummer from Etowah High School begins: *zzhh-zzhh-zzhh-zzhh* ...

Garner glows like a new parent. Aaron smiles appreciatively and glances at Angelo.

Dillingham tugs the cords slowly until the flag is fully revealed. "As my educated friend Tobin would say, Voilâ!" The drum roll ends with a rim shot smack. Dillingham beams at his acquisition and turns to us. Looks across the gathering. "You historians here know all about the Battle of Asheville just three days before Appomattox. Well, this here's the recently discovered Yankee battle flag from the 101st Ohio Infantry regiment that Asheville's Silver Grays repulsed on that occasion." The round of applause hurts my ears.

"Mr. Claude Garner," the senator calls, "could you please come forward?" Garner, all smiles, joins Dillingham. The senator takes Garner's hand. "Here's the man who found this flag for me. Claude Garner. From Flat Rock."

Garner nods, acknowledging the introduction. Aaron stands alongside.

Dillingham returns to his wheelchair. "Now, I'll officially purchase this flag from my new friend."

Tobin slides a small desk with an open check book to the senator and hands him a pen. Dillingham turns to Garner. "Shall we keep this incredibly large amount a secret between you and me?"

"Your call, sir," Garner says.

"I think we'll keep it confidential." Dillingham uncaps the pen, ready to write. "How would you like this made out?"

Aaron leans in and with practiced panache gently closes the check-book.

For Jocelyn and her plainclothes officers, Hubert Washington, Kalea and me, it's *Showtime!*

Dillingham stares up at Aaron, puzzled. Tobin Brantley registers angry surprise. Guests in the front row are bewildered. But perhaps this was planned. Maybe a prank? They look around but find no grins, so not a joke. What then?

I step into the breach. "Senator," I say, "We're sorry to interrupt, sir, but I wouldn't write that check if I were you."

Garner, under his breath, "What the hell?"

Dillingham's experiencing what Aunt Zelma would call a mighty vexation. He squawks: "What are you trying to say?"

"I think you'll find, sir," says Aaron, "that a competent appraiser would declare this flag essentially worthless."

A querulous buzz erupts.

Dillingham attempts to rise from his wheelchair. His face reddens, his nose flares. "Y'all are pullin' my friggin' leg," he shouts, and sits back down.

Garner comes toward me, glances uncertainly at Aaron

and, angrily, back to me. "What in hell do you know—"

The room erupts. Aunt Zelma pretends she doesn't understand what's happening. All I can make out is "bumfuzzled."

Madison and Cheyenne feign bewilderment.

On cue, Kalea slips toward the library. Tobin Brantley's jaw drops, a poster boy for incredulity.

Grover Knowles, a red and blue foulard in the neck of his white shirt, carries a bendy tubular package in our direction. He's accompanied by Hubert Washington, whose open-collar Madras shirt complements his cappuccino skin.

Angelo Scappare is now as confused as everyone else. And oblivious of the fact that he's about to be a cornered viper.

"Senator Dillingham," I say, "I'd like to introduce Mr. Grover Knowles." Knowles extends a hand to the senator.

Dillingham, perplexed, stares at the newcomer. Tobin Brantley steps back.

"Mr. Knowles," Aaron says, "would you show the senator what you've brought?" Knowles rips open his package, unrolls the flag and holds it aloft by two corners. Identical to the one on the easel. Dillingham gasps.

"Would you tell us where you obtained this flag and what you paid?" Aaron asks.

"Let's just say I paid a great deal of money and if the person I bought this from were still alive, I'd sue his butt for fraud."

Shocked silence. The senator puts his face in his hands. Garner glances left and right, begins to move. Jocelyn nods toward the French doors as a pair of burly plainclothes officers come in.

"I've also asked a certified Civil War appraiser to join

us," I say, as Hubert Washington walks up. Dillingham trembles like he's escaping from a barroom brawl. I hope we won't need a defibrillator.

"Senator," I say, "I'd like you to meet Mr. Hubert Washington. He's an I.S.A.-certified appraiser of militaria."

"I'm pleased to make your acquaintance," Dillingham says, muddled. "I guess."

"Mr. Washington," I say, "would you take a close look at Senator Dillingham's new flag?"

"May I?" he asks Dillingham who nods but seems fearful … or is it confusion? That he's being shown up as a fool easily parted from his money?

Washington rubs the material between a thumb and finger, holds a white stripe up to the light of a chandelier, checks the binding, and, using a jeweler's loupe, scrutinizes a hand-embroidered star.

Dillingham and Tobin watch intently, both seemingly on the cusp of a heart attack. Something about the star seems to catch the appraiser's interest. He moves the loupe to another. He brings the middle red stripe close and studies the embroidered lettering. He lets the flag fall back, pockets the loupe, and shakes his head. "I'm sorry, Senator. This flag is a reproduction and not a very good one at that. Appears to have been made by the same person who made the one for Mr. Knowles."

Garner slides out of the limelight and makes his way toward the French doors where he's confronted by the two plainclothes officers who lock his arms behind his back. I hear the muffled ratchet of handcuffs closing.

Watching this activity, Angelo undoubtedly wonders if other undercover officers are nearby, perhaps re-evaluating his plan.

Expect the unexpected, Grandpa Jack whispers. *Cornered vipers are unpredictable.*

"So what if I've bought a fake?" Dillingham growls, defeated. "If it's good enough to fool me, it'll look good enough to our museum visitors."

"Senator," Aaron says, "you haven't actually bought it yet." Aaron crooks a finger toward the library. Kalea reappears, using a strapped-on handle to heft a mover's fine art box.

Calmed, Dillingham says, "You're absolutely right, son. I haven't rightly bought the damn thing." A defibrillator won't be necessary.

Kalea carries the movers box to the little table. Hubert Washington helps her open it and together they hold up the framed flag for inspection.

"Ohhh." The senator sucks in a deep breath at the same time as the guests. "There's another one?"

Garner, flanked by the two officers, collapses in a chair.

Washington hands the senator his appraisal of this third one. "This one, sir, is the original." Dillingham has the same reaction as the crowd—stunned silence.

The senator looks up to Washington's confident face. "You sure about this, son?"

"As sure as I know you were the man my granddaddy voted for a long while back. He still has the picture you autographed. 'Thanks for your help, Mr. Washington,' you wrote. You might not remember, but he does."

Dillingham blinks back tears.

"We have a suggestion we think you'll like, Senator," Kalea says brightly. She's worked on this speech for the last two days. "If you're willing to write that check to Mr. Knowles for the same amount as you were ready to pay for the other one, then, on behalf of my moms, I can present you with the real one. I hope you'll be proud to have the original in your new museum … sir."

I start to clap and the assemblage becomes a sea of acclamation. When Dillingham regains his composure, he reaches to Kalea for a double handshake and rolls himself back to the check-writing table. "Pay to the order of …" He looks up to Knowles.

"Grover Knowles, Junior."

"Grover … Knowles … Junior," the senator says as he crafts the name and adds his signature.

"Now sir." He turns to face Knowles. "Shall we keep this figure confidential?"

"Reckon we should, sir."

The applause is deafening. The crowd gets to their feet. Cheyenne, grim, joins in the applause. Madison and Kalea share knowing grins.

I glance at Angelo. He's pulling a sharpened stick slowly from his jacket sleeve. The unexpected. Apparently decided to make his move while everyone's attention is on Dillingham and Knowles.

He moves closer. I stand to block him from Madison. Strangely, he looks directly at me and, almost in my face, growls just above a whisper: "Your turn."

Adrenalin fuels my attempt to seize the stick. He twists and all I can do is grab at his other arm. Several nearby men jump up to hold him. "Wayland's killer," I whisper to Madison. Shy, and Aunt Zelma back away from the scuffle. Kalea grabs for the stick and misses.

The angered viper, both arms restrained, waves the pointed stick helplessly. The tip is stained.

"Get back," I yell. "Poisoned tip!"

Kalea steps away as another man slams into Angelo's back and another pins the arm with the stick. A third man goes for the wrist and bends it backward. Way back. His fingers, forced to relax, allow me to take the stick.

Agent Brown and a pair of uniforms race through the French doors, come to our aid, and quickly twist Angelo's arms behind his back to be handcuffed. I give Lisa the stick while the two officers hustle their prisoner toward the French doors. "Careful," I blurt. "Curare on the tip."

"My God," Madison says, finally comprehending what's happened. "I can't believe …"

In that instant, I too realize what has just happened. Angelo has been under the impression that *I* was Wayland's daughter. The photo Angelo had seen in prison had been taken when Madison was a teenager —a blond teenager. My chest pounds.

He wasn't tracking Madison. The day we found Wayland, at the reenactment, and today, *I* was the second target.

The parallels in Madison's and my life began when we planned retribution for our parental betrayals. According to conventional wisdom, parallel lines don't ever meet. Yet, against all the odds since Euclid demonstrated the impossibility, today ours intersected.

Fear and incomprehension on Aaron's face. "Tell you later," I huff.

Momentarily distracted by the Angelo chaos, Dillingham turns his attention back to his checkbook. He rips the newly written check from the binder, hands it to Knowles, and looks up at Hubert Washington. "Please accept my thanks for your help, Mr. Washington."

Then he beckons to Kalea, raises her hand to his lips.

Another tear dribbles down his elderly cheek.

She'll have one hell of a story for the Junior Police Academy.

Chapter 55

"Bravo, Punkin."

Both of us were still breathing fast but slowly recovering our equilibrium. The big room seethed with surprised guests all talking excitedly, trying to make sense of the drama still unfolding.

Jocelyn and her two S.B.I. officers followed Agent Brown and the Angelo posse, propelling the handcuffed Garner out the French doors through which he had hoped to escape. The only words I could hear were "... anything you say may be used against you ..." He was, I presumed, under arrest for attempted felony fraud. On his way to booking, maybe he'd recall the envelope Aaron gave him—the one he'd hoped would hold a check for a million dollars. Unfortunately for Garner, it was the same $500. he'd advanced to Aaron. Possibly enough for a defense lawyer's first hour.

Cheyenne joined us, seemingly pleased at the resolution of this rapid-fire turn of events. We each shook Senator Dillingham's hand and wished him success with the new museum. He thanked Kalea and her moms again for the genuine flag.

"Happy we could help," said Kalea.

Madison and Hubert Washington huddled over a portfolio with a preliminary appraisal of Wayland's antiques. Aaron and Aunt Zelma returned to the bar, and Cheyenne, saying she'd take another look around the gardens, disappeared through the French doors to the Parterre Garden.

Kalea and I went to the hors d'oeuvres table to pilfer a snack for the trip home. I picked up a handful of nuts. "Just grab a fistful," I urged.

"Peanuts, pecans, walnuts," she recited. "Almonds ... cashews—" She paused. "What're these?" She held out two wobbly shaped nuts.

"Macadamias."

Kalea's wide eyes bulged and her mouth hung open.

"What on earth ... Kalea, what is it?"

"Wh-where do they come from?"

"Hawaii."

+ + +

My time with Aaron was about to end. He'd start back to King's Bay early tomorrow. If we were to make the most of it, I needed to get the gang back to Kalorama before the afternoon became evening.

Since I was unaccustomed to Southern farewells, getting everyone back to my aunt's SUV was the most awkward cat-herding I'd ever done. Cheyenne wandered in the Parterre Garden. Madison and Lynn were sipping wine with Aunt Zelma and Mera. Aaron was thanking Jocelyn for her assistance with our scenario. After a few minutes with Tobin and Dillingham, expressing our appreciation for their forbearance at our surprise alteration of the afternoon's program, I signaled discreetly to each of the Kalorama crowd: "wind it up, we're outta here."

On the road back to Flat Rock, we were quiet until Aunt Zee turned onto the Sandburg Pike. Out of the blue, she said, "I had an interesting chat with Colonel Clayton this morning."

"You mean Lorenzo Peters?" I said.

"No dear, *the* Colonel George Wesley Clayton. During my meditation."

"*Really?*" Cheyenne pronounced it like she'd just heard the earth was flat.

"I have no idea why he came, but then I never know when anyone's going to show up."

I swept aside my disbelief. "So what did you and the colonel talk about?"

I lurched against my seat belt as Aunt Zelma braked to avoid a young bicyclist crossing on a red light. An angry horn and brake screech behind us.

"Whatever else?" she said. "The Battle of Asheville."

Our light was still green as we moved across the intersection. "The colonel said he wanted to make sure I understood that when he rounded up his Silver Grays to meet the Ohioans he had no idea that the Appomattox surrender was imminent. He was certain the Ohioans didn't know either."

Zelma slowed for the left turn onto Beulah Road. "The colonel also asked if I knew about old Percival's nephew, Thaddeus. I said I'd never heard of him. He said it was Captain Thaddeus Porter who did himself proud that day as the ordnance officer in charge of the cannons."

"Did he say how many Thaddeus had?"

"There were just the two, the same as at the reenactment. But his crews were so well trained in rapid reloading," he said, "that the Ohioans thought they had at least six."

"No wonder they skedaddled back to Tennessee."

"I tell you," she continued, "it was a surprise to me. Don't you think it would be nice to have a photo of Captain Thaddeus at Kalorama? Among the thousands in the Mathew Brady collection at the National Archives, there's got to be at least one of him. I've asked Lorenzo if he can find one."

Chapter 56

As soon as Aunt Zee came to a stop, Kalea, saying nothing, jumped out, ran up the steps, and disappeared into the house. "I wonder what ignited her jets," Madison said.

Aaron and I had started across the lawn toward the swimming pool when Kalea, out of breath, caught up with us. "Found something," she huffed. It was the candy box from Madison's bedside table. She tapped a finger on one side.

I had to squint to read the tiny print.

The three of us hurried back to the veranda where Aunt Zelma, Cheyenne and Madison sipped amontillado from heritage goblets.

"My esteemed colleague has an announcement," I said. Aaron and I sat on the loveseat opposite Shy and Maddy, leaving Kalea to expound her theory.

"It was really very simple," Kalea began, sounding exactly like an elementary school play version of Sherlock. "The mystery of the ... idio—" she peered at me—

"Madison's diagnosis of idiopathic anaphylaxis," I said, assuming the multisyllabic diagnosis was the stumbling block.

Cheyenne extended her arm around Madison and pulled her close.

"In first grade," she said, "one day I was sick and had to stay home from school. I remembered Maddy-Mom telling me about how she was sick on your honeymoon."

I understood where this was headed.

"The doctor in Hawaii told you that you had that afanalax thing and it was because of eating something called macky-dames." She faced Madison. "I never understood. But I've been wondering what the *idio* thing was that Dr. Smythe said you had."

"Me too," Madison said.

"Well, today at Brantleigh I learned what a macky-dame is. A macadamia nut." She glanced at her moms. She held up the candy box and quoted the small print: "This product is made on shared machinery that processes milk, wheat, soy, *tree nut*, and peanut products. I looked up macadamias," she added. "They grow on trees."

Cheyenne and Madison regarded each other, incredulous.

"Therefore," Kalea concluded, "I rest my case—"

"Sweetheart," Shy cooed to Maddy, "I'd have never—"

"I know," Madison whispered, and pecked her partner's cheek.

"So it wasn't the candy, but *probably* some macadamias *in* the candy."

Kalea wore one of those smiles that reminded me of a sunrise. She was high-fived by both moms and hugged by Aunt Zelma. I was as proud as a surrogate aunt can be.

"Mom," Kalea whispered to Madison, "Please always check for allergy warnings."

"We promise," Cheyenne said. "No more nasty surprises."

"Good job, Punkin," I said, pulling her into an impromptu embrace.

"Now Aaron and I need to have a short conference, you know, top brass only?"

"You mean you need alone time." Kalea, clearly irked,

flipped her sable ponytail. "Whatever."

Aaron followed me down from the veranda. I grabbed his hand and waited until we were far enough down the path that the ancient boxwood hedge hid us from prying eyes. Past the unknown bushwhacker's gravestone, I pulled him into a full-body hug. "I want to show you how much I appreciate your help in nailing Garner and settling Wayland's debt."

"What'd you have in mind?"

"Probably the same thing that's on your mind, sailor."

He laughed and I probably grinned like the half-crazed person I was. I don't remember a whole lot after that, but the essence was that I asked him if he'd be interested in marriage. To me.

We stumbled into the same chairs where we'd concocted the story for Garner. On the far side of the pool, bright yellow Carolina Jessamine cascaded over the old stone retaining wall. At first Aaron said nothing. If he'd been a pipe-smoker, he might have puffed a few times and blown a smoke ring toward Mount Pisgah. But he wasn't and he didn't. Instead, he pulled me back to my feet and kissed me in several places, twice in a few.

"I thought you'd never ask," he quipped.

"I thought *you'd* never ask," I said.

"Yes, yes, and *yes!*" Another kiss. Shazam! In that instant, the distant echo of Josh's splash into the swimming pool faded. I had no idea nor cared where Saturn was at that moment, but the alignment of our planets seemed perfect.

"Shall we alert the media?" Aaron joked.

"We could start at the house."

My memory of the rest of the afternoon is a bit hazy.

Aunt Zelma always kept a bottle of champagne in her

fridge for "emergencies," she said. From a top cupboard shelf came five heirloom flutes. After Aaron untangled its cage, the cork blapped against the kitchen ceiling, and he managed to siphon most of the bubbles into the flutes. Smiling faces eventually blurred.

"We'll see you in the morning," I told Aunt Zelma, whose eyes twinkled. Kalea grimaced and made an exaggerated gagging sound.

+ + +

The next morning at the Lodge as we loaded Aaron's bags into the Mercedes' trunk, he said, as if it were an afterthought, "Would you be my date for the Summer Solstice?" He was almost as bashful as the red-headed kid who invited me to our junior high prom. But I had no idea what he was talking about.

"For what? Where?" The solstice was two weeks away.

"In two weeks. I'll have a ring."

"Give me a couple of days," I said. "I'll try to find something in Annapolis that weekend. If you're sure you can come north."

"Who knows? Clement Pritchard may have to check out an investment opportunity in Maryland."

"You're sly *and* silver-tongued."

"Don't laugh. They're prerequisites for advancement to Master Chief."

We locked up Wayland's apartment and headed to Flat Rock. I nodded, put my head on his shoulder and sobbed, for the first time, in happiness.

At Kalorama, Aaron kissed my aunt's cheek and hugged Kalea, promising they'd see him again soon.

Madison hobbled in for a hug. He assured her that she'd soon be free of the fixator, ready to tip-toe through as many tulips as she wanted.

Aaron's Mercedes and I awaited the completion of his requisite farewells.

Cheyenne's hug was perfunctory.

Aunt Zelma opened her arms to enfold the sailor into a proper Southern bear-hug. With a wink to me over his shoulder, she said, "I'll look forward to your next visit when you both can stay here with me."

"Count on it," he said, and stepped briskly toward me. "I never realized how much fun being a Civil War antiques collector could be."

"And how a real estate developer's wealth could show a girl a good time."

Aaron laughed aloud.

"Drive safe," I said. "Can't wait to see you in Annapolis." After a last kiss, Aaron shoved off for King's Bay and his world of submarines. Tears of sadness joined my happy ones.

Had my "second sight" genes foretold this? A few weeks ago, I would have dismissed the idea. Now, I decided I shouldn't mind having a few more Porter genes if they'd give me an occasional glimpse beyond the visible horizon.

+ + +

I took a long gander at Mt. Pisgah from my bedroom window and reluctantly shifted to the job at hand. Kalea hovered as I folded my tees, spare jeans, and undies back into my carry-on. I left the patriotic party dress in the closet with Aaron's bow tie clipped to the hanger. Perhaps, I thought, sometime in the future, we could laugh at the memories.

Grandpa Jack recalled another Yogi Berra maxim: *The future ain't what it used to be.*

I agreed that the future isn't ours to see. *Que sera, sera!*

"I'll see you back in Annapolis," said Kalea. My moms are thinking we'll probably go back next week."

"Counting on it," I said. "I'll need your help with a few things." She beamed.

"So give me a call and I'll pick up the cushions Cookie chewed."

I slipped the iPad into my backpack and hoisted my carry-on. Downstairs, Aunt Zelma was alone in her kitchen mixing tuna salad for lunch. "You're going to leave me rattling around in this big house, you know."

"Don't try to give me a guilt trip," I said with a derisive grin. "You have dozens of friends. When you kick out Kalea and her moms, plan a girls' night out. They're doing *Cats* at the Flat Rock Playhouse."

I snagged Madison in mid-stride. "Let's grab dinner at O'Leary's again when you and Shy get back. Can't wait to eat genuine Maryland crab cakes again."

"Deal," she said. And with a face that evoked her appreciation, her last words needed no elaboration. "Thank you."

As my aunt and I stepped down between the guardian lions, she said, "Now don't you be a stranger for as many years as it's been since the last time you were here." After a broad smile, she added, "By then I'd be teaching history to Saint Peter."

"I promise," I said, gave her a hug, kissed her cheek, tossed my bag on the back seat, thanked her for her great hospitality, and took off for the Asheville airport.

I had just accelerated to slightly above the speed limit on the interstate when my cell phone sounded. A 301 area code. Who would call me from Maryland? Maybe Kalea's neighbor who'd been roped into dog-sitting my Dobergirl?

"This is Ophelia Reid," the caller said. It took me a nanosecond. I'd never met my client's wife. And why would she call? Aidan must have asked her to rebuke me for postponing our meeting. Or they'd selected another designer. Neither option was good. I dreaded that my first important design commission, along with the gorgeous photos of the completed job that would have been prominent in my portfolio, was down the drain.

"Yes, Ms. Reid. I'm terribly sorry about having to reschedule our meeting. As you probably know, I've been out of town for longer than—"

"That's not why I'm calling, Miss Summers."

I sucked in breath. Waited.

"Aidan died last week."

"Oh ..." is all I said. Serious blow to my solar plexus.

"He wanted so much to work with you on the new design."

"I'm so sorry," I said. "Is there anything I can do?"

"Nothing, I'm afraid, except I'd like to discuss your preliminary design when you get back."

My apprehension subsided slightly. "I'll be in Annapolis tomorrow. I'll ring and we can set a date."

"I'll look forward to hearing from you, Penelope."

That was weird. I'd told Aidan my name was Penny and my business card didn't have my full name. Just Penny. But, I supposed, every Penny was always originally a Penelope.

"Likewise, Ms. Reid." I was ready to ring off.

"Penelope?"

There it was again.

"Yes ...?" I had no idea what might be coming. And dreaded whatever it would be.

"A bigger reason why I'm looking forward to our meeting is—" she inhaled a long breath as if trying to remember what she'd wanted to say "never mind. I'll explain when I see you."

Author's Note

A couple of years ago, a workshop leader who lives in western North Carolina was surprised to learn about a nearby historic estate she had never visited: Brantleigh Manor. I took pleasure in knowing that my imagination had constructed a manor house with an extensive garden without lifting a single brick or planting a single tree. An author's imagination is undoubtedly his most valuable resource. When a book is finished it's sometimes difficult for the author to tease fiction from fact.

Needless to say, Frederick Law Olmsted never met Governor Brantley because, only in fiction can a real person encounter a fictional one. Mr. Olmsted's last residential design was for George Washington Vanderbilt's Biltmore estate at Asheville, N.C.

The town of Flat Rock in Henderson County is very much alive and well as is the estate on which Kalorama is based. The owner welcomed this author in exploring the big house where, in fact, the original owner *was* murdered by a bushwhacker.

The Vanderbilt Inn in the story is loosely based on the Kenilworth Inn in Asheville, not built by Mr. Vanderbilt and nowhere near where it's depicted.

You can be forgiven if you've never heard of the Battle of Asheville because it was essentially a footnote to the history of the Civil War hereabouts. Sometimes known as a skirmish, it did take place three days before Appomattox.

My hat is tipped to the many Henderson County officials and first responders who improved the accuracy of several scenes. Without the suggestions of these folks, you might have screamed *Foul* where my imagination strayed.

Thanks is also due to Civil War historian Peter Lorenz who coached me in the procedure of loading a Civil War era musket and lent his persona to Colonel Peters who filled in for Wayland at the Battle of Asheville reenactment.

If you think it's unrealistic for a woman to seek justice thirty years after her childhood abuse, a retired federal prosecutor friend assured me that it's not at all unusual. He also educated me about how bad actors can slip under the radar of our parole system.

If the story piques your interest in visiting western North Carolina, I hope you'll enjoy discovering the locations that exist and are not terribly upset when you're unable to find the ones that don't. My defense? Hey, it's fiction!

Reading Group Discussion Questions

1. Grandpa Jack makes comments throughout the book. Discuss how his observations contribute to the story.
2. Discuss how the western North Carolina setting is important in *Brantleigh Manor.* Does it make you want to visit?
3. In what ways does the mention of food and drink add to the local color and the story itself?
4. The youngest character in this novel is 11-year-old Kalea. Would you like to meet her? Would you have any advice for her?
5. Penny is haunted by her little brother's drowning. Was she able to exorcise his ghost by revisiting the location?
6. To what extent are Madison's past traumas resolved in this novel?
7. The Civil War is central to this mystery. Were you surprised to learn about the one-day Battle of Asheville? Have you attended a Civil War reenactment?
8. Does Penny's Great-Aunt Zelma resemble anyone in your family? Or anyone you know? In what ways?
9. Discuss Master Chief Petty Officer Aaron Hunt's role in this story.
10. There are attempted murders and plot twists in *Brantleigh Manor* that build to an exciting denouement. Were you kept guessing all the way to the end?

CPSIA information can be obtained
at www.ICGtesting.com
Printed in the USA
FFHW011701170219
50563515-55891FF